The fiery brilliance of the Zebra Hologram Heart which you see on the cover is created by "laser holography." This is the revolutionary process in which a powerful laser beam records light waves in diamond-like facets so tiny that 9,000,000 fit in a square inch. No print or photograph can match the vibrant colors and radiant glow of a hologram.

So look for the Zebra Hologram Heart whenever you buy a historical romance. It is a shimmering reflection of our guarantee that you'll find consistent quality between the covers!

SWEET DESIRE

Moving with lightning speed, Blade had her in his arms before she could flee. His mouth came down on hers demandingly as he pulled her against him.

Suzanne struggled futilely against his powerful embrace.

Whispering her name, he moved his lips to her neck, trailing warm, exciting kisses down her throat. Suzanne felt herself weakening.

"No," she protested feebly. "Don't do this."

"It's too late," he murmured.

Lacing his fingers through her long hair, he sought her lips with his. She shuddered with rapture when his hands began moving over her creamy flesh. His lips soon followed the searing path his hands had taken.

Mindless with wanting, Suzanne was totally at his mercy; she was his for the taking, to do with as he pleased. She arched toward him, moaning with sweet desire . . .

FRONTIER FLAME

FRONTIER FLAME

ROCHELLE WAYNE

ZEBRA BOOKS
KENSINGTON PUBLISHING CORP.

ZEBRA BOOKS

are published by

Kensington Publishing Corp.
475 Park Avenue South
New York, NY 10016

First printing: January 1987

Printed in the United States of America

This one is for you, Sue.

Patrick Donovan stood on the porch beside his parents and watched the approaching carriage roll slowly down the long pine-bordered lane. At the age of thirteen, Patrick was an extremely handsome lad. The afternoon sun, casting its bright rays across the majestic plantation, caused the boy's golden blond hair to shine with lustrous highlights.

He glanced away from the distant carriage and turned his vivid blue eyes to his parents. First, he studied his father. Thomas Donovan was an imposing figure, and Patrick had always felt a certain awe in his presence. He was a rich, powerful man who ruled in lordly style over his flourishing plantation. He owned over three hundred slaves. In his opinion he always treated them fairly, but nonetheless, he exerted his superiority. He was their master, and it was in their best interest never to forget it. He demanded their respect and humble servility, and woe to any slave who didn't conform completely to his master's laws.

Averting his gaze from his father, Patrick centered his attention upon his mother. He loved the woman who had given birth to him, but he didn't especially like her. His own dislike for his mother was hard for Patrick to accept, and it aroused unrest and guilt in him. He wanted to like her, but she was not an easy person to like.

Ellen Donovan was selfish, haughty, and impossibly demanding. She firmly believed that Southern aristocrats were God's chosen people and reigned supreme over all others. Yankees were a coarse, vulgar lot and should not be allowed to disgrace Southern soil. Southerners whom she considered "middle class" were a necessary evil, but under no circumstances were they to be accepted as equals. Poor white trash were an abomination and an insult to the human race. As far as she was concerned, Negroes had only one purpose in life. They had been put on this earth so Southern aristocrats could turn them into obedient slaves. The South was dependent upon its slaves' labor, and it had been the Negroes' destiny to toil in Southern fields, and to wait hand and foot on their masters. The only rights they had were the ones their owners chose to give them.

Patrick looked away from his mother and peered back down the narrow lane. The carriage was drawing steadily closer. He fidgeted a little uncomfortably as he wondered how his righteous parents would welcome his arriving cousin. He was already sorry for the orphaned child. If she was used to warmth and expressive love, she wouldn't find it here in her new home. He had a distinct feeling that his mother would never truly accept her as one of the family and that his father would simply be indifferent to her. As he waited silently for the approaching conveyance, his thoughts drifted back to the afternoon when his father had suddenly announced that they would soon have a new member in their family.

He had taken Ellen and his son into the parlor, where

he had astonished them with the unexpected news. The thought of taking in the homeless child had caused Ellen to pale visibly, and for a moment Patrick had been afraid that she was going to swoon.

Thomas Donovan had been born fifteen years before his younger brother, and it had been Thomas who had inherited the plantation. His brother, Kevin, had not been neglected as their father had left his youngest son well off financially. At the time of the senior Donovan's death, Kevin wasn't twenty-one, so Thomas had been placed in charge of his inheritance.

Kevin was a likable, easy-going young man and seemed to have little interest in money or prestige. At the age of twenty, he had fallen hopelessly in love with a beautiful girl named Gloria. She was not of the Donovans' social class, but the daughter of what was commonly referred to as "poor white trash." When Thomas learned that his brother was involved with the girl, he demanded that Kevin stop seeing her. Kevin defied his brother and gave up his inheritance, and he and Gloria ran away to New Orleans, where they were married. Although Thomas learned of Kevin's whereabouts, he made no attempt to contact him.

Four years later, Thomas received a letter from a foundling home in New Orleans informing him that his brother's child had been orphaned. He had his lawyers go to New Orleans and investigate the situation, and they returned with the solemn news that both Kevin and Gloria had died during an outbreak of yellow fever. Their three-year-old daughter, Suzanne, had been placed in the foundling home. It was public knowledge that Kevin was Thomas Donovan's brother, so the head matron at the orphanage had promptly notified Thomas that his niece was now in her care. Kevin had been raised as a pampered aristocrat, and his employable skills were limited. He

9

and his wife had lived poorly and their daughter was left penniless.

A small frown knitted Patrick's forehead as he remembered how dead set Ellen had been against taking Suzanne into their home. The child's mother had been poor white trash, and Suzanne could never be a pure-blooded aristocrat, regardless of her environment.

Thomas, never one to shirk his duty, had insisted that they send for the orphaned child and raise her as their daughter. Gloria's family had moved away three years ago and their new location was unknown. Except for the Donovans, there was no one to help Suzanne.

But Ellen had held to her objections. Why not leave Suzanne at the foundling home and send money for her care? Why must they bring the girl to the plantation? Why should they be wholly responsible for Suzanne? It hadn't been their fault that Kevin had foolishly and thoughtlessly married beneath himself. Had he considered his obligations to the Donovans' name when he'd married below his station?

To Ellen's dismay, Thomas had remained adamant. Suzanne was a Donovan, and he'd not allow his brother's child to be raised in an orphanage.

Thomas always made the final decisions, so Ellen had had no choice but to relent. But she greatly resented her husband forcing her to take in Gloria's daughter. She was sure the child had inherited her mother's "bad blood." Someday Suzanne would disgrace the Donovans' name; Ellen believed it inevitable.

The carriage came to a stop in front of the columned home, and as the Negro driver leapt from his perch, Thomas moved down the short flight of steps to greet his guests. The conveyance was closed, and Patrick couldn't see the people inside. The boy continued watching as the driver opened the carriage door. He recognized the well-dressed man who quickly emerged. Marshall Lancaster was one of his father's lawyers, and he worked for a large firm in the nearby city of Natchez.

Shaking the lawyer's hand, Thomas said cordially, "Mr. Lancaster, I hope your trip was pleasant."

Marshall smiled. "It was very pleasant indeed. Everything went smoothly." His smile broadened as he reached inside the carriage and grasped the child's small hand. "Mr. Donovan, I'd like you to meet your charming niece."

Patrick studied the little girl as his father's lawyer lifted her from the carriage seat, then set her on the ground in front of her uncle. Patrick knew the child was only three years old, but he hadn't fully realized how young three really was until he actually saw her. Why, she's hardly more than a baby! he thought with surprise. Even from a distance he could see that she was a little frightened. Patrick, who was very much like his kind-hearted Uncle Kevin, felt a deep compassion for his cousin.

The young lawyer had thought Thomas Donovan would immediately embrace his own niece, and was surprised when the man made no move to do so.

Thomas took a step backward, then looked down at the child, who was gazing up fearfully into his face, apparently intimidated by his powerful presence.

He quickly noticed that she had inherited the Donovans' blond hair and blue eyes. He could see very little resemblance to her mother, but she was still quite young; when she grew older Gloria's characteristics might become more prominent.

During their journey from New Orleans, Marshall Lancaster had grown fond of Suzanne, and he placed an arm protectively about her small shoulders, drawing

11

her close to his side. She peered up at him, and he smiled down at her kindly. From the first moment Marshall had seen the little girl, he had been amazed by her beauty.

Suzanne Donovan was extraordinarily pretty. Her hair, the color of golden honey, was naturally curly, and the shining tresses radiantly framed her oval face. Her dark blue eyes were extremely large, and one could become impossibly lost in their azure depths.

"Suzanne," Thomas said evenly, "come and meet your aunt."

He stepped aside so the child could precede him. Although Suzanne's parents had been poor, they'd been rich with love, and she was used to adults treating her with an abundance of affection. Hesitating, she stared expectantly at her uncle, waiting for him to take her hand and lead her to the porch. When it became apparent that he had no intention of doing so, she moved past him and climbed the steps.

Suzanne's huge eyes widened with apprehension when she saw the stern and disapproving expression on her aunt's face. The child was too young to discern Ellen's countenance, but nonetheless she could sense the woman's annoyance.

Following behind Suzanne, Thomas told her, "This is your Aunt Ellen."

The woman studied the child critically for a moment, then, glancing toward Marshall, she asked, "Why is the girl dressed that way? Doesn't she have any decent clothes?"

Suzanne didn't completely understand Ellen's captious remarks, but she realized her aunt was somehow displeased with her clothes. The girl looked down at her simple cotton gown. It was her favorite dress. Her mother had made it a couple of months ago, and Suzanne had been thrilled when it was finished. It was her Sunday dress, and had been made to be worn to church. The Donovans were Catholics, and although Gloria hadn't shared her husband's faith, she had always accompanied him to Mass and had allowed their daughter to be baptized in the Catholic Church.

Marshall, still poised at the bottom of the steps, answered Ellen. "The dress Suzanne is wearing is her nicest gown. She doesn't have very many clothes."

With annoyance, Ellen replied, "I'll have Lettie take her measurements. The child must have an appropriate wardrobe."

Thomas touched Suzanne's shoulders and turned her around so that she was facing Patrick. "This is your cousin Patrick."

Stepping forward, the handsome boy flashed a grin so full of tenderness that Suzanne responded immediately.

Studying her smile, Patrick noticed a deep dimple in each cheek. He was already acutely aware of her beauty, but her enticing smile made her unbelievably lovely.

"Welcome to Southmoor," Patrick said amicably. Seeing confusion on her face, he explained, "This plantation is called Southmoor. When our grandfather bought this land and built this house, he wanted to give it a name. The word moor, spelled m-o-o-r, can mean to fix firmly or take up a position. Grandfather had no intention of leaving his home; he intended to remain here for the rest of his life. So he decided to call his home Southmoor."

At the age of three, Suzanne certainly wasn't capable of totally comprehending Patrick's explanation, but she had detected a friendliness in his voice that warmed her heart. Also, she could see an uncanny resemblance between him and her father, which made her long desperately for her papa. Her bottom lip trembled and tears smarted her eyes. Where were her papa and mommy, and when were they going to come get her? She had been terribly unhappy at the foundling home and had waited fretfully for her parents to come for her. She knew they were both very sick, but surely by now they were well! Why had Mr. Lancaster taken her away from the orphanage only to bring her here? Why hadn't he taken her back home?

Patrick was the only one who saw the tears that came to Suzanne's eyes, her sadness completely escaping the others' notice.

Thomas, wondering why the child hadn't spoken, asked the young lawyer, "Doesn't Suzanne ever speak?"

"Of course she does, but she's been a very quiet child. She probably misses her parents. When she becomes adjusted to her new life, maybe she'll be a little more talkative."

Agreeing, Thomas remarked, "If she's anything like Kevin, she'll never run out of things to say." He felt a pang of remorse as he thought of his brother's easy, likable manner. He had loved Kevin and wished he were still alive so they could find a way to make up their differences. But now it was too late. Yellow fever had robbed them of any chance for a reconciliation. As soon as I can manage to leave the plantation, he promised himself somberly, I'll go to New Orleans, visit his grave, and pray for his soul.

Bringing himself out of his deep thoughts, Thomas said cordially, "Come into the house, Mr. Lancaster. I'm sure you could use a glass of bourbon. We'll be having supper in a couple of hours, and we'd be honored if you would join us."

As the lawyer was accepting the invitation, Ellen ushered Suzanne into the house. Calling Lettie, she

14

handed the child over into the elderly slave's capable hands.

Suzanne barely had time to view her impressive and elaborate surroundings before Lettie began leading her up the marble staircase to the bedroom Ellen had already assigned to her niece.

Poised at the bottom of the stairway, Patrick watched the little girl obediently climbing the numerous steps. Lettie warned her to hold on to the banister so she wouldn't fall.

When Suzanne reached the top step, she seemed to feel Patrick's gaze, and turning slightly, she looked back at him.

He gave her an encouraging smile, and she timidly returned his smile. For a long moment, blue eyes met blue eyes, and inexplicably, they could sense the other's feelings. Patrick was conscious of her deep loneliness. Suzanne, in turn, knew he was her friend.

Patrick kept a close watch for Lettie, and when she descended the stairs, he gave his parents and Mr. Lancaster his excuses and left the parlor. "Lettie," he called, deterring her as she headed toward the kitchen. She paused, and when he reached her side, he inquired, "How is my cousin? Is she asleep?"

The woman shook her head. "No suh, Masta Patrick, but she's a-restin'." Lettie's wrinkled face frowned with concern. "Lawdy, I ain't never seen a chile so quiet. The poor baby must be a-grievin' somethin' powerful for her parents." Looking questioningly at Patrick, she added, "I needs to go to the kitchen and check on supper. Is there anything else you want, Masta Patrick?"

"No, thank you, Lettie," he mumbled vacantly,

looking thoughtfully toward the staircase. Deciding to check on the newest member of his family, Patrick hurried up to the second floor and down the hallway. When he reached Suzanne's room, he paused in the open doorway and peered inside.

The girl was lying in the middle of the huge four-poster bed, its massive size making Suzanne appear even tinier than she was. The room was entirely too large for a three-year-old child, and Patrick wondered why his mother hadn't had the nursery prepared.

Crossing the highly polished floor, Patrick went to the side of the bed. Smiling down into Suzanne's tear-brimmed eyes, he asked gently, "Do you miss your parents?"

Sitting up and crossing her legs Indian style, she nodded somberly. "I want my papa and mommy to come get me," she pouted.

"But Suzanne . . ." he began, before catching himself. Could it be possible that no one had told the child that her parents were dead? Carefully he asked, "Do you know what happened to your mother and father?"

"They don't feel good," she said sadly. "My papa and mommy are sick." Her huge blue eyes looked beseechingly into his. "When will they feel good again? I want them to come get me. I wanna go home!"

Patrick wished he knew the best way to answer her questions. Should he tell her the truth, or wait and let his parents try to explain everything? Deciding it was a problem best solved by his mother and father, he simply changed the subject. "Suzanne, do you like horses?" he asked, trying to sound cheerful.

She nodded enthusiastically. "Do you have a horse?"

"Yes, I do. Would you like to see him?"

She quickly agreed, and taking her hand, Patrick helped her from the bed. He continued holding her hand as he guided her down the long hallway and

16

toward the back staircase. For the first time since Suzanne had arrived at Southmoor, her steps were buoyant. Patrick noticed that her golden curls bounced with her quick, lively steps. Walking beside her, he realized how short she was and wondered if she was small for a three-year-old. Her chubby little hand, enclosed in his, held on tightly. Patrick smiled happily, glad that his little cousin had come to live with them. He had always longed for siblings, and now he had Suzanne, and he knew he would love her as dearly as a sister.

Suzanne's mood remained chipper as her cousin led her outside and toward the stables. Mr. Lancaster had said that she was a quiet child, but she rambled on continuously as she strode beside Patrick. The boy was impressed with her vocabulary and diction. She must be very smart, he thought.

Suzanne had been talking about horses when suddenly she changed the topic, "You look like my papa."

"Yes, I know," Patrick answered.

"Do you know papa?"

"Of course I do. He was . . . is my uncle," he stammered. "Your father used to live here at Southmoor. I was nine when he moved away."

"How old is nine?" she asked.

Patrick chuckled. "Before I can explain figures, you'll have to start learning how to count."

"I can count to three!" she declared proudly.

Letting go of her hand, he held up three fingers. "This is how old you are," he said. He then held up nine fingers. "This is how old I was when your father left Southmoor." He lifted another finger and told her to hold up three of hers. "This is how old I am now."

She was genuinely impressed. "I wish I could be that many!"

Slipping his hand back in hers, he said with a wisdom

beyond his age, "Don't wish your years away, Suzanne. Life is too short and precious to take lightly."

Standing in the stables' entrance, the slave Saul watched them approach. Grinning widely, he exclaimed, "This must be Miz Suzanne who has come here to live at Southmoor!"

Pausing in front of the tall, slim servant, Suzanne arched her neck and looked up into his kind face. "I don't live here. I am visi . . . visi . . ."

"Visiting?" Patrick helped.

She nodded eagerly. "Visiting," she repeated, speaking the word clearly.

Taken with the girl's astounding beauty, Saul said impressively, "Miz Suzanne, you is the prettiest chile I ever seen." Glancing at the boy, he continued teasingly, "Masta Patrick, in about twelve years or so you is gonna be busy keepin' the young gentlemens away from Southmoor."

Chuckling, he agreed. "Father and I will probably find it necessary to keep our shotguns loaded and ready to fire."

Suzanne was puzzled. Would Patrick and Uncle Thomas actually shoot young gentlemen if they came to Southmoor?

Intruding on her confusion, Patrick said, "Suzanne, this is Saul. He takes care of father's horses."

"Does he take care of your horse too?"

"Yes, he does," Patrick answered. Looking at Saul, he explained their visit. "Suzanne wants to see Lightning." Picking her up and carrying her inside the stables, Patrick told her that his horse's name was Lightning. Taking her to the roan gelding, he calmed the spirited animal, then set Suzanne on the horse's back.

He let her sit on the animal for a couple of minutes before asking, "Would you like to give Lightning a cube of sugar?"

She said that she would, and he lifted her from the horse's broad back and placed her on her feet. Saul handed him the lump of sugar, which he gave to Suzanne. He showed his young cousin how to place the cube in her palm before offering it to the horse.

She did exactly as Patrick instructed and laughed gaily when Lightning gently took the sweet tidbit from her outstretched hand.

"Patrick!" Thomas's voice suddenly bellowed. Striding briskly into the stables, he said sternly, "We have been searching the entire house for Suzanne! You shouldn't have taken her from her room without first telling someone."

"I'm sorry, father," he apologized.

Turning his attention to Suzanne, he said firmly, "It is time for Lettie to give you your supper so that you can go to bed."

The girl was wary of the strict man and carefully inched her way closer to Patrick. Gazing up at her cousin, she cried brokenly, "I don't wanna go back to the house! I want my papa and mommy to come get me!"

"She doesn't know?" Thomas questioned with genuine concern.

"No," Patrick answered.

"She must be told," his father said.

"I'll tell her," the boy volunteered. "Then I'll bring her back to the house." He dreaded telling Suzanne that she'd never see her parents again, but he believed it would be easier for her if the news came from him.

His father concurred and left the stables, taking Saul with him so Patrick could be alone with Suzanne.

The boy took a wooden bench and carried it close to Lightning's stall. Placing it on the dirt floor, he had Suzanne sit beside him.

He sighed heavily as he wondered if the child understood death. "Suzanne," he began gently, "do you know what it means when people die and go to heaven?"

She nodded hesitantly, and in spite of her young age, she sensed what Patrick was going to say next. Tears flooded her eyes, and the large drops rolled down her rosy cheeks.

"Your mother and father are in heaven," he said gently.

Her chin trembling, she asked sadly, "For always?"

"Yes, Suzanne," he whispered.

"They won't come and get me?"

"No, honey. Heaven is now their new home, and this is your new home."

Her small shoulders shook as deep sobs took over. "I want my papa and mommy!" she cried, heartbroken.

Sweeping her onto his lap, Patrick held her against his chest. Her little arms went about his neck and her copious tears wetted his shirt.

It was a long time before Suzanne's cries abated. The sun had set and long shadows were falling across the stables when she finally ran out of tears.

Although Patrick knew they should return to the house, he nonetheless remained, holding Suzanne in his lap. He sensed the child needed this quiet time alone with him.

Suzanne lifted her head from his shoulder, and her red, swollen eyes looked desperately into his. "Patrick, promise me you won't leave me and go to heaven!"

A faint smile touched his lips. "Honey, I can't make that promise. No one knows when they will die. But there is one promise that I can make."

"What?" she asked, her interest aroused.

"I promise you for as long as I live, I'll always be your friend, and I'll always be there for you whenever you need me."

"I promise too!" she exclaimed, and it was a vow the child had every intention of keeping.

She nestled her golden curls against his comforting shoulder, and finding security in her cousin's embrace, she soon drifted into sleep.

Gently, so she wouldn't awaken, Patrick cradled her in his arms and stood. Holding her securely, he began walking toward the magnificent house standing imperiously in the distance.

For a moment Suzanne came to, and her arms tightened about Patrick's neck. "I love you, Patrick," she murmured sleepily.

He placed a light kiss on her warm brow. "I love you too, Suzanne."

Soothed, she went calmly back to sleep.

Chapter One
1866

The day had been long as well as tiring, and Suzanne was feeling uncomfortable. She was sitting on the wagon seat and shifted her weight, hoping a different position might ease her weary body. She sighed with fatigue and absently brushed her hand over her moist brow. The hot sun was relentless and its scorching rays, which were now beginning their descent into the west, were still shining inexorably. The head wagons stirred up loose dirt and the grainy particles swirled thickly through the air. Suzanne could feel sand settling on her bare arms, and she knew if it weren't for her wide-brimmed bonnet, her face too would be coated with grimy dust.

Once again she wiped her flushed brow as she looked about, unimpressed with the landscape, thinking the extensive plains and the Platte River nondescript. She found the Wyoming territory seriously lacking when compared to the state of Mississippi. Studying the present vast terrain, she sorely missed the familiar scenery of home. She especially missed the cool forests of white oaks, maples, sycamores, and magnolias.

What she wouldn't give to find a large patch of woods and then seek comfort within its shade!

She turned her gaze to Saul, who was driving the mule team. He held the long reins entwined loosely through his fingers. Looking closely at the man, she allowed her perusal to deepen. She wondered how old he was. She had once asked him his age, but he hadn't known his birth date. Most slaves had birth records, but some of them, like Saul, had never had their births registered. Now, as she continued studying his face, she guessed that he must be in his late sixties or early seventies. His tightly curled hair was solid gray, and there were deep crevices about his eyes and mouth. She glanced down at his hands and saw a strength in them that belied his years. He was still strong and in good physical condition.

Her gaze returned to his face, and she saw that he was now watching her. She smiled fondly. "Saul, when we decided to make this trip, did you realize it was going to be so exhausting?"

He chuckled good-naturedly. "Yes'm, Miz Suzanne. But the trip is most over for us. Tomorrow mornin' we'll reach Fort Laramie."

Suzanne's pretty face brightened with anticipation. "Oh, Saul!" she breathed happily. "I can hardly wait to see Patrick!"

Saul grinned expansively. "I'm gonna be mighty glad to see Masta Patrick too!"

Their happiness only lasted momentarily. A feeling of consternation came over them as their eyes met with mutual understanding.

Although Suzanne longed desperately to see her cousin, she knew their reunion would not be a joyful one. Oh, Patrick! Patrick! she moaned inwardly. Why? Why did you betray the Confederacy? If only I knew why!

She grew tense and she clutched her hands together tightly. Tomorrow morning, after three long years, she'd finally see Patrick again. At the thought nervous perspiration accumulated on her palms, and her heart pounded heavily.

Her gaze centering on her lap, where her hands were resting, Suzanne's thoughts wandered restlessly into the past.

At the outbreak of the War Between the States, Patrick had joined the Confederate Army. Suzanne had been so proud of her cousin, and he had looked so dashingly handsome in his lieutenant's uniform. From childhood on, Suzanne had virtually worshipped her cousin; he was her idol, a man above reproach. She was sure he would eventually become the Confederacy's greatest hero!

The war was in its third year when Southmoor received news of Lieutenant Donovan's imprisonment by the Union. Patrick a prisoner of war! Suzanne had been devastated. There could be no more letters exchanged between them, or hope that he might come home on leave. For the first time, she was completely cut off from her cousin. If Thomas hadn't had a Yankee friend with political influence in the North, Patrick could have died in the Union prison without their knowledge. But this friend promised to keep the Donovans notified of Patrick's welfare, his vow to do so bringing a certain degree of comfort to the people at Southmoor.

However, the Donovans' comfort would be short-lived. Patrick had been captured for only two months when Thomas received a message from his friend notifying him that his son had been freed. At first Thomas was exultant, but as he continued to read the information, his heart filled with shame. Patrick had betrayed the Confederacy by taking an oath to the

Union and agreeing to go west and join the U.S. Cavalry. Hundreds of Confederate prisoners had been offered the same option, but to desert the South and take an oath to the hated Union was to many unthinkable! These brave, loyal soldiers preferred to rot in prison rather than turn against their beloved Confederacy. Thomas had wished to God that Patrick had chosen possible death over what he believed to be dishonor! Somehow the news became public knowledge. Although Thomas was not personally responsible for his son's betrayal, people nonetheless acted as though he were partially to blame. Unable to live down Patrick's shame, Thomas became a depressed and humbled man.

Her cousin's dishonor had been heartbreaking to Suzanne, but her faith in Patrick never wavered. She firmly believed he must have had a justifiable reason for disloyalty to the Confederacy. When she revealed this belief to her uncle, hoping to lighten his dark mood, he had lashed out at her, telling her there was no such thing as a justifiable reason for disloyalty to the Confederacy! Suzanne made no further attempts to soothe Thomas, but kept her faith in Patrick strictly between herself and Saul, whose beliefs coincided with hers. The slave's trust in his young master held as steadfastly as Suzanne's. They knew Patrick better than anyone else, and he was not capable of dishonesty. Then why had he deserted the Confederacy? They had no logical explanation to excuse his action; their faith in him was blind and beyond question.

When the war finally ended, Thomas had no intention of trying to locate Patrick. He had disowned his son, and if he'd had an inheritance to hand down, he would have left everything to Suzanne. But the war had left Thomas Donovan practically destitute. His majestic home had been burned to the ground, his fields were barren, and all his slaves, except for the few who had chosen to remain, had left the plantation to take advantage of their new-found freedom.

The war's aftermath left the Donovans living in the overseer's house, forced to feed themselves and their few servants from one small vegetable garden and whatever wild game they could shoot or trap.

When Thomas's northern friend had taken it upon himself to send a message to the Donovans, informing them that Patrick was stationed at Fort Laramie, the unexpected news had caused conflicting emotions to erupt. Suzanne had been determined to find a way to go to Patrick, but Thomas had been firmly against the idea. Patrick was no longer family, he was an outcast! But Suzanne was not about to relent. Somehow she would acquire the necessary means to travel to the fort. Suzanne was strong willed, and her deep love for Patrick gave her the needed strength to wear down her uncle's objections. Finally he submitted and gave Suzanne his permission to journey to Fort Laramie. A spark of love for his son still flickered deep in Thomas's heart, and he ordered Saul to dig up their buried silver, which he handed over to his niece. With her uncle's gift Suzanne had been able to obtain the necessary funds to cover the costs for her trip westward.

A woman's voice broke into Suzanne's troubled recollections. "When do you think we'll stop and make camp for the night?"

Turning her head, Suzanne looked back at the young woman who had spoken. She was sitting in the rear of the wagon, beneath the canvas enclosure. "I don't know, Molly. But the sun is starting to set, so I'm sure the wagon master will soon give the order to stop."

Molly sighed wearily. She had found the long journey not only strenuous but tedious. If she hadn't felt bound by her promise to marry Patrick, she'd never have consented to make this trip with Suzanne and Saul. But Patrick Donovan was her betrothed, and as his fiancée, it was her duty to go to him. She wondered bitterly why she should still feel a certain loyalty to Patrick; he certainly felt no devotion toward her. In Molly's opinion, he had not only deserted the Confederacy, but her as well.

Molly closed her eyes as the rocking motion of the wagon lulled her back to a different place and a different time. A wistful smile played fleetingly across her lips as she mentally envisioned the day Patrick had asked her to be his wife.

The sunny spring day when Molly O'Ryan became engaged to Patrick Donovan, she had been ecstatically happy. She adored her fiancé. Their proposed marriage had the complete approval of both sets of parents. The young couple had everything in common. They were both Southerners, descendants of the Irish, and Catholics. How could their future marriage possibly be less than perfect?

The O'Ryans had been especially pleased by the match. The Donovans were extremely wealthy, and someday Southmoor would belong solely to Patrick. Their daughter, and their future grandchildren, would live in luxury. Molly's father was a physician, but his income was small compared to the Donovans' riches.

Ellen would have preferred that her son marry a girl of higher status. But Irish Catholics were scarce in the South, and she would have firmly opposed Patrick marrying outside of his heritage and faith. Molly O'Ryan was well bred and a genteel lady, so Ellen had accepted her. In fact, their engagement had come as no surprise to either set of parents. Years ago they had taken it for granted that someday their son and daughter would marry. The O'Ryans, like the Donovans, believed Irish Catholics should marry their

27

own kind.

The sound of the wagon master's voice brought Molly out of her reverie. "We'll stop about a mile up ahead and make camp for the night," the man called as he rode his horse past their wagon, on his way to spread the word to the immigrants traveling farther behind.

Saul welcomed the news. He was anxious to call it a day. Like Suzanne and Molly, he had found the trip long and wearisome. He supposed it might have been less unpleasant if their final destination was more promising. He knew that each of them, in his own way, was dreading reaching Fort Laramie.

Saul sighed worriedly. Masta Patrick, he thought, why did you dishonor your home and your papa's name? Why did you do them things? I'm sure you had a good reason! I know you, Masta Patrick, and I know you wouldn't do nothin' bad without just cause!

When Suzanne had announced her wish to travel to Fort Laramie, Saul hadn't had to think twice about accompanying her. He knew she would need a man's protection, and besides, most wagon masters would not agree to a woman or women traveling alone. It was usually the rule that each wagon had a man, as the westward journey was much too strenuous and dangerous for a woman to handle without the help of a man. Although Saul had eagerly agreed to join Suzanne on her trip, he realized that Molly had been hesitant to do likewise. But he couldn't really blame her. Her fiancé had made no attempt to contact her, so why should she seek him? Saul was very disappointed in Patrick for neglecting Molly so. Well, they would reach the fort in the morning. It was only a matter of hours before Patrick would explain his actions.

Saul frowned deeply. What possible explanations could Masta Patrick offer?

Perspiration beaded his forehead, and he wiped his

arm across his brow, letting his shirt-sleeve absorb the moisture. His faith in Patrick held inflexibly. You'll have a good reason for what you done, Masta Patrick! I'm sure you will!

Suzanne's thoughts coincided with Saul's. "Tomorrow morning we'll know everything," she murmured. "When Patrick finishes explaining what happened, we'll know that we were right to believe in him."

"Yes'm, Miz Suzanne," Saul acquiesced. "We know Masta Patrick as well as we know ourselves, and he ain't capable of them things he's been accused of. Maybe he's workin' undercover for the Confederacy."

"There is no longer a Confederacy," Suzanne said dryly.

Saul gave her a shrewd look. "We don't know that for sure. How can we be sure the South has really given up?"

Suzanne smiled tolerantly. "I'd like to believe that the Confederacy isn't dead, but that's wishful thinking. The damned Yankees won and our men lost." Her large blue eyes flashed angrily. "Yankees!" she spat. "Fort Laramie will be full of them! Everywhere I look I'll be confronted with blue uniforms!"

"And Masta Patrick will be one of them men wearin' a blue uniform," Saul added carefully.

"Oh, Saul," she cried desperately, "I can't imagine Patrick wearing the enemy's colors!"

"I can't neither, Miz Suzanne," he admitted. "But we got to prepare ourselves for seein' it."

Overhearing their conversation, Molly said bitterly, "You two might be able to prepare yourselves for such a sight, but I never will!"

Suzanne understood Molly's feelings and sympathized with her. She couldn't even begin to fathom why her cousin had apparently abandoned his fiancée. Patrick, what is wrong with you? she pleaded silently.

29

Tears came to her eyes, but she blinked them back. If she started crying, Molly would probably join her, and then Saul would have two hysterical women to try and calm.

"The head wagons are beginnin' to circle," Saul observed. "It's time to set up camp."

"Our last night on the Oregon Trail," Suzanne said thoughtfully. She favored Saul and Molly with an encouraging smile. "Tomorrow morning we'll be with Patrick. Everything will be all right, I'm sure of it."

Intensely Molly replied, "Suzanne, how I wish I had your faith!"

Enclosed in the covered wagon, Molly and Suzanne were preparing for bed. Suzanne sat on her pallet in a cotton nightgown, brushing her long, curly blond hair.

Sitting across from her, Molly watched her companion. Suzanne's astounding beauty never failed to amaze her. She had often wondered how a woman could be so flawlessly beautiful. Although Molly loved her good friend, she had always been a little jealous of her. But she supposed her jealousy was a normal reaction; how could any woman help being envious of Suzanne's perfection? Molly smiled inwardly. More amazing than Suzanne's beauty was the fact that she possessed not a shred of vanity.

Molly was right, Suzanne Donovan wasn't vain. But neither was she blind. She was perfectly aware that nature had been more than generous to her, but she accepted her extravagant good looks modestly. When she was still a child, Patrick, worried that his cousin's beauty might make her conceited, had often reminded her that beauty is as beauty does. Suzanne unquestioningly accepted everything her cousin told her, so she grew up believing that true beauty came from within, and it was a belief she still practiced.

Suzanne had inherited her honey-blond hair and blue eyes from her father, but her full, sensual lips and high cheekbones were identical to her mother's.

You couldn't take one of Suzanne's features and say it was her prettiest; they were all beautiful. Her blond hair was naturally curly and the thick tresses cascaded gracefully to her hips in full, deep waves. Her dark blue eyes were round and extraordinarily large, framed by well-arched brows and heavy lashes. Her prominent cheekbones and sultry lips set off her oval face faultlessly. Her only flaw, if it could be called a flaw, was that she was shorter than the average woman, and her frame was very petite. Her breasts, waist, and hips were small, but perfectly proportioned.

Becoming aware of Molly's scrutiny, Suzanne put down her brush and met the woman's eyes. "Is something the matter?" she asked gently.

"No," Molly answered. "I was just admiring you. I wish I was as beautiful as you are." Somberly she added, "Maybe then Patrick wouldn't have deserted me."

"You don't know that he has deserted you," Suzanne quickly replied. "And you are a very pretty woman, Molly O'Ryan!"

Suzanne hadn't spoken frivolously. Molly was an attractive woman. Her beauty wasn't as outstanding as Suzanne's, but her looks were pleasing. Her auburn hair shone with reddish highlights, and her brown eyes had a mystic charm that men found intriguing. Molly despised the mass of freckles that were splashed haphazardly across her small nose and rosy cheeks. Although she was twenty-five years old, people always thought she was much younger. Molly blamed her adolescent appearance on her freckles, which made her despise them all the more. She wished for sensuality,

31

not youthfulness. She was average height, her softly contoured curves making her slim build look very feminine.

"Suzanne," Molly began hesitantly, "do you really believe Patrick will have a plausible explanation for his conduct?"

"Yes, I do," she answered immediately. "Molly, you must have faith in Patrick."

Molly sighed impatiently. "My faith faltered a long time ago."

"Then why did you agree to come on this trip?"

"I guess I felt it my duty."

Suzanne didn't like Molly's answer, but she tried not to judge her. Maybe Molly didn't love Patrick as deeply as she did. After all, she herself didn't see him as a fiancé but as a cousin, so it was probably much easier for her to forgive him for his actions.

Lying down on her pallet, Molly sighed. "Well, tomorrow everything will be settled. Patrick will answer all our questions and the puzzle will be solved."

Standing up and slipping on her robe, Suzanne said softly, "I'm going to tell Saul good night. I'll be back in a few minutes."

Emerging from the covered wagon, she saw Saul resting beside the campfire drinking a cup of coffee. Joining him, she sat at his side. A coyote's forlorn cry sounded in the distance, and Suzanne inched closer to the servant.

Chuckling, Saul asked, "Are you scared of a little ole coyote, Miz Suzanne?"

Realizing she was behaving foolishly, she smiled. "Maybe I'm just not used to wild animals crying in the night."

"It ain't wild animals that you got to worry about out here in the wilderness, but savage Indians."

Frightened, she exclaimed, "Is there a chance that we

32

might be attacked by Indians?"

"I reckon there's always a chance of them attackin' a wagon train, but the scout ain't seen no signs of Indians. Besides, I guess we're too close to the fort to run across any savages."

Relieved, Suzanne spoke with a bravery she didn't truly feel. "Well, we survived the Yankees, so I'm sure we can overcome the Indians." A bitter frown crossed her face as she remembered the Northern invaders riding up to Southmoor, raiding and burning everything within sight. The captain in charge had allowed the overseer's house to remain unharmed so the Donovans would have a place to live. Suzanne had known that the young captain had expected her to thank him for his generosity, but she had seen no reason to thank him for letting her and her family keep what was rightfully theirs.

"I suppose we might as well turn in for the night," Saul muttered. "We got a busy day facin' us tomorrow."

Suzanne tensed. "We've waited so long to see Patrick again!" Her voice broke with a sob. "Oh, Saul, I love him so much!"

"I do too, Miz Suzanne," Saul said sincerely.

She looked up into his face, and her eyes met his. There was no need for words; each understood exactly how the other felt. Before Patrick had gone away to fight in the war, the three of them had been very close. They shared a mutual love that time could never erase.

Although Saul loved Patrick, there was no one on the face of the earth who loved him more than Suzanne. Her adoration for her cousin had been born the first day she had arrived at Southmoore, and it had grown stronger with the passing years. There was a special bond between them, a bond so private that not even Saul could be a part of it. It belonged exclusively to Patrick and Suzanne.

Saul's bedroll was under the wagon, and before Suzanne rejoined Molly, she remembered to bid him good-night. Moving to her pallet, she lay down and closed her eyes. A warm smile crossed her lips as she recalled the pact that she had made with Patrick when she was only three years old. They had promised always to be friends and always to be there for each other.

"Tomorrow," she whispered. "Patrick, I know you need me, and tomorrow I'll be there for you."

Chapter Two

The westward pioneers on the wagon train looked forward eagerly to reaching Fort Laramie. The women dressed in their nicest clothes and arranged their hair in flattering styles. The men were anxious to leave their wagons and visit the enlisted men's bar, where they could relax while enjoying a glass of beer.

The wagon train set up a temporary camp just outside the fort walls. The travelers would remain there for a few days, during which time supplies could be replenished from the trading store at the military post.

Suzanne and her party would not be moving onward with the others, so they guided their wagon away from the camp and toward the opened gates of Fort Laramie.

Suzanne's thoughts were exclusively on Patrick, and she paid scant attention to her surroundings as her wagon rolled into the large courtyard. Fort Laramie was built in the form of a square, and its high walls were made of adobe. Most of the buildings inside the fort were constructed of stone or log.

The fort was crowded, and so many people were moving about that Suzanne knew it was highly unlikely that she would spot Patrick among them.

There was a spacious area reserved for wagons remaining at the post, and Saul guided their mule team to the designated location.

Suzanne was sitting beside Saul, and taking her wide-brimmed bonnet from her lap, she quickly donned it, tying the silk ribbons beneath her chin. "You and Molly stay here," she told Saul, "while I see if I can find Patrick."

Lifting the hem of her gingham gown, she climbed down from the wagon. She looked about thoughtfully as she tried to decide which direction to take. She spotted a young captain close by, and calling to him, she hurried to his side.

She had caught his attention and he paused to wait for the lovely woman who was approaching. As she drew closer, her beauty was more distinguishable, and the captain became fascinated.

Suzanne's simply cut gown emphasized her soft, sensual curves, and her long, golden hair flowed freely. When she reached the captain and looked up into his face, he noticed the way her blond curls peeked out from beneath her bonnet to fall teasingly across her forehead. He gazed down into her huge blue eyes and was immediately mesmerized. He felt as though he could drown in their deep, dark pools.

"Excuse me, captain," Suzanne said eagerly. "Could you possibly tell me where I might find Trooper Patrick Donovan?"

"Did you say Patrick Donovan?" he gasped, apparently surprised.

My goodness, she thought testily, what's wrong with these Yankees? Can't they understand simple English? "Yes, Trooper Donovan," she repeated impatiently.

She could tell he was reluctant to offer any information. "He isn't here," the captain mumbled hesitantly.

"What do you mean, he isn't here?"

"Trooper Donovan is no longer at Fort Laramie," he explained.

Suzanne had a sinking feeling all the way to the pit of her stomach. "Has he been transferred?"

"No, ma'am," he answered.

"Where is he?" she cried.

The captain appeared quite disturbed. "I don't know exactly how to tell you this, ma'am . . ."

Interrupting, she gasped in fright, "He isn't dead, is he?"

"No," he replied quickly, seeing the fear on her pretty face.

Suzanne sighed gratefully. "Captain, Trooper Donovan is my cousin and I have traveled a great distance to find him. Will you please tell me where he is?"

"I wish I could, ma'am, but I don't know where he is." He wished there were an easier way to break the news. Carefully he told her, "Trooper Donovan has deserted."

It took a moment for his words to seep into her consciousness. She certainly didn't blame Patrick for leaving the Yankee-infested cavalry. But now, how would she ever find him? "When did he desert?" she asked, wondering how many days he had been gone.

"Ma'am, if you want more information, I think you should talk to Major Landon."

"What does this major have to do with my cousin?"

"He was Donovan's commanding officer."

"Very well, captain," she agreed. "Will you please take me to him?"

"Yes, of course," he agreed politely. He reached out to take her arm, but she drew away from his touch. Her accent had left no doubt that she was a Southerner, and the captain smiled and understood that this beautiful little rebel probably despised Yankees. Well, she has still another Yankee to confront, he thought, and Major Landon will have no patience with her hostility. And when he learns that she's Donovan's cousin, he'll have even less patience. He wondered if he should warn her to tread cautiously with the major, but then decided it was none of his business.

Suzanne fell into stride beside the captain as he led the way to the major's quarters. Realizing she was not going to see Patrick caused a sob to rise in her throat. She blinked her eyes to hold back the tears that were threatening to overflow, and swallowed deeply in an effort to rid herself of the sob aching to be released.

When they reached the major's quarters, the captain told the sentry that the young lady with him needed to see Major Landon. As the guard left to announce Suzanne's presence, she studied the stone building where the major apparently had his office and living space. It resembled a barracks, and was typically military.

The sentry returned and told Suzanne that the major would see her. He held open the door for her, and after hastily thanking the captain for his help, she entered Major Landon's office.

Glancing about the room, she saw that the interior, like the exterior, reflected an army decor. The major was standing behind his desk with his back turned, studying a wall map. He wasn't wearing his dress uniform, but was dressed in blue trousers with a matching shirt. He was a tall man, with broad, sinewy shoulders, and the rolled-up sleeves of his shirt displayed his powerful arms.

Suzanne grew impatient for him to acknowledge her presence. Obviously the major was not only a despicable Yankee, but a rude one as well! "Major Landon," she said sharply, "I do not have all day to stand here and wait for you to turn away from that map and speak to me!"

"I'll be right with you," he answered, keeping his back turned as he continued giving the map his full attention.

Losing her temper, Suzanne placed her hands on her hips, and stamping her foot, she snapped, "Major Landon, it is imperative that I talk to you immediately!"

He whirled about, and for such a big man, he moved with incredible grace. A retort had been on the tip of his tongue, but when he was unexpectedly met by such a lovely vision, he completely forgot what he was going to say. His dark eyes took in every inch of her beauty as he gave himself plenty of time to relish fully this enticing vixen standing before him.

Major Landon's masculinity was blatant, and Suzanne was overwhelmed by his aura of male dominance. He was indeed an attractive man, and his virile presence never failed to captivate a woman; Suzanne Donovan was no exception. His chestnut-brown hair matched the color of his eyes and thick lashes. A well-trimmed moustache tapered handsomely to his firm lips.

He suddenly smiled, and his smile was so sensual that it took Suzanne's breath away. "Why do you need to talk to me, and why is it so imperative that you do so immediately?"

"I need to talk to you about Trooper Patrick Donovan," she replied.

Suzanne was startled by the sudden cold rage that flickered in his dark eyes. "Donovan!" he whispered furiously. "Who are you, and what is your business with Trooper Donovan?"

"My name is Suzanne Donovan, and Patrick is my cousin. I have traveled all the way from Natchez to find him."

"Did you arrive on the wagon train?"

"Yes, I did," she answered.

"Who's traveling with you?"

"Patrick's fiancée and my servant, Saul."

"Well, Miss Donovan," he said impatiently, "all of you might as well return to Natchez because you won't find your cousin at Fort Laramie."

"Yes, I know," she replied shortly. "I have already been notified that Patrick deserted."

He raised an eyebrow. "Then why did you want to talk to me?"

"I think I have a right to know the details. Why did Patrick run away?"

His lips curled into a snarl, and his deep voice was heavy with resentment, "Your cousin ran away because he's a spineless coward!"

"Don't you dare call him a coward!" she raged.

"If I wasn't in the company of a lady, I would call him something much worse than a coward!"

Her anger fully aroused, she retorted, "I don't blame Patrick for leaving! Why would he want to stay here in your Yankee-controlled army?"

"Why indeed, Miss Donovan!" he seethed.

Lifting her chin defiantly, she asked coolly, "Major Landon, are you going to give me the details concerning my cousin's desertion, or must I go elsewhere for the information?"

Gesturing to the chair in front of his desk, he said calmly, "Sit down, Miss Donovan, and I will gladly enlighten you. I'm sure you are very anxious to hear all about your cousin's cowardice."

Finding his last remark insufferable, she was about to tell him to go straight to the devil, but her urgent need to know about Patrick prevailed. Repressing her angry words, she sat in the chair and waited silently for

Landon to continue.

He eased his large frame into his own chair and watched her across the span of his desk top. Her eyes met his without wavering. He cleared his voice before speaking. "Two weeks ago Patrick Donovan deserted his comrades during battle. A company of my men were engaged in warfare with the Sioux. Lieutenant Wilkinson, who was in charge, sent Troopers Donovan and Jones for assistance. The rest of my men and I were a few miles to the north, and the lieutenant's orders were for them to locate us so we could come to the aid of the soldiers who were fighting. Lieutenant Wilkinson and his men were greatly outnumbered by the Sioux. When your cousin and Trooper Jones had ridden out of sight of the Indians and the remaining soldiers, Donovan shot Jones in the back, then deserted. It was merely by chance that, over an hour later, my men and I happened to come across the wounded Jones. Before he died, he told me what had happened. By the time we reached the battleground, five soldiers had died and twelve were wounded. If Donovan hadn't deserted but had carried out the lieutenant's orders, chances are those five men wouldn't have died. We could've gotten there in time to save them." A hard glare came to his eyes as he continued harshly, "Your cousin not only murdered Trooper Jones, but was also indirectly responsible for the death of five good soldiers."

"No!" Suzanne cried desperately. "You are lying to me! Patrick would never do anything so horrible!"

He rose swiftly, and placing his hands on the desk, he leaned toward her. The fury on his face was frightening, and she unknowingly cringed. "I am telling you the truth, Miss Donovan! And if it's the last thing I do on this earth, I will see Trooper Donovan court-martialed!"

41

"Court-martialed!" she repeated shakily. "Will he be . . . be . . . ?"

"Executed?" he finished for her, his tone dangerously cold. "Have no doubt, madam, he will go before a firing squad!"

Leaping to her feet, she said frantically, "You can never make me believe Patrick did what you are accusing him of! I know my cousin, and he could never do anything so detestable!"

"I don't give a damn whether you believe me or not!" he shouted angrily. "If you will excuse me, Miss Donovan, I have a lot of things to take care of before I leave in the morning. At sunrise my scout and I will be leaving this fort to hunt down your cousin and bring him back to face a court-martial!"

"Take me with you!" she pleaded.

He looked incredulous. "Are you out of your mind?"

"No, I most assuredly am not!" she spat. "But I have serious doubts concerning your sanity! You must be half mad to believe Patrick would desert his comrades!"

He sighed heavily. "Miss Donovan, are you as blind as you are beautiful? Trooper Donovan is guilty as charged."

"He is innocent until proven guilty!" she remarked firmly.

"Very well, have it your way. I don't have time to argue with you."

"Are you going to let us go with you?"

"Us?" he asked.

"Saul and Patrick's fiancée," she explained. "And myself, of course."

"Absolutely not!" he grumbled.

"Major Landon, you must let us accompany you!"

"Why? So one of you can stab me in the back when I least expect it?"

She eyed him shrewdly. "Although I find your speculation very tempting, I can assure you my only reason for wanting to join you is because I know I'll need your help to find my cousin."

He studied her thoughtfully. If he had Donovan's cousin and fiancée traveling with him, their presence might make it easier for him to trap the man. But did he want to be responsible for the safety of two women?

"Major Landon," she began collectedly, her mind set, "if you refuse us permission to travel with you, then we'll search for Patrick on our own."

"Miss Donovan, if you leave this fort without proper protection, then the next time I see your lovely blond hair it'll be hanging from a Sioux warrior's lance."

Suzanne gasped, and her huge eyes widened. With a bravery she was far from feeling, she answered calmly, "Nonetheless, I will search for my cousin, and if I die while doing so, then I hope my death weighs heavily upon your conscience."

Admiring her spirit, the major chuckled. "Not only are you a courageous little rebel, you're a very sly one."

"I will make a deal with you, major. If you refrain from calling me a little rebel, then I will reciprocate and not refer to you as a damned Yankee."

This time, instead of a mere chuckle, he broke into a full laugh. "Touché, Miss Donovan, it's a deal."

"Does this mean you have decided to let us accompany you?" she asked, excited.

"I don't see that I have any other choice. I certainly wouldn't want your death on my conscience."

"Thank you, Major Landon," she said amicably. "We will be ready to leave at sunrise."

"My scout, Justin Smith, will come to your wagon in the morning. In the meantime, I suggest that you visit the traders' store and replenish any supplies you might need."

"Major," she asked, "how long do you intend to search for Patrick?"

"Until I find him," he said inflexibly.

"Can you stay away from the fort indefinitely?"

"My commanding officer has given me permission to hunt down Trooper Donovan, however long it takes."

Seeing the determination on his face, she said softly, "You won't give up your quest, will you? Not even if it takes you years to find him."

She didn't wait for his response, but turned away and walked quickly out the door.

Slowly the major returned to his chair. He wondered if his decision to let Miss Donovan and the others accompany him would turn out to be a mistake. His handsome face became deeply worried. Well, he had given her his permission and he wouldn't go back on his word. Besides, it probably wouldn't take long to locate Trooper Donovan, and the man's cousin and fiancée might prove useful in locating the deserter.

A smile crossed his lips as he recalled Suzanne's beauty. He certainly couldn't object to having such a charming traveling companion. She was not only beautiful but also spirited, and he had a feeling that she possessed integrity. But considering her cousin, it was apparently a trait that didn't run in the family.

Dismissing Suzanne from his thoughts, he stood and went back to studying the map that covered the Wyoming territory. He centered his attention on the area where Lieutenant Wilkinson and his men had been ambushed by the Sioux. Concentrating intently, he tried to figure out the most logical route for Trooper Donovan to have taken.

"I don't believe it, Miz Suzanne!" Saul groaned. "I don't believe Masta Patrick would desert his friends

44

under gunfire, and he wouldn't shoot another soldier in the back!"

"Of course he wouldn't!" Suzanne agreed resolutely. She was sitting in the back of the covered wagon with Saul and Molly. Upon her return, she had let them know about Patrick. "There must be some kind of conspiracy going on."

"What do you mean?" Saul asked, somewhat confused.

Suzanne wasn't sure what she had meant; she was merely grasping at straws. She knew her cousin as well as she knew herself, and he was not capable of cold-blooded murder or desertion under fire. Her thoughts flowing randomly, she said anxiously, "This fort is filled with Yankees. But Patrick is a Southerner. Maybe some of these Yankee soldiers didn't like him and plotted against him. Maybe he was framed."

"Surely you don't believe that!" Molly remarked, speaking for the first time since Suzanne had floored them with the shocking news of Patrick's desertion.

"What else can I believe?" Suzanne cried desperately. "Molly, you know as well as I do that Patrick is innocent!"

Molly was sitting across from Suzanne, and leaning forward, she looked closely at her friend. "You have overlooked one very feasible explanation."

Suzanne and Saul both stared questioningly at her.

Molly went on intensely, "You haven't considered the likely chance that this Trooper Donovan isn't our Patrick."

"Of course!" Suzanne exclaimed, her face bright with optimism. "Uncle Thomas's friend probably made a mistake. There was a Patrick Donovan stationed here, but he wasn't the right Patrick!" Smiling with new hope, she leaned toward Molly and hugged her with enthusiasm.

"This Trooper Donovan," Saul began, "he must've left some of his things behind. Miz Suzanne . . ."

Interrupting and leaping to her feet, she declared, "I'm one step ahead of you, Saul. I'll examine his personal belongings. If he's our Patrick, I'll recognize his possessions."

Suzanne left the wagon hurriedly, and her hopes raced zealously as she rushed back to Major Landon's quarters. She brushed past the young sentry, and flinging open the door, she darted into the office.

Following her inside, the soldier said urgently, "Ma'am, you can't walk in here without first being announced."

Major Landon was seated behind his desk, and rising, he looked at Suzanne with amazement. "Miss Donovan," he said sternly, "do you think I have a guard at my door just for the hell of it?"

She glared at him for a moment, then whirling lightly, she marched back out the door and waited for the sentry to follow. As he emerged, she said clearly, so the major would overhear, "May I please have an audience with Major Landon?"

"Miss Donovan!" she heard him bellow from inside the office.

She smiled saucily at the young guard, and her enticing smile made him feel flushed.

"Ma'am," he stammered, "I . . . I think the major is expecting you."

She laughed gaily, and sweeping past him, she stepped back inside. Major Landon had walked out from behind his desk and was now leaning against it with his arms folded across his chest.

Looking at her reproachfully, he remarked evenly, "Are you always so defiant, my little Confederate?"

Scowling, she spat, "You promised not to refer to me in that manner!"

He cocked an eyebrow. "I said that I would not call you a little rebel, I said nothing in reference to addressing you as a little Confederate."

Lifting her chin and meeting his steady gaze, she answered defensively, "Yes, I am usually quite defiant; especially where Yankees are concerned."

He grinned wryly, and once again Suzanne was acutely aware of his sensual smile.

"I didn't expect to see you again until tomorrow morning," he remarked. "I suppose you have an important reason for returning."

"Yes, I do," she said anxiously. "Major, I need to see Trooper Donovan's personal belongings. I have reason to suspect that this Patrick Donovan isn't my cousin."

He was very interested. "For your sake, I hope your suspicions are true. Will you describe your cousin to me?"

"He's average height and has blond hair and blue eyes."

The major's expression was inscrutable. "Any discrepancies?" he asked.

"Patrick was wounded in his left leg during the first year of the war, and he walks with a slight limp."

He sighed heavily. "I'm sorry, Miss Donovan, but your description fits Trooper Donovan perfectly."

"No!" she cried despairingly. "This man can't be my cousin!"

Gently he asked, "Do you still want to see Donovan's personal belongings?"

"Yes, please," she whispered brokenly.

The major hastened to the door and ordered the sentry to bring him Trooper Donovan's possessions. Returning to his desk, he told Suzanne to be seated.

She complied numbly, as a feeling of depression came over her. She had been hoping so desperately that this Trooper Donovan would not be her Patrick.

Major Landon studied her sympathetically. Her distress touched him deeply. He wished he could say something to lighten her mood, or give her hope. But what could he possibly say? If Trooper Donovan wasn't her cousin, then he was the man's identical counterpart.

The major kept their conversation on a light note until the sentry returned and handed the major a cloth bag. He dismissed the sentry, then placed the bundle on his desk. "Miss Donovan," he said quietly, "these are Donovan's belongings."

She stood and stepped to the desk, untied the bag slowly, and cautiously reached inside. Removing two pairs of trousers and a couple of shirts, she looked them over carefully. They were not familiar. She reached back further into the bag and her fingers closed on a stack of letters. She quickly brought them forth. Staring down at the letters in her hand, she gasped and tears filled her eyes. Raising her gaze to the major, she moaned, "These are from me! These are letters that I wrote to Patrick!"

She suddenly felt faint and her knees weakened, causing her to sway unsteadily against the major. His strong arms went about her, holding her supportively.

Drawing her closer, he murmured tenderly, "I'm sorry. I was hoping he wasn't your cousin."

Without conscious thought, she leaned into his embrace, where she found the comfort she needed so badly.

Major Landon was startled by the intense emotions this enticing little rebel and the feel of her soft body pressed to his had stirred within him.

Coming to her senses, Suzanne squirmed out of his arms. Good Lord, she had actually allowed a Yankee to embrace her! He was not only a Yankee, but also the man who intended to capture Patrick and have him executed!

Reading her thoughts, the major chuckled. "You aren't quite as defiant as you thought, are you, my lovely little Confederate?"

Her eyes flashed angrily. "Don't let the embrace we shared give you the wrong idea, Major Landon! I wouldn't desire you if you were the last man on the face of the earth!"

"Do you mind telling me why?" he asked calmly.

"I love Patrick with all my heart and soul! You are the man who wants to see him killed! Need I elaborate further?"

"No," he answered levelly. "But allow me to add emphasis to an important part of your statement. It's true that I want to see Trooper Donovan executed, but if the necessity should arise, he'll die by my own hand."

"Not if I can help it!" she promised.

"Forewarned is forearmed, madam." He grinned insolently.

She cast him an icy glare, then turned away and hurried outside. Clutching the letters to her heart, she headed quickly toward her wagon.

Chapter Three

"Do you realize what you are asking of Saul and me?" Molly demanded, her eyes staring into Suzanne's incredulously.

The two women were standing close to the wagon as Saul was unhitching the mule team. Immediately upon her return from Major Landon's office, Suzanne had told her companions that Trooper Donovan was apparently their Patrick. She had then proceeded to inform them that they would be leaving first thing in the morning to continue their search, with Major Landon and his scout accompanying them.

Suzanne was puzzled by Molly's startling reaction. "I don't understand why you are so upset."

Striving for patience, Molly answered, "I can't believe that you expect us to leave this fort to go trekking across the wilderness! Suzanne, we are not in Mississippi. This land is dangerous, there are wild Sioux who are on the warpath."

"Nonsense!" Suzanne refuted with a certainty she didn't truly feel. "If it was really all that dangerous, the major and his scout wouldn't leave. And Major Landon wouldn't have given us permission to accompany them."

Annoyed, Molly argued, "Soldiers knowingly place their lives in jeopardy. I'm sure the major and his scout are fully aware that this quest is a very perilous one."

"Then why is Major Landon allowing us to go with them?" Suzanne asked pointedly.

Turning away from the mules, Saul took it upon himself to answer Suzanne's question. "That Yankee major is most likely plannin' to use us as bait. He probably figures it'll be easier for him to catch Masta Patrick if he has us travelin' with him."

His speculation made a lot of sense and convinced Suzanne, who spat resentfully, "That sneaky, low-down varmint! So he intends to use us, does he? Well, we'll just play along with his underhanded game. Then, when he finds Patrick, he'll wish he didn't have us with him, because we'll help Patrick escape."

"That might be easier said than done," Saul surmised, unable to repress a grin.

Deciding that helping Patrick was a bridge they would cross when they came to it, Suzanne remarked, "When the time is right, we'll outsmart that Yankee."

"If we don't get scalped by Indians first," Molly put in.

Considerately Suzanne told her, "If you want to stay here at the fort, I'll understand. When I asked you to come on this trip with me, I didn't intend you to risk your life for Patrick."

Molly's emotions were in conflict. Considering the way Patrick had treated her, she felt she didn't owe him her undying loyalty. In fact, she wasn't even sure if she still loved her fiancé. But she loved Suzanne as dearly as a sister. Could she stay behind while her good friend embarked on such a dangerous mission? If it were the other way around, would Suzanne desert her? No, Molly thought, she would remain my ally and support me dauntlessly. Smiling ruefully, Molly murmured,

"I'm going with you."

Reaching for her friend, Suzanne hugged her affectionately. Then looking at Saul, she said kindly, "If you want to remain here . . ."

Interrupting, he declared firmly, "Miz Suzanne, you and Miz Molly ain't goin' nowhere without me along to protect you two." Somberly he added, "Besides, I love Masta Patrick, and I want to find him as badly as you do."

Suzanne was deeply touched, and misty-eyed, she replied softly, "I don't know how to thank you two. You are both very brave."

"I'm not sure if I'm all that brave," Molly said crisply, controlling her own sudden tears, "but I am practical. Saul, if you're finished unhitching the team, would you mind accompanying me to the traders' store? We need to buy some extra supplies."

"Yes'm, Miz Molly," he consented. "I'll go with you."

After they had left for the store, Suzanne took a blanket from the wagon and placed it on the ground. She still held the letters she had written to Patrick, and sitting on the blanket, she laid them on her lap. She gazed down at them through a tearful blur. Oh, Patrick, she moaned inwardly. Why are these Yankees accusing you of such horrible deeds? You could never do the terrible things they say you have done!

Her eyes remaining downcast, Suzanne's thoughts were swept away into the past.

"Patrick! Patrick!" the five-year-old Suzanne called urgently. She had been exploring in the woods behind the house, and emerging from the thicket, she had spotted Patrick on his way toward the stables.

The boy paused to wait for his young cousin. He

noticed that she carried something in her hands. Looking closely, he saw that it was a bird.

Reaching him, she gazed up into his eyes, her face flushed with worry. "I found this little bird in the woods and it's hurt." Her fear for the feathered creature began to wane. Patrick would know what to do for the bird. Patrick knew everything!

"Let me see it," he said gently. She handed him the patient, and he cradled the bird carefully. Looking it over closely, Patrick diagnosed that it had a broken wing.

"Will it die?" Suzanne gasped, her blue eyes alarmed.

"I don't know," Patrick answered gently.

"Do birds die when their wings are broken? People don't die when they break their arms."

Patrick held back the urge to smile. "It won't die because of its wing. But it's a wild creature, and if we set its wing, it'll have to remain in captivity until it heals. Sometimes wild animals can't survive confinement."

"But it's sure to die if we don't help it!" she remarked thoughtfully.

"That's true," Patrick agreed. "Let's take it to the stables, maybe Saul can help us."

Falling into stride beside her cousin, Suzanne asked, "What kind of bird is it?"

"A bobwhite quail," he answered.

Without losing step, she reached over and petted the bird, which was still resting in Patrick's hands. "Poor little bobwhite," she soothed.

"Suzanne," he began carefully, "don't become too attached to this bird. Chances are he won't survive."

"Yes, he will, Patrick! You can make him well!" She looked at him with complete trust.

The boy was perfectly aware that his young cousin utterly worshipped him. He wasn't overly concerned. He believed all children needed someone to look up to with high regard. He had idolized his Uncle Kevin. But the thought of disappointing Suzanne worried him. She was putting too much faith in him. How could he possibly keep this wild creature alive? It would mourn for its freedom until eventually its malaise would probably bring on its death. He decided if it were humanly possible to keep the bird alive, Suzanne would not be disappointed, for he had every intention of trying his damnedest to live up to her expectations.

True to his word, Patrick dedicated his time and energy the next few days to saving the wounded bobwhite. His diligence was rewarded, and the bird made a remarkable recovery.

When the day finally came for the bobwhite to be set free, Suzanne was firmly against the idea. She had grown fond of her feathered friend and wanted to keep it as a pet.

Patrick had insisted that she accompany him into the woods, where he planned to free the bird. Suzanne agreed reluctantly. If she hadn't loved Patrick so much, she would have refused, but her feeling for her cousin went much deeper than those for the bird.

Now, as they strolled into the wooded area, Suzanne walked silently beside Patrick, keeping her solemn mood to herself.

The boy knew exactly how she was feeling. Somehow he must make her realize that the bird had been born to be free, and to keep it confined would be cruel.

There was a creek in the woods, and taking her there, Patrick told her to sit down. He joined her on the bank, and she gazed sadly at the bird held gently in his hands. The bobwhite was calm, totally trusting the boy holding it. It had known only kindness and healing from the hands enclosing its body.

Looking around, Patrick said casually, "The forest is beautiful, isn't it?"

"I suppose so," she admitted, her pretty face sullen.

"Would you like to live in the woods?" he asked.

"Of course not," she answered quickly.

"Why not?" he pressed.

"People aren't supposed to live in the woods," she remarked.

"Who does live in the forest?" he asked.

"Animals and birds," she replied easily.

"That's right, Suzanne. The woods are home to wild creatures. It isn't right to take anyone away from their home, is it?"

"No, I guess not," she muttered, his reasoning making headway.

"Would you like it if someone took you away from Southmoor and made you live in the woods?"

Tears welled up in her eyes. "I know what you are trying to tell me. But Patrick, our little bird might be scared. Maybe he forgot that he's supposed to live in the woods."

"Do you know what instinct means?"

She shook her head.

"It means something that is inborn. God gave this natural gift to all his wild creatures. It is the only way they have to survive."

"Does our bird have instinct?"

"Yes, he does, and that is why he won't be scared. He will fly to his own kind."

"But will he be happy?" she insisted.

He smiled warmly. "Yes, he will be happy."

"Then set him free, Patrick."

Lifting the bird, Patrick pitched him upward. It took a moment for the bobwhite to stretch his wings and fly, and when it appeared as though he were going to fall, Suzanne gasped fearfully. But then he gracefully flapped his widespread wings and soared smoothly into the air. They watched him as he circled about, then flew to a tree branch and perched on it.

Pointing into the sky, Patrick said, "Look, Suzanne. He has already made a friend."

Suzanne looked on with amazement as another bobwhite landed on the limb beside him.

Chuckling, Patrick said, "I think he has just found himself a girlfriend."

"He's happy now, isn't he, Patrick?" she asked, her large eyes glazed with joy.

Slipping his arm about her shoulders and drawing her closer to his side, Patrick answered, "Yes, honey, I'm sure he's very happy."

She snuggled against him. At the age of fifteen, Patrick was beginning to take on a manly appearance. Glancing down at his hands, Suzanne could see their strength; yet they had been so gentle when doctoring the wounded bird. At this moment she loved him so much that she felt as though her heart would overflow.

Suzanne, engrossed in her memories, didn't hear the man walking up quietly behind her. She wasn't aware of his presence until he leaned over and dropped a pocket watch onto her lap. The timepiece fell atop the letters, and startled, she raised her head and stared up into Major Landon's eyes.

"The watch was among Donovan's possessions," he explained. "It appears to be quite expensive, and I thought you might like to have it."

"Thank you," she murmured, picking up the watch and studying it reflectively. "Uncle Thomas gave this to Patrick on his twenty-first birthday."

The major knelt at her side. "When I walked up, you seemed to be very deep in thought. Were you thinking about your cousin?"

"Yes," she confessed. "I was remembering . . ." Her

voice faded abruptly as she realized to whom she was speaking. She wasn't about to reminisce about Patrick to this man who wanted to see him executed!

"Remembering what?" he coaxed soothingly.

"It doesn't matter," she said briskly.

"Why don't you tell me about your cousin?"

"Why should I? You already know him."

"Yes, I know him, but certainly not very well. Officers and enlisted men don't usually socialize."

"Patrick was an officer in the Confederate Army."

"But he wasn't an officer in the cavalry. Southern prisoners who agreed to come west did not keep their commissions. They were still considered hostile, and the army was not about to give them power of any kind."

"Did very many Confederate officers choose the cavalry over imprisonment?"

"No, nor were there very many enlisted men. The Southerners who agreed to betray the Confederacy were outcasts, cowards and men of little value."

Suzanne's eyes flashed daggers. "Are you insinuating that Patrick is an outcast, a coward, and has no values?"

"Your cousin is a traitor, Miss Donovan."

Leaping to her feet, she raged, "You dirty, low-down Yankee, you aren't fit to wipe his boots!"

Standing upright, he gazed steadily down into her angry face. "Not fit to wipe his boots?" he repeated. "Madam, I intend to wipe your cousin off the face of this earth!"

"Why do you hate him so much?" she pleaded.

"He murdered a good soldier and caused the death of five more."

She turned away from his gaze. Stepping to the wagon, she kept her voice even. "I don't think we have anything further to discuss, major."

"Do you always try to run away when you're backed into a corner?" he challenged.

Whirling around to face him, she snapped, "You won this battle, Major Landon. But I intend to win the war."

"I didn't know we were at war," he replied calmly.

"Oh?" She raised her eyebrows shrewdly.

He smiled handsomely. "It's already been proven that a Yankee can beat a Southerner. But if you insist on fighting, just remember to the victor go the spoils."

"Don't be impertinent!" she spat.

Chuckling and moving away, he called, "I'll see you in the morning, my hostile little Confederate."

She glared at his departing back, then hastily climbed into the wagon. The man was insufferable! She wished he wasn't so sensually handsome; it would be easier for her to hate him.

Entering the Officers' Club, the major caught sight of Justin Smith, who was sitting at a corner table. Going to the man, he pulled out a chair and joined him.

"Are you ready to leave in the morning?" Justin asked. He was a big man, his physique brawny, reflecting the man's great strength. His black hair grew to collar length, and he had a full beard that matched the color of his hair. His dark brown eyes added to his rugged but attractive aura.

Hesitantly the major told him, "There's been a change in our plans."

Justin looked puzzled.

"It won't be just the two of us on this mission," he disclosed, then waited with feigned calmness for his friend's response.

"Damn it, Blade!" Justin fussed. "We don't need

58

anyone else ridin' with us. We can make better time alone."

Leaning back in his chair and stretching out his long legs, the major replied firmly, "I don't intend to change my mind about this."

Justin recognized Blade's set expression and knew he meant what he said. "Who's going with us?" The man frowned, not trying to hide his irritation.

"Donovan's fiancée, his cousin, and their servant. They arrived on the wagon train this morning."

"Fiancée!" Justin bellowed. "We don't need a woman travelin' with us!"

"Women," Blade corrected evenly.

"Is the servant a woman?"

"I don't think so, since his name is Saul."

"Then the cousin is a woman?"

Blade grinned. "She is definitely a woman, and the most beautiful one I've ever seen."

"What in the hell is wrong with you?" Justin demanded. "This mission is too dangerous for women to be a part of it!"

Sighing, Blade admitted, "I totally agree. But if I hadn't given Donovan's cousin permission to join us, she was determined that she and the others would search for him on their own. Two women and a servant wouldn't stand a chance out there on the plains by themselves."

"Is she that desperate to find Donovan?"

"She's dead set on finding him."

Justin smirked. "If he was my kin, I'd disown him."

"Disown him?" Blade chuckled. "She thinks the sun rises and sets on him."

"Doesn't she know what he's done?"

The major shrugged. "Sure she knows, but she refuses to accept it."

Justin looked worried. "I don't like being responsible for two women."

"Neither do I, but we've got them whether we like it or not." Sitting upright, he continued, "Besides, having Donovan's cousin and fiancée might work in our favor. Their presence could make it easier for us to catch him."

Justin nodded reluctantly. "Maybe," he mumbled, "but I still don't like it."

The waiter stepped to their table, and Blade ordered a glass of brandy. Justin watched his friend thoughtfully as he leaned back in his chair once again and lit a cheroot. He'd known Blade for twelve years, during which time their friendship had deepened into mutual respect, and they loved each other like brothers. Justin was forty-three, which made him ten years older than Blade. He had first met the major when Blade was a lieutenant fresh out of West Point.

Continuing his close perusal, Justin remarked quietly, "Donovan's cousin made quite an impression on you, didn't she?"

"I've never met a woman like her. She's got spirit, courage, and dignity. It's hard to believe she's kin to Donovan. How can two people who are so opposite come from the same family?"

Justin didn't offer a solution; instead he grumbled, "I've got a feelin' this woman is goin' to cause trouble."

Although Blade's eyes met Justin's, he made no comment concerning his friend's prediction. He sensed the man's words would come to pass. Suzanne Donovan was trouble, he didn't doubt it for a moment.

Chapter Four

On the morning of their departure Molly finished dressing before Suzanne, and deciding to help Saul hitch the team, she climbed down from the back of the wagon. Noticing a tall, bearded man approaching, she paused hesitantly and wondered if he was the major's scout who was supposed to come to them this morning.

He wore a buckskin shirt that fit snugly across his wide shoulders and broad chest. When he reached Molly, he doffed his weather-worn hat. "Miss Donovan?" he inquired.

"No," she replied a little breathlessly, overwhelmed by his strong presence. "I am Miss O'Ryan. Are you Major Landon's scout?"

"Yes'm. Justin Smith's the name." He studied her with mild puzzlement.

"Is something wrong?" she asked, wondering why he was staring.

"If you aren't Donovan's cousin, then you must be his fiancée," he replied, his eyes still perusing her.

"Yes, I am," she answered, beginning to feel somewhat flustered.

His expression thoughtful, he questioned, "How long have you and Donovan been engaged?"

She thought his question too personal, but remaining cordial she answered, "We have been betrothed for five years."

"I always heard that Southern women marry young, but you couldn't have been more than thirteen when you became engaged. Ain't that just a little too young?"

Bristling, she said testily, "I was twenty years old when Patrick asked me to be his wife."

"No kiddin'?" he responded, taking a step backward and looking her over from head to foot. "I could've sworn you weren't a day over eighteen."

"Mr. Smith, you are very rude!" she retorted.

"Rude?" he repeated. "Why, most women consider it a compliment when a man guesses them to be younger."

Folding her arms beneath her breasts and eyeing him severely, she answered, "Well, I am not most women. I hate it when people take me to be younger than I am."

Justin was chuckling heartily when Suzanne emerged from beneath the canvas. The sight of her caused his deep laughter to fade abruptly. Admiration filled his eyes as he watched her descend from the wagon. One look at the lovely woman told him why the major was so taken with her. He had never seen anyone so beautiful.

"Suzanne," Molly said, "this is the scout, Justin Smith."

When she smiled, he found the deep dimples in her cheeks downright enticing. "How do you do, Mr. Smith. I am Suzanne Donovan."

He touched the brim of his hat. "Ma'am, the major is ready to leave. We'll wait for all of you at the main gate."

"Very well, Mr. Smith. We'll be there momentarily."

He nodded his approval, then walked away. The two women watched his departure, then Suzanne asked,

"What was Mr. Smith laughing about?"

"Suzanne, the man is rude and uncouth," Molly spat.

"What did he do?" she asked anxiously.

"He asked me personal questions, and he told me I look like I'm eighteen."

Suzanne repressed an amused grin. She knew how her friend hated her youthful appearance. "Molly, there's nothing wrong in looking younger."

"That's easy for you to say," she argued. "Your youthfulness is beautiful, but mine is . . . is adolescent!"

"Well, I'm sorry the man upset you, but I'm sure he's a Yankee, so you can't expect him to act like a gentleman."

Blade and Justin were mounted on their horses and waiting for Suzanne and the others as their wagon rolled toward the opened gates. Suzanne tried to refrain from looking closely at the major, but against her will her eyes trailed over him appreciatively. She was surprised to see that he wasn't in uniform, but was dressed in a buckskin shirt and tan trousers with a gun belt strapped about his hips. As the wagon drew closer, she could see that his shirt was partially unbuttoned, revealing the dark hair that grew thickly across his muscular chest.

When Saul pulled up the team, the major's eyes gleamed insolently into Suzanne's. "Good morning, Miss Donovan."

"Good morning," she replied, lifting her chin haughtily.

Finding her arrogance amusing, he responded with a mocking chuckle.

Keeping her composure, she asked evenly, "Exactly

where are we going, Major Landon?"

"West," he answered.

She looked startled. "My goodness, if we are traveling westward, why don't we wait and journey with the wagon train?"

"We'll be making a few detours along the way," he replied.

"Along the way where?" she asked impatiently.

"California," he answered. "Unless we find your cousin between here and there. If we should, then we'll return to Fort Laramie."

"California!" she exclaimed. To Suzanne it sounded like the ends of the earth.

"Most deserters end up in San Francisco," he explained. "They can easily get a job on a ship and be out of the country in no time."

"Do you really want to find Patrick so badly that you'd chase him all the way to San Francisco?"

"If need be, madam, I'll chase him around the world. The question is, are you willing to do likewise?"

She squinted resentfully. "Major, I want to find my cousin worse than you do."

"I doubt it, Miss Donovan. Your quest is compelled by love, but I am driven by hate." Meeting her gaze with an intensity that was almost frightening, he added, "Hate is a much stronger compulsion than love."

She refused to flinch beneath his hard scrutiny. "If you believe that, then apparently you have never loved anyone with all your heart and soul. Otherwise you would know that love is the strongest of all emotions."

"That goes both ways, madam," he said firmly. "Obviously you have never truly hated anyone."

Interrupting their bickering, Justin remarked, "Shouldn't we be leaving?"

Blade agreed, and Justin led their pack mule to the back of the wagon and tied it securely, whereupon Saul slapped the reins against the team and the wagon moved through the open gates.

On the first night of their journey, the travelers stopped at dusk and set up camp. The day had been uneventful but tiring. Suzanne found riding in a wagon uncomfortable and wished she could travel horseback. If she'd had a horse, she would have carried out her wish, but all she had was a team of mules.

Following the evening meal, Molly helped Suzanne wash the dishes in the wooden tub they carried for that purpose. Then, deciding to retire, Molly walked to the wagon and was about to climb inside when Justin suddenly appeared.

"Ma'am," he said softly, "I'd like to thank you for supper. The major and I are carrying our own grub, but you and Miss Donovan can cook a lot better than either one of us."

"Mr. Smith, I hope you and Major Landon will join us at every meal. I wouldn't dream of making two men cook for themselves."

Smiling disarmingly, he replied, "Thank you, ma'am." His gaze grew thoughtful. "Miss O'Ryan, your freckles make you as cute as a speckled hound pup."

Blushing, and somewhat irritated, she said coolly, "Mr. Smith, if that was supposed to be a compliment, then it was not appreciated."

Crossing his arms over his chest, he eyed her darkly. "Dad-gum it, woman! What's wrong with you? Don't you like compliments?"

Flustered, she stammered, "Of course I do, but I don't like to be reminded that I look eighteen, and . . . and I hate my freckles!"

He guffawed heartily, his mirth piquing Molly's

temper. "Stop laughing!" she commanded. "How would you like it if you were compared to a speckled hound pup?"

His eyes gleaming with amusement, he answered, "Why ma'am, there ain't nothin' any cuter than a speckled hound puppy."

Deciding the man was too uncouth to understand her reasoning, she said curtly, "If you'll excuse me, Mr. Smith, I think I will retire. Good night, sir."

She turned to enter the wagon, but swiftly his hand was on her arm, deterring her. His masculine strength easily had her pinned against him. He was such a powerfully big man that she felt he must be as strong as a bear. As she gazed warily up into his black bearded face, she became aware of a savage magnetism about him that was not only overwhelming but exciting as well.

"Let's get one thing straight, Miss O'Ryan," he said, his tone mildly threatening. "I don't like women who are haughty and put on airs. Now I don't want to place you across my knees and spank you, but I will if you push me too far."

"How dare you!" she gasped out.

"Don't dare me, ma'am, 'cause I'm mighty curious to see if you also have freckles on your pretty little behind." He grinned devilishly.

She tried desperately to free herself from his tenacious hold, but her attempts were futile. "I have never met a man as rude as you are!"

"Ma'am, you ain't never met a man like me, period. And considering who you are engaged to, you probably don't know what a man really is." He released her brusquely.

Her wrath fully aroused, she seethed, "I refuse to discuss my fiancé with you!"

"Good!" he remarked. "Skunks have never been one

of my favorite topics."

"You are not only ill-mannered but also totally impossible!"

His grin cocky, he responded, "And you're still as cute as a speckled pup, even more so when you're angry."

"You . . . you insolent cad! Will you please go away and leave me alone!"

"I'll leave for now, ma'am," he consented. "But just remember, we have a lot of miles to travel together, and there's no way we can avoid each other's company."

He quickly bade her good night, then turning away, he strolled over to his horse to bed it down for the night.

Suzanne sat alone beside the campfire. Molly had retired and Saul was sleeping in his bedroll, which was beneath the wagon. The major and his scout were standing a short distance away, deep in conversation. Suzanne knew she should go to bed, but she wasn't feeling sleepy. Her concern for Patrick was too acute, and these worries kept her wide awake. Considering how deeply she loved her cousin, she was amazed that she still had a certain degree of control over her emotions. She wondered how much more she could take before she'd completely break down.

She lifted the coffeepot from the hot coals and poured herself a cup of the warm brew. Sipping the drink, she stared reflectively into the darting flames. Suzanne treasured her memories of Patrick, and as she sat quietly beside the flickering fire, she allowed herself the pleasure of indulging in yet another.

Searching for six-year-old Suzanne, Patrick found

her in the woods sitting beside the creek. His mother had informed him that the child had stormed out of the house, simply because she had been told she was to go away to boarding school. Ellen's decision to send the child away had infuriated Patrick. He believed Suzanne was too young to leave home. He had lashed out at his mother, telling her he would not stand by and allow her to treat the girl unfairly. He knew Ellen wanted to get rid of Suzanne, because she had never wanted to take her into their home in the first place. Patrick had insisted that a tutor be hired for Suzanne so she could receive her schooling at home. At first Ellen had firmly refused, but Patrick had voiced his objections so strongly that she'd finally relented. After receiving his mother's promise to employ a tutor, he left the house to look for his cousin. He had sensed that he would find her down at the creek.

Now, strolling up to Suzanne, he sat down beside her. She gazed up at him, her large eyes filled with tears. "Aunt Ellen is sending me away!" she sobbed. "Oh, Patrick, I don't want to leave you!"

"You aren't leaving," he murmured. "I had a long talk with mother, and she has decided to hire a tutor for you."

Suzanne's face brightened. "Honest?"

"Yes, honest," he replied, grinning fondly.

Excited, she asked, "How did you get Aunt Ellen to change her mind?"

His blue eyes twinkled. "It doesn't matter."

Feeling warm and happy in her cousin's presence, she glanced about their surroundings, then said, "Patrick, let's call this place our own special place."

"All right," he agreed, indulging her.

Her face quite serious, she told him, "We'll always come here to our special place whenever we are worried or . . . or need to think about something. And if we are separated but need to feel the other's presence, we can always feel that we are together here in our special place."

He studied her with wonder. Suzanne's intelligence never failed to impress him. She could speak with a wisdom far beyond her years.

Watching him expectantly, she asked, "Is it a deal, Patrick?"

Offering her his hand, he answered, "It's a deal; let's shake on it."

She gladly complied. Patrick loved his young cousin with all his heart, and was struck anew with how precious she was to him. He drew her into his arms and hugged her affectionately.

"Thinking about your cousin again?" Blade's voice broke into Suzanne's reverie.

Startled, she glanced up to find the major standing beside her. "Yes, I was," she admitted crisply, ready to defend Patrick should this man come back with a snide remark.

He joined her beside the campfire. "You should be in bed. Tomorrow will be a long and tiring day. You need your rest."

"I'm not sleepy," she murmured, placing her coffee cup aside.

They lapsed into silence. A coyote's howl suddenly sounded in the eerie quiet. The beast's cry sent an uncontrollable shiver through Suzanne.

Her feelings didn't escape Blade's observation, and taking advantage of the moment, he said with feigned seriousness, "Miss Donovan, I want you to remain perfectly calm, but I think we are being watched."

She was confused. "What are you talking about?"

"The Sioux often imitate coyotes. They can move in

69

close to their prey, and at the same time, let the others know their exact position by imitating a coyote's howl." Blade's eyes gleamed mischievously. He knew there were no Sioux for miles around, and the howling was that of a coyote.

Gullibly, she cried, "Do you think we are being surrounded by Indians?"

"Sh . . . sh," he whispered cautiously. "If there are Sioux out there, they possibly don't plan to attack. They're most likely just curious. If we don't let on that we are aware of their presence, they'll probably just observe us for awhile, then move on."

"All right," she agreed bravely, her eyes surreptitiously scanning the dark background. Another long, forlorn howl came from the distance, and she unconsciously moved closer to the major's side.

Blade smiled inwardly. He had her right where he wanted her, snuggled next to him. Carefully he slipped his arm about her shoulders. When he felt her stiffen, he said pressingly, "Miss Donovan, for your own sake, pretend that you're my wife."

"Why?" she demanded.

"If one of these warriors get the impression that you are unattached, he might decide to kidnap you and take you for his own."

She found the thought terrifying.

"Furthermore," he continued, "I think it would be very wise if you were to put your arms around me and kiss me."

"Isn't that going just a little too far?" she argued, but the words had scarcely passed her lips before a loud, persistent howl was heard. Promptly she threw her arms about the major, then lifted her face to his so he could kiss her.

Triumphant, his mouth claimed hers, and the taste of her sweet lips stirred warm emotions within him.

Against her will, her lips soon parted beneath his, and as he intensified their kiss, she couldn't prevent herself from responding.

The sound of footsteps interrupted them, and Suzanne pushed away from the arms enfolding her. Seeing Justin approaching, she said intensely, "We are surrounded by Indians."

Before he could manage a reply, he had to recover from the shock of having witnessed their kiss. He had gotten the distinct feeling that Miss Donovan harbored hostile feelings toward the major. Then, as her warning seeped into his conscious thought, he asked, astonished, "What makes you think we are surrounded by Indians?"

"Those aren't coyotes out there howling."

Bestowing a discerning look upon Blade, Justin roared with laughter.

Realizing she had been deceived, Suzanne bounded to her feet. Her blue eyes flashing angrily, she glared down at the major and raged, "You lying, contemptible Yankee!"

Keeping his expression innocent, he replied, "All's fair in love and war, and after all, you were the one who said we are at war. Personally, I prefer love over war."

Seething, she retorted, "I'll get even with you for this! You dirty, low-down, sneaky, no-good varmint!"

Whirling about, she hastened to the wagon and climbed inside without a backward glance.

Sitting beside his friend, Justin chuckled as he repeated Suzanne's tirade. "Dirty, low-down, sneaky, no-good varmint?"

Gaily, Blade said, "Miss Donovan does have a way with words, doesn't she?"

Meanwhile, inside the wagon, Suzanne was still steaming inwardly. She had never before been so angry, but her wrath was aimed partly at herself. She had actually responded to that Yankee's kiss! Going to her pallet, she lay down and tried to calm her feelings. Well, if he ever tries to kiss me again, she decided stubbornly, I'll belt him a good one right across his arrogant jaw!

Chapter Five

The second day of their journey was beginning to look as though it would be uneventful when unexpectedly a large swirl of dust appeared on the horizon. This evolved into a squad of mounted soldiers, followed by a covered wagon, its white canvas top billowing like a floating cloud.

Blade told Saul to pull up the team, then he and Justin rode out to meet the advancing troop. Suzanne was seated on the wagon seat beside Saul, and she looked on with curiosity. She and the others watched in silence as the major and his scout talked with the officer in charge. They waited anxiously, and within a few minutes Blade left Justin with the soldiers to return to their wagon.

"Has something happened?" Suzanne asked him.

"A shipment of army rifles from Fort Laramie to Fort Fetterman was stolen by the Sioux," he explained.

"What does this mean?" she asked.

"This means we'll have to postpone our quest temporarily. Captain Goldsworthy and his men are searching for the warriors with the rifles, and Justin and I will join them."

"Why have you decided to accompany them?" Was

Patrick somehow involved?

"Although I want to find Trooper Donovan, my job takes priority."

Suzanne wasn't sure she completely believed him. Had he told the truth, or was he hiding something? "What are we supposed to do while you and Mr. Smith are off hunting Indians?" Her tone was laced with sarcasm.

"A few of the captain's men will escort you all to Fort Fetterman. You will remain there until Justin and I come for you." He glanced up at the sky, noting the sun's descent into the west. "It's too late for you to leave today. We'll set up camp with the soldiers, then first thing in the morning you'll be taken to the fort."

"Are we settin' up camp here?" Saul asked.

"No, there's a better place a couple of miles to the west."

The mounted troopers moved their horses aside, preparing an opening for the wagon belonging to the civilians. Gesturing toward the gap, Blade explained, "As a precautionary measure, the soldiers will surround the wagon."

"Are we in danger?" Suzanne asked.

"There are armed Sioux close by, and as of now we don't know their intentions." Looking at Saul, he ordered, "Move this wagon up so they can surround you, and as we travel to the location where we plan to camp, keep this wagon safely within the confines of the soldiers." He turned his eyes on Suzanne, and his tone brooked no opposition. "I don't want you sitting in the open. Get under the canvas with Miss O'Ryan, and stay there."

He waited until she obeyed before telling Saul to move out.

*   *   *

Suzanne sat beside the campfire between Molly and Saul. The soldiers, still keeping them surrounded, were camped on all sides.

"I never thought I'd be relieved to be encircled by blue uniforms," Molly said quietly. "But it's comforting to know these soldiers are between us and the Sioux."

Suzanne offered no comment, even though she reluctantly agreed with her friend. She wished they weren't indebted to Yankees. Deciding she preferred not to sit by idly and stare at blue uniforms, she got to her feet and said tiredly, "Well, I'm going to bed. Good night."

She moved away from the fire and went to the wagon. Before she could climb inside, Blade seemed to appear from nowhere. He grasped her arm, and trying to jerk free, she said sharply, "Let go of me!"

"I want to talk to you," he replied sternly. Tightening his hold, he urged her away from the wagon.

As he encouraged her to walk at his side, she demanded, "Where are you taking me?"

"Where we can be alone," he answered shortly.

"Isn't it dangerous to leave the camp? After all, we might be surrounded by hostile Sioux!"

Grinning wryly, he added, "Or howling coyotes."

Piqued, she once again tried to pull away from his grasp. "Have you stopped to consider that I might not want to be alone with you?"

Still keeping her in his grip, he retorted evenly, "Frankly, madam, I don't give a damn. I need to talk to you, and you're going to listen."

They were now a couple of yards from the large campsite, and halting their steps, Blade released his hold. They were standing in darkness, and the surrounding blackness made Suzanne feel uneasy.

Sensing her fear, he said reassuringly, "Don't be

afraid. Justin is close by, and he's keeping a lookout. You won't be attacked by Indians." His eyes twinkling, he continued, "Or wild animals."

"Does he also intend to protect me from sneaky varmints?" she snapped.

"If you are referring to myself, then the answer is no. He'll not protect you from me. You are totally at my mercy."

"I wouldn't be so sure about that!" she flared. "One scream from me, and every soldier here, including the captain, will come running."

"That's quite true," he agreed with a smile. "But, my little Confederate, in the army rank has its privileges. At present I am the superior officer, and my orders will unquestioningly be obeyed. Let me remind you again that you are totally at my mercy."

Vexed, she ranted, "You are a despicable, insolent, discourteous . . ."

He interrupted, "Miss Donovan, I think I already have a general idea of your opinion of me. There is no reason for you to keep repeating yourself."

"What do you want to talk to me about?" she demanded, letting the argument rest.

His tone became serious. "I want your promise to wait for me at Fort Fetterman. I know how hot-headed you are, and I also realize how determined you are to find your cousin. I want you to give me your word that you won't take off by yourself to search for him."

When he didn't receive an immediate reply, he placed his strong hands on her shoulders and pulled her against him. His eyes boring into hers, he said seriously, "Suzanne, if you don't do as I tell you, then you will most likely get yourself, Saul, and Miss O'Ryan killed. If not for your own sake, then for theirs, give me your word!"

"All right!" she consented. "You have my word!

Now will you please release me?"

He sighed with relief, then removed his hands from her shoulders.

Resentfully, she remarked, "Major, don't be so presumptuous as to address me again as Suzanne. I didn't give you permission to use my first name."

His handsome face hardened with anger. "Miss Donovan, your hostility is typically Southern."

"And your arrogance is typically Yankee!" she countered.

Tired of quarreling, he proposed, "Until this crisis with the Sioux is over, let's call a temporary truce, shall we?"

Suzanne was beginning to feel drained. These altercations with the major always left her upset, and, for some strange reason, depressed. "Very well," she assented. "I'm willing to try and keep peace between us."

He was surprised that she agreed so readily.

"Major Landon, why don't you tell me about yourself?" she suggested.

"For instance?" He raised an eyebrow.

"Where are you from? Why are you in the cavalry? Do you plan to make a career of the army?"

"Well, I was born in Missouri," he began after a moment. "But I can't claim the state as my homeland. At the time of my birth, my parents just happened to be in Missouri. My father and his father before him were militiamen. In 1811 my grandfather fought the Shawnees. He fought under General Harrison at Tippecanoe. My father became a Mounted Ranger and was actively involved in guarding the route from Indepenence, Missouri, to Santa Fe, which you may know as the Santa Fe Trail. My mother was living in Independence when I was born. The Mounted Rangers were an elite regiment, and only lasted for a year. In

1833, the year I was born, Congress merged the Rangers with the First Regiment of Dragoons to produce our nation's first true cavalry outfit. My father was one of the first cavalrymen. It wasn't until 1855 that President Pierce's secretary of war, Jefferson Davis, who later became your Confederate president, decreed the formation of four new army regiments. Two of these regiments were mounted, but this time they were not called Dragoons but the First and Second Cavalry."

"When did you join the cavalry?" she asked.

"Shortly after I graduated from West Point."

"What happened to your grandfather and your father?"

"My grandfather was killed during our war with Mexico. He was with General Zachary Taylor and died in the Battle of Palo Alto. My father died in 1858, fighting the Comanches."

"Why did you leave the cavalry to participate in the War Between the States?"

"I wasn't exactly given a choice in the matter. The war was into its second year when I received orders to leave the cavalry and join the Union Army."

"Would you have preferred to stay out West?"

He shrugged. "I certainly wasn't looking forward to fighting other Americans. Brother killing brother was enough to sicken any man's soul. But I was wholeheartedly against the country separating. To stay strong, this country must remain united."

"And how do you feel about fighting the Indians?"

He sighed deeply before answering, "The Indians own their land by natural right, and true justice is ultimately on their side. But it is power that rules rather than justice, and the Indians are doomed by the white man's superior strategic skills. I can foresee only one end for the Indians: they will either be killed or forced

78

to live on reservations. They are the innocent victims of the white man's lust, greed, and aggression. There are military men like myself who respect and sympathize with the Indians. But we know their fate is inevitable. If we were to leave the cavalry because we feel for the Indians, in the long run we wouldn't be doing them a favor. We must stay actively involved in this war with the Indians. When treaties are signed, maybe then we can see to it that the Indians receive their fair share. Also, officers like myself believe in taking prisoners. You'd be surprised how many men of high military rank have no qualms about butchering an entire village."

"How do you feel about the Indians when you are engaged in battle with them?"

"They are the enemy; it's kill or be killed. It doesn't matter if you're fighting an Indian in war paint or a man in a Confederate uniform." He added gravely, "In the midst of battle there is no neutral zone."

"Do you plan to stay in the army?"

"I know no other life," he answered. "I guess the military is in my blood, handed down to me from my father and grandfather."

Her eyes well accustomed to the darkness, Suzanne studied the man standing close to her side. He was looking away from her, but she could see his profile clearly. Regardless of their personal differences, she found him extremely attractive. His sensual and virile masculinity couldn't possibly escape a woman's notice.

Slowly he turned to face her. He towered over Suzanne and she had to lift her head to meet his eyes. "You are very beautiful," he murmured, admiring her perfection.

A blush came to her cheeks as she said softly, "Thank you."

Their eyes met with a driving urgency that made

Suzanne feel strangely flushed. She couldn't totally understand what she was feeling; she only knew that this man's hypnotic gaze was sending her into a kind of trance.

Although Blade was taken with Suzanne's astounding beauty, his feelings for her were not superficial. Her spirit, courage, and integrity he held in high esteem. But at this moment it was her sultry lips that had him mesmerized, and he longed desperately to kiss them.

He moved with incredible speed, and before Suzanne knew what was happening, he had her enfolded in his powerful grip. He pressed her pliable, softly contoured frame to his tightly muscled body. Bending his head, he captured her mouth with his.

She leaned submissively into his ardent embrace and surrendered completely to his kiss. Her senses were reeling as he swept her away into their own private world. But Patrick's existence suddenly loomed between them as the memory of his face flashed vividly before Suzanne. She struggled out of the major's arms, and stepping back, tried to regain her composure.

Blade understood how she felt, for Trooper Donovan had also entered his thoughts when Suzanne had been in his embrace. He sighed disconsolately. How could he and this lovely woman ever find their way to each other with Donovan standing between them?

Her presence of mind restored, Suzanne began to feel a terrible anger toward herself. Why had she once again responded to this man who wanted to see Patrick before a firing squad?

Her eyes reflected her self-condemnation, causing Blade to ask with concern, "What are you thinking about?"

Petulantly, she snapped, "I am too angry to think rationally!"

"I'm sorry," he said gently. "And I apologize for

kissing you."

"I'm not upset with you!" she blurted out. "I am angry at myself. Why couldn't I live up to my resolution?"

"What resolution?" he asked.

"After the last time you kissed me, I promised myself that if you tried again, I'd belt you a good one right across your arrogant jaw!"

Blade had to place his hand to his mouth and feign a cough to keep from bursting into laughter.

"And what do I do instead?" she raged on. "I become a shrinking violet and melt in your arms!"

"Suzanne," he said soothingly, reaching for her.

Eluding him, she stepped quickly to one side. "Don't touch me!" she ordered sharply. "And don't call me Suzanne! Our temporary truce is officially over!"

He eyed her cunningly. "One of these days, my defiant little Confederate, when I have you backed into a corner you're going to stand and fight instead of running away."

"Perhaps!" she huffed. "But it certainly won't be tonight!" Whirling about, she left him to hurry back to the safety of the wagon.

Saul was sitting alone beside the fire when he caught sight of Blade returning to the campsite. Getting to his feet, he hurried over to speak to him.

"Major, suh," he called, gaining Blade's attention. "Is it all right, suh, if I talk to you for a moment?"

Nodding toward the fire, Blade answered, "Why don't we talk over a cup of coffee?"

When the two men were seated with their cups of coffee, Blade thoughtfully studied the ex-slave. "Saul, you speak as though you have received some education." Blade was aware that very few slaves

81

were ever educated.

"No, suh," he answered. "Masta Thomas never wanted his slaves to get any schoolin'. It was Masta Patrick who taught me readin', writin', and cipherin'."

"Donovan!" Blade muttered, his tone heavy with dislike.

Saul detected the major's bitterness, and although he felt the need to defend Patrick, he kept it suppressed.

"What do you need to talk to me about?" Blade inquired.

"Major, I got somethin' important to ask you, and I'm hopin' you'll tell me the truth."

"All right," he agreed.

"Does Masta Patrick have anything to do with these stolen rifles?"

"Why do you think he's involved?"

"'Cause you wouldn't be plannin' to hunt down the Indians who stole them if you didn't believe you'd find Masta Patrick along with them Sioux."

Blade took a drink of his coffee. It was a long moment before he finally spoke. "This gun shipment originated in the East. It was to be sent to Fort Laramie, then to Fort Fetterman; its final destination is Fort Casper. All military personnel knew about this shipment, including Trooper Donovan. Although the soldiers taking the rifles to Fort Fetterman were attacked by the Sioux, there was a survivor. This soldier reported a white man riding with the Indians. He described him as a man of average height with blond hair. He was wearing cavalry trousers. The surviving soldier was not from Fort Laramie, so he had never seen Trooper Donovan, and there is no way I can be certain that this white man is Donovan. But the description fits, and Donovan knew about the rifle shipment."

"But why would Masta Patrick tell them Indians

about the guns?" Saul moaned.

"I don't know," Blade replied. "A bargain to save his life maybe."

"I don't believe this man is Masta Patrick!" Saul announced firmly.

Blade finished his coffee, then set aside the cup. Tonelessly he remarked, "I take it that your loyalty is as blind as Miss Donovan's."

"Our loyalty ain't blind, major," he said earnestly. "Miz Suzanne and I, we know Masta Patrick better than anyone. And he ain't capable of these things he's been accused of."

"His desertion is not an accusation," Blade argued. "It's a fact. Neither is it an implication that he murdered a man in cold blood. His victim lived long enough to identify him."

"Masta Patrick couldn't kill nobody in cold blood!" Saul gasped.

Blade sighed impatiently. Trying to reason with this man was as fruitless as trying to reason with Suzanne. They were both too blindly enamored of Donovan. Standing, Blade looked down at Saul and said urgently, "I hope you don't mention this conversation to Miss Donovan. At present there's no reason for her to know that her cousin might be involved with the theft. If he is an accomplice, she'll find out soon enough."

Saul concurred. "I ain't gonna say nothin' to her about it." His eyes met the major's, and their expression was unyielding. "But you're dead wrong about Masta Patrick, Major Landon, he's innocent. He didn't do none of the things that you and the others say he did. Masta Patrick, he's got too much goodness in his heart to ever hurt anyone on purpose."

Giving up, Blade turned on his heel and walked quickly away. He couldn't even begin to fathom why

Suzanne and Saul refused to face the truth. Patrick Donovan was becoming a constant thorn in his side, a thorn that embedded itself deeper and deeper.

Saul remained sitting beside the fire, his eyes gazing dreamily into the darting flames. The Patrick Donovan that he remembered cared dearly about human life. One incident in particular came to mind as he let his thoughts drift into the past.

Saul and Patrick were on their way back to Southmoor. They had gone into town to buy food for the horses, and the rear of the buckboard was loaded with sacks of grain.

On this day Patrick seemed unusually quiet, and wondering why he was so preoccupied, Saul asked, "Masta Patrick, is somethin' botherin' you?"

Patrick was now eighteen years old, and had become an exceptionally handsome young man. Although slim, he was strong. He had the kind of boyish charm that would stay with him for years. Turning in the wagon seat and looking at Saul, he answered, "As you already know, next month I'll be leaving for college. I'm a little worried about Suzanne. You know as well as I do that mother has never truly accepted her, and father simply ignores her. When I leave home, she's going to be terribly lonely."

Nodding, Saul replied, "That sweet chile is gonna miss you real bad."

"I hope I can depend on you to help her. Give her a lot of your time."

"I will, Masta Patrick. I love Miz Suzanne, and I always enjoy her company."

Patrick glanced into the distance, and seeing saddled horses standing on the side of the road, he said, "I wonder what's going on."

Saul knew immediately who owned the riderless horses. There wasn't a slave in the South who didn't fear the slave patrollers and learned early in life to recognize the cruel men as well as their mounts.

As the buckboard neared the horses, Patrick found them familiar. Although the house itself was not in sight, they were within the boundaries of Southmoor. "Why are slave patrollers on my property?" he said angrily. Patrick despised these men, who made their living rounding up runaway slaves and exploiting their misery.

Suddenly Saul gasped.

"What's wrong?" Patrick asked urgently.

His words racing with fear, the man answered, "Big Abe, he ran off again yesterday mornin'! Do you reckon the slave patrollers got him?"

The slave known as Big Abe was always slipping away to visit the woman he loved, a slave on a plantation a few miles from Southmoor. But Big Abe never failed to return home. Patrick didn't blame the man for wanting to see the woman he apparently adored. Numerous times he had asked his father to purchase her so she and Big Abe could live together. But Thomas was always angry at the slave for disobeying and leaving the plantation. To punish him, he refused even to consider buying the woman.

When the unmistakable sound of a whip lashing against bare flesh reached Patrick's ears, he shouted for Saul to stop the buckboard. The sound had come from the nearby woods, and leaping from the wagon seat, he raced headlong into the thicket. Securing the wagon's brake, Saul jumped to the ground and ran after Patrick. The striking whip sounded three more times before they reached the slave patrollers, who had Big Abe tied to a large tree. His shirt had been removed, and his bare back, which was turned toward the torturer, was bleeding from the deep lacerations.

Advancing on the man holding the whip, Patrick snatched it from his hand. His face red with rage, he yelled furiously, "Who gave you permission to whip this slave?"

Remaining outwardly calm, the man replied, "Mr. Donovan, I have your father's approval. He is tired of this nigger running away. His orders were for me and my men to locate him, then give him a dozen lashes."

"The hell you will!" Patrick sneered.

Saul looked on with shock. He had never seen the young master so angry; he had always seemed so gentle.

Patrick glared murderously at the slave patroller. "Cut him loose!" he demanded.

The patroller spoke to one of his comrades. "Cut that damned buck loose." To young Donovan he said gruffly, "Your father ain't gonna like you interferin' with his orders."

"You let me worry about my father!" he raged.

As soon as Big Abe was freed, Saul rushed to his side. The beaten man was weak, and he leaned on the elderly slave.

"Masta Patrick," Big Abe pleaded, "I didn't run away. I was comin' back home when they catched me and strung me up."

"I know you weren't running," Patrick told him warmly. "Help him to the wagon," he said to Saul. Throwing down the whip, he was about to follow them when the patroller spat out nastily, "You damned nigger lover!"

Patrick moved so speedily that his adversary was caught completely off guard. His fist struck the man's jaw, sending him plunging to the ground.

The patroller, as well as his companions, would have relished beating Patrick to a pulp, but young Donovan was a rich aristocrat, and in the South, aristocrats represented too much power. They were the lords of the manor. Ordinary men like these patrollers had to use slaves to unleash their anger, so Negroes became their whipping boys.

Patrick assisted Saul with Big Abe, and they soon reached the buckboard, where Saul pushed aside the bags of grain to make room for Abe.

As the injured man crawled into the back of the wagon, Patrick looked at the elderly slave who was also his friend. "Saul, no man should have the right to string up another man and whip him! It just isn't right!" His blue eyes shone with feeling. "And no man has the right to own another human being! God should doom all of us slaveowners straight to the fires of hell!"

"Masta Patrick," Saul intruded hastily, "there ain't no way God is gonna doom you to hell. Besides, you don't own no slaves. We belong to your papa." He hesitated, then continued movingly, "If every man on the face of this earth, regardless of his color, had the goodness in their hearts that you have, this old world would be a fine place to live."

"Goodness?" Patrick refuted. "Saul, a few minutes ago I was so angry I could've killed that patroller. There's a streak of violence in all of us."

The older man smiled with love. "Masta Patrick, you might have been mad enough to kill, but you wouldn't have done it. There's a big difference."

Saul stared into the fire, which by now was dying down to a glowing ember.

He never did learn what was said between Patrick and his father concerning the incident with the slave patrollers. But two days after the whipping Thomas purchased the woman Big Abe loved, which put a stop to his slipping away from the plantation.

Feeling his age, the elderly man slowly got to his feet. He put out what was left of the fire, then walked sluggishly to his bedroll beneath the wagon. Snuggling into his blankets, he uttered a quick but sincere prayer before falling asleep. "Dear Lord, please let me live long enough to prove that Masta Patrick is innocent. Then I can die with my mind and heart at peace."

Chapter Six

Saul's thoughts were troubled as he finished hitching the team to the wagon. Although the worry over Patrick weighed heavily, he was also very concerned about Suzanne. He was aware of how much his young mistress worshipped her cousin, but what if Patrick should turn out to be guilty of these charges against him? Would Suzanne have the inner strength to sustain such a shock? Firmly Saul cast these doubts aside. What in the world was wrong with him? Of course Patrick wasn't guilty! Why had he allowed himself to question his former master's integrity? Saul was ashamed for letting his faith weaken. He swore solemnly never again to lose his trust in Patrick.

Suzanne had been inside the wagon, and leaving it by the rear entrance, she walked around to the front. Seeing Saul, she smiled as she moved to his side. "Good morning," she greeted him.

"'Mornin', Miz Suzanne," he responded.

Her brow furrowed with worry. "I wonder how long we'll be stuck at Fort Fetterman."

"It could take a long time for the major and the soldiers to hunt down them Sioux, so you might as well prepare yourself for a long wait."

She sighed. "We may never find Patrick if we are held up indefinitely."

"Well, Miz Suzanne," Saul drawled, "we ain't got much choice in the matter." The sudden sound of a horse racing toward the camp caught his attention. "There's someone comin'."

They watched as the visitor, a mounted trooper, quickly dismounted. The captain and Blade were in sight, and after saluting, he reported his news to the two officers.

Suddenly Blade turned and looked in their direction, then uttered a few words to the captain before starting toward them.

Suzanne kept her eyes on him as he drew closer with long, self-assured strides. Today he wasn't wearing buckskins but had changed back into his uniform. The blue shirt and trousers fit his large, muscular frame like a second skin. His handsome physique provoked an overwhelming desire within her. In an effort to rid herself of this rushing need, she looked quickly away and reminded herself that he was not only a hated Yankee, but also the man who wanted to see Patrick executed. She took a deep breath and succeeded in putting the major in perspective, then turned back to face him.

As Blade walked up to them, Saul asked, "Is anything wrong, major?"

His worry reflected in his eyes, he answered, "A few days ago Lieutenant Holmes and his men left Fort Fetterman. They haven't returned to the fort. They should have been back yesterday. The lieutenant doesn't know about the stolen rifles, so he isn't aware that there are armed Sioux in the vicinity. Before we try to find the Indians with the rifles, we'll search for the lieutenant and his men."

"Are we still going to Fort Fetterman?" Suzanne asked.

He turned his gaze to Suzanne, and her loveliness struck him full force. Although she was wearing a simple, modestly cut gown and her long hair was pinned up into a tight bun, she was as beautiful as a picture. "Yes," he answered. "I want all of you at the fort where you'll be safe. For the first few miles we're all going in the same direction, so the entire column will travel with you until it's time to take different routes. Then your escort will take you on to the fort." Speaking to Saul, he said briskly, "It's time to move out. Keep the women inside the wagon."

Without further comment, Blade walked over to the young trooper who was holding the reins to the major's saddled horse. As he was mounting, Saul told Suzanne to get inside the wagon.

But she was not about to stay under the stifling canvas. She defiantly climbed up onto the wagon seat, and her stubborn expression dared Saul to utter one objection.

"The major ain't gonna like you sittin' up here," he said as he climbed up beside her.

"He isn't going to tell me where I can and cannot sit!" she said peevishly. When Saul made no move to start the wagon rolling, she ordered, "Slap the reins against those mules and stop treating me as though I'm a naughty child!"

"Yes'm, Miz Suzanne."

They had traveled only a short distance before Blade became aware of Suzanne's position. The wagon was in the center of the column, and although Blade was riding in front, he had glanced over his shoulder to check on the procession. Seeing Suzanne sitting in the open, he turned about and rode back to the wagon.

He kept his mount in stride with the mules. "Miss Donovan, I gave explicit orders for you to stay inside!"

He was riding at her side, and giving him a smug look out of the corner of her eye, she replied scornfully, "I will stay where I damned well please!"

Raising his hand, he shouted, "Company halt!"

The procession came to a sudden stop, and as Saul pulled up the team, Blade leaned toward Suzanne. His strong arm quickly encircled her waist and he lifted her from the seat and onto his horse.

She fought ineffectively against his strength. "How dare you! Put me down this instant!" she shouted.

Capturing her with one arm, he jerked the reins with his other hand and guided his horse to the rear of the wagon. He tossed her roughly through the opening in the canvas, and when she unceremoniously hit the wooden floor, he was inundated with screaming insults.

"You obnoxious, ill-bred, loathsome, detestable . . . bully!"

"If you don't stay where you are, I'll have you restrained." Slapping the reins against his horse, he returned to the head of the column.

When they were moving once agian, Suzanne looked over at Molly, who hadn't spoken a word since the major had pitched her friend into the wagon.

"I hate Major Landon!" Suzanne spat.

"He's only trying to protect you," Molly reasoned.

"I can take care of myself!"

The other woman sighed impatiently, but she didn't argue with Suzanne. She was very familiar with her friend's stubborn nature. Smiling inwardly, she began to wonder if Suzanne had finally met her match in Major Landon.

*　　*　　*

They were about an hour into their journey when two of the three scouts the captain had sent ahead appeared on the horizon. The men were urging their mounts to go as fast as possible, and clouds of loose dust rained about the horses and their riders as they quickly crossed the open ground. Reaching Captain Goldsworthy and Blade, the scouts brought their horses to an abrupt stop.

Although Suzanne was sitting inside the wagon, she had taken a position behind the seat, and by looking over Saul's shoulder she could see what was taking place.

As Saul pulled the wagon to a halt, Molly moved to Suzanne's side, and she also watched the activities. The excited gestures of the scouts who were relaying information to the captain and Blade told them that something serious had happened.

The three civilians watched with strained silence as Blade moved his horse to Justin's side. The two men shared a short discussion, then Justin rode over to the wagon.

Speaking to all three of them, he reported solemnly, "Lieutenant Holmes and his men have been found. They were massacred about two miles from here."

"Oh my God!" Molly groaned. "There are no survivors?"

"No, ma'am," he replied. He looked from Molly to Suzanne before saying somberly, "Ladies, we're going to the scene of the massacre. It will be necessary for the soldiers escorting you to Fort Fetterman to take the bodies back to the fort." He turned to Saul. "For the sake of the ladies, keep this wagon a distance from the battle scene."

"Yes, suh," Saul answered.

Justin's eyes fell upon Suzanne. "Major Landon gave strict orders for you and Miss O'Ryan to stay inside and away from the area."

Suzanne didn't argue. The thought of the dead soldiers wrenched her heart, and she certainly didn't want to view the tragedy. "How many men were killed?" she asked.

"Thirty-two," he said gravely, then urged his mount back to the front of the column.

A heavy sadness fell across the procession as they journeyed toward the site. The silence was so heavy that the sounds of the horses' marching hooves and the creaking of wagon wheels seemed eerily amplified.

Suzanne remained sitting behind the seat, and as they drew nearer to the site of the massacre, she saw a large flock of vultures circling in the sky. The carnivorous birds were a hideous sight, and she quickly looked away.

The scout who had been left behind to guard the exposed bodies rode out to meet the arriving soldiers. Saul brought the mule team to a stop, and as the troopers passed by, Suzanne moved to the back of the wagon and climbed down.

"Major Landon said for you to stay inside," Molly reminded her.

"I need fresh air," Suzanne explained faintly, breathing in deeply. She leaned against the wagon and tried not to think about all the dead bodies that were lying close by.

Suzanne had been standing outside only a few minutes when she heard a horse approaching. Glancing to her side, she saw the major. He pulled up his mount and swung down from the saddle. "Miss Donovan," he said sternly, "can't you obey one simple command? I gave an order . . ."

Her temper flared. "To hell with your order! I needed a breath of fresh air!"

In no mood for an altercation, he changed the

subject. "In a few minutes Justin and I will be leaving with the captain and his men. A rider has been sent to Fort Fetterman for wagons to carry back the bodies. All of you will stay here until they arrive, then you'll be taken to the fort."

"How long do you think you'll be gone?" she asked.

"I don't know."

Although Suzanne understood why the major wanted to find the Indians responsible for the massacre, she was anxious to keep searching for Patrick. "Major, it is imperative that our plans not be delayed too long. Each day I am at the fort is another day that my cousin will move farther away from me."

"Your precious cousin!" he sneered. The major knew that Lieutenant Holmes and his men had been killed by the Sioux who had stolen the rifles, and believing Patrick to be involved, his anger emerged recklessly. "Don't mention that son of a bitch's name in my presence!"

From the violent rage flashing in his eyes, Suzanne once again sensed that he wasn't telling her everything. Did he think that Patrick was a part of this terrible massacre? "Major Landon," she began furiously, "if you believe for one moment that my cousin is even remotely responsible for what happened to those soldiers, then you must be deranged!"

"Deranged?" he said viciously. "It's your murdering cousin who is deranged!"

Saul could overhear their angry words, and afraid the major's rage might make him tell Suzanne too much, he jumped down from the wagon in the hope of reaching them before it was too late.

Suzanne drew back her arm, but as she swung forward to slap Landon, he caught her wrist in mid-flight.

She struggled to free herself from his firm grasp.

"What does Patrick have to do with all this? Answer me, damn you!"

Saul quickly moved up behind them and tried to catch the major's eye, but Blade was beyond rationality. He released his hold on her wrist and stared darkly into her flushed face. "All right, Miss Donovan, if you insist on hearing the truth, then I'll enlighten you. When the Sioux attacked the soldiers taking the rifles to Fort Fetterman, there was a survivor who reported a white man riding with the Indians. He described this man as of average height with blond hair, and wearing cavalry trousers. Trooper Donovan knew about this gun shipment, and, probably in an exchange for his life, he told the Sioux about it. And so help me God, if I find your cousin with these Indians, I'll kill him!"

Suzanne threw herself at the major, her small fists flailing violently against his chest. "No! You're wrong! . . . Patrick had nothing to do with this massacre! . . ." she shrieked.

From behind Saul grabbed the hysterical woman and forcefully pulled her away from the major. Fighting against him, she cried, "You're wrong, Major Landon! . . . Dear God, you're wrong! . . . Patrick could never do anything so horrible! . . ." Her knees weakened, and falling into Saul's arms, she moaned heartbrokenly, "Oh, Saul, tell him he's wrong."

She broke into tears, and her heartache touched Blade deeply. He made a move to console her, but knowing he was the last person to do it, he turned to his horse, grasped the reins, and walked away.

Standing at a distance, Justin had witnessed the scene between Blade and Miss Donovan. He waited until the major had moved away before making his approach. Saul was helping Suzanne step up into the wagon when Justin reached them. He considered offering the distraught woman some kind of encouragement, but what could he possibly say?

After assisting Suzanne, Saul looked at the scout. "Can I do somethin' for you, suh?"

"I'd like to speak to Miss O'Ryan."

"Miz Molly!" Saul called. "Mista Smith wants to see you."

Molly appeared quickly, and Justin's large hands were suddenly on her waist, lifting her from the wagon.

She hadn't expected to be literally lifted into the air, and as he gently placed her on her feet she said somewhat breathlessly, "What can I do for you, Mr. Smith?"

His smile was suggestive. "Well, ma'am, I can think of quite a few things, but at the moment I merely need to talk to you."

His subtle implication hadn't gone unheeded. "I don't think we have anything to discuss," she said coolly.

"Of course we do," he insisted, taking her arm and ushering her a short way from the wagon where they couldn't be overheard. "Miss O'Ryan, I'm worried about you. This new development concerning your fiancé must've hit you pretty hard."

His kindness surprised her. "I . . . I had no idea that you cared."

"Well, I do care," he assured her. "In fact, I care very much."

"I'm mostly numb," she admitted. "I find it very hard to believe that Patrick has done any of these terrible things that he's been accused of. I remember him as a very compassionate and warm man. And I can't help wondering if this Trooper Donovan is an imposter."

"I suppose he could be," Justin said. "But ma'am, if I

were you, I wouldn't hold too strongly to that hope. Trooper Donovan's description fits your fiancé's. He also had Miss Donovan's letters and the watch that was given to Patrick on his twenty-first birthday."

"But this man could've stolen those things," she reasoned.

"Maybe, but he couldn't have stolen Donovan's blond hair, height, and lame leg."

"Patrick is very handsome, but he has a boyish appeal that makes him look younger than his age. Does the Trooper Donovan you know have a boyish look?"

Justin shrugged. "I guess you could say he has a young appearance. I never really looked at him all that closely."

Molly sighed sadly. "I feel so sorry for Suzanne. If this man is Patrick, I don't know if she'll be strong enough to bear it."

A puzzled frown crossed his brow. "Why does your concern lie with Miss Donovan? How about yourself? You must love Donovan as much as his cousin does, if not more."

Before she knew what she was doing, Molly found herself voicing her inner most feelings, "No, I don't love Patrick more than Suzanne loves him. To be perfectly honest, I'm not even sure whether or not I still love my fiancé at all."

Justin was pleased. He was becoming very attracted to this lovely woman, and he preferred not to have a rival. But keeping these thoughts to himself, he asked with a casual air, "If you aren't sure of your feelings for Donovan, why did you come west to find him?"

"I'm not sure why," she confessed. "Maybe I felt it my duty to do so, or maybe I just couldn't find it in my heart to refuse Suzanne. She wanted me to come with her so desperately."

"Then she doesn't know how you really feel about Donovan?"

"I don't think so," she replied. "Suzanne is totally blind where Patrick is concerned. Her faith in him is beyond question. She utterly adores him; her love borders on worship."

Justin's expression was concerned. "In that case I feel sorry for Miss Donovan, because she's probably in for a tragic awakening. I'm quite sure Trooper Donovan and her cousin are one and the same."

"I also am afraid it's true." Tears came to her eyes as she whispered with heartfelt sympathy, "Poor Suzanne. Her love for Patrick may very well destroy her."

Noticing the captain and his soldiers preparing to leave, Justin said hastily, "Miss O'Ryan, it's time for me to go." He placed his hands on her shoulders, and gazing warmly into her eyes, he spoke urgently. "When the soldiers at Fort Fetterman and their families learn that you are Donovan's fiancée and Miss Donovan is his cousin, they aren't going to treat you very cordially. You must prepare yourself for this, and warn the others."

"Good Lord!" she moaned. "I hadn't thought about the people at the fort and how they would accept us. To them, we will represent the man who helped the Sioux kill thirty-two of their soldiers."

"I promise you, Miss O'Ryan, that the major and I will come to the fort as quickly as possible." His hands on her shoulders tightened comfortingly. "Major Landon and I care about all of you, and we don't want to see any of you get hurt."

He walked swiftly away from her, and she looked after him as he hurried over to join the soldiers. His kindness had touched her deeply, and she began to see the rugged Justin Smith in a different light. She placed a hand over her heart, startled to find that it was beating rapidly. The Fort Laramie scout was indeed an imposing figure of a man, and most assuredly provoked disturbing feelings within her. He was so different from the Patrick she had loved. Justin's masculinity was an aggressive, domineering force, whereas Patrick's virility had always seemed unobtrusive and reserved.

Chapter Seven

When Justin had warned Molly of the hostility that awaited them at Fort Fetterman, he had not spoken lightly. The soldiers and their families treated the three visitors as though they were the plague itself. No one approached their wagon, which was parked in an isolated area of the fort. They bypassed it as if it weren't even there. Suzanne and the others stayed close to their wagon, spending most of their time inside and out of sight.

They had been at the fort for seven days when their supply of coffee had dwindled to less than a pound. Suzanne dreaded going to the military store to buy more coffee, but because she had been the one to instigate this search for Patrick, she felt it was her place to confront the hostility that waited beyond the privacy of their wagon.

Saul was against Suzanne's leaving, but she insisted. His concern for his young mistress prompted him to follow her.

Suzanne was totally unaware of Saul's protective presence as she strolled briskly toward the mercantile. She walked proudly with her head held high, keeping her eyes straight ahead. The closer she drew to the store, the more populated were her surroundings. She made a point of not looking directly at anyone, thinking if she completely ignored them, perhaps they would show her the simple courtesy of doing likewise.

Suzanne was just beginning to hope that she might make it to the store and back without incident, when two troopers who were lounging in front of the enlisted men's bar, stepped forward and blocked her path.

Sneering coldly, the larger of the two men asked harshly, "Are you Donovan's fiancée or his cousin?"

"I'm his cousin." She made an attempt to move on.

He took a step to the side, which prevented her from passing him. "Donovans ain't welcome on this fort," he declared.

"Please let me by," she pleaded.

"If you care anything about that cousin of yours, you won't be here when the captain and his men bring him to the fort. There ain't enough officers or guards on this fort to keep us enlisted men from your no-good bastard cousin. We're going to tear him limb from limb, and by the time we finish, there won't be enough left of him to feed to the vultures."

"Leave me alone!" she cried.

"There's thirty-two fresh graves in the cemetery, Miss Donovan, and your stinking cousin is gonna pay for each one of them," the man said.

Saul had seen the two troopers confront Suzanne. He hurried to catch up to her, and taking a protective stance at her side, he asked, "Are these men botherin' you, Miz Suzanne?"

The larger of the two soldiers spoke again, "You ain't no longer her slave. We fought to free you and all of your kind. Don't you understand that you don't have to do anything she tells you to do? You're your own man."

Saul stood tall as he answered with dignity, "Yes,

suh, I understand that I am a free man. But there's something you don't understand. Patrick Donovan didn't tell the Sioux about them rifles." Turning to Suzanne, he said in a tone that brooked no argument, "Give me the money for the coffee. You go back to the wagon and stay there."

She gladly handed him the money, then departed quickly, anxious to put distance between herself and the two troopers.

Returning to the wagon, she saw that Molly was taking a nap, so she quietly took a blanket, spread it out on the ground, and sat and leaned back against the large wagon wheel. She tried not to think about what those men had told her, but how could she erase their words from her troubled mind? Your cousin will pay for each grave, one of them had said. Thirty-two graves? My God, Patrick respected life, he could never be even indirectly responsible for a massacre! The cousin that Suzanne remembered and loved cared about human life. She drew up her knees, and folding her arms across them, rested her head on her arms. She couldn't control the flow of tears that rolled down her cheeks as she left the unpleasant present to return to the past.

Although Suzanne had eagerly agreed to her cousin's invitation for a picnic with just the two of them, she nonetheless was despondent throughout the entire meal.

Traveling by buggy, Patrick had taken them to a peaceful green meadow that lay within the boundaries of Southmoor. He had a specific reason for wanting to share this time alone with Suzanne. He would be leaving in the morning to go to college in the East and wouldn't see his young cousin again until Christmas vacation. He knew his leaving was the cause of her solemn mood.

Now, sitting on the blanket across from Suzanne, he studied her carefully. At the age of eight, she was still an extraordinarily pretty child. Dressed in a blue frock with her curly hair pulled back from her face, she was a picture of perfection. Patrick had often tried to find a flaw in her beauty, but in his opinion, none existed.

Sensing his scrutiny, she lifted her gaze to his. Smiling wistfully, she murmured, "Oh, Patrick, I wish you didn't have to leave."

"Suzanne, you must understand that it's very important for a man to receive an education."

"I don't understand why it's important for you," she entreated. "You're going to inherit Southmoor!"

"It means a lot to me, Suzanne," he tried to explain. "I long for more education. There are so many things that I still don't know."

"But why do you want to know about these things?" she asked, exasperated.

"My thirst for knowledge is unquenchable," he answered with a smile.

Suzanne's pretty face puckered into a pout. "But you already know everything you need to know."

He chuckled humorously. "Maybe I know all that's necessary to run this plantation, but did you ever stop to consider that I might not want to be a planter?"

Her huge eyes widened with surprise. "You don't want to run Southmoor?"

"No, I don't," he confessed soberly. "But Suzanne, promise me you won't say anything about this to father."

"All right," she quickly agreed. "But you'll have to tell him someday."

"I'll wait until the time is right," he said thoughtfully.

"When will that be?"

"When I know what I want to do with my life." His vivid blue eyes looked deep into hers. "Suzanne, I have a feeling that Southmoor is not my destiny. I believe there is some other purpose to my life, but I don't know yet what it is."

She was confused. "A purpose? What do you mean?"

"I wish I knew," he sighed heavily. He picked up the picnic basket, and getting to his feet, he said briskly, "Well, it's time to start back home."

She folded the blanket, then followed him to the buggy, where she placed it on the floorboards. He helped her into the conveyance, then sitting beside her, he picked up the reins.

They said little to each other on the short ride to Southmoor. Patrick was looking forward to attending college, but he was sad about leaving Suzanne. He loved his young cousin, and he knew how dependent she was on him.

They approached the house from the rear entrance, and as the buggy turned into the dirt lane, he said cheerfully, "We can write to each other often."

"I'll write you every day!" she said enthusiastically.

His sudden laugh was jolly. "If you can find time to write every day, then the least I can do is answer each letter the day I receive it."

A long row of slave cabins lined the narrow lane. There were children playing about as their mothers washed clothes or worked in the small vegetable gardens behind each cabin.

Suddenly Patrick stiffened, and peering at one of the log houses, he exclaimed, "I think I see smoke coming out of that window!"

Suzanne started to follow his gaze when a woman's piercing cry sounded close by. She had been visiting another slave and had caught sight of the smoke at the same moment that Patrick had spoken.

Now, running past their buggy, the frantic woman screamed, "My baby! . . . My baby's in there!"

Jerking back on the reins, Patrick pulled up the team. Moving quickly, he grabbed the blanket, and leaping to the ground, he yelled to Suzanne, "Stay here!"

Suzanne looked in fright as more women raced to the burning cabin. All the men were toiling in the fields and there was no one to help, except for Patrick.

The slave women were aware of their young master's presence, but they weren't expecting him to do much to help the trapped baby. White men didn't risk their lives for Negroes, especially not for a black baby, who wasn't worth much financially.

The hysterical mother hurried to the front door, but on flinging it open, she was engulfed by so much smoke that she had to turn away.

Meanwhile Patrick headed swiftly for a laundry tub and dunked the blanket in the water. When it was thoroughly soaked, he swung it over his shoulders. Protected by the wet covering, he made a beeline for the cabin window, and slinging away the partially closed shutters, he climbed inside.

Suzanne felt as though her heart had stopped beating and that time itself had ceased to exist as she waited fearfully for Patrick to climb back out of the window.

When she saw him emerge, she jumped down from the buggy and ran toward him. Against his chest he held the baby, who wasn't moving. He knelt to the ground and cradled the infant in his arms. Pinching the baby's nostrils with his fingers, Patrick placed his mouth over the child's and breathed air into his lungs.

Suzanne and the infant's mother reached Patrick at the same moment, and they both dropped to their knees beside him. "Dear Lord!" the frantic mother prayed. "Oh Lord, don't let my baby die!"

The burning cabin had been spotted, and as the fire bell rang loudly over the plantation, the child in Patrick's arms began to stir. His movements grew stronger, and when Patrick removed his mouth, the baby let out an angry wail.

Patrick handed the crying infant to his mother. Taking the child, she held him against her bosom, then grasping her young master's hand, she kissed it over and over again. "Thank you, Masta Patrick. You is a good man, masta. God bless you!"

He caught the eye of the woman standing by and told her to help the mother. As she assisted her toward her own cabin, Patrick guided Suzanne away from the fire and to the buggy. The flames were making the horses nervous, and stepping in front of the team, Patrick tried to calm them. Men who had been in the fields were alerted by the fire bell and rushed to the scene. Organizing a bucket brigade, they began to put out the fire.

Suzanne moved to stand beside Patrick. The horses were now quiet, and placing her hand on his arm, she got his attention. "Patrick, you are so brave!" she exclaimed, her eyes shining with love.

He was about to tell her modestly that in his opinion, his deed hadn't been all that heroic, but by now everyone had learned that Master Patrick had saved the baby at the risk of his own life, and he was suddenly surrounded by grateful slaves.

"Miz Suzanne," Saul said, waking her from her memory.

She hadn't been aware of his presence, and she

glanced up with surprise.

He held a five-pound bag of coffee, which he placed inside the wagon before he turned back to Suzanne and said gravely, "The soldiers and Major Landon have returned."

She bolted to her feet. "Is Patrick with them?"

"No, ma'am," he answered. "They ain't got no white prisoners, but they do have them Sioux who stole the rifles. The major spoke to me, and he said to tell you that he'll be here in a little while. He needs to talk to you."

Suzanne glanced inside the wagon. "Molly, wake up. Major Landon and the others are here."

Molly came awake instantly, and Saul helped her down. "Do they have Patrick?" she inquired breathlessly.

"No," Suzanne replied.

"The major's comin'," Saul said, catching sight of him walking briskly in their direction.

Suzanne watched Blade as he drew closer and noticed that he appeared tired. She wondered how much sleep he'd had in the past week.

For a tense moment, Blade studied the three people standing before him. He dreaded revealing his news. They were not going to like what he had to tell them, especially Suzanne. He found himself gazing into her questioning eyes. Damn it, why did he have to be the one to break her heart! He would give anything to offer her a reason to smile; instead, he was about to destroy her. With each passing day, Blade's hatred for Trooper Donovan grew stronger.

Deciding there was no way to soften the blow, he said with a composure he was far from feeling, "We captured the Sioux who stole the rifles and massacred Lieutenant Holmes and his men. A few of these warriors speak English, and they admitted that a white man informed them of the rifle shipment. They said this white man's name was Patrick Donovan, and that he was a deserter from the cavalry."

"No!" Suzanne moaned.

Blade continued quickly. He still had more to say, and was anxious to get it over with. "Donovan told them about the rifles in exchange for his life. He stayed with the warriors for a couple of days, then, when two trappers came to the Sioux camp, Donovan left with them."

Suzanne was now totally convinced that this man was not Patrick, but an imposter. "Trooper Donovan is pretending to be my cousin," she said firmly. "There is no doubt in my mind."

"If that's true, then how do you explain their identical descriptions?" Blade asked.

"Coincidence."

"Your letters and the watch?"

"He stole them from Patrick."

"Trooper Donovan limps slightly because of a war wound. Can you really believe this also is a coincidence?"

"It has to be!" she cried desperately. "Patrick couldn't do the things that this man has done!"

"If you truly believe this, then why don't you let me send you and the others back to Fort Laramie? There's no reason for you to continue this search, since you are so sure that Trooper Donovan isn't your cousin."

"There's a very important reason, Major Landon," she said. "This man stole Patrick's identity and possessions, and I want to know why." Her voice became faint. "He probably killed Patrick. I can't go the rest of my life wondering if my cousin is dead or alive. And only through Trooper Donovan can I learn

109

what happened to Patrick." She swallowed. "When you find Trooper Donovan, I intend to be there."

Blade took her arm and gently urged her a short way from the others. "Will you have dinner with me tonight?" he asked, releasing his hold.

Her first impulse was to refuse, but then it came to her that this man was no longer an adversary. It wasn't her cousin he was determined to arrest, but the man posing as Patrick, and she wanted him captured as badly as the major.

She smiled amiably. "Thank you, Major Landon, I'd love to have dinner with you."

Blade was pleased. He hadn't expected her to agree so readily. "I'll come for you at eight." Touching the brim of his hat, he smiled pleasantly and left.

Suzanne looked after him for a moment, then rejoined Molly and Saul, who were still standing behind the wagon.

"Miz Suzanne," the elderly servant began worriedly, "if this trooper is an imposter . . ." His voice faded and he had to take a deep breath before continuing. "Where is Masta Patrick, and how come this man has his things?" A trace of tears came to the old man's eyes. "Do you think he killed our Patrick?"

Pain gripped Suzanne's heart. "I don't know, Saul. But I think we'd better prepare ourselves for the possibility that Patrick is dead."

"If he is dead, Miz Suzanne, how will we ever stop grievin' for him?" He sounded heartbroken.

She stepped to him, and as she had often done as a child, she nestled her head against his comforting shoulder. His arms encircled her tenderly.

Finding solace in each other, they didn't notice Molly slip away. She walked aimlessly, paying little attention to her surroundings. *I shouldn't have agreed* to come on this trip, she was thinking. *I don't belong here with Saul and Suzanne. If we learn that Patrick is dead, I'll not be able to fully share their grief. I positively adored Patrick when we became engaged, but God forgive me, I no longer love him! I now know this to be true. It's beginning to look more and more as if Trooper Donovan isn't Patrick, but the man who killed him. Yet I cannot feel the sorrow that Saul and Suzanne are feeling, which means I have stopped loving my fiancé. If he is dead, I will mourn him, but only as one mourns the loss of a friend.*

Engrossed in her solemn thoughts, Molly had unknowingly strolled toward the fort stables.

Justin, having finished seeing to the care of his horse and the major's, caught sight of her approach. Leaving the stables, he hastily headed in her direction.

Spotting the large, rugged scout, she paused to wait for him.

"Miss O'Ryan," he chided gently, "you shouldn't be walkin' around this fort by yourself." From her doleful expression, he concluded that the major had told her the latest about Donovan. He said kindly, "Ma'am, I'm sorry about your fiancé. I wish Major Landon and I could've brought more encouraging news."

"I think Patrick is dead," she answered tonelessly. "This Trooper Donovan probably murdered him." Justin started to intervene, but she interrupted, "No! Don't try to convince me otherwise." Her feelings rushing to the surface, she pleaded, "I want to go home! I have no wish to continue this search for Patrick's murderer! I should never have come on this quest! I don't belong here! My love for Patrick no longer exists; over the past three years it died a long and painful death!" She was suddenly sorry for her outburst and wished she could withdraw the words she had uttered

111

so impulsively. Why had she confided in this man who was practically a stranger? Why had she found it so easy to tell him her innermost feelings, when she couldn't even tell them to Saul or Suzanne?

Flushed, Molly apologized. "Please forgive me for carrying on so foolishly."

Justin smiled kindly. "You don't owe me an apology, and you didn't behave foolishly." Slipping his hand into hers, he offered to walk her back to the wagon.

Molly felt she should dissuade him from holding her hand, but his strong grip was comforting. She was a Southerner, and this man had probably fought for the Union. Maybe the time has come to let the war die in peace, she reflected, her fingers interlacing with his. Gazing up at his attractive profile, she inquired, with no offense intended, "Mr. Smith, did you fight for the North?"

"Yes, I did," he replied. He turned his head and met her gaze. "I wish you'd call me Justin."

Feeling a little shy, she looked away from his friendly face and murmured, "Please call me Molly."

When they drew within sight of the wagon, Suzanne and Saul were still outside. As Suzanne became aware of Molly and the Fort Laramie scout, she was surprised to see them holding hands.

A moment of anger surged within Suzanne, and she whirled sharply toward the wagon and was about to climb inside when she was deterred by Saul's voice. "Miz Suzanne, don't you go a-judgin' Miz Molly. She's got every right to fall in love with another man."

Her resentment dissipated. "You're right, of course. Molly should get on with her life. She needs a husband and children." Her expression grew introspective.

Discerning her thoughts, Saul suggested with a warm smile, "You might consider takin' your own advice."

"No," Suzanne said quickly. "Finding out what happened to Patrick is all I have on my mind." She stepped up into the bed of the wagon. Marriage! she mused impatiently. Even if I was interested in marrying any time soon, which I'm not, who would I find for a husband in these parts? This countryside is inundated with damned Yankees!

Chapter Eight

The Officers' Club at Fort Fetterman wasn't quite as impressive as the one at Fort Laramie, but Suzanne found the small dining room cozy and warm. She remained relaxed and amiable throughout the delicious meal that Blade had ordered for them. Neither of them wanted to say anything to put a damper on the enjoyable evening, so they carefully kept their conversation on a light note.

Blade thought her exceptionally desirable that night. She was wearing an ivory-colored dress with a heart-shaped bodice that emphasized the soft curves of her breasts. She had arranged her honey-blond hair into an upsweep, and her golden curls were a radiant crown setting off her beauty. A dainty chain adorned with a cameo hung from her slender neck, the engraved stone resting gracefully upon her sensual, womanly cleavage.

"Your cameo is an exquisite piece of jewelry," Blade said, admiring both the necklace and the woman wearing it.

Her smile was enticing. "Thank you. It was a gift from Patrick. He gave it to me on my sixteenth birthday."

Blade grimaced. All evening they had managed to

avoid her cousin, but now his name had popped up. He took a sip of his coffee. Well, so far it had been a pleasant evening, and if he steered the discussion away from Donovan it would remain so. He was about to change the subject, but before he could, Suzanne spoke up.

"Major," she began, her tone laced with excitement, "I have been giving Patrick's disappearance a lot of thought, and I think maybe I know what happened."

"You don't know that your cousin has disappeared," Blade pointed out. "You're taking it for granted that he isn't Trooper Donovan."

"Nonsense. I am thoroughly convinced that the man is an imposter."

Snatching the napkin from his lap, Blade wadded it up, then threw it down on the table. He shoved back his chair and got brusquely to his feet. Damn it, he hadn't asked Suzanne to dinner so he could listen to her talk about her no-good, murdering cousin! She might believe the trooper was only pretending to be Patrick Donovan, but he was certain that the man he was searching for and her cousin were one and the same.

He stepped behind her chair. "It's time to take you back to your wagon," he said levelly. "We'll be leaving the fort early in the morning, and you need your rest."

She stood, coming into close contact with his large, muscular frame. The top of her head barely reached the wide breadth of his shoulders. Finding his proximity strangely disturbing, she hastily stepped to the side and began walking toward the front entrance. Waiting at the door, she watched Blade as he paid for their dinner. A waiter fetched the major's hat. Suzanne watched Blade, spellbound. The snug fit of his dress uniform emphasized his physique.

Joining her, he placed a hand on her arm to usher her outside, but for a moment she was too mesmerized to move and could only stare at him. His dark brown eyes were attractively framed by thick brows and long, heavy lashes, and his well-trimmed moustache matched the chestnut of his hair.

"Are you ready to leave?" he asked, exerting more pressure on her arm.

Suzanne looked away from his face and allowed him to escort her from the club and out into the refreshing night air.

As they strolled toward her wagon, Blade reached inside his jacket pocket and withdrew a cheroot and a match. "Do you mind if I smoke?" he asked.

"No, of course not," she assured him. Dreamily she added, "I like the smell of a cigar. Patrick enjoyed a smoke after dinner, and now the aroma from a cigar always makes me think of him."

"On second thought," Blade remarked testily, "I don't think I want a smoke!" He shoved the cheroot and match back inside his pocket.

"Major . . ." Suzanne began.

"My name is Blade! Why in the hell can't you use it?"

She didn't understand his anger. "I'm sorry if I offended you."

"No, I am the one who should apologize. Please try to overlook my rudeness. I guess I'm just in a foul mood."

"Blade, I think Patrick ran away from the Confederate Army to become a priest."

Her statement took him completely off guard and he came to an abrupt halt. "I've never heard anything so incredible!"

Her words raced zealously. "Blade, it isn't as far-fetched as you might think!"

"All right, explain on our way to your wagon."

They resumed their walk, and although Blade resented her desire to discuss Patrick, he nonetheless slowed their steps, giving her sufficient time to explain her revelation in detail.

"I was nine years old," she began, "when Patrick came home from college for the first time. It was Christmas vacation. It had only been four months since I'd last seen him, but to me it seemed forever. I tagged along behind him practically everywhere he went. I was probably a nuisance, but Patrick never complained. He had been home three days when one morning I couldn't find him. I searched the house, the grounds, and even the stables. He was nowhere to be seen. I knew he hadn't left the plantation because his horse was in its stall. There was a large patch of woods behind the house, and in these woods there was a creek. Patrick and I used to go to this area often, and we called it our own special place. I decided to look for him there, but I seriously doubted I'd find him. It was bitterly cold that day, and I couldn't imagine why he'd brave the chill to visit the creek."

Suzanne's pleasant voice, with its melodic southern drawl, held Blade's undivided attention. Listening attentively, he felt as though he were drifting back into another moment in time and could actually visualize the nine-year-old Suzanne trekking through the woods hoping to find her cousin.

Hearing a twig snap in the woods, Patrick turned away from the creek to look behind him. Seeing Suzanne coming his way, he greeted her with a welcome smile.

She huddled her shoulders against the frigid wind and buried her gloved hands even deeper into the fur-lined pockets of her heavy coat. "Patrick!" she gasped, reaching his side and snuggling against his warmth. "I

117

thought I might find you here. Don't you think it's a little cold for an outing?"

He wrapped an arm about her, drawing her closer. "I needed some time alone to think."

"Couldn't you do that in your bedroom, standing in front of a warm, blazing fireplace?"

"I suppose," he chuckled. "But I always feel more attuned to God when I'm in the midst of nature."

"Did you come here to talk to God?" she asked with a child's simple faith. If Patrick wished to communicate with God, she never doubted that he could do so.

A tender smile played across his handsome face. "I didn't exactly come here to talk to Him; I needed to be alone with my thoughts. I guess you could say I was meditating."

She wasn't sure she understood. "What does that mean, Patrick?"

"Meditate?" he repeated quietly. "It means to think something over in your mind."

"What are you thinking about?" she asked curiously.

His sudden laugh was jovial. "Am I not allowed any secrets?"

Gazing up at him very seriously, she swore, "Patrick, if you have a secret, I promise not to tell." Her small hand moved qiuckly across her chest. "Cross my heart and hope to die!"

"Well, you don't have to go quite that far to protect my secret," he responded, playing along with her game. "Besides, there's nothing to hide. Lately I've been giving my future a lot of thought, and I believe I have a spiritual calling."

"Are you considering the priesthood?" she exclaimed.

"Yes, I am," he answered earnestly. "But it's too soon to make a final decision. I still have college to finish. And before I take such a big step, I want to be absolutely sure that I'm doing the right thing. So for now, let's just keep this between us, shall we?"

"I won't tell anyone," she hastily assured him. "But Patrick, if you should decide to become a priest, what will Uncle Thomas say?"

His blue eyes clouded with worry. "I don't know. But father is Catholic, and in his own way he's a God-fearing man. If I decide on the priesthood, surely he won't try to stand in my way."

The gusty wind picked up speed and its increasing force whistled eerily across the bare tree tops. Patrick shivered, but he wasn't sure if it was from the cold or a premonition that his father wouldn't be as understanding as he hoped. Patrick believed Thomas Donovan was a God-fearing man, but he was also aware that his father's plantation came first, taking priority over his religion as well as God Himself. He was utterly devoted to Southmoor. It had been handed down to him from his father, and someday he'd give it to his own son. Southmoor would shelter future Donovans for generations to come. But Patrick knew if he became a priest, there would be no more Donovans. Suzanne had Donovan blood, but her children would carry her husband's name.

Although Patrick was afraid his father would find a way to stop him if he decided to dedicate his life to the Church, he kept these thoughts to himself as he slipped his hand into Suzanne's.

The major and Suzanne were only a few feet from the wagon when Blade took her arm, bringing them to a standstill. With arms akimbo he said, "You aren't thinking rationally. Just because your cousin once told you that he was considering the priesthood, you have now convinced yourself that he's run away to a seminary!"

"But Blade, you don't understand! There's more to it than that!" she attempted to explain.

"I don't want to hear any more!" Suddenly he moved closer and grasped her shoulders. His dark eyes bore into hers, but beneath their heated gaze a note of pleading lingered. "Suzanne, do you realize what you have been doing? When you learned of the charges against Donovan, you very conveniently believed him innocent. You couldn't admit to yourself that he had deserted his comrades and committed cold-blooded murder, so you chose to believe that the army had falsified their accusations. Then, when you could no longer deny these charges as false, you tell yourself that this Trooper Donovan is an imposter. But for you to believe in an imposter, you must conclude that your cousin was murdered. How else could this man who is pretending to be Patrick Donovan come by his possessions? But your closed mind cannot accept the possibility of your cousin's demise, so in order to keep your idol alive, you persuade yourself that he gave up his identity to become a man of God!"

She wrested herself from his tenacious grip, her large blue eyes radiating anger. "I should have known you wouldn't understand! To you everything must be cut and dried. I suppose it's your army background that makes you this way. Even though your fellow soldiers have been killed, you can still keep yourself emotionally detached, evaluating all the evidence with your stoical, military mind. Well, Major Landon, it's not that easy for me! I am emotionally involved! So don't you dare analyze me with your superior, cold-hearted attitude! You can't possibly understand how I feel! No one you love is involved!"

Blade spoke quietly, but his tone was tinged with such fury that Suzanne cringed beneath his granite-hard scrutiny. "I am not as uninvolved as you think! Trooper Jones, the man Donovan murdered, was my half-brother!"

He turned about swiftly and began walking away. For a moment Suzanne was too stunned to move, then, regaining a semblance of composure, she ran after him. Catching up, she clutched his arm. "I'm sorry," she cried. "But I didn't know! Why did you wait until now to tell me about your brother? Why didn't you tell me sooner?"

"Would it have made you feel any better if I had told you that your cousin killed my brother?" he lashed out.

"Trooper Donovan murdered him, not my cousin!" she said emphatically.

Their unyielding gazes met and locked.

Blade reached over and gently brushed aside a tendril of hair that had fallen across her forehead. "Where do we go from here?" he asked sadly.

She moved back from his touch. "What do you mean?"

"Don't play games with me, Suzanne. You know exactly what I'm talking about. From the first moment we met, we were both acutely aware of the attraction between us. I'm not like you, I can't run away from my feelings. I prefer to stand firmly and face them." He stepped very close to her, and gazed tenderly down into her beautiful azure eyes. "Suzanne Donovan, I'm falling in love with you."

She wasn't sure if she wanted Blade to love her, nor was she sure of her own feelings. Denying her ambivalent emotions, she turned to flee to the sanctuary of her wagon.

But Blade stopped her with his strong hands gripping her shoulders. "Once again, my little Confederate, you run when I back you into a corner. If you want to escape, then by all means do so. But first I'm

121

going to prove just how powerful this attraction truly is."

His arms went about her, and holding her close against his large frame, he bent his head and kissed her. His lips seared hers with a brutal force that took Suzanne's breath away. His strong arm, encircling her waist, pressed her thighs up against his. Her full skirt and petticoats couldn't prevent her from becoming aware of his hard desire. She was completely dominated, and intense longing filled her senses. Leaning into his embrace, her lips parted beneath his, and when he deepened their kiss with his probing tongue, she welcomed the intimacy.

She felt his tightly muscled frame tremble with need as he drew her thighs even more powerfully to his. His solid maleness rubbed against her with a friction that sparked a fiery flame within her loins.

Blade was reluctant to release her, but he knew if he didn't break their embrace, he'd lose control, throw caution to the wind, and carry her to the shadows, and make love to her.

He set her free. Suzanne was shaken. She had never imagined that a man's kiss could awaken such a hungry longing within her.

Blade's passion was so aroused that it took a great effort for him to keep his voice even. "Now that I have made my point and you can no longer deny our need, I'll ask you again. Where do we go from here?"

Suzanne had to take a couple of deep breaths before achieving a certain degree of calm. "Where we go from here depends on what we learn of Patrick."

He frowned. "In other words, if Trooper Donovan proves to be an imposter and your cousin is dead, or else playing priesthood, then we have a future together. But if Trooper Donovan isn't an imposter, but your long-lost cousin, then there's no hope for us."

Her eyes pleaded with his. "Oh, Blade, don't you understand? If this Trooper Donovan is my cousin, and you were to kill him or be responsible for his execution, I would never want to see you again!" Her eyes now downcast, she continued brokenly, "If Patrick has done all these terrible deeds, then I can never again love anyone. My heart will be totally devoid of feeling."

"Do you love him that much?"

Raising her tear-filled gaze to his, she murmured pathetically, "Yes, I do." She made a desperate stab at making him understand. "My parents died when I was three years old, and I was taken in by my aunt and uncle. They didn't want me; they only offered me a home because they considered it their duty to do so. I was so lonely and so afraid. Patrick was my salvation. He loved me, and he was always kind and considerate."

Blade didn't want to hear about her past with Patrick. "To hell with the man you think the sun rises and sets on! Don't you realize you're living a fantasy? The chance that Trooper Donovan isn't your cousin is such a slim one that it barely exists."

"Nonetheless, Major Landon, I will continue to hold on to that hope until it is no longer alive!" She cast him a defiant look before starting back to her wagon, which sat starkly alone on the quiet fort, the gentle night breeze rippling its white canvas top.

Blade watched her until she had climbed safely inside, then he turned sharply about. As he headed for his temporary quarters, his hate for Trooper Donovan increased, jealousy now taking its place among all his reasons for despising the unscrupulous deserter.

Chapter Nine

Leaving Fort Fetterman behind them, Blade and his fellow travelers continued their westward course. It was mid-July, and the weather was extremely warm, the sun's burning rays relentless.

Their journey was into its second day when Luther's Trading Store appeared as a hazy mote on the far horizon. The log cabin, sitting alone on the vast, grassy plains, resembled a mirage. Suzanne felt the vision might vanish like a puff of smoke. But as they drew closer and the cabin remained in sight, she knew her eyes had not been deceiving her.

Blade and Justin were riding ahead of the mule team, and turning his horse about, Blade trotted the animal to the wagon's side.

For a change, Molly had joined Suzanne and Saul on the wagon seat, and the three of them looked expectantly at the major.

"The cabin up ahead is called Luther's Trading Store," he explained, his eyes meeting Suzanne's. "Chances are good that Trooper Donovan and the two trappers accompanying him stopped here to buy supplies. Hopefully Luther can give us information that will prove vital."

124

He didn't wait to hear if they had any comments to offer. Slapping the reins against his horse, he returned to ride beside Justin.

Minutes later, when Saul pulled up the team in front of the trading store, Suzanne, who was sitting between Molly and Saul, said briskly, "I'm going inside with the major." Standing and lifting the hem of her long dress, she moved past Molly, and before either she or Saul could object, she climbed down to the ground.

Dismounting along with Justin, Blade became aware of Suzanne's intent. Stepping to her side, he grumbled brusquely, "There's no reason for you to go inside with us."

She swept past him. "When you question this Luther, I intend to be there to hear his answers."

Following her to the door, he taunted, "Don't you trust me, my doubting little Confederate?"

"Where my cousin is concerned, I trust you no farther than I can see you!"

He caught her and grasped her arm. "That goes both ways, Miss Donovan," he retorted.

"At last, Major Landon, we understand each other!"

Undisturbed, he chuckled lightly as he opened the cabin door, then stepped aside for her to precede him and Justin.

Her eyes were accustomed to the bright sunlight, and it took a moment to adjust to the darkness inside the disorderly store. Tables placed randomly about were piled with blankets, furs, and clothing, the articles heaped in a chaotic disarray.

Taking a stance close to the entrance, Suzanne watched Blade and Justin as they walked to the counter to speak to the man standing behind.

Luther knew the two men, and although Blade was wearing buckskins instead of his uniform, the store owner said cordially, "Howdy, major." He nodded to

125

Justin. "Mr. Smith. What can I do for you gents?"

"We're looking for a deserter," Blade answered, then proceeded to give him Trooper Donovan's description and the information they had recently acquired.

Chawing a wad of tobacco, Luther said in a lazy drawl, "Yep, the man you're lookin' for was here, and he had two trappers with 'im. They was here 'bout two days past. Bought themselves up a whole bunch of supplies. Said they was goin' into the Black Hills and trap for the winter, and also do a little prospectin'. Then come spring, they plan to sell their furs and take whatever gold they panned to San Francisco."

"Damn!" Blade cursed.

"What's wrong?" Suzanne asked urgently, crossing the room.

"We can't follow Trooper Donovan into the Black Hills."

"Why not?"

It was Justin who answered, "The Black Hills are Sioux territory. Besides, a man could hole up in those hills and stay hidden for years. To find Donovan in the Black Hills would be like lookin' for a needle in a haystack."

"Then what are we going to do?" Suzanne exclaimed, her question aimed at Blade.

He thought for a moment. "We'll return to Fort Laramie, then next spring head for San Francisco."

"Surely you can't expect me and the others to winter at Fort Laramie!"

"Your only other choice, Miss Donovan, is to go back to Natchez." Blade didn't feel nearly as emotionally uninvolved as he had sounded. What if she should decide to take his advice? Could he let her leave?

"I'm not returning to Natchez!" she avowed, unaware that her words had eased Blade's heart. "I intend to find out what happened to Patrick, and I will

126

not go home until I know!"

"In that case," Blade said calmly, "we may as well start for Fort Laramie."

The sun had dipped into the west and long shadows were falling across the wide landscape when the travelers stopped to set up camp. Blade and Justin had chosen a fertile patch of land located beside a small stream of water.

Blade had left to scout the immediate area and Justin was helping Saul start a fire, when Suzanne decided to take a bath in the narrow river. Gathering up clean clothes, a large towel, and a bar of jasmine-scented soap, she headed quickly downstream. Finding an ideal spot sheltered with green foliage, she draped the clothes she carried across a bush and dropped the towel to the ground. Then she undressed hastily, letting the discarded garments fall haphazardly over the shrubbery. A southerly breeze was drifting gustily, and her long, curly hair blew about her face as she waded into the crystal-clear water. When she was knee-deep, she sat down and waves washed over her. Enjoying the refreshing coolness, her mood was lightened as she lathered herself with the sweet-smelling soap. Once she had herself sufficiently sudsed, she splashed the water over her smooth skin, rinsing away the film of soap. She then wet her hair and shampooed it thoroughly. She was reluctant to quit her bath; the mountain-cooled water was heavenly. But knowing Molly would need her help preparing supper, she grudgingly got to her feet. Rivulets of water rolled off her silken flesh as she moved gracefully through the rippling waves to return to the bank. The warm wind was now stronger and its gusty force blew her long, damp tresses. This wind is going to dry my hair in a hundred tangles, she reflected, if I don't hurry back to the wagon and get it brushed.

Stepping onto dry land, she bent over and picked up the towel, and wrapping it about her, she went over to the bushes to retrieve her clothing. Finding the foliage minus at least half of them, she looked about frantically. Who had slipped up to the shrubbery and taken her things? A Sioux warrior? She gasped, fear gripping her heart.

A horse's whinny suddenly sounded in the near distance, and frozen with fear, Suzanne stood motionless.

Her huge eyes widened expectantly as a man's form took shape in the shadowy thicket, then recognizing the buckskins he wore, she sighed with effusive relief.

Ambling leisurely into the open ground, Blade, leading his horse, smiled wryly as he beheld Suzanne wearing nothing but a towel. He carried her missing clothes across his arm, and nodding toward them, he asked casually, "Did you lose something?"

Her relief was quickly supplanted by anger. "How dare you steal my clothes! You . . . you peeping cad! . . . You rude, sex-starved Yankee!"

"Whoa there, my hot-headed little Confederate! I am not a peeping cad, nor am I a rude Yankee."

"Sex-starved Yankee!" she repeated tersely.

"Well, I have to admit that implication is open for debate," he answered, his eyes roaming boldly over her skimpily clad flesh. "May I suggest that the next time you decide to wash in the river, you anchor your clothes if the wind is blowing. I was on my way back to camp when your dress blew across my path, which I might add, startled my horse and almost made him throw me."

Suzanne giggled.

Raising an eyebrow, he studied her questioningly.

"You find my near mishap funny, do you? It couldn't possibly be more humorous than you wrapped in a towel, believing yourself decently covered while unaware that the wind is periodically giving me glimpses of your desirable attributes."

Glancing down, she was abashed to see that the wind was blowing aside her towel, revealing her bare thighs to his scrutiny. Blushing and holding her cover together, she ordered sharply, "Give me my things, then go away!"

"Very well," he complied, handing her the clothes draped over his arm. "But Suzanne, I think I should warn you that it isn't safe for you to wander away from camp. This land is uncivilized and full of lurking dangers—Indians, desperadoes, and snakes, to name a few."

When he turned away, she demanded, "Don't leave!"

"First you tell me to go away, now you tell me not to leave. Can't you make up your mind?"

"You just stay where you are while I step into the shrubbery and get dressed!"

"Are you scared of all the lurking dangers? Don't you realize, my beautiful little Confederate, that I am your greatest danger?"

She watched him warily. A strange expression shadowed his face, one she couldn't analyze.

Moving abruptly, he stepped to his horse and mounted. Guiding the sleek gelding to Suzanne's side, he leaned over, wrapped his strong arm about her waist, and lifted her onto his saddle.

She wanted to fight him, but her arms were laden with her bundle of clothes. "What do you think you are doing?" she lashed out angrily.

"I'm taking you where we won't be disturbed by the others," he replied with an arrogance that merely added fuel to her anger.

"If you don't put me off this horse, I'll scream!"

Blade sent his mount into a fast gallop. "Go right ahead. By the time Saul can respond, we'll be a long way from here."

Deciding screaming was useless, she asked apprehensively, "Why do you want us to be alone?"

"I'm going to make love to you," he disclosed calmly.

"You must be mad!"

"I am," he agreed. "Mad about you."

"Surely you don't intend to force yourself on me!" she said breathlessly.

"No, I don't," Blade assured her, his tone level. "I intend to seduce you."

"Seduce me? It'll snow in hell before I succumb to a damned Yankee!"

"We'll see about that."

"I can't believe this!" she suddenly gasped.

"You can't believe what?" he chuckled, pressing her closer to his manly chest.

"I can't believe I am actually sitting on this horse, nude, wearing only a towel for protection, while you are taking me God only knows where in order to seduce me!"

"Believe it, little one."

Suzanne noticed they were traveling downstream, remaining close to the river. He reined in the gelding. "This seems to be a good place."

He dismounted, then reached up and lifted her from the horse. Easing her to the ground, he let her soft body slide down his, the feel of her intensifying his passion.

The setting sun had descended far into the west, and the landscape was now blanketed with a charcoal hue.

"We'll need your towel," he said, reaching for it.

Stepping back, she exclaimed, "Good Lord, you are mad, totally mad!"

Gesturing down toward the grassy area where they

stood, he explained, "Although it looks comfortable, it can be prickly against the bare skin. So if you'll hand me your towel, I'll spread it out for us to lie on."

"I'm not lying anywhere with you! You might think you can seduce me, but it'll be over my dead body!"

He smiled sensually. "Quite the contrary. Your lovely body will be very much alive and wonderfully responsive."

Moving with lightning speed, he had her in his arms before she could flee. She still carried her bundle of clothes, and snatching them, he dropped them to the ground. His mouth came down on hers demandingly as he pressed her flesh against him. He pried her lips apart and his tongue darted between her teeth.

His fervent kiss made Suzanne feel strange inside, and as his mouth continued to relish hers, she weakened and leaned into his powerful embrace. Her eyes closed, she surrendered to the sensations flowing within her.

Whispering her name with deep longing, he moved his lips to her neck, sending warm, exciting kisses over her throat. Suddenly his mouth was back on hers, and she gasped for breath. Lacing his fingers through her long hair, he kept her lips pressed to his as he continued kissing her forcefully.

Giving in to a need she could no longer restrain, she laced her arms about his neck and clung tightly.

"Suzanne," he whispered hoarsely, his lips next to her ear. "I love you, and I think you love me too."

Did she love him? She didn't want to be in love with him. "No," she protested feebly, "don't love me."

"It's too late," he murmured, before kissing her once again. Carefully his hand moved to the part of the towel that was wrapped securely about her breasts. He released the knotted ends and her wrap descended to the ground to lie at her feet. Bending his head, he caressed her full mounds with his mouth, his tongue teasing and circling their taut peaks. Suzanne trembled with awakening ecstasy as his warm mouth aroused waves of pleasure that overwhelmed her. She felt as though she was drowning in a stormy sea.

Relinquishing her, he picked up the fallen towel and spread it upon a patch of grass. Then, sweeping her into his arms, he knelt and gently laid her down. Lying beside her, he sought her lips with his. She shuddered with rapture when his hand began moving over her naked flesh, his fingers deftly exploring her curves and hollows. His lips soon followed the path his hand had taken as he kissed her breasts, her stomach, and then the golden V between her delicate thighs.

By now Suzanne was totally at his mercy; she was his for the taking, to do with as he pleased. She arched toward his intimate touch, and succumbing, she writhed as his mouth and tongue tasted her sweet nectar.

"Suzanne, my beautiful darling," he murmured thickly as his lips caressed her stomach before moving upward to kiss her breasts.

Entwining her fingers into his dark hair, she pressed him ever closer, loving the erotic pleasures he was provoking within her. "Oh, Blade! . . . Blade!" she whispered timorously.

"I love you, Suzanne," he whispered, then his lips descended upon hers, his kiss one of fiery ecstasy. He left her slowly, a little reluctantly, as he stood to shed his clothing.

Her eyes filled with admiration as she watched him disrobe. When he removed his shirt, she studied his muscular chest and was thrilled by the sight of his rippling muscles. She continued to look on as he peeled off the remainder of his clothes. Lowering her gaze to his erect manhood, she inhaled sharply, a little frightened by his size.

Returning to lie with her, he said soothingly, "Don't be afraid, sweetheart. There will be pain, but it'll only last a moment."

Capturing her lips to his, he moved over her small frame. He used his knees to part her legs, and as his hardness probed against her, she stiffened. Placing his hands under her buttocks, he moved forward and entered her quickly. He heard her gasp softly as he took her virginity. He paused and waited for her discomfort to subside, then pressed himself even deeper into her velvety depths.

His penetration soon caused wondrous sensations to course through her trembling body, and moving her hand to the back of his neck, she urged his lips down to hers.

"Blade . . . Blade," she purred throatily, blissfully soaring upward to reach love's highest plane.

Responding to her ardent response, he placed his mouth on hers and kissed her fiercely.

Lost to each other, and to the sensations that were now all-consuming, they drifted gloriously into a world all their own.

Molly, becoming worried about Suzanne, approached Justin who was sitting beside the campfire talking to Saul. Pausing and wringing her hands a little nervously, she said, "I'm afraid something might have happened to Suzanne. She went down to the river to bathe."

"I'm sure she's fine," Justin said reassuringly, "but if you want, I'll check on her."

"Would you please?" she asked.

Molly watched him with growing apprehension as he walked away and started farther downstream.

"The major ain't anywhere around either," Saul muttered.

"What exactly are you implying?"

He shrugged. "Just makin' a comment, Miz Molly." He was holding a cup of coffee, and turning his attention to the warm brew, he took a big drink. The old man's forehead wrinkled with worry. He could foresee only trouble for Miz Suzanne and Major Landon if they were to fall in love. Nothin' but lots of trouble! he mused solemnly.

Meanwhile, reaching the area where Blade had found Suzanne, the tracks left in the damp earth close to the river's edge told Justin all he needed to know. Eyeing the clothes that had been left draped across the bushes, the scout's brow furrowed with mild puzzlement. Nothing like being in a hurry, he thought with amusement.

"Justin!" he heard Molly call from the distance.

Not wanting her to find Suzanne's clothes still lying about, he left the scene to head her off.

"There you are," Molly said as Justin suddenly appeared in her path. "Did you find Suzanne?"

"She and the major have gone for a ride," he mumbled, not quite meeting her eyes.

"How do you know?"

"Ma'am, it's my job to read tracks, and believe me, Miss Donovan and Major Landon rode off on his horse."

"I wonder why?" she pondered.

"Would you like me to help you start supper?" he asked, anxious to change the subject.

She smiled pleasantly. "It's very kind of you to offer, but I'm sure I can manage."

He grinned sheepishly. "Which is probably for the best, 'cause I ain't a very good cook."

Tilting her head to the side, she looked at him pertly,

totally unaware of the enticement she presented. "On second thought, maybe I can use your assistance. You can peel potatotes, can't you?"

Taking her unprepared, he stepped so close that his brawny frame was mere inches from hers. "You're a comely woman, Molly O'Ryan."

"Th . . . thank you," she stammered, blushing.

"I know I ain't the kind of man you're used to. I don't have much education, but I can read and write. But that doesn't put me in your social class, and I'm aware that you southern aristocrats set a great store by such things."

Confused, she asked guardedly, "What are you trying to say?"

He looked somewhat embarrassed, but it was hard to tell with a full black beard covering his face. "I guess I'm tryin' to tell you that I want to court you." Expecting a rejection, he raced on, "Ma'am, I realize you're a virtuous lady, I mean I understand how you southern women are protected and always chaperoned. And I'm far from the ideal gentleman, at least I ain't the kind you're used to associating with. I have a bad habit of saying what I mean and taking what I want. And, Molly O'Ryan, I want you somethin' bad, but 'cause you're a real lady, I'm goin' to keep myself in check and pay court like a true gentleman. That is, if you'll let me."

Molly's emotions were confused. She was flattered, pleased, even responsive, but most of all, she was gripped with guilt. He believed her a virtuous lady, a woman untouched! He had her on a pedestal, where she didn't belong. She should tell him the truth, but ashamed, she murmured evasively, "I am still engaged to Patrick, and I do not feel free to give you, or any man, permission to call on me."

He didn't buy her excuse. "You're lyin' to me, Molly.

There's no reason for you to be dishonest. Why don't you just tell me the truth? You don't think I'm good enough for you, do you?" Before she could try to convince him otherwise, he grumbled, "Can't say that I blame you. I sure ain't much of a catch." Doffing his weather-worn hat, he apologized, "I'm sorry, ma'am, for runnin' off at the mouth and sayin' things I had no business sayin'."

He walked away quickly, giving her no chance to stop him. She watched him until he disappeared from her sight. For a moment she was tempted to go after him, but decided it was best to leave well enough alone. She liked Justin Smith and was attracted to him, but she wasn't sure if a relationship between them would be wise. They were so different, and had absolutely nothing in common. Or so she tried to convince herself.

Chapter Ten

"What are you thinking about?" Blade asked Suzanne, wondering why she was so quiet. They were lying on the towel, cradled in each others' arms, enjoying the feel of the wind as it drifted refreshingly over their naked flesh.

"All kinds of thoughts are racing through my mind," she sighed, sounding perplexed.

"Care to name a few of them?" he asked.

Moving out of his arms, she sat up and answered somberly, "My thoughts don't matter."

"Of course they do," he insisted, raising up to sit beside her.

She looked into his eyes. "Well, for one thing, I'm wishing we hadn't made love."

"Why?" he questioned gently.

"I was raised to believe that a woman should save herself for her husband."

He smiled tenderly. "What makes you think I won't be your husband?"

Suzanne appeared surprised. "Is that a proposal?"

Standing, he stepped to where her jumble of clothes were lying on the ground. Sorting through them, he found a pair of pantalets, a petticoat, and the dress that earlier had blown across his horse's path. Handing her the garments, he asked carefully, "If I were to ask you to marry me, what would be your answer?"

Getting to her feet and starting to dress, she said truthfully, "I'd tell you that I had to think about it."

Slipping into his trousers, he responded, "Then why don't we spend the next few days thinking? I'll think about proposing and you can think about an answer."

"Isn't it all hypothetical?" she asked, smiling.

"Cautious is a better word. After all, marriage is a big step."

"Especially between a Yankee and a Southerner."

He frowned impatiently. "The war is over and done with! It should be allowed to rest in peace. My reservations concerning marriage between us are caused by your cousin."

She finished dressing, then, moving close to his side, she murmured, "When you asked me to tell you my thoughts, Patrick was a large part of them."

"I figured he was," Blade said shortly. "He's about all you ever think about."

"But Blade, my cousin is no longer between us. Trooper Donovan, the man you hate, isn't Patrick."

He took her hands into his and clasped them tightly. "Suzanne, you don't know that for sure. You have to prepare yourself for the worst. Trooper Donovan could very well be your cousin."

She jerked her hands free. "I tell you, he isn't Patrick!"

Giving up, he said with ill-temper, "We better return to camp."

She agreed and went over to the horse. He helped her mount, then handed her the towel and the rest of her clothes. As he swung into the saddle, she asked tentatively, "Blade, why are you so sure that Trooper

138

Donovan is Patrick?"

"I'm not absolutely sure. But all the evidence seems to point to them being one and the same."

"Physical and material evidence," she argued.

"In a court of law, they carry a lot of weight."

She said no more about Patrick. In his mind, Blade had her cousin guilty and there was nothing she could say to change his belief. Only Trooper Donovan himself could prove Patrick's innocence, and she would find this man if it was the last thing she did in her life!

Molly had supper prepared when Suzanne and Blade returned. There wasn't much talking during the meal. Although no one referred to their absence, Suzanne nonetheless felt that they all knew what had happened. As soon as the dishes had been washed, she excused herself and went to the wagon. She was slipping into her nightgown when Molly joined her.

"Are you going to bed so early?" Molly asked. "It's only eight o'clock."

"I'm tired," Suzanne murmured, looking guiltily away from her friend's questioning eyes. Moving to her pallet, she lay down and turned her back toward the other woman.

Molly started to ask her if something was wrong, but afraid that her mood might be connected somehow with the major, she decided not to pry. She wondered if Suzanne and Major Landon had made love; if they had, then she could personally sympathize with Suzanne. She knew exactly how her friend was feeling; remorseful, ashamed, and yet like a woman in every sense of the word. She hoped this man who had taken Suzanne's innocence would also marry her—unlike Patrick, who had taken her own innocence only apparently to desert her afterward.

Deciding to have a cup of coffee before retiring, Molly left the wagon and walked over to the campfire. Justin was taking the first watch and was nowhere to be seen. Glancing about, she saw Saul strolling toward the major, who was lying on his bedroll.

Blade watched the elderly man's approach. Seeing his grim expression, he readied himself for a confrontation. He knew his intentions toward Suzanne were about to be questioned. He didn't blame the man for wanting to protect his beautiful mistress.

"Major, suh, can I talk to you for a few minutes?" Saul asked.

Sitting up, Blade answered, "Of course."

Slowly Saul eased himself to the ground to sit beside the major. "There seems to be a storm brewin'," he drawled.

Looking up at the star-studded sky, Blade replied, "Even though the wind is blowing strongly, I don't think it's going to blow up a storm."

"I wasn't referrin' to no storm in the sky, I'm talkin' 'bout the storm brewin' down here on earth."

Blade understood. "Saul, why don't you just come right out and say what's on your mind?"

The old man found the present situation uncomfortable. He'd been a slave practically his whole life, and a slave didn't oppose a white man. He took a deep breath and gathered his courage. Regardless of the outcome, he was going to have his say in the matter. "I love Miz Suzanne," he began calmly. "With Masta Patrick gone, she's all I got left. Her happiness is very important to me. Major Landon, if you do one thing to hurt that little gal, I'm gonna kill ya."

Blade hadn't expected quite so much hostility. "Isn't murder going just a little far?"

"If Masta Thomas or Masta Patrick was here, they'd

140

call you out." Blade could sense a cold rage lurking beneath the servant's outward composure. "When a man has lived as many years as I have, he knows things without bein' told. And no one has to tell me what happened this afternoon between you and Miz Suzanne. I already know. But I believe Miz Suzanne let it happen. If I didn't believe that, you'd be a dead man."

"What do you want from me, Saul? Do you want my promise to marry her?" Blade sounded impatient.

"Major Landon, if you're a gentleman, which I believe you are, then that's exactly what you'll say."

"Saul, I'd marry her tomorrow if I thought that was the answer. I'm in love with Suzanne."

The older man looked confused.

"Don't you understand?" Blade pressed.

"I ain't sure," he mumbled.

"Then let me explain. Let's say, just for the sake of argument, that I marry Suzanne when we return to Fort Laramie. Do you think my wife is going to give me her support when I leave in the spring to hunt down her cousin? And when he's standing before a firing squad, do you think my wife will still love me?"

Saul shrugged off Blade's speculations. "Trooper Donovan ain't Masta Patrick."

Losing his patience, Blade exclaimed irritably, "Well, until we know for a fact that they aren't one and the same, a marriage between Suzanne and myself might be impossible!"

His anger surfacing, Saul demanded, "Then why didn't you leave that little gal alone?"

"That's a good question, Saul. I just wish I had a good answer. But damn it, love has no logic! Haven't you ever been in love?" He was beginning to feel exasperated.

It was a long time before the servant answered. "Yes, suh, I was in love. But that was fifty years ago, and sometimes I forget how it feels to be young and in love. All I got out of it was a broken heart, and I got a feelin' that's all Miz Suzanne is gonna get from you."

"Not if I can help it," Blade said firmly.

Slowly Saul got to his feet, then looking down at the major, he said gravely, "I ought to shoot you and save Miz Suzanne all the heartache you're gonna bring her."

"You've got it wrong, Saul. I'm not the one who will break her heart. It's Patrick Donovan who's going to completely shatter her. I only wish I could be the one to pick up the pieces and put her world back together again, but I'll be the last person she'll turn to for comfort. You're the one who will have to help her through it. I can only hope that someday she'll let me back into her life."

Saul's eyes bored into the major's. "You done got Masta Patrick tried and found guilty. If you knew him like Miz Suzanne and I know him, you'd know he's innocent."

"But I don't know him in that way, do I? I only know him as a deserter and a murderer."

Saul looked haggard and older than his age as he groaned brokenly, "I keep askin' the good Lord to let me live long enough to prove Masta Patrick's innocence." It was a tired, beaten man who turned away from the major and walked sluggishly toward the campfire.

Blade watched him closely. He had a feeling there was a lot more to the ex-slave than anyone knew, including Patrick and Suzanne. He wondered about the old man's life. It couldn't have been an easy one. It was difficult for Blade to imagine life in bondage, belonging bodily to someone else. He lay back down and closed his eyes, but he knew the gesture was futile, for he was wide awake. Suzanne, Saul, and Trooper Donovan filled his thoughts, causing him to toss and turn restlessly as sleep eluded him.

Suzanne was also suffering. As hard as she tried, she couldn't make herself fall asleep. She was too guilt-ridden. Why had she gone against her own beliefs? She had always thought it wrong for a woman to give herself to a man who wasn't her husband. She had sinned, there was no doubt in her mind. But in spite of her guilt, she felt a certain glow. She had never dreamed that making love could be so heavenly. And if Blade were to come to her right now, lie at her side and take her into his arms, she knew she wouldn't have the will power to refuse his advances.

I have no self-control where he's concerned, she thought, defeated. Hadn't she told him that it'd snow in hell before he could seduce her, and hadn't she also told him if he tried, it'd be over her dead body? Well, figuratively speaking, he had made her eat her words! Why have I no defense against him? she wondered.

A worried frown crossed her face. Aunt Ellen always swore that I'd never be a genuine lady. Could she have been right? She said I had my mother's bad blood, and that when I grew up, I'd be just like her. Suzanne's memories of her mother were vague. As a child, she had never understood what her aunt meant by her mother's so-called "bad blood." She still wasn't sure precisely what Ellen had been implying. Had what had happened this afternoon between herself and Blade been what her aunt was referring to? Had she surrendered to the major because of this bad blood that flowed through her veins? Or did it have nothing whatsoever to do with a trait she may have inherited? Did she submit to Blade because she was falling in love with him? And if she was in love with him, what then? Marriage? No, she didn't have time for marriage! She

143

must continue devoting all her time and energy to finding out what happened to Patrick!

Suzanne sighed deeply. Patrick, she mused dreamily. Whenever Aunt Ellen tried to belittle me, you always stood up for me. You never thought I had bad blood or would grow up to dishonor my family.

Rolling to lie on her side, Suzanne fluffed her pillow, and burying her face into its downy softness, she allowed her thoughts to roam into the past.

Suzanne dressed hurriedly. This was Patrick's last day of Christmas vacation. He'd be leaving in the morning to return to college. Wanting to spend the day with him, she had awakened early and was now slipping quickly into her clothes. Lettie, looking on, chastised the girl for her haste. The servant tried to get her young mistress to let her arrange her hair, but brushing aside the woman's request, Suzanne darted from the bedroom and fled down the staircase. Detecting voices inside the parlor, she headed in that direction. The door was ajar, and as she neared the room, she heard her aunt mention her name. Hesitantly Suzanne slowed her steps, and when she reached the open doorway, she paused.

Ellen, pacing the room, was speaking to Patrick. "Suzanne is becoming impossible to deal with. Her tutor, Miss Simpson, says the child is a serious problem. Suzanne refuses to concentrate on her schoolwork, and spends the biggest part of the day fidgeting or daydreaming."

"Maybe you should shorten her school hours," Patrick suggested. He was sitting on the sofa, watching his mother pace back and forth. "After all, her studies last from nine in the morning until five in the afternoon, with only an hour free at lunch. Honestly, mother, isn't that overdoing it a bit? I only had studies from nine to eleven, and then again from one to three."

She sat in the chair across from Patrick. "Well, I admit the hours are a trifle long, but it's for the child's own good."

"Why, pray tell, do you think that?"

"It keeps her out of mischief," Ellen remarked as though her answer made everything crystal clear.

Patrick looked thoughtfully at his mother. She's a beautiful woman, he reflected. It's a shame her beauty is only skin-deep. His tone edged with annoyance, he asked, "What kind of mischief, mother?"

"If it weren't for her studies, the girl would spend all her time down at the stables, or else trekking in the woods. Heaven only knows why she wants to dally at the smelly old stables or walk around in the woods. Mark my words, that child has a wild streak in her, and she isn't normal."

Stiffening, Patrick spoke angrily. "Don't ever again tell me that Suzanne isn't normal! On the contrary, she's as smart as a whip!"

"I didn't mean she wasn't intelligent; there are other ways of being abnormal."

His patience at an end, Patrick bounded to his feet and bellowed, "Mother, you're a malevolent, cold-hearted woman! How can you be so cruel to a nine-year-old child? My God, have you no compassion at all?"

Leaping from her chair, Ellen retorted furiously, "You're just like your Uncle Kevin. He was completely possessed by Gloria, and now the woman's daughter has you possessed!" Her eyes glaring, she hissed, "Just remember, Patrick, she is your first cousin! You had best guard your feelings, and pray to God for guidance!"

Patrick was shocked. His face ashen, he rasped,

"Surely you aren't implying what I think you are!"

"Son, you are so naive," she implored. "Women like Gloria can tempt men into committing all kinds of sin. And Suzanne is her mother's daughter. Her beauty is already outstanding. Someday she'll have the power to lead even the most honorable man astray. Oh, Patrick, I beg you, beware of her wicked charms!"

He looked strangely at her. "Mother, you're jealous of Suzanne, aren't you?" Suddenly a memory from childhood crossed his mind. "Dear God!" he groaned. "I just remembered something. I was about six years old, and I was supposed to be taking a nap, but I couldn't sleep. I came downstairs looking for you. The door to the parlor was closed, and I opened it quietly. I saw you and Uncle Kevin, and you were clinging to him. Naturally I didn't think anything of it, but I did sense that you'd be angry if you knew I had left my room, so I closed the door and went back to bed. I know the kind of man Uncle Kevin was, so I doubt seriously that he instigated the embrace I witnessed. You were in love with him, weren't you, mother? And that's why you hated Gloria so much, because Kevin loved her and not you. Now you have transferred that hate to Suzanne. Once again, you believe you are losing someone you love to a rival. Only this time, it's me you think you are losing, instead of my uncle." He seemed totally disgusted. "Mother, if anyone in this household is abnormal, it's you!"

"Believe what you want!" Ellen shrieked. "But I'm telling you, your feelings for Suzanne are not platonic!"

"She's only a child!" he reasoned.

"But she won't always be a child! What then, Patrick?"

"Then I hope she falls in love, gets married, and has children!"

For a moment Ellen looked deranged. "With you as her husband and the father of her children?"

"Mother, you're pathetic!" Patrick spat, disgusted. He turned brusquely to leave the room when suddenly he became aware of Suzanne's presence. She was standing as though glued to the spot and her face was pale. "Oh my God!" Patrick whispered. Glancing back to Ellen, he ordered tersely, "Leave us alone."

Complying, she left the room, wondering gravely if her relationship with her son could ever be restored. She had a sickening feeling that Patrick would never truly forgive her for the things she had said. But she had only been trying to help him. She should have known that he was beyond help! He was too much like Kevin. Hadn't she tried to make Kevin see that Gloria would ultimately be his downfall? But he had refused to listen, and now her son was making the same mistake!

"Come here," Patrick said gently to Suzanne.

Hesitantly, she did as he requested.

Returning to the sofa, he encouraged her to sit beside him. Placing an arm about her small shoulders, he drew her close. "Did you understand the things mother was saying?"

"Not all of them," she admitted. "But they weren't very nice, were they?"

"Mother very seldom says anything nice," he replied. "She is to be pitied. She is so filled with malice and jealousy that she makes herself more miserable than she makes the people around her."

"Why is she like that, Patrick?"

"I don't know why, honey. I wish I did, maybe then I could help her."

Her face brightened as she asked excitedly, "Patrick, are you really going to marry me and be the father of my children?"

He laughed. Even when his mood was at its lowest,

147

Suzanne could always cheer him. "First cousins shouldn't marry," he explained. "Besides, I'm thinking about becoming a priest, remember?"

"If you do become a priest, will you marry me and my . . . and my . . ."

"And your who?" he asked, smiling.

"My fiancé," she said, remembering the word.

"Of course I will."

"Promise?" she insisted.

"Suzanne, you must refrain from trying to extract promises from me that I can't make. If it's at all possible, then I will gladly marry you and your intended."

"He'll be tall, dark, and handsome," she murmured.

"Your husband?" he queried.

"Yes, and he'll also be strong and brave, and you two will be the best of friends."

The best of friends, Suzanne thought bitterly. Well, if I marry Major Blade Landon, I certainly won't be marrying Patrick's friend. Quite the contrary. I'll be marrying the man who believes my cousin is a deserter as well as a murderer!

Oh, Patrick! she cried inwardly. How did it all come to this? What happened to all those wonderful dreams we shared? You were going to be a priest and I was going to marry my knight in shining armor! But maybe the dreams will still come to pass! You could very well be in a seminary right this very moment, and my destiny might lie with Blade. Could it possibly be true?

Never in her life had Suzanne Donovan hoped so fervently that her speculations could come to pass!

148

Chapter Eleven

On the last night before reaching Fort Laramie, Suzanne was sitting alone at the campfire. Saul had retired, Molly was inside the wagon, and Justin was tending to the horses. Blade, having decided to take the first watch, was preparing to take a protective position a short distance from the camp. But catching sight of Suzanne, he veered his course and walked over to her.

Aware of his approach, she glanced up and watched him as he drew closer. His good looks were striking, and she couldn't decide if he was more handsome in the buckskins he was now wearing, or in his uniform.

Pausing at her side, Blade asked, "Suzanne, will you accompany me for a few minutes? I'd like to talk to you." Detecting her hesitation, he added quickly, "I'm not going to try and take advantage of you."

"Very well," she assented, although her better judgment warned her to be wary of this man who had such power over her emotions.

Blade carried a rifle, and as she fell into step beside him, he placed his free hand on her arm. He waited until they had put a reasonable distance between themselves and the campfire before leading her to an isolated tree. He propped his rifle against the trunk,

149

then placing his hands on her shoulders, he gazed directly into her large blue eyes. "Suzanne, I want to apologize for what happened the other afternoon. I did not behave like a gentleman. I have only one excuse to justify my behavior. I love you very much, and since the first day I saw you, I dreamed of making love to you."

Defensively, she moved away from his firm grip. Just the feel of his hands on her shoulders filled her with an intense longing. She knew if he were to take her into his arms and kiss her, she'd not only surrender, but wantonly return his passion. "You don't need to apologize," she murmured. "You certainly didn't force yourself on me. If I remember correctly, I was quite willing."

"You're a very admirable young lady," he said sincerely. "Most women, under the same circumstances, would give the impression that they had been done a terrible injustice."

"I am not like most women, Major Landon, as you will soon find out."

"I am already aware that you are unique and very special." He studied her closely as he asked, "Why did you call me Major Landon? Is that your way of telling me that our relationship is no longer one of friendship?"

Her emotions in turmoil, she sighed, "I don't know what I want from our relationship. I only know that I find you irresistible."

He smiled tenderly. "The feeling is quite mutual. But Suzanne, we don't have to make any decisions at present. For now, let's just take each day as it comes and remain perfectly honest about our feelings."

"You say that you love me, but Blade, I'm not sure if I'm in love with you." Her heart told her she was a fool. Of course she loved him, otherwise she wouldn't desire him so desperately! But Suzanne pushed this truth to the far recesses of her mind. She wasn't yet ready to admit to herself that she had fallen in love with a man who was not only a Yankee, but who also believed Patrick was a deserter and a murderer.

Blade understood the reasons behind her uncertainty. "Our problems cannot possibly be resolved until we unravel the puzzle that surrounds Patrick Donovan."

Suzanne whole-heartedly agreed. "We aren't going to find those answers tonight, are we? So let's change the subject."

"All right," he complied. "What would you like to talk about?"

Relaxing, she inquired curiously, "Blade is a strange name. How did you come by it?"

"In a way, I was named after my grandfather. His Christian name was Wolford James. He was not only a perfect marksman with a rifle, but was also uncannily good with a knife. As I told you before, he was a militiaman. His fellow comrades gave him the nickname of Blade because he could handle a knife so well. My mother named me Blade James."

"You said Trooper Jones was your half brother. Were your parents divorced?"

"My mother couldn't cope with her husband being away from home so much. She pleaded with him to settle down and spend his time with his wife and son. But father was an adventurous man. He always wanted to climb the mountain just to see what was on the other side. Finally my mother gave up and moved back to her home in New York and divorced her husband. A few years later she married Samuel Jones. They had one child, my brother Sam. My father didn't lose contact with me. He always made a point to travel east at least every year or so to visit me. I was greatly impressed with him, and wanted to be just like him. When I told my mother I planned to become a military man, she was strongly opposed. But my mind was set, so she relented and sent me off to West Point with her blessings. But she was bound and determined that my younger brother didn't follow in my footsteps. I was fourteen years older than Sam, so we were not especially close. I wasn't even aware that he wanted to be in the army, until last year when he suddenly showed up at Fort Laramie. At the time he was eighteen and old enough to make his own decisions. He signed up with the cavalry. I wrote my mother and stepfather to let them know where Sam was. My mother wrote back, asking me to please keep him safe. It was less than a year later that I had to write and notify her that Sam was dead."

"Did you and your brother become close?"

"Officers and enlisted men do not usually socialize. But at times, we'd visit as brothers. If you want to know whether or not I loved him, then the answer is yes. I loved him as a brother, admired him as a man, and in my estimation, he was a damned good soldier." Suddenly his dark eyes hardened. "Then a sorry bastard like Trooper Donovan comes along and shoots Sam in the back!"

"Will you please stop calling him a Donovan! Don't you realize the man is an imposter?" she demanded crossly.

Blade frowned. "Somehow our conversations always end with your cousin, don't they?"

"They also end on an angry note!" she replied sternly.

He moved so swiftly that Suzanne was taken off guard, and before she could object, he had her imprisoned in his arms; her soft body pressed against his solid frame. "All my life I have waited for a woman like you," he confessed hoarsely. "Now that I have found you, I'm afraid losing you is inevitable. If Trooper Donovan is your cousin, you'll be lost to me forever, won't you?" When she failed to reply immediately, he commanded gruffly, "Answer me!"

"Yes!" she cried brokenly.

He released her so abruptly that she tottered for a moment. "I don't understand!" he groaned. "If your cousin is guilty of these crimes, how can you still love him?"

"I refuse to believe Trooper Donovan is Patrick!" she said emphatically.

"And if it should be proven otherwise?" He watched her closely.

"I don't know what I'll do." Turning from his intense scrutiny, she gazed away thoughtfully. "Blade, you are asking for answers that I can't give."

He took her gently into his embrace. "I love you, Suzanne," he murmured, and pressed his lips to hers. She responded to his kiss; she had no defense against Blade Landon.

He turned her loose with reluctance. The taste of her sweet lips had stirred his desire, but he had promised not to take advantage of her. Besides, he was supposed to be on watch, and so far guarding the camp had not been uppermost in his mind. Suzanne was too distracting, and he shouldn't have asked her to accompany him. "I think you'd better return to the fire," he suggested.

She concurred. "Good night, Blade." She made a move to leave, but turning back to face him, she suddenly asked, "How will the others and I be treated at Fort Laramie? Will the soldiers and their families be as hostile to us as the people at Fort Fetterman were?"

"I don't know," he sighed heavily. "Some of them might be."

"I have a feeling it's going to be a long, lonely winter

for Molly, Saul, and me."

Although she carried a heavy burden on her shoulders, she nonetheless moved proudly as she walked away from the major. Her courageous manner didn't escape Blade's notice.

It was the middle of the night when Molly woke up abruptly from her troubling dream. At first she was disoriented, and it took a moment for her head to clear. Sitting up on her pallet, she brushed a hand across her forehead, surprised to feel that she was actually perspiring. She was shaken, and inhaled deeply as she attempted to calm her thoughts. The dream, still vivid in her mind, flashed before her. She had dreamed of Patrick and their last night together before he'd gone off to war.

They had taken a buggy ride, and finding a secluded spot, Patrick had spread out a blanket beside a billowing oak. When they were seated, he had begun talking to her about the war, but she hadn't wanted to hear about it. She had no way of knowing how long it would be before she'd see him again. He could even be killed! She loved him so desperately; she wanted to be in his arms! Why must he go on and on about the war? Didn't he desire her at all?

As she continued to recall her dream, Molly's cheeks reddened with the memory. In graphic detail, she remembered how she had suddenly stood in front of Patrick and brazenly removed her clothes. He had been so shocked by her wanton behavior that he'd been struck speechless. Posing nude before him, she had stroked her hands over her body, caressing her most intimate parts as she seductively dared him to take her.

Dear God! Molly moaned inwardly. It didn't happen like that! I never tempted Patrick in that shameful way!

154

She wished she could wipe the dream from her thoughts, but against her will it ran on, making her cringe. Patrick had turned away from her nakedness, begging her to put her clothes back on. She had been wretched and cried out to him, demanding to know why he didn't want her. Keeping his eyes averted from her bare flesh, he had shouted harshly that she was a shameless hussy and he'd not be tempted by her wicked and sinful ploy. Defeated and heartbroken, she had then knelt beside her fallen clothes.

Suddenly she had felt a hand on her shoulder, and glancing up, she had been astounded to see Justin smiling down at her. She'd glanced hastily over at the blanket, expecting to see Patrick, but he had mysteriously vanished. Justin's strong, rugged hands drew her to her feet and into his powerful arms. Holding her nude body tightly against his brawny frame, he had kissed her aggressively. A fiery need burned within her, and she returned his passion, boldly pressing her naked thighs to his male hardness. His buckskin trousers couldn't keep her from feeling how badly he wanted her.

At that point the dream had ended and Molly had come brusquely awake. Now, falling back on her pallet, she tried to calm her feelings. Her body was still on fire, and its intense heat was centered at her feminine core. If Justin were really to kiss her, would she truly surrender so passionately?

Deciding sleep was not possible at present, she slipped on her robe and climbed down from the wagon. The campfire was kept burning so whoever was on watch could always have a cup of coffee, and the pot was resting on the hot coals.

She walked over, and kneeling beside the flames, she was pouring herself a cup of the warm brew when suddenly a hand touched her shoulder. Startled, she

155

glanced up to find Justin smiling down at her. The moment was so ironically related to her dream that Molly gasped in shock.

Justin's strong hands easily drew her to her feet and into his arms. Molly knew he was going to kiss her, and she raised her face to his. When his mouth came down urgently on hers, she wrapped her arms about his neck. Her knees weakened, and her head was spinning with ecstasy. His kiss was as exciting as she had dreamed it would be!

Justin hadn't expected such an ardent response, and fully aroused, he moved his hands to her thighs and pinned her against his hardness.

Her senses returning, Molly roughly pushed herself out of his embrace. Good Lord, she was behaving as shamefully as she had in her dream! Why was she acting like a brazen hussy?

Breathlessly, she offered an apology, "I'm sorry. I can't understand why I behaved so outrageously."

It took a moment for Justin to compose himself. His passion had been very much aroused. It'd been a long time since he'd had a woman, and his male urge was demanding. Eyeing her sternly, he warned, "Molly O'Ryan, if you intend to save your virginity for your husband, then never kiss me like that again."

She wanted to cry out to him, What makes you so sure I'm still a virgin? Couldn't you tell by my fervent response that I have experienced the pleasures of love? But believing her secret shameful, she kept it guarded. "What just happened between us will not take place again. I promise you."

"Don't make promises you can't keep," he retorted.

"Oh?" she asked questioningly. "What makes you think I can't keep my promise?"

When he'd walked soundlessly to the campfire, he

had placed his rifle on the ground. Now he leaned over and picked it up. Cradling the Winchester across his arms, he replied calmly, "I understand your kind of woman. You put on southern aristocratic airs, but beneath all that haughty facade, you're a woman cravin' a man. You're twenty-five years old, and for the past three years you have been ripe, yet you continue to deny yourself what you need the most. From what you have told me, I don't think you're saving yourself for Donovan, so why in the hell won't you give another man a chance? I offered to court you as a gentleman. But that offer no longer stands. Although I can tolerate a snobbish female, a teasing one I can't abide." He touched the brim of his hat. "Good night, ma'am."

"Wait!" she pleaded. "You are mistaken about me. I am not what you think I am. Oh, Justin, please believe me! I don't consider myself better than anyone else, and I'm not the kind of woman who leads a man on. I am truly sorry to have given you that impression."

He wasn't sure he trusted her, but deciding to give her the benefit of the doubt, he answered, "Your apology is accepted. And I'm sorry for passing judgment on you. I had no right to do so."

"I want us to be friends," she said sincerely.

With a crooked smile, he replied, "So do I. For some reason, Molly O'Ryan, you have come to mean a great deal to me. I had begun to believe I'd never again find a woman who can make me feel the way you do."

"Again?" she asked. "What do you mean?"

"I was once married, and I loved my wife very much."

"Are you a widower?"

"My wife died over fifteen years ago," he muttered tersely, then walked away.

Molly watched him until he had disappeared into the

157

blackness of the surrounding night. She had a feeling that Justin's marriage was a topic he preferred not to discuss.

Saul, lying in his bedroll beneath the wagon, had overheard everything said between Molly and Justin. He waited until Molly had reentered the wagon before rising and going to the campfire. Sitting, he poured himself a cup of coffee. First Miz Suzanne and the major, and now Miz O'Ryan and Justin Smith. He saw a ray of hope for the scout and Molly. Saul had always considered himself a good judge of character, and in his opinion Justin was a good and honorable man. If Miz Molly chose to marry him, it would probably be a wise decision. He chuckled inwardly. But her parents wouldn't approve. If their daughter married a Yankee, they'd most likely disown her. Southern aristocrats! he thought bitterly. I thank God that I lived long enough to see their reign come to an end. But not all aristocrats were bad, he reminded himself. There's no one on the face of this earth whom you admire more than Masta Patrick.

His aged face grew sorrowful. Would he and Miz Suzanne ever find Patrick Donovan? Or was this frantic quest useless? Was his former master dead? Had this Trooper Donovan murdered him? The old man gave in to his grief, his shoulders shaking with his deep sobs. "Why, Lord?" he pleaded aloud. "Why would you take a good man like Masta Patrick but allow a man as evil as Trooper Donovan to live? Oh God, I just don't understand!"

Unknown to Saul, Blade, who was lying on his bedroll in the distance, was not asleep. He had been awakened earlier by Molly and Justin talking. Now he could hear Saul's desperate prayer along with his broken sobs. Blade couldn't begin to fathom why an ex-slave should love a man who had once held him in bondage; it went beyond his comprehension. He was tempted to ask Saul to explain why he could worship a man who had bodily owned him, but he didn't want the servant to know he was witnessing his grief. The old man thought his sorrow was strictly between himself and God.

Quietly, Blade rolled to his side, turning his back to Saul and the glowing fire. His expression was grim as he closed his hands into tight fists. Patrick Donovan, he seethed inwardly, you are an enigma! You have completely possessed Saul and Suzanne, and now, so help me God, you are starting to become an obsession with me! Who in the hell are you? Are you the devil reincarnated? I swear, if you and Trooper Donovan are one and the same, I will personally send you back to the fires of hell where you belong! Blade groaned painfully. Even if destroying you costs me the woman I love!

Chapter Twelve

The sight of Fort Laramie did nothing to lift Suzanne's spirits, for she was expecting the people behind the fort walls to greet her and the others with open hostility. She braced herself for the cold welcome she believed awaited them.

The great gates opened, and with Blade and Justin leading the way, they entered the fort, which was filled with soldiers drilling or engaged in other perfunctory activities. Trappers, trading Indians, and military dependents occupied the courtyard.

Saul drove the wagon behind the major and his scout, and when they pulled up in front of Blade's quarters, the servant brought the mules to a halt.

Blade and Justin dismounted and were about to walk back to the wagon when all at once a woman called out.

"Blade!" she shouted happily, and with Colonel Johnson at her side, hurried toward the major and Justin.

The two men paused. Blade was surprised to see Almeda Johnson. He hadn't been expecting her return to Fort Laramie.

Smiling radiantly, the young woman flung herself

into Blade's arms and hugged him enthusiastically.

Looking on, Suzanne tried vainly to ignore the jealousy that was slowly rising in her.

Disentangling himself from Almeda's smothering embrace, Blade held her at arms' length. Gazing down into her emerald green eyes, he said cordially, "Almeda, I certainly didn't expect to see you."

She feigned a solemn expression. "My grandmother passed away last spring. Father wrote and asked me to come here and live with him."

"I thought you didn't like fort life," he reminded her.

Pouting prettily, she answered, "Well, I didn't especially care for life at a fort when I was here last summer, but that was a year ago, and I have matured a lot since then." Stepping to Colonel Johnson's side, she slipped her arm into his. "I am looking forward to spending time with father. We have seen so little of each other."

Blade studied the young woman. She was even more beautiful than she had been last year. Colonel Johnson was a widower, and his daughter had lived in the East with her grandmother. The previous summer she had come to Fort Laramie to visit her father and had practiced her feminine wiles on Blade, trying desperately to snare him. Although he had found her very tempting, he had nonetheless kept their relationship casual. He had easily seen through her veneer of innocence, sensing she could be as dangerous as a black widow spider.

Stepping away from her father, Almeda favored Justin with a radiant smile. "Hello, Mr. Smith," she said in a low, sultry voice, as her eyes surreptitiously took in his handsome physique. Almeda's fascination with Blade didn't prevent her from admiring the rugged scout; no attractive man failed to capture her attention.

Touching the brim of his hat and returning her smile,

Justin responded, "Miss Johnson, it's a pleasure to see you again."

Sitting on the wagon seat beside Suzanne, Molly was also beginning to feel pangs of jealousy. She had never seen a more sensual woman.

Blade turned his attention to the colonel, and showing due respect, he came to a military position and saluted. "I'm sorry, sir," he apologized.

Returning his salute, Colonel Johnson replied, "That is perfectly all right, major. My daughter didn't really give you a chance to acknowledge me in military fashion."

Almeda moved back to Blade, and taking his hand into hers, she gazed up invitingly into his eyes. "When I arrived a few days ago, and Father told me you weren't here, I was devastated. He said he didn't know how long you'd be away." She smiled sweetly. "I'm so glad you have returned."

"I should have told you that Almeda was coming here," the colonel explained, "but in her letter she made me promise not to tell you."

"I wanted to surprise you," Almeda said brightly.

Like a gentleman, Blade lifted her hand and placed a light kiss upon it. "I am flattered. I had thought by now you would've forgotten all about me."

"I could never forget you," she said softly, then squeezed his hand provocatively before releasing it.

"Major," the colonel began, "if you'll join me in my office, you can fill out a complete report."

"Father told me why you left the fort," Almeda remarked. She stole a quick glance at Molly and Suzanne. "He explained that you and Mr. Smith were traveling with Trooper Donovan's family. Did you locate the dreadful man?"

Suzanne cringed and was about to speak her piece, but Saul silenced her with a solid nudge against her side.

Before Blade could reply, Captain Newcomb, who had been strolling close by, joined the gathering. He spoke politely to the major and Justin, then, turning his gaze to the wagon, he carefully studied the two women, first Suzanne and then Molly. He found both of them attractive. Although he quickly decided the blonde woman was the prettier, he centered his thoughts on Molly. Gary Newcomb was a sensually handsome man, who was well aware of his good looks. For some time he had been seriously considering marriage. Fort life was lonely, and he longed for a woman to share his bed on a permanent basis. But a beautiful wife like Suzanne was out of the question. A gorgeous woman might be too wrapped up in her own beauty to become totally devoted to him. He wanted a wife who would admire him as much as he admired himself. So as he continued to eye the two women, he made the decision to pursue the one with the auburn hair.

"Good afternoon, ladies," the captain said cordially. "Allow me to introduce myself." Bowing elegantly, he announced, "Captain Gary Newcomb at your service."

They said good afternoon in unison, both of them quite aware of the captain's good looks.

Blade spoke to Saul. "You can park the wagon in the same area where you had it before."

"Yes, suh," he answered, and slapping the reins against the team, he headed the wagon in that direction.

Before Blade could leave with the colonel to make his report, Almeda asked, "Blade, you will have dinner tonight with father and me, won't you?"

"Of course he will," Colonel Johnson answered for him, then gestured for Blade to accompany him to his office.

As they walked away, Almeda called to Blade, "I'll

expect you at eight o'clock."

For a moment she watched Blade's handsome physique, then turning back to Captain Newcomb and Justin, she cast them both a charming smile. Speaking to Justin, she asked, "Which one of the ladies is Trooper Donovan's cousin?"

"The blonde," he replied. "Why do you ask?"

"Before you all left, Blade talked to father about Donovan's cousin, and father said he got the feeling that Blade was quite taken with her."

Justin grinned. Like Blade, he understood Almeda Johnson and her lascivious charms. "Afraid of competition?" he teased.

She lifted her chin smugly. "Donovan's cousin cannot compete with me."

Justin's grin broadened. "Do you have that much confidence in your beauty, or does your self-assurance stem from the fact that your father is Blade's commanding officer?"

She glared at him. "Mr. Smith, you are very rude!"

"So I've often been told," he chuckled, grabbing the reins to his horse and the major's.

He was about to lead the animals to the stables when he was detained by the captain inquiring, "The other lady, the one engaged to Trooper Donovan, is she still in love with her fiancé?"

Justin's visage hardened. "Isn't that her business?"

Gary Newcomb shrugged. "Perhaps, but women are scarce on this fort, and it's only natural for a man like myself to find a woman as comely as Donovan's fiancée very appealing. She may be engaged, but she is still a free woman, so as far as I'm concerned, she's unrestricted game."

"You refer to her in that manner again," the other man warned, "and I'll knock the hell out of you!"

Gary smiled knowingly. "You're very touchy about

the lady, aren't you? Well, Justin, I am a man who tries to remain open and aboveboard, so I think it's only fair to let you know that I intend to become closely acquainted with the lady in question."

"You're right about *one* thing, she *is* a lady, and you'd better remember it!" Justin grumbled. Then turning away abruptly, he began leading the horses toward the stables.

"It seems we both have rivals," Gary said to Almeda, his tone unconcerned.

"Justin Smith and Donovan's cousin have already lost," she responded, having faith in her own charms as well as Gary's.

He lowered his voice, speaking secretively. "Since you plan to entertain Blade tonight, I don't suppose you'll be coming to my quarters."

She smiled. "No, not tonight, and if things progress as I hope they will, I'll have no need ever to return to your quarters." She let her eyes travel over him appreciatively. He was indeed a good lover, and he always satisfied her every desire. If they weren't so much alike, she might even have contemplated marrying him, but their egos would be constantly in competition. Besides, although Gary was a very desirable man, in her estimation he couldn't even begin to compare with Major Landon. Since meeting Blade, she hadn't been able to get him out of her mind. When she had returned east, after spending the summer at Fort Laramie, every man she'd met had seemed lacking when compared with Blade. Last summer she had failed with the major, but this time she'd succeed. She was more experienced now, and she'd use her knowledge to the fullest. She had every confidence in herself and her well-endowed femininity. In no time at all, she'd have Blade pleading for her hand in marriage. Then, after they were married, she'd convince her father to see to it personally that Blade received a transfer to the East, preferably to Washington. From there she could encourage her husband to consider going into politics. She would love the prestige connected with being a congressman's wife, or perhaps a senator's. And the icing on her cake would be Blade himself; her virile, handsome husband!

Tearing herself away from her musings, she told Gary, "Good luck with your newest love. Now if you'll excuse me, I think I'll go home, take a long, relaxing bath, then decide which dress to wear tonight."

"Wear the crimson gown," he suggested. "It not only complements your silky black hair, it accentuates your desirable curves to perfection."

"Thanks for the advice," she responded, then, turning gracefully, she moved away.

"That woman reminds me of Aunt Ellen," Suzanne muttered tartly.

"Suzanne!" Molly gasped reproachfully.

They were seated in the back of the wagon as Saul unhitched the team. "It's true!" she insisted. "I could tell you a few things about my aunt that would shock you." Suzanne didn't approve of malicious gossip, so she refrained from elaborating.

"Miss Johnson is very attractive," Molly murmured reflectively. Depressed, she recalled the admiring gleam she'd detected in Justin's eyes when he had been speaking to the woman.

Deciding to dismiss the colonel's daughter from her mind, Suzanne changed the subject. She spoke thoughtfully as she glanced about the wagon's close confinement. "We can't possibly live in this wagon for an entire winter. We'll have to find proper quarters."

Molly agreed. "But where can we stay?"

"I don't know. I'll talk to the major; maybe he can find us a place."

"When do you plan to talk to him?"

"I'm sure he'll come here soon to check on us, and when he does, I'll ask him."

Suzanne believed it would be only an hour or so before Blade showed up, and she was prepared to wait patiently. But as the hours slowly dragged on without his appearing, her patience wore thin.

When the shadows of dusk began creeping across the fort and Blade still hadn't arrived, Suzanne decided to pay him a visit.

Leaving the wagon, she strolled quickly to his office. She thought there would be a sentry posted, but no one was about, so she knocked on the closed door. When she didn't receive an answer, she turned the doorknob, and finding it unlocked, she stepped inside. Pausing, she looked about the office. The open door at the rear of the room led into the major's private quarters. Wondering if Blade was in his bedroom, she called, "Blade, are you here?"

She was answered by silence. Deciding to wait for his return, she walked farther inside. She was heading toward his desk when she caught sight of a liquor cabinet against the wall. She helped herself to a glass of sherry, and finding the drink warm and soothing, she finished it off quickly, then poured another one. Going to the desk, she eased herself into Blade's huge leather chair and snuggled into its softness. It was entirely too large for Suzanne's small frame, and she had plenty of room to draw up her legs and tuck them about her. Comfortable, she sipped on her sherry and the potent brew soon had her completely relaxed. She was beginning to feel light-headed, as well as a little sleepy.

The darkness of night shrouded the office, but Suzanne felt too drowsy to get up and light a lamp.

Instead she drank more sherry. Her eyelids grew heavy, and while trying to stifle a yawn, she placed her glass on the desk top. She then leaned her head against the back of the chair, and giving in to her fatigue, she closed her eyes. Soon she was sound asleep.

The moment Colonel Johnson made his excuses and left the parlor to retire, Blade seized the opportunity to do likewise. He was sitting on the sofa beside Almeda, and finishing his brandy, he put the empty glass on the coffee table. Getting to his feet, he said politely, "Thanks very much for dinner."

Rising and standing close to him, Almeda said with a sweet pout, "Surely you don't have to leave so soon. We haven't seen each other in ages and ages."

He smiled tolerantly. "We don't have to try and make up for all those ages in one evening. After all, you plan to stay here indefinitely. I'm sure we'll see each other often."

"Promise?" she insisted, daringly reaching up to lace her arms about his neck.

"This fort isn't quite large enough for us to avoid one another," he replied, gently prying her arms loose.

Almeda was frustrated. The man was still impossibly unresponsive. Well, last summer was not going to repeat itself! This time it would be different. One way or another, she'd get him to cooperate.

She leaned sensually against him, and inadvertently his arms went about her. She pressed herself to his chest, then moved back a little so he'd have a clear picture of the deep cleavage between her breasts. The low décolletage of her crimson gown barely covered her ample bosom.

Resisting temptation, he stepped back. "Almeda, you are a very desirable young lady, but I've had a long day and I need a good night's sleep."

"Blade Landon!" she fussed, her tone honey-laced. "You are insufferable! Don't you like me?"

He cuffed her playfully on the chin. "Of course I like you. Good night, you seductive little cat."

Without further words, Blade strode out of the parlor, grabbed his hat off the rack, and made his departure.

Stepping inside his dark office, Blade went to the lamp closest to the front door and lit it. As the soft light fell across the room he looked toward his desk, where he was pleasantly surprised to see Suzanne curled up in his chair, asleep. Smiling tenderly, he sauntered over to stand beside her. Gazing down into her face, which was serene in sleep, he noticed she seemed to be totally at peace. If only it were true, he thought. If only she weren't so troubled.

He allowed his gaze to linger, and her vulnerable sweetness caused warm emotions to stir within him. He found her so precious, and was falling more in love with each passing day. Was a future between them impossible? Had he finally met the woman who was right for him, only to lose her? Could he stand losing her? He supposed he had the inner strength to survive, but he knew he'd never be the same; nor would he ever stop loving her. She's in my heart forever, he sighed inwardly, the revelation bittersweet.

Gently he touched one of her golden curls, wrapping it about his finger. Suzanne awakened slowly.

Her eyes fluttering open, she saw Blade standing beside her. Still caressing her silky lock between his fingers, he smiled engagingly. "Hello, my sleepy little Confederate. Were you waiting for me?"

"Yes, I was," she answered, sitting upright.

He leaned back against the desk, and crossed his arms over his chest.

"Blade, the others and I can't possibly stay in a wagon for the winter. We need proper quarters. Do you have any suggestions?"

"I'll work something out," he assured her. "Give me a couple of days to arrange everything."

"What time is it?" she asked, wondering if it was late.

"About nine-thirty," he answered.

"My goodness, I had no idea I slept so long." Curiously she asked, "Where have you been?"

"I had dinner with Colonel Johnson and his daughter."

"Miss Johnson," she muttered, her tone edged with dislike.

He arched a brow. "Are you jealous?"

"Of course not!" she denied hastily.

"You are a very poor liar, my jealous little Confederate," he murmured, moving swiftly and lifting her into his arms. Cradling her close, he continued sensually, "I love you, Suzanne, and I want no other woman."

"I told you not to love me," she reminded him with faltering conviction.

"And I told you, it was too late," he retorted. He began carrying her toward his bedroom.

Realizing his intentions, she demanded sharply, "Blade, do you always just take a woman whenever the mood strikes you? Haven't you ever heard of asking?"

"If I ask, I might be denied," he said with a grin.

"Can't you take rejection?"

"Not where you're concerned," he answered, carrying her to his bed and laying her down with care.

She watched him as he went to the door and closed and bolted it. Returning, he lay beside her and took her into his arms. His lips met hers, softly at first, then increasing in intensity. "Suzanne," he moaned hoarsely, his passion aroused.

As she began to unbutton her dress, this signal of her willingness to make love with him thrilled Blade.

He slipped his hand beneath her chemise, and the feel of her soft breasts sent his blood racing. Again his lips sought hers, and she returned his caress with a need that matched his own.

Standing, Blade drew her from the bed, quickly helping her undress. Wanting him as badly as he wanted her, she then assisted him, until at last there were no clothes separating their bare flesh.

He eased her onto the bed, Suzanne's heart beating wildly as his mouth descended to hers. She accepted his kiss completely, tasting and relishing the wonderful joy of his lips upon hers.

Their hands began to move over each other, each welcoming the other's exploration. Suzanne moaned and arched against him as his touch drove her to heights of desire.

"Come to me, Blade," she whispered, urging him by parting her thighs so they could become as one.

His strong frame trembled with passion as he moved between her slender legs. He entered her swiftly, and his maleness filled her with ecstatic pleasure.

Wrapping her arms about him tightly, she yielded gloriously to the wondrous sensations she was feeling.

They were soon totally engulfed in their own lovers' world; time and reality ceased to exist. This moment was forever.

Blade drew her even closer, and as her womanly heat surrounded him, he thrust deep within her. Her hips arched beneath his, and her exciting movements sent his senses whirling.

His climax came powerfully, tremors racking his body as he released his seed into her velvety depths.

Suzanne clung to him and cried out softly as her own completion washed over her in turbulent, erotic waves.

He kissed her tenderly, then holding her close, he rolled to lie on his side.

Her head came to rest on his shoulder. They were quiet for a moment, then Suzanne sighed heavily.

"Is something wrong?" he asked gently.

"I can't love you," she remarked, as though they had been discussing the possibility.

She didn't need to explain; Blade understood only too well. "You mean you won't let yourself love me. You're too afraid that I'll be the man responsible for your cousin's execution."

"Until we find Trooper Donovan, I'll not give in to my heart and fall in love with you."

"Suzanne, don't you think you are already in love with me?"

Did she love him? Her heart cried that she did, but suddenly a vision of Patrick standing before a firing squad flashed across her mind. The mental picture sent a cold chill coursing throughout her. Impaled with guilt, she decided to hurry back to the wagon and away from this man who could so easily trouble her emotions.

She sat up quickly, and leaving the bed, she began to dress. "I need to get back to the wagon. Molly and Saul are probably worried about me."

"As usual you're going to run away from your feelings, aren't you?" He watched her as she hurriedly slipped into her clothes, concealing her beautiful body from his appreciative gaze. Blade had to muster all his willpower to keep himself from grabbing her, ripping off her clothes, and drawing her naked form back into his bed.

Her eyes pleaded with his. "Please try to under-stand!"

"I do understand, but I don't agree with you. Why in the hell can't you accept our love?"

She didn't answer until she was fully dressed. "I won't promise you my love until I can do so without reservations."

"And when will that be?" he asked impatiently.

"When we find this man who is posing as my cousin."

Deciding to let the subject rest for the time being, Blade swung his long legs over the bed and offered, "If you'll wait until I get dressed, I'll walk you back to your wagon."

"That won't be necessary," she answered hastily. For a moment Suzanne allowed herself the pleasure of studying his splendid male flesh, but when the sight of his nakedness caused a fiery need once again to burn within her, she quickly looked away. Before he could insist that she let him accompany her, she bid him a curt good night, then left the bedroom and hurried across the office and outside.

Chapter Thirteen

Blade was sitting at his desk taking care of paperwork when the sentry opened the door and announced Colonel Johnson. He told the young guard to admit the colonel, and to leave the door open, as the office was as little stuffy.

As his commanding officer entered the room, Blade rose to his feet.

The colonel told the major to be seated. "I have important business to discuss with you. While you were away, I sent a runner to find Black Wolf."

"Has the army decided to negotiate a peace treaty?"

"Yes," Colonel Johnson replied. "That is why I sent for Black Wolf. He's the ideal man to help us. He has a lot of clout among all the Sioux. He's greatly respected, and can speak English better than any Indian I know. If the treaty is successful, he's the best warrior to meet with the government officials from Washington. Next week two generals and other high officials are expected to come here. They will tell Black Wolf what this treaty consists of, and he will then take the army's proposal to every Sioux tribe he can locate. He'll return here and let me know how the Sioux chiefs responded. Hopefully, they will agree to the army's terms. Then, with Black

Wolf acting as an interpreter, the peace treaty can be signed. I want you and Justin to accompany Black Wolf on this important mission. The warrior likes and respects both of you, so he'll not object to your company. This assignment will take a long time, but you should be back before winter sets in."

"This treaty—are you familiar with its contents?"

"I know a little about it. When we talk to the generals and the officials next week, we'll be told everything."

"Can you give me some idea of the terms?"

"Basically, it comes down to one thing. If the Sioux will remain at peace, the United States government will give them the land in the Black Hills. They will not be bothered so long as they stay on this land and not declare war on whites."

Blade looked skeptical. "Colonel, you know as well as I do that many people believe there is gold in the Black Hills. Just how long do you think the government will abide by this treaty? It's only a matter of time before that land will be taken away from the Sioux. And the army will have all the Sioux right where they want them, where it'll be easy for them to round them up and send them to a reservation."

"Major, it's not your place to question orders!" the colonel said sternly.

"The Indians," Blade sighed heavily. "They always end up getting the short end of the stick."

"How can it be otherwise?" Colonel Johnson sounded resigned. Firmly he added, "Major Landon, you are a damned good soldier, but there are times when I worry that you might let your compassion for the Indians rule your judgment."

"You needn't worry, colonel," he assured him. "Although I do feel a deep compassion for the Sioux, and for all Indians, my loyalties lie with my fellow comrades. First, and above all, I am a soldier in the

United States army, and I love my country."

They weren't aware that the sentry had stepped through the open door with Black Wolf at his side. When the Sioux warrior suddenly spoke, both men looked up with surprise. "Major Landon, you speak the words of an honorable man."

Smiling broadly, Blade stood and walked over to greet his friend. Familiar with the white man's gesture, Black Wolf shook hands with Blade. The physiques of the two men were almost identical. The warrior's height was close to the major's, and his frame was muscular.

Power emanated from the Sioux brave, reflected in the style in which he stood tall and in his self-assured movements. Black Wolf was dressed in tan leggings and moccasins and a fringed shirt decorated with colorful beads. His long black hair was braided and he wore one feather, which was attached to a leather band about his head. His coppery complexion was flawless, and his light blue eyes were in contrast to his dark skin.

His smile revealed even, white teeth. "Major Landon, my trusted friend, it is good to see you again."

Standing and joining them, the colonel asked, "Did the runner explain why I sent for you?"

"Yes," Black Wolf answered.

"There is no reason for me to go into details at present," Colonel Johnson proceeded. "Next week, when the officers and the others arrive, we'll have a long conference. Until then, I have made arrangements for you to use the barracks that are occupied by our Indian scouts. I hope that will be satisfactory."

"That will be fine, colonel," he replied.

"Well, I'll leave you two alone so you catch each other up on the latest. I know you are close friends."

They waited until the man departed, then Blade gestured for Black Wolf to be seated. Leaning against his desk, he studied the warrior with interest. "You look in good health, Black Wolf."

"My body is well, but my heart is sick," he said somberly.

"I'm sorry, Black Wolf. I wish I could say something to ease your pain, but you know as well as I do that the fate of the Sioux is inevitable."

"My people will not surrender easily. There will be much bloodshed on both sides."

"But both sides are your people," Blade pointed out.

"No," he sighed. "The whites are not my people. I carry part of their blood, but I am not one of them."

The sentry reappeared. "Excuse me, major, but Miss Donovan is here to see you."

"Show her in," Blade answered.

At Suzanne's entrance, Black Wolf got to his feet. He admired her beauty as she was greeted by Major Landon.

Placing an arm about her waist, Blade led her over to the imposing warrior. "Suzanne, this is Black Wolf, whose father is a Sioux chief."

She was deeply impressed with the brave's savagely handsome presence.

"Black Wolf," Blade continued, "I'd like you to meet Miss Donovan."

Taking her hand, the warrior kissed it lightly. "It is a pleasure to meet you, Miss Donovan."

Suzanne was astonished by his elegant manners. Discerning her surprise, Black Wolf explained, "My mother was white, and she not only taught me to speak English fluently, but also taught me the white man's etiquette."

Anxious for his good friend to become well acquainted with the woman he loved, Blade encouraged Black Wolf to sit behind the desk, then he saw to it that Suzanne was seated in the other chair.

Blade took a stance beside the desk and leaned his large frame against it.

Speaking to Black Wolf, Suzanne remarked, "You said your mother was white. Was she kidnapped by the Sioux?"

"Yes. She was eighteen years old when my father, Running Horse, abducted her. Her family were homesteaders, and she had wandered away from the house when Running Horse happened to come upon her. For my father, it was love at first sight. He knew he must have her for his own."

"Did she fall in love with him?" Suzanne asked.

He smiled. "It took a little while for my mother to return his love, but in time she came to love him very much." Black Wolf's perusal of Suzanne deepened. He had often wondered how his father could have loved a woman upon first sight, but now as his gaze remained on the lovely Miss Donovan, he suddenly came to realize why Running Horse had been so suddenly smitten.

"Is your mother dead?"

"Yes, she died three years ago of smallpox."

"Excuse me, sir," the sentry once again interrupted.

"Yes?" Blade inquired.

"Miss Johnson is here."

Blade grimaced as he remembered that the previous night she had extracted a promise from him to take her to the club for lunch. Reluctantly he told the trooper to admit her.

Almeda bustled gracefully into the room. She was wearing a stylish blue dress, and its long folds swayed rhythmically with her light steps.

The men stood at her approach. On her previous visit to the fort she had seen the Sioux warrior on a couple of occasions and had found him unbelievably handsome and sensual. She had never dreamed that an Indian could be so good-looking. Now, appraising him, she was again amazed by his sensuality. "Hello, Black Wolf," she said softly, offering him her most provocative smile.

Black Wolf admired the woman's extravagant beauty, but he believed it was merely skin deep. Suzanne, whom he thought even more beautiful than Miss Johnson, was full of beauty, he felt, the kind that came from the heart as well as the body. "Hello, Miss Johnson," he responded cordially.

Turning her smile upon Blade, Almeda asked charmingly, "Are you ready to take me to lunch?"

Stammering, he replied, "Well . . . to be perfectly honest, I forgot our date."

"Blade Landon, you are quite impossible!" she scolded affectionately. "This time, darling, I'll forgive you. But I am famished, so let's leave, shall we?"

Feeling uncomfortable, Blade looked at Suzanne, his expression apologetic. "I'm sorry," he murmured. Damn it, why had he agreed to this luncheon engagement!

"You will excuse us, won't you, Miss Donovan?" Almeda asked, her tone sugar-coated.

Rising from her chair, Suzanne tried to suppress her anger. "Please don't let me keep you." She held her gaze away from Blade, afraid he would see her resentment. She certainly didn't want him thinking she was jealous!

"Black Wolf, why don't you join us for lunch?" Almeda invited, blatantly omitting Suzanne.

"You know Indians aren't allowed in the Officers' Club," Blade snapped. He was irritated with her.

"Oh yes, I forgot," she lied smoothly. She had merely wanted the pleasure of leaving Suzanne out of the invitation.

"Black Wolf," Suzanne began, "when I left the wagon, my friend Molly was preparing a pot of stew. Why don't you have lunch with us?"

The warrior was pleased. "Thank you very much. I will be honored."

Suzanne started to leave the office, when Blade interrupted her. "Was there a special reason why you came here? Did you need to talk to me about something?"

Continuing on her way to the door, she said casually, "What I had to discuss with you can wait. It wasn't important."

With Black Wolf close behind, Suzanne left.

"The stew is ready," Molly told Saul, stirring the pot that stood over the open flames.

Saul was inside the wagon, changing clothes. "I'll be right there, Miz Molly," he called.

Catching a movement out of the corner of her eye, she turned away from her cooking. Seeing Captain Newcomb strolling toward her, she smiled pleasantly.

"Good day, ma'am," he said, pausing close at her side. Glancing at the simmering stew, he continued, "I stopped by to ask you if you'd have lunch with me. It looks like I was just in the nick of time. If I'd been a moment later, you would've already started eating."

Molly was surprised by his invitation. "Thank you, Captain Newcomb, but as you can see, my dinner is prepared."

"That's no reason not to accompany me to the Officers' Club. I'm sure the food will be eaten by your servant and Miss Donovan."

She was confused. In a way, she wanted to leave with

him. Lunch in a dining room sounded very tempting. But she was wary about accepting a date with this man whom she barely knew.

Seeing her hesitation, Gary said charmingly, "I promise to be a perfect gentleman."

Impressed with his chivalry, she replied, "Captain Newcomb, we have not been formally introduced. My name is Molly O'Ryan."

Removing his hat and bowing from the waist, he asked elegantly, "Miss O'Ryan, will you please do me the honor of having lunch with me?" Replacing his hat, he proceeded with a touch of sentiment. "Western forts are isolated, and a soldier such as myself grows very lonely for a woman's company."

After such a touching plea, how could she possibly refuse? "Very well, captain, I'll be happy to accept your kind invitation."

Victorious, Gary was confident that he'd soon have this lovely woman anxious to do his bidding.

Saul emerged from the wagon simultaneously with the arrival of Suzanne and Black Wolf. The servant had overheard the captain's invitation, and he studied the officer with interest before turning to Suzanne and her Indian companion. He wasn't sure which surprised him more, Molly going to lunch with this stranger, or Suzanne showing up with a savage warrior.

Gary, recognizing Black Wolf, watched the brave with ill-concealed dislike. He had no use for Indians, and in his opinion, half-breeds were the worst.

Black Wolf was aware of the captain's antagonism and didn't bother to acknowledge him.

Resenting the warrior's presence, Gary took Molly's arm and urged, "It's getting late, and I think we had best leave before the club stops serving the midday meal." He nodded politely to Suzanne, then tightening his grip, he ushered Molly away.

Although Suzanne was a little astonished about their luncheon date, she refrained from saying anything about it. She introduced Black Wolf to Saul, then they all sat on the blanket that was spread close to the campfire. Suzanne dished out three bowls of the delicious stew, as Saul poured glasses of water.

Noticing the way the old servant's eyes kept shifting warily toward Black Wolf, Suzanne smiled inwardly. She wondered humorously if Saul was worried about his scalp.

Black Wolf, also aware of the man's distrust, decided to put him at ease. Using his best white man's manner, he said, "This stew is quite savory. My compliments to the cook."

Saul came dangerously close to dropping his bowl, and suppressing a giggle, Suzanne asked him, "Saul, is something wrong?"

"No, ma'am," he answered hastily.

Black Wolf laughed brightly, and his deep chuckles rang out pleasantly. "Of course something is wrong, old man," he insisted. "You didn't know savages could practice decorum."

Embarrassed, Saul mumbled, "I'm sorry, Mr. Black Wolf, suh. But I don't know much about Indians. I reckon I had the wrong impression."

"You probably aren't too far wrong," Black Wolf replied with friendliness. "I am an exception. My mother was white, and she insisted that I learn how to communicate properly with her people. She was a very strict woman, and taught me well."

"Why was she set on you learning so much?" Suzanne asked.

"My mother knew the ways of the Sioux could not survive. She believed if I could fit in with the whites, maybe my fate will not be the same as that of the Sioux."

"Do you believe this?" Suzanne asked.

"No," he replied without elaboration.

"Black Wolf," she continued, "have you tried to locate your mother's kin?"

"I do not want to find them. I have part of their blood in my veins, but I am not one of them. The Sioux are my people."

It was Saul who questioned him next. "Do you have slaves in your village?"

The Indian gave him a discerning look. "Old man, your question comes from the heart. You know what it is to be a slave, don't you?"

"Yes, suh, I know only too well."

"Yes, we have slaves in our village. They are people from enemy tribes."

"Do you have any white captives?" Suzanne inquired.

"We have no white slaves. On the day Running Horse married my mother he promised her when he became chief, his village would never keep whites as slaves."

"Black Wolf, will you tell me about your people?" she requested.

"What do you want to know?" he asked, grinning disarmingly.

She blushed. "Romance. How do wives and husbands treat one another? How does a young brave go about proposing?"

"A woman's questions," he murmured, finding her interest amusing. He set aside his empty bowl, then his crystal-blue eyes met Suzanne's own blue ones. "A husband and wife do not show affection in public. This does not mean they are uncaring; they prefer to display

183

their love for each other in the privacy of their tepee. An overt expression of affection in public is considered poor taste. Courting among our young people is relatively simple. When a young brave wishes to meet and talk to a maiden, he usually does so in front of her tepee. There he can enfold the girl in his robe, and together, with heads covered from view, they can converse in private, although they are in public. Of course, there is always a chaperon on hand. Lovers who wish to marry announce their intentions to their close relatives. In the event that their families mutually agree to the match, arrangements are immediately set in motion. The proposal is carried by a close friend or a brother of the young man to the girl's brother or some male standing in a similar close relationship to her. It is between these young men that the details of the bride price is determined, and it is the girl's relative, the *hakatakus,* to whom the fee is paid. It is understood that the greater the young woman's social position, the higher the price. A price that can include many horses."

Listening attentively, Suzanne became even more impressed with the man's English. "Black Wolf, your faultless speech completely dumbfounds me."

He was used to people finding him amazing, and smiling tolerantly, he replied, "Whenever my father raided whites, he brought back books for my mother. It was through this abundant supply of reading material that I learned your language so well. I have read books by Dickens, and even Shakespeare."

"Running Horse didn't object?" Suzanne asked.

"I think he was a little resentful, but he loved my mother and could deny her nothing."

"Black Wolf, please tell me more about your people," Suzanne prompted.

He understood that her curiosity was genuine. She is the kind of woman, he thought, who could learn to care deeply about the Sioux. Perhaps he should follow his father's example, kidnap this woman of his choice, take her into the Black Hills to his village. Maybe, when the time is right, I will do just that, he mused.

Suzanne had no idea of the course his thoughts had taken as he continued to tell her about the ways of the Sioux.

Chapter Fourteen

Justin had his own small cabin, which was in a remote location on the large fort. On his way home, he happened to be passing the Officers' Club as Molly and Gary were leaving. The unexpected sight of the two of them together brought the scout's long strides to an abrupt halt.

At the big man's apparent surprise, Captain Newcomb smiled complacently. "Good afternoon, Mr. Smith," he said, his tone heavy with mocking cordiality.

Molly found the present situation uncomfortable, although she wasn't sure why. She had simply shared a harmless meal with the captain; besides, her social affairs were none of Justin's concern. After all, they were merely friends. Nonetheless, for some strange reason she felt guilty and was hesitant to meet the scout's gaze. But she could feel his eyes on her, so with a semblance of composure she acknowledged him. "Hello, Justin," she said politely.

His countenance hard, he muttered, "I thought you had better taste where your friends are concerned, but then considering who your fiancé is, I should have known better."

She was astounded by his hostility.

Gary laughed. "Don't be such a poor sport."

Justin turned his steely gaze upon the captain. He had never liked Gary Newcomb, and the man's interest in Molly merely deepened his dislike. "Poor sport?" he sneered. "I don't play games, captain." Suddenly he cast his heated gaze on Molly. "And you would be wise to keep that in mind, madam!" Without further ado, he walked quickly away.

Watching him leave, Molly said with puzzlement, "Why do you suppose he was so rude?"

"He's jealous," Gary replied casually. Slipping her hand in the crook of his arm and dismissing the scout's anger as insignificant, he suggested, "Let's take a stroll, shall we? I'll give you a tour of the fort."

Molly agreed absently, her thoughts were filled with Justin. Was the captain's analysis correct? Could Justin be jealous? The possibility thrilled her.

Molly tried to give the captain her full attention as he guided her about the fort, but despite herself, her concentration faltered continually. She couldn't clear her mind of Justin. During their tour, Gary pointed out the head scout's log cabin, and she took careful note of its location. Although she didn't consciously admit it to herself, she knew she'd soon be visiting the isolated cabin.

Knowing he must return to his military duties, Gary bid her good day, leaving her near her wagon. He would have walked all the way with her, but thinking Black Wolf might still be there, he preferred to avoid the Indian's presence. Under no circumstances would he socialize with a Sioux warrior. He didn't give a damn if the man's mother had been white, nor was he impressed with his savoir-faire. In spite of his elegant airs, he was still an Indian, and Gary Newcomb hated all of them, especially Black Wolf! How dare the savage act as though he were as good as a white man! Just because his mother had educated him, he believed himself special. Black Wolf's intelligence infuriated the captain. It was Indians like this son of Chief Running Horse who encouraged the Indian Bureau and Mormons to proclaim that these savages could be civilized and take their proper place among the white man's society. Captain Newcomb was a firm believer in the axiom that the only good Indian was a dead one!

Molly waited until Gary had walked out of sight, then, instead of going to the wagon, she headed back in the direction of Justin's cabin. She didn't know what excuse she'd give the scout for paying him an unexpected visit, but she didn't let herself dwell upon it. That was a minor detail. The chance that Justin might be jealous was all that was important. She was almost afraid to hope that he might care that much about her. No man had ever been jealous of her. Patrick hadn't had a jealous bone in his body! The mere thought that such a man as the rugged, powerful scout could actually resent her association with another man was exciting to Molly. She had always been somewhat of an introvert and had never had men vying for her attention. She was indeed flattered that Justin had seemed annoyed.

Why am I so attracted to Justin Smith? she wondered anxiously as she continued walking in the direction of his cabin. She remembered the night he had kissed her, and the way she had responded. The memory brought a deep blush to her cheeks. She had shared passionate kisses with Patrick, but compared to Justin's they had been mild. But then, her fiancé and the scout were as different as night and day. Patrick never had Justin's aggressive style. Maybe that is why I find Justin so irresistible, she decided. I want a man who is domineering.

Reaching the cabin, Molly went to the front door and knocked firmly.

"Come in," she heard Justin call from inside.

She entered without hesitation, but the sight that confronted her caused her to stop suddenly. Her eyes widened, and as she gasped, her hand flew to her mouth.

Standing in the middle of the one-room cabin was a round wooden tub, and Justin was in it, taking a bath. His back was to the door, and glancing over his shoulder to acknowledge his visitor, he was astonished to see Molly.

His surprise fading, he grinned insolently. In her shock, she had left the door open. "Would you mind closing the door?" he asked nonchalantly. "There's a draft."

Numbly, she complied. Her voice shaky, she stammered, "Do you always invite people inside when you are taking a bath?"

"Usually," he remarked flatly. "But then, I wasn't expectin' a woman." He was still looking over his shoulder. "Molly, do you mind moving over this way? I'm getting a crick in my neck." As she hesitated, he added, "Ma'am, you ain't gonna see nothin' you shouldn't see unless you come close enough to peek over the rim of this tub."

Keeping a respectable distance between them, she stepped unsteadily away from the door and took a stance facing him. His bare chest caught her eyes, and she couldn't stop herself from studying his obvious strength. The man's build was impressively strong, and she could see the rippling of his muscles as he rubbed the wash cloth over his muscular arms. A mass of dark, curly hair covered his broad chest, and for a fleeting moment she wondered what it would be like to feel her bared breasts pressed against his manly form.

While washing, he watched her curiously, waiting for her to explain why she had called on him. When she appeared to have no intention of explaining, he said, "I suppose you have a reason for being here."

She had not conjured up a plausible explanation for her presence, and stuttering, she answered evasively, "I . . . I thought we . . . should talk."

"Talk?" he asked, his eyebrows arched.

Deciding her best recourse was honesty, she replied, "Captain Newcomb made a certain comment that has me very perplexed."

Her reference to the captain brought a scowl to his face. "What did he say?"

Although embarrassed, she remained candid. "He said that you are jealous."

"Jealous of what?"

Her embarrassment deepened. "Of me."

Justin guffawed heartily.

His mirth was perturbing. She had come here to talk openly with him, and he had the rudeness to laugh at her! "You might find the captain's speculation funny, but I don't!"

Suppressing his chuckles, he replied, "Don't go gettin' your dander up. And don't flatter yourself, Molly O'Ryan. I ain't jealous of what doesn't belong to me. You're a free woman, and you have every right to do whatever you want."

"If you aren't jealous," she pressed, "then why were you so curt when you saw us together?"

"I don't like Captain Newcomb, but I do like you, and I hate to see you get involved with a no-good skunk like him."

"Captain Newcomb seems to be a very considerate gentleman," she protested.

"You're entitled to your own opinion," he drawled. The man's indifference grated on her nerves. She should have known that the captain was wrong; Justin wasn't in the least jealous. She had been a fool to believe that he was, and an even bigger fool to come here and confront him with it! She was about to bid him an uncivil good day when all at once, he stood up in the tub. Shocked beyond words, she stood riveted, her face mirroring disbelief.

Grabbing the towel hanging over a nearby chair, Justin said evenly, "Like I said, I'm only jealous of what belongs to me."

Molly was only vaguely aware of what he was saying. The magnificient sight before her eyes, held her spellbound. Good Lord, the man was a perfect specimen of masculinity. His hard-muscled body emphasized his powerful strength, and lowering her gaze, she saw that he was aroused. The unexpected sight of his erection caused her to inhale sharply.

Noticing where her eyes were fixed, Justin chuckled amusedly. "You'll have to excuse my condition, but you seem to have that effect on me." He tied the towel about his waist, and stepping out of the tub, he continued, "If you want me to get all riled and jealous over you and the captain, then first you are gonna have to become mine."

Feeling flustered, she lowered her gaze and stared down at the floor.

He moved to her on long, confident strides. His arm snaked out and wrapped about her waist before she knew what was happening. Pulling her flush against him, he used his free hand to tilt her face up to his. His dark eyes bore into hers. "Now, you listen to me, Molly O'Ryan, and you listen closely. I'm a helluva lot older than you are, and I stopped playing games a long time ago. If you want me as badly as I want you, then you just come right out and say so. If you're waitin' for me to chase you like some love-sick schoolboy, then you got a damned long wait comin'. I once asked your permission to court you like a gentleman, but you turned me down."

"But you don't understand why I turned you down!"

"Of course I do!" he retorted angrily. "You don't think I'm good enough for you!"

"No!" she exclaimed. "I'm not good enough for you!"

Her statement taking him by surprise, he released her and stepped backward. "Why do you believe that?"

Her feelings rushed forth. "Oh, Justin, you think I am a virtuous lady, but I'm not!"

"Are you tryin' to tell me that you aren't a virgin?"

Lowering her gaze, she murmured, "Yes."

"Donovan?"

She nodded. "It happened on his last night home before he left for the war."

Smiling tenderly, he drew her back into his arms. "Molly, I don't think any less of you because of what happened between you and your fiancé. I shouldn't have taken it for granted that you were still untouched. I've always had a bad habit of speaking without thinking first. It's perfectly understandable why you'd want to make love to Donovan before he had to leave. I'm sure he needed you very badly, and since you loved him, you couldn't very well have denied him."

"But it didn't happen like that!" she cried, twisting out of his arms. "He didn't need me, I needed him! I was the one who wasn't denied!" Suddenly breaking into tears, she sobbed out her shame. "I practically threw myself at his feet! I behaved brazenly and disgracefully!"

Justin's large bed was within reach, and taking her hand, he sat her down beside him on the edge of the soft feather mattress and draped his arm about her shoulders. "Molly, you wanted to make love to the man you adored. There's nothing wrong with that, so why do you feel so guilty?"

"Because I used my feminine wiles to tempt Patrick into doing something he didn't truly want to do. You see, he made love to me with his body, but not with his heart. Afterward, I felt cheap and terribly ashamed."

"Why don't you explain exactly what happened?"

She sighed unhappily. "I utterly adored Patrick. I had loved him for years. I thought he loved me in the same way I loved him, but now I'm sure that he never did. When war was declared, I pleaded with Patrick to marry me before he left to join his regiment. But he refused, saying he didn't want me to end up a young widow. On our last night together, we went for a buggy ride. We stopped in a secluded spot and spread out a blanket beneath a tree. The war had upset Patrick very much, and he dreaded going into battle. Don't misunderstand what I'm saying. He wasn't a coward, but he was a very compassionate man. He had never killed anybody, and wasn't sure if he could bring himself to do so, even in self-defense.

"Now, as I think back on that night, I realize he needed desperately to speak his innermost feelings. I should've listened and tried to help. But I was a young woman passionately in love. I didn't want us to talk about the war and death, I wanted us to cling to each other and profess our love. I took the initiative and put my arms about him. I not only kissed him, I pressed myself against him in a way that was shamefully provocative. Like a gentleman, Patrick tried to cool our embrace, but I kept kissing him. I even took his hand and put it on my breasts. I asked him to make love to me; over and over again I pleaded with him.

"Well, a man can only stand so much, then his resolve will weaken. Patrick took me, and he was a tender, considerate lover. But Justin, I now know that his heart wasn't in it. I have also come to believe that he never really wanted to marry me; I think he proposed to me to please his father. Thomas Donovan wanted grandchildren. In his own way, Patrick loved me, I'm sure he did. But it certainly wasn't a very romantic, passionate love."

When she fell silent, Justin drew her closer to his side. "Molly, I don't see any reason for you to feel guilty. We all need love, and you weren't wrong to reach out for it. Apparently you just picked the wrong man."

She smiled, and gazing softly into his eyes, she asked, "Are you the right man?"

"I don't know, but I can promise you one thing."

"What's that?"

"If I make love to you, I'll do so from the heart."

"Then Justin, will you make love to me?"

"I thought you'd never ask," he grinned, before bending his head and claiming her lips.

He eased her down onto the bed, then stretched out beside her. He kissed her again, and when his tongue sought entrance, she parted her lips and received him.

"Molly," he moaned, his voice hoarse with need. His mouth came again down on hers, but fiercely this time. His hand moved to her breasts, caressing their fullness beneath the cotton bodice of her dress.

His touch ignited a fire within her and her arms encircled his neck, bringing his lips ever closer to hers.

"Justin," she whispered timorously, "let me get undressed."

He moved so she could rise from the bed. He sat on the edge of the mattress, his eyes like hot irons branding her flesh as she removed her clothes, revealing her beauty to his intense scrutiny.

Her boldness excited Justin, and when he lowered his gaze to the tight red curls between her ivory thighs, he said fervently, "Woman, I want you!" Moving quickly, he reached out and grasped her waist, pulling her between his legs. Holding her slim hips with his strong hands, he pressed his lips against her smooth stomach and his tongue flickered over her warm flesh.

Entwining her fingers in his black hair, she crooned huskily, "Justin, my wonderful darling." Her passion flowing hotly, she arched her hips to his mouth.

His lips moved upward to suckle her breasts, teasing and nipping at their erect nipples. She shivered with ecstasy when she felt his mouth trail downward across her stomach and to the softness between her thighs, tasting and savoring her womanly mound. Molly gasped as wondrous tremors racked her body.

Justin's manhood was throbbing for release, and his brawny strength easily lifted her from her feet and onto the bed. Flinging off the towel, he moved over her, and separating her legs with his knee, he buried himself deeply into her moist heat. Her warm depths caressed the full length of him, and pulling out, he drove into her again, more powerfully than before.

His demanding penetration made her cry out with rapture, and clinging tightly, she wrapped her legs about his waist.

His thrusts were hard, aggressive, and his kisses verged on brutality as he made love to the woman writhing beneath him.

Justin's release came to him with an almost violent force, and grasping her hips, he jerked them up against him as he reached his fulfillment. His deep, breathless sobs mingled with hers as Molly experienced her own exquisite pleasure.

He kissed her fondly, then rolled over to lie at her side. It was a moment before he could manage to find his voice. In his wildest fantasies, he had never imagined that Molly would respond so wonderfully.

"You are most assuredly a woman who knows how to satisfy her man," he said.

Raising herself up to lean on one elbow, she gazed lovingly into his face. "Are you my man, Justin?"

"You're damned right I am," he said firmly. "And now that you belong to me, there's something I think you should know."

"Oh?" She smiled pertly.

"If I ever again catch you with that no-good skunk Captain Newcomb, I'm gonna put you over my knees and give you the spanking of your life."

She laughed gaily and moved into his arms.

Chapter Fifteen

Blade strolled toward the area where Suzanne's wagon was parked. He was sure she resented his luncheon date with Almeda, and he couldn't blame her. Why had he allowed Almeda to extract an invitation from him? He knew Colonel Johnson's daughter was a manipulative young woman, but before he realized what was happening, she had got him to promise to take her to lunch at the club.

Nearing the wagon, Blade saw Black Wolf, Saul, and Suzanne sitting by the campfire. They seemed to be deep in conversation.

The Sioux warrior was speaking, but at Blade's approach he stopped. The three of them looked up at the major, then Suzanne quickly glanced away. She was very much aware of the man's presence, but, still annoyed with him for having lunch with Miss Johnson, she pretended total indifference.

It was Saul who politely invited Blade to join them. Complying, the major sat down on the blanket, purposely taking a position close to Suzanne. He turned his gaze upon her, but she kept her eyes on Black Wolf, giving the impression that she couldn't care less if Blade was present or not.

Blade, very much aware that her attention was centered on the warrior, experienced a strong surge of jealousy. Black Wolf was an impressive man, and more than once Blade had seen how the Sioux brave could captivate a woman—not only Indian maidens, but white women as well. Why should Suzanne be an exception? Returning his gaze to Black Wolf, Blade said evenly, "You were talking—please don't let me interrupt."

"I was tellin Saul and Miss Donovan the ways of the Sioux. We were discussing bravery." Black Wolf returned to his two avid listeners. "Bravery is inculcated in the minds of our children from earliest childhood. It is strongly emphasized in the stories told by old people, and in the rules taught by parents, and in the games the children play. But bravery is not something only heard about and never seen, it is a way of acting, of being and doing. Small boys are guided and encouraged to behave fearlessly. Braves exhibit their courage on the battlefield. If a warrior strikes an enemy he is said to have 'counted coup.' Whether or not the enemy is killed or wounded does not matter. The fact that the brave was courageous enough to touch an opponent and risk death rather than shoot him from a safer distance shows the brave has great courage."

"Why do Indians whoop and yell when they attack?" Saul asked curiously.

Black Wolf smiled good-naturedly. "The wild battle cry is supposed to intimidate the enemy, but it also seems to reinforce the warrior's own courage."

Suzanne questioned him next. "How do the Sioux come by their names?"

"There are many different ways, and it is not unusual for adults to have different names from those they had as children. To change one's name is not only acceptable but expected." Black Wolf was sitting directly across from Suzanne, and his vantage point made it easy for him to see her lovely face. His clear blue eyes softened dreamily as they looked deep into hers. "If you were to live in my village, I would call you Little Dove."

Black Wolf's voice caressed the name, causing Blade to tense and cringe inwardly.

"Why would you call me Little Dove?"

"You are very small, and also beautiful and graceful like a dove."

"Little Dove," she repeated thoughtfully.

"If you do not object," the warrior began, "from now on I will call you Little Dove."

Blade had heard enough, and interjecting gruffly, he asked, "Black Wolf, are you ready to go to the barracks and settle in?"

Black Wolf agreed, and getting to his feet, he said to Suzanne, "Thank you for the meal."

The others also rose. "You're very welcome," Suzanne answered sincerely. She had thoroughly enjoyed the warrior's company.

Taking Suzanne by surprise, Blade reached over and grasped her wrist. "Black Wolf," he said, "will you excuse us for just a moment?" His hold firm, Blade led her a short way from the wagon.

Resentfully she jerked her arm free. "Don't man-handle me!" she said sharply.

"Suzanne, there's no reason for you to be upset because I had lunch with Almeda Johnson."

Her temper flared. "What makes you think I'm upset? You can lunch with whomever you please!"

He didn't want to argue. "Why did you come to my office this morning?"

"It doesn't matter," she muttered.

"When you were leaving you said that it could wait,

so why don't you tell me now?"

Evasively she murmured, "Well, actually it couldn't wait."

"Why?" he asked.

"I was going to ask you to have lunch with me here at the wagon!" she blurted.

Blade groaned, feeling thoroughly contrite. "I'm sorry," he murmured. "But let me make up for it. Have dinner with me tonight at the club."

She was stubborn. "No, thank you."

"I won't take no for an answer," he insisted. "I'll come for you at seven."

"Blade, you must learn to accept rejection," Suzanne advised coolly.

"I have already told you that I won't accept rejection where you're concerned. So be ready at seven o'clock." His tone brooked no opposition, and his eyes blazed into hers. Then, turning smoothly, he walked away and over to Black Wolf.

Blade beckoned to the warrior to accompany him, and they moved off in the direction of the barracks.

Strolling beside the major, Black Wolf said, "Little Dove is a very special woman."

Blade grimaced.

"I never believed in love at first sight, but now I know that it can happen," the brave said with feeling. Had Black Wolf known that Blade was in love with Suzanne, he would honorably have stepped out of the picture. But the warrior had no way of knowing that he and his friend were in love with the same woman. "Now I can understand why my father adored my mother upon first sight, for I loved Little Dove from the moment I set eyes on her."

Seething inwardly, Blade muttered tersely, "Suzanne Donovan has no time for love."

"Because of her quest?" Black Wolf asked.

"So she told you about her cousin?"

"Yes, she did."

"Then you should know that she has only one thing on her mind. Patrick Donovan."

Black Wolf smiled confidently. "A woman's mind can be changed."

Blade offered no comment, but the jealousy burning inside him intensified. He studied Black Wolf surreptitiously. The Sioux warrior was indisputably an attractive man. Why shouldn't Suzanne find him appealing? More important, Black Wolf had one very crowning qualification in his favor; he had no reason to despise Patrick Donovan, and unlike Blade, wasn't determined to see the deserter court-martialed! His emotions in turmoil, Blade looked away from his companion. Never before in his life had Major Landon had reason to feel jealous, but now he was consumed with it.

Suzanne watched Blade and Black Wolf as they walked away. They were truly impressive, with their long, self-assured strides. As they faded from view, she climbed into the wagon, and going to her pallet, sat down. She wondered if she should have dinner tonight with Blade. Recalling his arrogance, she felt she should absolutely refuse. But she had a strong feeling that he wouldn't tolerate a rebuff. Deciding her best recourse was to join him for dinner, she resigned herself to spending the evening with him. I won't let him make love to me, though, she thought angrily. If he thinks he can have me and Almeda Johnson at the same time, then he has another think coming!

Tired, she lay back on her blankets and rested her head on the feather-filled pillow. Her musings wandered to Black Wolf. She liked the Sioux warrior, and had enjoyed talking with him. He makes me think of Patrick, she thought. There was no physical resemblance between the two men, but their similarities went much deeper than an outward one. Not since her cousin had Suzanne found a man who could so easily captivate his audience. She could sit and listen to Black Wolf for hours on end, just as she had listened to Patrick.

She sighed sadly as her thoughts centered on her cousin. Oh, Patrick, she moaned inside, you would have made a wonderful priest. When you spoke of God, your congregation would surely have listened to your every word.

Suzanne turned to lie on her side, and closing her eyes, she let her thoughts float backward into time.

When Patrick graduated from college, he decided the time had come to notify his father of his future plans. He dreaded telling Thomas Donovan that he wanted to become a priest. But there was no longer any doubt in Patrick's mind that he had a spiritual calling and felt the need to dedicate his life to the Church.

Suzanne, knowing of Patrick's decision to confront his father, waited until her cousin and uncle were closeted in the study before slipping up to the door. Her eavesdropping was natural enough, for by now, at age twelve, she was quite sure that Thomas Donovan would disapprove of Patrick's vocation. She was gravely worried about Patrick; she knew how desperate he was to apply for the priesthood, and was afraid her uncle would find a way to dissuade him. If Thomas won out and Patrick bowed to his father's wishes, would the final outcome destroy Patrick? Would he ever again be the same? Was anyone ever the same after they had lost their dream? Suzanne groaned.

Yes, some people are strong and can handle disappointments, but they are the survivors. In the far recesses of her heart, she knew Patrick was not a survivor.

She glanced about stealthily, relieved to see no one was around. Then, pressing her ear against the closed door, she listened.

Thomas, sitting behind his desk, gestured to Patrick to take the chair across from him and asked fondly, "What do you need to talk to me about?"

Patrick looked at his father uneasily. He knew the man was going to find his news upsetting. "I want to discuss my future."

"Your future!" Thomas repeated heartily. "Why son, your future is right here at Southmoor. Now that you are a full-grown man, it's time for you to take your rightful place on this plantation. You can relieve me of many of my responsibilities." He smiled tentatively. "After all, I'm not getting any younger."

Sitting rigid, Patrick replied carefully, "Father, I don't want to be a planter."

For a moment Thomas was too stunned to acknowledge his son's revelation. Then slowly his voice came to him. "You can't mean that."

"I'm afraid I do," Patrick answered softly.

His face depicting his confusion, Thomas asked weakly, "If you don't want to be a planter, then what do you want?"

Outwardly composed, Patrick said, "I want to become a priest."

Thomas paled. "A priest!" he choked. "Are you out of your mind?"

"No, of course not. I've felt for a long time that I had a spiritual calling. Now I'm sure I want to dedicate my life to God."

Anger replacing his shock, Thomas said gruffly,

"Then dedicate your life to the Lord while you run this plantation! You can worship God without becoming a priest!"

"Father," Patrick began tolerantly, "I can't truly give myself to God and also run Southmoor. You don't seem to understand that I want nothing to do with this plantation. I intend to devote myself fully to the Church."

"Over my dead body!" Thomas raged, bounding to his feet. Leaning over his desk, he glared at Patrick. "A priest!" He practically spit out the word. "Son, don't you realize that only certain kinds of men become priests? They aren't men like you and me. They don't possess a man's natural drive. It doesn't bother them to take a vow of celibacy." Suddenly a look of horror shadowed his face. "Patrick, you aren't . . . that way . . . are you?"

Reclining in his chair, Patrick smiled. "No, father, I'm not 'that way.'"

Effusive in his relief, Thomas demanded, "Then how can you even consider being celibate?"

"There are more things to life than sex," Patrick replied lightly. "All priests feel the same way I do. Men of God are not abnormal."

"If you don't marry, there will be no more Donovans! I long for grandchildren, lots of them. I wished for a large family, but for some reason God blessed your mother and me with only one child." Thomas groaned brokenly. "But I always believed that through you the Donovan line would continue."

"I'm sorry, father, but my mind is made up. You may as well change your will and leave Southmoor to Suzanne."

"No!" Thomas yelled furiously, his hand slamming on the desk. "My niece will not inherit my land; it belongs to my son!" Then, frightened by Patrick's set expression, Thomas moved swiftly to his son's chair and pleaded, "Must I get down on my knees and beg you? Patrick, if need be, I will grovel at your feet. But son, please, please don't do this to me. God has many to do his work, but I have only one son to give Him."

Suzanne, still listening at the door, turned away and ran outside. She shouldn't have eavesdropped! Hearing her uncle actually break down and beg had made her feel sick inside. It was terribly wrong for her to have witnessed his humiliation.

Without conscious thought, she headed into the woods and toward the creek, making her way through the verdant thicket to the water's edge. Dropping to her knees, she tried to calm her rapid breathing. Gradually she began to relax, and sat down slowly. Tucking her long skirt about her legs, she lifted her knees and folded her arms across them.

Vacantly she stared across the creek to the lush vegetation that grew abundantly in the virgin soil. Although Southmoor overflowed with cotton and other crops, these woods had remained untouched by the plow or the ax. It was nature at its purest.

Her thoughts were somber. Patrick wouldn't become a priest; he'd give up his dream. A painful sob caught in her throat. Uncle Thomas would have his way by preying on Patrick's love and compassion.

Time seemed to stop as she remained sitting by the creek, her heart aching for her cousin. She had no idea how long she had been there when she sensed a presence at her side. She didn't need to look up to see who had joined her. Her eyes, clouded with tears, were still staring off into the distance. "Patrick, I'm so sorry," she lamented.

He sat beside her. His voice was almost inaudible. "How did you know?"

She didn't look at him; she couldn't bear to see his

pain. "I listened at the door, but when I heard Uncle Thomas start begging, I left."

"Suzanne," he said sadly, "father completely broke down. I couldn't stand knowing I was causing his misery."

"You don't have to explain, Patrick. I can imagine what he said, and everything that happened. I knew you wouldn't have the heart to refuse him." She swallowed. "Your dream is dead. You'll never be a priest." She began to feel angry, and her tone was sharp. "He had no right to do that to you! He took your love and used it against you!"

In her anger she forgot why she hadn't looked at him, and her gaze swept to his. Disappointment and sorrow were written all over his handsome face. Seeing his sadness, she flung herself into his arms.

He held her gently, but as he spoke his hold tightened almost painfully. "I'll run his precious plantation, marry, and give him grandchildren. But Suzanne, my heart will never be in it. I'll be alive on the outside, but dead on the inside. I'm only twenty-two years old, but I'm already a beaten man."

"In time, Patrick, you'll feel differently," she said encouragingly.

"No," he moaned. "I'm finished."

Sitting up on the pallet, Suzanne rubbed a hand over her brow. "Patrick," she whispered to herself, "you were never the same after that day."

Entering the wagon, Molly asked, "Were you talking to me?"

She hadn't heard her friend's arrival, and startled, she stammered, "No . . . no, I was just rattling on to myself. How was your lunch with the captain? And where have you been all this time?"

Molly wondered if she should tell her about Justin and the wonderful love they now shared, but uncertain of Suzanne's reaction, she decided against it. Suzanne's loyalty to Patrick was unyielding, and she might resent her involvement with the scout.

"Lunch was fine," she answered, then murmured evasively, "After leaving the club, I had a few things to do and lost track of time."

Deciding to take a nap, Suzanne lay back down on her blankets. Her thoughts still filled with her cousin, she said softly, "Molly?"

"Yes?"

"Did Patrick ever tell you that he once wanted to become a priest?"

Molly was astonished. "No, I had no idea!"

"Well, he did. In fact, he wanted it very badly, but Uncle Thomas talked him into staying at Southmoor."

Molly's expression grew thoughtful. Had that been the reason why Patrick hadn't loved her above all else? Had his first love been the Church? "Suzanne," she asked, "did he every truly get over giving up the priesthood?"

"I don't think so," Suzanne whispered. Her mind returned to the day at the creek. Finished. He had said he was finished. Oh, Patrick, if only I could understand what you meant!

When Blade asked Suzanne to join him for a drink in his quarters, she hesitated, but then accepted crisply. Her mood was far from friendly, and she practically stormed into the office. As Blade closed the door behind them, she whirled about. Her blue eyes were flashing daggers. She had never had a more unpleasant meal, and was still infuriated.

The evening had started out pleasantly enough, and

Suzanne had made a point of behaving amiably to Blade. She saw no reason to hold a grudge simply because he had taken the colonel's daughter to lunch, but her urbanity had dissolved immediately upon their arrival at the club.

The moment she and Blade had entered the dining room, they had been accosted by Almeda and her father, and Almeda had insisted that they all have dinner together. In Suzanne's opinion, Blade had not been very assertive in his refusal, for the woman had merely ignored his objection. Throughout the entire meal she had completely occupied Blade's attention, while secretively casting catty looks in Suzanne's direction.

Now, facing Blade in the privacy of his office, Suzanne snapped irritably, "Miss Almeda Johnson clings to you like a leech!"

"Don't you think you're exaggerating?" he said nonchalantly. Sauntering toward his liquor cabinet, he asked, "Would you like a glass of sherry?"

"I thought we were going to have a quiet dinner with just the two of us!" Her temper was still flaring.

Pouring a sherry for Suzanne and brandy for himself, Blade replied, "Believe me, I would have preferred a dinner for two, but Colonel Johnson is my commanding officer and there is certain etiquette in the military. One rule is you never refuse a social invitation from a superior officer."

"But it was his daughter who insisted that we join them," Suzanne pointed out.

Handing her the glass of sherry, he answered, "In this case, they were one and the same."

"Oh, you're impossible!" she spat.

He smiled. "I think you're jealous."

"Ha!" she refuted. "Don't be so pompous!"

"You're looking very lovely tonight," he said, his

208

eyes traveling over her with admiration.

Suzanne glanced down at her pale pink gown. It was old, but still in good condition. She was sure it had been out of style for quite some time. "Thank you," she murmured.

Feigning indifference, Blade asked, "What do you think of Black Wolf?"

He was startled by the gleam that came to her eyes. "I like him very much. He reminds me of Patrick."

"You've said some incredible things since I've known you, but that has to be the most outrageous."

"I didn't mean that they look anything alike. Their resemblance goes much deeper."

Blade finished off his brandy, then, placing his glass on the cabinet, he turned back to Suzanne. He was perfectly aware of how much Suzanne worshipped her cousin, and Black Wolf made her think of him. Afraid of losing her to the Sioux warrior, anxiety now coupled itself to Blade's jealousy.

Having no idea of his thoughts, Suzanne innocently began to elaborate on Black Wolf. "I could sit for hours and listen to him talk. And he's so impressive. I never dreamed that a Sioux warrior could be so elegant and such a gentleman. He's also a very handsome man."

"That's enough!" Blade bellowed suddenly. In two long strides he was at her side. "You always go on and on about your cousin, and now you've decided to carry on about Black Wolf! For once, why don't you try talking about us and our future?"

His wrath set off her own anger. "We don't know yet if we have a future to discuss!"

"Of course!" he declared testily. "Our future depends on Patrick Donovan! If he's the deserter I'm searching for, then we are finished, but if he's dead or else a priest, then we can spend the rest of our lives together!" Snatching the glass from her hand, he dropped it on the floor. His strong hands grabbing her shoulders, he said fiercely, "To hell with your cousin! Madam, either you love me or you don't!"

His harsh remarks regarding Patrick provoked more vexation within her. Violently she pushed his hands away. He had hurt her, and longing to hurt him in return, she said scornfully, "I don't love you! I could never love a brute like you!" Although her words tore at her heart, she denied the pain she was suffering. She wouldn't let herself love him, not now or ever!

"So you think I'm a brute, do you?" he snarled. "Then maybe I should start acting like one!" He moved so fast that she was taken totally unaware. Before she had time to react he had her in his arms, her soft body pressed firmly against him. His mouth captured hers in a kiss so demanding that his touch was brutal. She tried to fight, but he had her pinioned so she couldn't move. His lips continued their ardent assault, and she was beginning to feel faint. He had never before kissed her in this savage, aggressive way.

When at last he freed her mouth, her knees were so weak that she was afraid they would fail to support her if he were to release her from his supportive grasp.

Suddenly he had lifted her into his arms and was carrying her to his bedroom.

"Put me down!" she demanded.

"Why should I?" he smirked. "We both know that I never ask for your favors!"

Taking her to the bed, he dropped her onto the soft mattress. Leering down at her, he said with barely controlled rage, "Tonight your cousin will not stand between us. This is one time you'll give all of yourself to me. I'll not share you with another man, not even his memory!"

Suzanne felt as though she were with a stranger, and a very dangerous one. The fury in his dark eyes frightened her.

He took his place beside her, stretching out his long frame next to her smaller one. She opened her mouth to speak, but his sudden fierce kiss silenced her.

Suzanne told herself not to respond but to remain coldly submissive and let him have his way with her. But Blade's fiery kiss quickly melted her resolution, and soon a burning need was ignited throughout her entire being. As though they had a will of their own, her arms wrapped about his neck. Her moist lips parted, and when his tongue entered the deep recesses of her mouth, she received him with abandon.

He pressed himself against her, and she could feel his hard desire touching her thigh. Surrendering, she turned toward him as his hand moved down to her buttocks, and grasping her, he shoved her up against his throbbing erection. Even through her clothes she could feel his splendid arousal, and wanting him closer, she thrust forward until they seemed inseparable.

His anger completely forgotten, Blade whispered thickly, "Suzanne—God, how I want you!"

"Oh yes, Blade!" she responded throatily, conscious of nothing except the passion that this man could so easily awaken within her.

Leaving the bed, they undressed hurriedly, anxious to find the rapture they knew awaited in each other's embrace.

Easing her naked body down to his, Blade positioned her on top. Settling her knees on the mattress, she straddled him, and as he clutched her waist, she slid down onto his hard shaft. His entry sent erotic chills coursing wildly through her, and she cried out her true feelings. "Darling, I need you. I need you so much. Love me, please, love me!"

"I do love you, sweetheart," he moaned, increasing his hold on her waist and urging her to move up and down. His breath came passionately as his manhood rode in and out of her.

Leaning over, she pressed her lips to his, and daringly her tongue sought entrance, her unbridled lovemaking driving Blade to cresting heights of desire.

Smoothly, without breaking contact, he rolled her onto her back, and taking the dominant role, he thrust into her rapidly. Arching beneath him, she equaled his strong drives by crossing her ankles over his waist, and wanting him ever deeper, she moved her legs farther up his back.

Their troubles ceased to exist as they became gloriously engulfed in the throes of ecstasy. Nothing mattered except for this powerful longing for each other. They must quench it, conquer it, and achieve the thrilling sensations that awaited their ultimate victory.

Chapter Sixteen

Suzanne awoke slowly, and stretching gracefully, she turned to lie on her side. The morning sun was shining brightly through the opening in the canvas, and she squinted her eyes against the glare. It took a moment for her to recall last night, but as the evening flooded through her mind she frowned testily and chided herself for having once again surrendered to Blade. What was wrong with her? Why did she continually allow this man to destroy her resolutions? She had sworn not to let him make love to her. Apparently she had no resistance where he was concerned. All it had taken was one kiss, and her defenses had crumbled.

A warm blush came to her face as she remembered Blade's aggressiveness. He was certainly not a man to trifle with, and could become very domineering when the urge struck him. She moved her hand to her lips and caressed them gingerly, finding they were still tender from his vigorous assault. His kisses had been almost brutal in their force, and his lovemaking had been excitingly demanding. Her heart beat wildly as she continued mulling over the night before. Why had she even tried to fight her desire for Blade? It was useless to do so. He's always telling me that I run away from my feelings, and he's right. Well, I won't run anymore. I'll stand firmly and face them. Regardless of Patrick, I love Blade Landon. I know this to be true. I suppose I've known it all along, but just couldn't admit it to myself, or to him.

She smiled dreamily as she made the decision to profess her love to Blade. When she saw him again, she'd reveal her true feelings for him. Whatever the future held, they'd face it together.

Filled with resolve, she threw off her covers and dressed hastily. She brushed her hair vigorously, then pulled it back from her face with a blue ribbon that matched the color of her cotton gown.

As she climbed down from the wagon, she saw Molly and Saul sitting beside the campfire drinking coffee.

The servant rose at her approach and said cheerfully, "Good mornin', Miz Suzanne."

She greeted him warmly. "Good morning, Saul. I'm sorry I slept so late. Have you two already had breakfast?"

Molly answered, "Yes, we ate about an hour ago. If you want, I can fix you something to eat."

"No, thank you," she replied, pouring herself a cup of coffee. "I'm not hungry."

"We're about to have a visitor," Saul said, spotting Captain Newcomb heading toward their wagon.

Putting down her cup, Molly got to her feet and said pleasantly, "Good morning, captain."

Gary murmured the appropriate greetings, then turned his attention to Molly. "Miss O'Ryan, next week Fort Laramie will be visited by two generals and some government officials from Washington. Miss Johnson, along with the officers' wives, is planning a ball for the occasion. I would be very honored if you were to allow me to escort you to the festivity."

"I'm sorry, but I can't possibly accept your invitation." Molly liked the captain and felt bad about turning him down.

He appeared crestfallen. "May I ask why?"

She couldn't possibly tell him about Justin. First she must let Suzanne know, and this was not the way to break the news to her good friend. Evasively she stammered, "Captain Newcomb, I would prefer not to accept a date with you. At present I do not feel free to do so."

It was reasonable for Gary to assume erroneously that she wished to remain faithful to her fiancé. He felt no jealousy; he did not consider Donovan a serious threat and had every confidence in his own charms. He'd soon have her hopelessly in love with him. "I understand," he said graciously. "Miss O'Ryan, would you please consider attending the dance as Colonel Johnson's guest? I'm sure you agree the colonel will not jeopardize your reputation or infringe on your engagement vows." He gave Suzanne a cursory glance before planting the deceitful seed Almeda had asked him to embed. "Major Landon will be taking Miss Johnson to the ball, so I'm sure the colonel would welcome your company."

It took a great effort for Suzanne to remain composed. How dare Blade take Almeda Johnson to the dance! Oh, she had been a fool to think he sincerely loved her and they could face the future together! He was merely using her to satisfy his male lust! I bet he never forces Miss Johnson into his bed! she thought angrily. After all, she's the daughter of his commanding officer, so he places her on a pedestal while taking advantage of me! Oh, the sneaky, low-down, two-timing varmint! Well, if he wants to squire Almeda

Johnson about the fort, then he can do so with my blessing!

Molly sought a plausible excuse to give the captain. If only she had told Suzanne about Justin, then she could tell Captain Newcomb that she was now involved with Mr. Smith and had no wish to attend social functions without him. Avoiding a direct answer, she asked, "Captain Newcomb, may I think about it for a couple of days?"

"Yes, of course," he replied politely. He could sense that she was hedging with him, and wondered if Miss Donovan was the reason why. Perhaps Miss O'Ryan only felt obligated to her fiancé when she was in his cousin's presence. Well, there was only one way to find out. "May I speak to you alone?" he asked Molly, and without waiting for her consent, he took her hand. He quickly led her a short way from the wagon, then insisted gently, "I want you to tell me why you are being so evasive."

Molly decided to be honest. "Captain Newcomb, I am in love with Justin Smith, but Miss Donovan doesn't know."

Gary kept his expression impassive, although inwardly he was seething. Damn Justin! Slowly his anger dissolved as he wondered how much Molly actually knew about the scout. Had he told her of his past? Gary seriously doubted it, for if she knew, she'd not be in love with him. He felt very smug. Well, when the time was right, he'd take it upon himself to tell Molly about Justin's dark past.

Now, with calculated deceit, he lifted her hand to his lips and kissed it fleetingly. "I wish you and Justin Smith happiness. He's a very lucky man to have such a beautiful and gracious lady in love with him."

He bid her a pleasant good day, then walked away

and headed straight for Colonel Johnson's house, where he knew Almeda was waiting for his report.

Ushering Gary into the small, tastefully furnished parlor, Almeda questioned him anxiously. "Did you get a chance to mention casually in front of Miss Donovan that Blade is taking me to the ball?"

"Yes, I did." He looked at her quizzically. "How do you know she won't ask Major Landon if it's true?"

"I don't know," she replied, apparently not unduly concerned. "If she does, then you can simply say you were mistaken." A wicked smile crossed her full lips. "But if Miss Donovan is the kind of woman I think she is, her pride will keep her from confronting Blade. Trust my feminine intuition, Gary. Blade will be escorting me to the ball, just wait and see." She turned her flashing green eyes to him. "Are you escorting Miss O'Ryan?"

Scowling, he said bitterly, "It seems Molly O'Ryan is involved with Justin Smith!"

Almeda was genuinely surprised. "Mr. Smith doesn't seem the type of man a southern aristocrat lady would choose. The man is terribly uncouth and ill-bred."

"He's also a murderer," Gary added maliciously.

"What!" she gasped. "What do you mean, he's a murderer?"

"I mean exactly what I said, and when the time is right, I intend to deliver the shocking news to Miss O'Ryan. When I tell her everything, believe me, she'll have nothing more to do with Justin Smith."

Taking his arm, Almeda urged him to the sofa. Sitting beside him, she asked with insistent curiosity, "Who did he murder, and when? Gary, you must give

217

me all the juicy details."

"You must promise not to breathe a word to anyone. I don't want Miss O'Ryan learning about this through gossip. I want to be the one to tell her. And most important, don't let Major Landon know that you are aware of what happened."

"I promise," she swore impatiently, dying to hear the whole sordid tale.

Leaning back on the sofa and making himself comfortable, Gary proceeded to tell her what he knew about Justin Smith.

Leaving Justin's cabin, Blade headed in the direction of Suzanne's wagon. He had arranged proper living quarters for her and the others, and was anxious to tell her that everything had been taken care of. But Blade was even more anxious to ask her to have dinner with him tonight. Afterward, he planned to take her to his office, and there in the privacy of his quarters, he intended to ask her to marry him. It was not a decision that he had made on the spur of the moment; he had thought of nothing else since the afternoon he had first made love to her. He knew a marriage between them would be a perilous one, but true love could win over insurmountable odds. Did Suzanne love him? She had never said that she did.

Of course she loves me! he told himself firmly. She's just too stubborn to admit it. She couldn't have given herself to me so sweetly and passionately if she didn't love me.

Trooper Donovan infringed on his thoughts, but Blade quickly wiped him from his mind. He'd not let anyone prevent him from marrying the woman he adored, not even her unscrupulous cousin. His better judgment tried to warn him that he was behaving foolhardily. His and Suzanne's love for each other couldn't possibly surmount the problem of Patrick Donovan! He'd never give up his determination to see the deserter punished for his crimes, but if he should become directly responsible for Donovan's execution, Suzanne would never forgive him. God, he thought frantically, maybe the man really is an imposter! Blade knew the possibility was a slim one, but nonetheless, he prayed it would be true. But what it if isn't true? his common sense intruded. Could you bring yourself to arrest, or even kill, your wife's cousin? Angrily he brushed the thought aside. He must continue to see Donovan as a deserter, and the man who had killed his brother in cold blood. He must not think of him as Patrick Donovan, the cousin who was so kind and loving to Suzanne.

As he neared the wagon, he resolutely cleared all doubts from his troubled mind. He would marry the woman he loved, and Patrick Donovan was a bridge they would cross when they came to it.

Suzanne was climbing down from the wagon when Blade arrived. As always, his virile presence affected her strongly, but she managed to look at him with feigned indifference.

The sun's glowing rays touched Suzanne, causing her blond hair to shine with radiant highlights, and her large blue eyes perfectly matched her cotton dress. She was a beautiful vision, and Blade had to call upon all his willpower not to draw her into his arms and kiss her.

"Where are Saul and Molly?" he asked.

"They went to the store," she answered shortly.

"I found a place where all of you can stay for the winter," he informed her. Why were they standing here conversing like casual acquaintances? She was the woman he loved, and he believed she shared his

219

feelings. So why were they behaving so formally? He longed to embrace her, but there was a strange coldness about her that dissuaded him.

"Oh?" She sounded nonchalant. "And where might that be?"

"Justin has a cabin here on the fort. He's going to move into officers' quarters so that all of you can stay at his place. It's only a one-room cabin, but there's a storage area leading off the back that can be converted into a bedroom for Saul."

"When you see Mr. Smith, please give him my thanks. But I feel badly about imposing on him."

"He doesn't mind. In fact, it was his idea. You can move in tomorrow morning."

"Very well, major," she responded coolly. I hate him, she seethed inwardly, while retaining an outward semblance of composure. He's an arrogant, deceitful scoundrel! How dare he use me to secretly appease his lust while he openly courts Almeda Johnson! I despise him! He's a no-good, dirty, two-timing . . . despicable Yankee!

Her frigid attitude had Blade totally perplexed. After the passionate love they had shared last night, how could she now be so distant? He frowned testily. Damn it, why must she be so hard to get along with?

Although he was tempted to ask her about her present aloofness, he chose not to do so. He had a day's work waiting for him and didn't have time to delve into her puzzling mood. He would wait and question her tonight. "Suzanne," he began, "will you have dinner with me?"

He was startled by the anger that suddenly flashed vividly in her eyes. Losing control over her temper, she snapped furiously, "Do you intend to buy my favors with dinner? Major Landon, I am not your whore!"

"What in the hell are you implying?" he demanded forcefully.

Her resentment flowed heatedly. "If you need a dinner companion, then I suggest you seek Almeda Johnson. Maybe afterward she'll repay you by joining you in your bed!"

"Surely you aren't still upset because she manipulated us into having dinner with her and Colonel Johnson," he replied, striving for patience.

Suzanne was about to inform him coldly that she knew he was taking Miss Johnson to the ball, when she happened to spot Black Wolf walking in their direction.

Lowering her voice, she spat, "Major Landon, I will not have dinner with you tonight, or any other night!" Then stepping away from him, she greeted Black Wolf with a warm smile.

Joining them, the handsome warrior said cordially, "Good morning, Little Dove." He looked at Blade. "Good morning, major."

Blade responded with a curt nod.

Black Wolf said to Suzanne, "I came here to ask you if you'd like to take a ride with me. It will do you good to get away from the fort for awhile."

"I would love to, but I don't own a horse," she answered.

"That is no problem. I am sure the army will loan you one. I will see to the horses, then come back for you."

"All right. I'll be ready," she assured him, looking forward to his company.

Blade came very close to venting his rage, but was prevented by the return of Saul and Molly, which coincided with Black Wolf's departure.

Casting Blade an icy look, Suzanne turned and

entered the wagon. Fighting back the urge to follow her and demand an explanation, he whirled on his heel and left, his anger so aroused that he forgot to speak to Molly and Saul.

It wasn't until Suzanne had climbed inside the wagon that it dawned on her that she didn't have any riding clothes. She knew it would be very awkward to wear one of her cumbersome dresses. She supposed she could find Black Wolf and tell him she couldn't accept his invitation, but an outing sounded so wonderful, and she was anxious to get away from the fort—and from Blade!

Deciding to visit the trading store and purchase some riding garb, she went to where she kept her money hidden beneath a stack of blankets. Her funds were meager, and she felt a little guilty about spending any part of it frivolously. Telling herself that in this instance it was all right to splurge, she took some of the money and slipped it into the pocket of her dress.

Before leaving, she told Molly to have Black Wolf wait for her if he should arrive before she returned.

Suzanne hurried to the store and asked the proprietor if he had ladies' riding apparel. She was disappointed to learn that he didn't carry such finery. She frowned impatiently; she should have known that a military store wouldn't handle such attire. She supposed women who lived on the fort brought their riding clothes with them, or else bought the material and made the garments. She, of course, didn't have time to sew a proper outfit, and was on her way out the door when a table piled with trousers caught her attention. Pausing hesitantly, she pondered the possibility, then decided, why not? Rummaging through them, she located a pair of boys' tan breeches that looked as if they would fit.

To complete her new outfit, she also purchased a boys' plaid shirt and riding boots. Carrying her wrapped bundle, she rushed back to the wagon, relieved to find that Black Wolf hadn't yet arrived.

Saul and Molly remained outside as Suzanne hurried inside the wagon, where she quickly changed clothes. She had just slipped on her boots when she heard Black Wolf asking for her.

She hurried out of the wagon. Unprepared for the shock her appearance would have on Molly and Saul, she was surprised to see astonishment on their faces. Turning her gaze to Black Wolf, she noticed that he didn't seem to be in the least surprised. Quite the contrary, his eyes were traveling over her with obvious admiration.

Suzanne's breeches clung seductively to her womanly hips and shapely legs. In her haste she had left the top two buttons of her shirt undone, the opening teasingly revealing the soft fullness of her breasts.

It was Molly who finally broke the strained silence. "Suzanne, don't you think your outfit is a little . . . scandalous?"

"On the spur of the moment, it was the best I could do." Growing impatient, she said defiantly, "Besides, why should I care if the people on this fort find me scandalous? We have been treated just as coldly here as we were at Fort Fetterman. So I don't give a damn what they think of me!"

"Bravo!" Black Wolf exclaimed. "Little Dove, you have a lot of spirit." A teasing grin played across his sensual lips. "Are you sure you don't have a touch of Sioux blood in your veins?"

She laughed gaily. "I hardly think so."

Taking her arm, he ushered her over to the horses. He had chosen a sorrel mare for her to ride, and he

223

assisted her into the saddle before mounting his pinto.

As Black Wolf and Suzanne rode toward the gates, they caused quite a stir among the people mingling in the courtyard. The imposing warrior and the lovely woman riding at his side were a striking vision. The soldiers on duty turned away from their activities to admire the way Suzanne's trousers hugged her curvaceous thighs and slender legs. Although most of the women residing on the military post harbored great hostility toward the Sioux, they nonetheless were greatly impressed with the handsome warrior. His sexual appeal caused more than one lady to fantasize being whisked away by him into the wilderness and taken savagely; the exciting thought sent their hearts beating wildly.

Leaving the fort behind, Black Wolf and Suzanne encouraged their mounts into a full gallop.

Suzanne soon found the ride exhilarating. The wind in her face was rejuvenating, and its refreshing force blew through her long hair, causing the golden tresses to whip about her face.

Black Wolf's restless stallion was impatient to stretch his powerful legs and run full out, but knowing his horse would quickly leave the mare in its wake, the warrior kept a tight rein, curbing the pinto's spirit.

They had been riding about thirty minutes when Black Wolf guided them to the bank of the Platte River. Pulling up, they dismounted. He took Suzanne's hand in his and led her to the river's edge.

Sitting on the ground beside him, she studied the vast landscape. "The West is so open and unpopulated."

"It won't be for long," he predicted. "Now that the War Between the States is over, more and more settlers will invade this land."

"You sound as though you'll resent their presence."

He shrugged. "It is useless to resent it. They will arrive in droves, and they will keep demanding more land until they have it all."

She looked at him with deep feeling. "Where will that leave the Sioux?"

"On reservations," he said bleakly.

"Would that be so terrible?" she asked.

He answered harshly. "How would you like to be confined to a tract of land and told you can't leave it?"

"I wouldn't like it," she admitted. She tried to sound optimistic. "But Black Wolf, maybe it won't be as bad as you think. The government realizes the Indians were here first. Surely they will let your people have a large portion of land where the Sioux can live in peace and not be bothered."

"Apparently you don't realize your country is very greedy."

"My country?" she said, scowling. "This country is now ruled solely by Yankees."

He chuckled with amusement. "Now who is sounding bitter?"

Thinking of Blade, she spouted petulantly, "Yankees are sneaky and despicable."

"I hate to disagree with you, but Major Landon is a Yankee, and is one of the most honorable men I know."

"Hah!" she blurted out. "Then you must not know him very well!"

Studying her speculatively, he got the feeling her animosity toward the major wasn't political. Could she possibly be in love with Blade? Come to think of it, he realized, Major Landon has been acting strangely too. Although he was disappointed to know that he was too late to win Little Dove's heart, he smiled inwardly as he came to the conclusion that Suzanne and Blade were enamored of each other. He didn't need to wonder what was keeping them apart. Patrick Donovan was undoubtedly the cause.

Softly he asked, "Little Dove, are you in love with Blade Landon?"

"Of course not!" she denied, her tone clipped. Wishing to change the topic, she asked impulsively, "Why are you called Black Wolf?"

Considerately he let the subject of Blade rest. "My father named me Black Wolf. Before I was born, he had a dream which he believed was a prophecy. He dreamed of a pack of wild dogs, and among them was a cross between a wolf and a dog. Although this half wolf loved the dogs, who were the only family he ever knew, he was nonetheless restless to know the wolves. Eventually he left the wild dogs to live with the wolves."

"What do you suppose his dream meant?"

"Running Horse believes that some day I will leave the Sioux to live with the white man."

"Do you believe this?"

"I don't want to believe it, but I can't deny that my father's dreams are often a vision of what is to come."

"Considering your mother's determination for you to learn so much about her people, her teachings must have had some influence on you."

"Yes, of course they did. She even gave me a white man's name. She had a Bible, and in it she recorded my birth. She named me after her father, Charles Lansing. But she called me Chuck. She never used this name in public. She only referred to me as Chuck when there was no one around, except for Running Horse."

"Your father didn't object?"

"As I told you before, he loved my mother and could deny her nothing. But she never belittled him in front of his people. They thought she had fully adopted the ways of the Sioux."

"Did she ever visit her parents?"

"No. She knew if she returned to her family, they

would make her stay with them. To reclaim his wife, Running Horse would be compelled to take her by force, which would have brought forth bloodshed."

"Then her family never learned her fate?"

"No," he answered.

"You should find them and let them know that she was happy and loved her husband."

"Over thirty years have passed since Running Horse abducted my mother. At the time she was living in northern Texas. I seriously doubt if her family still resides there."

"Chuck Lansing," she said, savoring the name. Perusing him closely, she murmured, "You apparently inherited your black hair and dark complexion from your father, but your facial features must be from your mother's side of the family. With your hair cut short, and wearing white man's clothing, your resemblance to the Sioux would not be very noticeable."

"I have no wish to look like a white man. My loyalties lie with my father's people."

Intensely she asked, "But Black Wolf, what about your father's dream?"

He offered no answer to her question; instead, he stood and helped her to her feet. "It's time to go back to the fort." His dark eyes probing hers, he said profoundly, "Little Dove, listen closely to what I have to say. Major Landon is a good man. Don't let your cousin keep you away from him."

She turned from his steady gaze and mumbled evasively, "I have no idea what you are talking about. I couldn't care less about Major Landon."

She headed back to her horse, and Black Wolf quickly followed her. Helping her mount, he said with decision, "Your relationship with the major is none of my business. I'll refrain from offering any more advice."

Settling herself into the saddle, she replied, "Good, because as far as I'm concerned, Blade Landon is not even worth discussing. I don't trust him any further than I can see him. He's a lying, contemptible, detestable varmint! I don't care if I ever see him again!"

Cocking an eyebrow, he chuckled. "You said he wasn't worth discussing, yet you seem more than willing to talk about him."

She blushed scarlet, and when he was mounted she jerked the reins and headed the mare toward Fort Laramie. Black Wolf easily caught up to her to ride protectively at her side.

Chapter Seventeen

As Suzanne and Black Wolf entered the fort, the warrior spotted Blade standing in front of his office, watching their arrival. The jealous scowl on the major's face caused Black Wolf to smile inwardly. He now had no doubt that the man was in love with Little Dove. Casting Suzanne a sidelong glance, he saw that she also was aware of the major's presence. The stubborn set of her chin and the anger flashing in her azure eyes told him all he needed to know. She was obviously very much in love with Major Landon. He admired and respected both of them and hoped they would find a way to resolve their differences. But apparently their love was a stormy one, and considering their stubborn natures, calming the storm would not be easy.

When they drew closer to the major's quarters, Blade stepped forward. "Suzanne!" he said sharply. "I want to talk to you!"

The riders reined in their mounts. Eyeing Blade coldly, Suzanne said, "We have nothing to talk about."

Trying to control his rage, Blade said threateningly, "You will either dismount and step into my office, or I will literally lift you from your horse!"

He moved toward her, and realizing he would

indeed carry out his threat, she replied hastily, "Major, there is no need to resort to force." Turning to Black Wolf, she said sincerely, "Thanks for the ride. I enjoyed it immensely."

Taking the reins to her horse, he replied, "So did I. Good day, Little Dove."

She dismounted, then, as Black Wolf headed for the stables, she went over to Blade and stared at him defiantly.

His heated gaze trailed over her from head to foot. "Why in the hell are you wearing trousers? Don't you realize those pants are skin-tight? There isn't a soldier on this fort who isn't ogling you!"

"I don't own ladies' riding apparel!" she retorted. "So what was I supposed to wear?"

"And button your shirt!" he continued.

"What?" she asked, confused. Glancing down, she suddenly realized that she had forgotten to close the two top buttons. "I hadn't noticed."

His arms akimbo, Blade thundered, "Well, I bet Black Wolf noticed!"

Perturbed, she spat, "Honestly, Blade, stop acting as though you're jealous. We both know better. You just relish ordering people around. No wonder you love the army, it gives you the opportunity to make a career out of being a bully."

His temper simmering dangerously, he said gruffly, "Either you walk into my office quietly, or I'll drag you in there!"

She squinted angrily. "I'll go quietly, but once we are inside and away from watching eyes, don't expect me to be peaceful!"

"Since the first day I met you, I have come to expect your hostility, my love."

Coolly she responded, "Let's get one thing straight, Major Landon; hostile I might be, but I am not your love!"

She brushed past him and walked proudly to the door, and as the sentry opened it, she stepped inside.

"Trooper, I don't want to be disturbed!" Blade ordered.

"Yes, sir!"

Following Suzanne into the office, Blade slammed the door shut behind him.

Suzanne had taken the major's favorite stance and was leaning against the desk with her arms folded across her chest. Eyeing him severely, she asked, "What do you want to talk about?"

"I want an explanation!" he demanded, stalking toward her.

"I don't have to explain myself to you. What I do is none of your business."

Pausing mere inches from her, his cold leer met her unwavering gaze. "That's true, Miss Donovan!" he seethed. "You owe me no explanations! You are free to do as you please!"

"You talk as though I was yours and you have decided to set me free. Major Landon, you cannot free what has never belonged to you!"

A violent rage suddenly shone in his dark eyes, and its dangerous glint caused Suzanne to cringe. She had a frightening feeling that Major Landon was not a man to push too far.

Unexpectedly, a calm seemed to come over him, and in an inexplicable way, it was more threatening than his anger. "You're right, my independent little Confederate. You have never belonged to me."

Mustering a semblance of indifference, she said collectedly, "Well, I'm glad we have that settled. Now may I please leave?"

Her haughtiness infuriated him. But remaining ouwardly composed, he said evenly, "No, you may not leave."

Her temper barely under restraint, she fumed, "I am

not one of your soldiers, and I don't have to obey your impossible demands." Attempting to sweep past him, she continued firmly, "I will not remain in this office one moment longer!"

His strong arm reached forward, and grasping her around the waist, he jerked her against him. She tried to resist, but his strength pinned her easily. He had never known a woman so defiant, so unruly. "You infuriating little vixen!" he growled hoarsely, before bending his head to capture her lips in a kiss so passionately demanding that its impact was explosive.

Suzanne longed desperately for the willpower to remain unresponsive. But as always, the feel of his lips on hers sparked a burning need within her. As flames of desire spread throughout her like wildfire, her arms went about his neck. How could she possibly refuse him; she loved him with all her heart and soul!

"Oh God, Suzanne!" he groaned. "You have the power to bewitch a man completely, drain his strength, and bring him to his knees!" Cupping her face with his hands, he kissed her forehead, and cheeks, then reclaimed her mouth with his.

He took her hand to lead her into the bedroom, but his kisses had left her so weak, her legs faltered. Effortlessly he swept her into his arms, and cradling her against his muscular chest, he carried her to the other room. Pausing beside the bed, he set her on her feet.

Immediately her arms wrapped about him, and when his lips descended upon hers, she thrust her thighs to his. The feel of his manly hardness was thrilling, and longing to touch him there, she moved her hand down his masculine frame. Grasping him, she pressed her palm against his solid erection before daringly opening his trousers. Slowly, teasingly, her hand slipped inside his pants, where her fingers encircled him.

His passion aroused to its limit, Blade lifted her onto the bed. Quickly and impatiently, he removed her boots, trousers, and undergarment. The golden triangle between her ivory thighs was a tempting sight, and kneeling beside the bed, he drew her legs forward, placing them over his shoulders. Moving his hands beneath her buttocks, he elevated her thighs, then his mouth sought her womanly softness.

Lying back, Suzanne gasped with pleasure, his lips and tongue driving her wild with rapture. Wondrous, tingling sensations became all-consuming, and she couldn't hold back an ardent cry when her body was suddenly racked with uncontrollable, satisfying tremors.

Standing, Blade hastily shed his boots and pants, then leaning over, he positioned himself between her parted legs. He entered her powerfully, and his intrusion revived her passion, whereupon she locked her ankles about his waist.

He pulled out, then dove back into her time and time again, his rapid thrusts demanding and excitingly forceful.

Love's culmination came to them with a rapturous frenzy, and they clung to each other tightly as they achieved their ultimate fulfillment.

Remaining inside her soothing warmth, Blade kissed her endearingly. Then, withdrawing, he moved to lie next to her.

A tense silence hovered as each waited for the other to speak. Finally Blade decided to break the uneasy quiet. "Suzanne, when I came to your wagon this morning, why did you treat me so coldly?"

It was on the tip of her tongue to tell him she knew all about him and Almeda Johnson, but why should she give him the satisfaction of knowing she resented his relationship with the colonel's daughter? He'd

233

probably merely gloat. She firmly believed he only wanted her in the same way a man wanted his mistress. All his talk of love and marriage had been lies! Lies to get her into his bed.

Sitting up, she reached for her clothing, and answered elusively as she began to dress, "You take too much for granted, Major Landon. Just because we have shared a few passionate encounters, you seem to think that I should be totally enamored with you. Well, I hate to shatter your ego, but I still think of you as a despicable Yankee. But I can't help finding you attractive, and that is the only reason why I respond to you." There, she thought rebelliously, I guess I put him in his place! She knew there wasn't a word of truth in her statement, but she'd be damned if she'd let him know how much she truly loved him. He'd not have the satisfaction of knowing he had made a fool of her!

Blade's anger rose, but keeping it in check, he left the bed. Retrieving his clothes, he dressed quickly. Then, striding from the room and entering his office, he went to the liquor cabinet. Grabbing a bottle of bourbon, he wrenched off the cap, tilted it to his mouth and helped himself to three generous swigs. He had been a fool to believe Suzanne loved him! He meant nothing to her! She was merely using him for her own enjoyment; he was a plaything for her to amuse herself with while she whiled away the days waiting for spring so she could resume her search for Donovan! Well, two can play her heartless game! he fumed.

As she stepped into the room, he turned about and faced her. His expression inscrutable, he raised the bottle in a toast. "Here's to you, Miss Donovan. As always, your favors were not only delightful, but satisfying as well."

His mockery wounded her deeply, but she didn't let on. Her retort was spoken smoothly. "I'm glad you enjoyed yourself, but then, I had a good teacher. After all, you taught me all I know. I can only hope my next lover will appreciate my expertise."

He swallowed a large portion of the potent bourbon, then, with an aloofness he was far from feeling, he said tonelessly, "I suppose Black Wolf will be the next recipient. Well, I'm sure he'll not find you lacking."

Repressing the urge to slap his arrogant face, she retaliated, "If he should find me lacking, I'm sure he can teach me what I don't know. I have a feeling that Black Wolf is a very proficient lover."

She lifted her chin defiantly, then, turning away from his gaze, she walked to the door, opened it, and left. She was tempted to slam it shut, but keeping her composure, she allowed the sentry to close the door behind her.

Suzanne had taken only a few strides when she suddenly caught sight of Almeda walking toward her. She wished she could avoid the woman, but in order to do so she would have to change directions. She wasn't about to give Miss Johnson the pleasure of knowing she preferred not to face her, so she didn't alter her course.

Almeda's fashionable gown accentuated her voluptuous curves, and her thick black hair was arranged stylishly. "Miss Donovan," she murmured in her usual sugar-coated voice. Her eyes traveled critically over Suzanne's manly attire. "Why are you dressed so horribly?"

"I went horseback riding," Suzanne answered, finding it very difficult to keep her voice even.

"Don't you own riding apparel?" Almeda sounded as though the very idea was unheard of.

"No, I don't," Suzanne replied tersely, resentment now creeping into her voice.

"I have numerous sets of riding clothes. Come to my

house tomorrow, and I will give you one of the outfits I no longer care to wear. Of course, you'll have to alter it. My figure is much fuller than yours." Almeda was thoroughly enjoying the conversation.

Suzanne was simmering. "When I ride, I prefer to wear trousers."

"Nonsense," Almeda refuted snobbishly. "You are foolishly allowing your pride to keep you from accepting charity. I also have quite a few old gowns, and you are welcome to them. Since you are so proud, you may not consider my gifts as charity. My house needs a good cleaning, and if you do a satisfactory job, the clothes are yours."

Suzanne's temper ran amuck. "If your house is in need of a good scouring, then I suggest that you put your lazy butt to work and clean it yourself!"

Without further ado, Suzanne walked away in the direction of her wagon.

Saul had gone to the stables to tend to the mules, and Molly was taking a stroll with Justin. Left alone, Suzanne spread out a blanket beside the wagon. She was still wearing the trousers, and sitting Indian-style, she rested her elbows on her knees. Then, cupping her chin in her hands, her gaze became fixed on nothing in particular.

So far the day had been upsetting, and she was still feeling unnerved. It had begun early this morning with Captain Newcomb's visit and his remark concerning Blade squiring Almeda to the ball. Suzanne pouted sullenly. She would have relished going to the dance with Blade. She loved balls, and it had been years since she'd last been to one; the war had long since put a stop to all such festivities in the South.

I don't care if Blade takes Miss Johnson! she told

herself stubbornly. Even if I went to the ball, I wouldn't be welcome! The people on this fort despise me because they think Patrick is Trooper Donovan. As far as I'm concerned, Fort Laramie and everyone in it can go straight to Hades! . . . Especially Almeda Johnson!

Suzanne didn't want to think about her last encounter with Blade, but against her will the memory flashed before her. The man was a rogue and a scoundrel, so why did she love him so passionately? If only she could find the strength to deny him. Suzanne sighed disconsolately. How can I possibly deny him, when I love him from the depth of my soul?

Tears welled up in her eyes, but with determination she forced them back. I won't cry! she swore, afraid that if she did, it would take a long time before her tears abated.

Suzanne frowned irritably as her thoughts returned to Almeda Johnson. The woman is a haughty . . . bitch! she decided, startled at herself for using such a term. Well, it's true! She's just like Aunt Ellen!

Drawing up her knees, Suzanne folded her arms across them. Ellen Donovan, her musings continued. She never thought of anyone but herself. She was selfish and deceitful. If only her evil hadn't finally infected Patrick's life.

Suzanne placed her head on her folded arms, and closing her eyes, she let her thoughts drift back in time.

Suzanne and Patrick had gone horseback riding. Stopping to let their mounts graze, they had decided to take a stroll. They were on Donovan property, but this part of the land was unplowed and the surrounding tableau was rich with green grass and numerous trees.

At the age of thirteen, Suzanne was beginning to lose her girlishness and was starting to take on the appearance of a young lady. Now, as she walked beside Fatrick, he happened to glance at her in a way that made him aware his cousin was blooming into a beautiful woman. She was looking especially pretty in her trim beige riding habit. He smiled to himself. It wouldn't be long until she'd have a string of beaux visiting Southmoor, each seeking to win her hand in marriage. He hoped she'd fall in love with a man worthy of her.

Walking hand in hand, they headed toward a small patch of woods, but as they drew closer, they suddenly noticed two saddled horses.

Pausing, Patrick's expression became thoughtful. "Isn't one of those horses mother's red mare?"

"Yes," Suzanne answered, looking closely at the two animals. "And I think the other one belongs to Uncle Thomas's lawyer, Marshall Lancaster."

Patrick tensed, and when he spoke, his voice was strained. "Let's go back."

They moved to leave, but it was too late. Before they could make their departure unnoticed, Ellen suddenly stepped out from behind one of the trees. Her clothes were in disarray and her hair was disheveled. Catching sight of her son and niece standing in the near distance, she gasped as her face paled noticeably.

Marshall Lancaster was still in the process of doing up his trousers when he emerged from behind the same tree. Unaware of Patrick and Suzanne, he said clearly, "Darling, when can I see you again?"

When Ellen didn't answer, he glanced at her questioningly. Becoming aware of her distress, his eyes followed her frozen gaze. "Oh, my God!" he groaned.

Patrick took Suzanne's arm, and as he turned her around to lead her back to where they had left their own horses, Ellen cried, "Wait!"

Reluctantly, Patrick hesitated. His hold on his

238

cousin's arm tightened considerably.

Ellen hurried to their side, but when she reached them she was uncertain of what to say. Her hands moved nervously to her hair, and while trying to smooth the mussed tresses, she attemped an explanation. "Patrick, you are twenty-three years old. You're a grown man, so surely you can understand how something like this can happen."

Her son appeared totally disgusted. "Mother, I really don't give a damn."

Her heart beating fearfully, she pleaded, "You won't tell your father, will you?"

"Why should I? It wouldn't undo what has already been done. If he knew, it'd only hurt him."

She sighed with relief. "Thank you, Patrick." Turning her questioning gaze to Suzanne, she asked, "Do you intend to tell your uncle?"

Patrick answered for her, "No, she won't say anything either." His eyes hardened severely. "Go back to your lover, mother. He's waiting for you. And I'm sure he's anxious to know if there's a chance of father challenging him to a duel."

Patrick was still holding onto Suzanne's arm, and his grip increased painfully as he forced her to keep up with his long, angry strides.

He was moving too quickly for Suzanne, and when his demanding pace made her stumble, she jerked free of his tenacious grip. Stopping and rubbing her sore arm, she complained, "Patrick, you were hurting me, and I can't possibly walk as fast as you can!"

"I'm sorry," he murmured, his eyes pleading with hers to forgive him.

"It's all right," she assured him. "You don't have to apologize."

All at once, he whirled away to a nearby tree. When he suddenly began hitting his fists against the solid

239

trunk, she rushed over to him.

Trying vainly to grab his hands, she cried, "Patrick . . . Patrick!"

Roughly he shoved her aside as he continued his wild assault. His fists struck repeatedly against the rough bark as he took out his anger on the fixed object instead of his mother and Marshall Lancaster.

Suzanne kept her distance as she wept and begged him to stop. She had never seen this violent side of Patrick's nature, and it frightened her.

When finally his rage was spent, he dropped to his knees and bowed his head.

Hastening over, she knelt beside him. "Patrick," she whispered with heartfelt emotion, tears streaming down her face. She couldn't bear to see him so troubled.

Patrick sat down and drew her onto his lap, and she wrapped her arms about his neck. Minutes passed before he spoke, "Do you remember the first time you sat on my lap? It was the day you came to live at Southmoor. We were inside the stables and I had told you that your parents were dead."

"I remember it very well," she replied softly. "We made a pact always to be friends and always to be there for each other." She paused, then whispered, "I'm here for you now, Patrick. I know you need me."

He groaned. "God, Suzanne, you probably have no idea how badly I have always needed you. Sweetheart, you're very precious to me, and you're the only person in my life who has never disappointed me."

She reached down to take his hand, but as she did, she saw that it was bleeding where the rough bark had cut into it. "Oh, Patrick," she gasped. "Look at your hands!"

He seemed indifferent to his injuries. "They'll heal."

"Why did you keep hitting the tree? Why did you

want to do something so crazy?"

He smiled ruefully. "I have a violent temper, Suzanne. Usually I can control it. But there are times when it explodes. I fear this smoldering rage inside me. What if someday I can no longer keep it repressed and it should overpower me? What kind of man would I become? A murderer, perhaps?"

A cold chill ran down her spine. "Patrick, don't talk like that! You could never murder anyone."

"Couldn't I?" he smirked. "The devil is in all of us."

"You say that because you've never stopped feeling guilty for letting Uncle Thomas talk you out of becoming a priest. Are you afraid God is going to punish you by letting the devil have you?"

He chuckled. "Suzanne, no matter how solemn my mood, you can always say something to make me laugh." Frivolously he added, "How can the devil get me when I have a guardian angel like you in my corner?"

Suzanne raised her head from her folded arms, and concentrating intently, she once again recalled Patrick's reference to his violent temper. She didn't want even to consider the possibility that his prediction had actually come true. Had he turned into a murderer? Was this Trooper Donovan her cousin? No! she cried silently. It isn't true! Again her head came to rest on her crossed arms. Moaning, she prayed, "Oh God, don't let it be true!"

Chapter Eighteen

After months of living in a covered wagon, Suzanne found Justin's rustic cabin a welcome change. Although small, her new home was comfortable and cozy.

It hadn't taken Suzanne and the others very long to get completely moved in. The cabin was adequately supplied with cooking utensils as well as linens and other essentials, so it hadn't been necessary for them to bring a lot of supplies from their wagon.

Settled in, Suzanne decided to write a letter to Thomas Donovan. She had been putting it off, as she dreaded telling him what she had learned about Patrick. But it had to be done, so she might as well get it over with. She knew her uncle was waiting anxiously for news, and she shouldn't keep procrastinating. She was being terribly unfair to the man; after all, if it weren't for Thomas she could never have made this trip. He had given her the Donovans' silver to pay expenses. Suzanne knew her letter would depress him; if only she had encouraging news to send. At least she had Saul and Molly for comfort, but her uncle had no one to console him. Ellen had died of pneumonia a few months before the war. As a child growing up on

Southmoor, Suzanne had never dreamed that the day would come when she'd actually feel sorry for Thomas Donovan, but now, as she picked up pen and paper, she pitied the man.

Saul and Molly were sitting at the round wooden table, where Suzanne joined them.

She was about to start writing when Molly said, "Suzanne, before you become involved in your letter, I need to talk to you."

Putting the pen down beside the inkwell, Suzanne looked across the table and met her friend's gaze. "All right," she agreed.

"Do you want me to leave?" Saul asked Molly.

"No, what I have to say is for both of you."

"You sound serious."

"I am," Molly answered. She paused, and her eyes moved back and forth between Saul and Suzanne. She loved both of them, and hoped they would accept her relationship with Justin. Saul and Suzanne were reasonable, compassionate people; surely they would understand why she had stopped loving Patrick! Her hands were resting in her lap, and clasping them nervously, she began, "I need to talk to you about Justin Smith. I am in love with him."

Molly waited for one of them to speak, but when they offered no comment, but merely stared at her, she continued, "I'm sorry if you find my news upsetting. I can't help it if I no longer love Patrick. I certainly didn't plan to fall in love with Justin, but now that I have, he has come to mean everything to me. I am hoping he'll ask me to be his wife, and if he does, I'll happily marry him."

"Patrick is probably dead," Suzanne murmured tonelessly. "Saul and I don't expect you to remain true to his memory."

Molly's voice edged on desperation. "Please don't

243

use that logic to accept my love for Justin."

"Miz Molly's right," Saul spoke up.

Suzanne sighed, then looking closely at Molly, she asked, "Does Justin love you?"

"I think he does," she answered.

"He hasn't told you?"

Molly was about to answer when a few rapid knocks sounded on the front door. Getting to her feet, Suzanne said, "I'll see who it is."

She walked across the room and opened the door. A trooper she had never seen before was standing on the porch. Removing his hat, he smiled tentatively. "Miss Donovan?"

"Yes," she replied, returning his smile politely. He was a nice-looking man, his full moustache matching the color of his flaming red hair.

"Ma'am, could I talk to you?"

She stepped aside so he could enter. "Yes, of course. Won't you come in?"

"My name is Jesse Rowland," he told her as he entered.

She introduced him to Molly and Saul, then invited him to sit at the table. Complying, he fidgeted apprehensively with his hat as he stammered, "I've been debating with myself for days about payin' you this visit."

Suzanne had remained standing, and taking a position close to the trooper's chair, she looked down at him with mild puzzlement.

"I finally decided comin' here was the right thing to do," he went on. "You see, ma'am, I was pretty good friends with Trooper Donovan. I've heard rumors that you believe Trooper Donovan is an imposter. I don't know, maybe he isn't your cousin, but if he ain't, then he sure knows a hell of a lot about the man. I think I ought to tell you everything he told me about his life, then leave it up to you to decide whether or not he's posing as Patrick Donovan."

Suzanne could barely contain her excitement. "Go ahead, Mr. Rowland, tell me what you know."

"Miss Donovan, you don't by chance have a picture of your cousin, do you?"

"No, I don't," she answered. "When our home was burned, all the pictures and paintings were destroyed."

"That's too bad," the soldier mumbled. "A picture would sure solve everything for you." Studying her studiously, he proceeded, "Several times Donovan showed me a daguerreotype he has of you. In it you're wearin' a low-cut gown and your hair is loose and falling over your shoulders."

"Before Patrick left for the war, he took me into Natchez and had the picture taken."

"Well, like I said, he showed it to me time and time again. And each time he had me look at it, he'd ask me if I had ever seen a woman more beautiful than his cousin." The trooper smiled a little bashfully. "I'd tell him you were the prettiest lady I ever set eyes on. And it was the gospel truth, Miss Donovan."

"Thank you," she murmured.

"He talked about you all the time."

"What did he say?" she asked anxiously.

"Well," the man drawled, "he told me about the day you came to live at Southmoor. You were only three years old and no one had told you that your parents had passed away. You and Patrick were alone in the stables when he told you that they were dead. You broke down and cried for a long time, then afterward you and Patrick made a pact always to be friends and always to be there for each other."

Suzanne gasped. Had she written about that day to Patrick? Had this Trooper Donovan learned about it from her letters? Concentrating hard, she couldn't

245

recall ever writing to her cousin about her first day at Southmoor and the pact they had made. Quickly she turned her gaze to Molly. "Did Patrick tell you about that day? And if he did, could you by chance have mentioned it in a letter to him?"

"No," Molly answered. "I knew nothing about it."

"I wonder where your letters to Patrick are?" Suzanne pondered. "They weren't among the possessions Trooper Donovan left behind."

The visitor looked at Molly apologetically, then returning to Suzanne, he mumbled, "Donovan destroyed her letters. I was with him when he burned them. He said he didn't have any wish to keep holdin' on to 'em. Your letters were the only ones he wanted to keep."

The man's words wounded Molly severely, and she had to swallow back the tears that threatened to emerge. Apparently Patrick had never truly loved her!

"What else did he say about me?" Suzanne asked urgently.

"He told me about the time you found the bobwhite, and how he tried so hard to keep the bird from dying. He knew you worshipped him and believed he could do anything. He didn't want to disappoint you, and that's why he worked so hard to keep the bird alive."

Once again, Suzanne's eyes turned to Molly's.

Shaking her head, Molly said, "I didn't know about this either. Maybe you or Patrick's father wrote about it in one of your letters."

"No," Suzanne moaned. "Thomas never wrote to Patrick. He left it up to me to correspond with him. I'm sure I never wrote about the bobwhite."

"Miss Donovan," the trooper began, "it's kind of hard for me to remember everything he told me about his life. But he did talk a lot about Southmoor and his relationship with you. Why don't I just tell you what I can recall?"

"All right," she answered. Her knees were weakening, and she had to lean against the table for support.

Reflectively he continued, "Donovan told me about the day he saved the Negro baby from the burning cabin. I know all about the creek behind the main house and that you two called it your own special place. He wanted to become a priest, but his father talked him out of it. One day you two caught his mother having a dalliance with a lawyer named Marshall Lancaster. The revelation hit Patrick real hard, and he lost his temper. You witnessed his anger, and he confessed to you that he feared this uncontrollable rage inside him."

With a moan, Suzanne folded her arms across her stomach as though to stop the pain that was cutting into her like a knife. She couldn't remember writing about any of this to Patrick. Then how had Trooper Donovan come by his knowledge? Grasping for an answer, she said intensely, "Maybe this Trooper Donovan was once friends with my cousin, and Patrick told him all these things."

"Maybe," the soldier muttered. "But ma'am, I kinda doubt it. If Donovan learned about your cousin through hearsay, I don't think he could've talked to me about it so vividly. When a man is only repeating what he's heard, he tells it in the same way I'm talkin' to you now. Another man's life doesn't make such an impact on you that you can repeat what he's confided to you in precise detail."

Suzanne didn't want to agree, but how could she argue against such logic?

The trooper mumbled his excuses and rose to his feet. Suzanne and Saul were both too numb to show him out, so it was Molly who escorted their guest to the door.

Returning to the table, Molly placed her hand on

Suzanne's arm. She was about to try and console her, but Suzanne brusquely brushed aside her touch. She moved to the center of the room, then she whirled about and looked wretched at Saul. "My God, he's Patrick! This deserter and murderer is really our Patrick!"

Glancing away from her, Saul placed his elbows on the table, and leaning his head into his hands, he groaned brokenly, "I wished I hadn't lived to see this day! Oh Lord, why did you let Masta Patrick turn bad?" The old man burst into heaving sobs. "God, he was such a good boy and grew into such a gentle man! Why did he become a monster? What happened to him? What happened to my boy? . . . Masta Patrick! . . . Masta Patrick!"

Molly thought Suzanne would hurry to Saul and comfort him, and she was surprised when her friend made no move to approach the grieving man. Hesitantly Molly went to the servant, and resting a hand on his shoulder, she patted him soothingly. "Oh, Saul, I'm so sorry."

Slowly, as though in a dreamlike trance, Suzanne walked to the bed and sat on the edge. I'm not strong enough to bear this, she thought, dazed. I can take no more disappointments. Blade has disillusioned me, and now so has Patrick. The two people I love the most are not even worth loving.

Molly turned away from Saul to look at Suzanne. She was prepared to offer her friend her deepest sympathies and expected to see Suzanne in tears. She was startled to find Suzanne dry-eyed, her expression devoid of emotion.

Saul was regaining control of his grief, and getting his attention, Molly whispered secretively, "Saul, I'm worried about Suzanne. She's acting strangely."

His concern for his mistress overcame his own

248

distress. He stood and looked at Suzanne. Like Molly, he had expected to see her crying. Going over to the bed, he said softly, "Miz Suzanne, are you all right?"

She didn't answer.

"Are you all right?" he insisted gently.

She lifted her eyes to his. "No, I'm not all right, and I don't think I ever will be again."

The coldness of her voice worried him. "Right now you're in shock, but sooner or later you got to make yourself face the truth about Masta Patrick."

"The truth!" she said bitterly. "And what exactly is the truth, Saul? How do I make myself accept the fact that Patrick is a cold-blooded murderer? Why did he become the kind of person who is totally at variance with the man I knew and loved?"

Slowly he eased his frame onto the bed and sat beside her. "Maybe Masta Patrick was always capable of this kind of violence. You was aware of this rage in him, and so was I. We've both seen it. I remember one time when Masta Patrick became so enraged that he most nearly killed a man."

Suzanne looked at him questioningly.

"You remember that time Masta Thomas and Miz Ellen took a trip to New Orleans and Masta Patrick was left in charge of the plantation?"

"Yes, I remember. It was the year before the war started."

"One night Mista Hopkins had a visitor." Saul's face hardened at the thought of Mr. Hopkins, who had been the overseer at Southmoor. The man had been brutal and had relished inflicting his cruelty on helpless slaves. "He was visited by Mista Greer."

"Mr. Greer?" Suzanne contemplated the name. "Didn't he own the bar in town?"

"Yes'm," Saul answered. "He and Mista Hopkins had been drinkin' heavily, and they were both pretty drunk. Mista Greer decided he wanted a wench. It seemed he had a likin' for young virgins. So Mista Hopkins sent for little Missy."

Suzanne inhaled in shock. "But at that time, Missy couldn't have been more than thirteen!"

"She was only twelve," he mumbled. "Well, when her pappy learned that the overseer had sent for Missy, he was real upset. You got to realize, Miz Suzanne, that it's awfully hard for a slave to oppose a white man. He knows he'll either get whipped or killed if he don't do exactly as he's told. But Missy's pappy couldn't just stand by and do nothin, so he finally came to me. He begged me to go to Masta Patrick and tell him what was happening. All the slaves at Southmoor believed Patrick a fair man, and he was Missy's only hope. When I got to the big house, I was told that Masta Patrick was in the study. As soon as Lettie showed me in, I told him about Mista Greer and Missy."

Saul paused for a moment and wiped a hand across his brow. "Masta Patrick was furious. We stormed out of the house and down to the overseer's. When we barged inside, Mista Greer had Missy on the bed. The poor chile was naked, and the man was standing over her with a whip. He enjoyed whippin' his wenches before . . . before . . ."

"I understand," Suzanne murmured.

"He'd gotten in quite a few lashes before we got there, 'cause Missy's back was cut and bleedin'. Masta Patrick stalked over to Mista Greer and grabbed the whip from his hand. Miz Suzanne, he turned on the man somethin' furious. He started a-whippin' him. Mista Greer tried to avoid the blows by runnin' outside, but Masta Patrick followed him, still attackin' him with that whip. Mista Hopkins made an attempt to stop him, but Masta Patrick turned about and struck out at him. Well, the overseer wasn't about to get himself whipped, so he backed off. When Masta Patrick went back to attackin' Mista Greer, I got scared that he'd whip the man to death. To this day, I don't know how I managed to get Masta Patrick to stop beatin' the man, but somehow I got through to him and he dropped the whip. Mista Greer was in bad shape, and when Patrick came back to his senses and seen what he had done, he was shocked. The whole time he was a-whippin' the man, he'd been out of his head. Later, after we were back in the big house, Masta Patrick told me how scared he was of his own violence. Masta Thomas came home the next morning and if he hadn't paid Mista Greer off, I reckon Masta Patrick would've gotten into a lot of trouble with the law."

Suzanne wished Saul hadn't told her the story. She didn't want to hear about Patrick's violent temper. She didn't want to hear about him at all! She was too beaten, too defeated. She only wanted to escape from the horrifying present.

Saul rose to his feet and Suzanne went and lay down on the bed. Turning her back to the others, she curled up on her side. Molly and Saul called to her, but their voices seemed to come from somewhere far away. Closing her eyes, Suzanne shut out the world and sank peacefully into a deep, endless void.

Chapter Nineteen

Blade, Justin, and Black Wolf were planning their journey into the Black Hills when the young sentry opened the office door and announced, "Major, Miss O'Ryan wants to see you."

"Show her in," Blade answered, wondering why Molly was calling.

She entered quickly, but upon seeing Justin, she rushed toward him. Seeing her distress, he opened his arms and drew her into his embrace.

"Molly, what's wrong?" he asked gently.

She didn't want to leave the haven of his arms, and she stepped back from him reluctantly. "It's Suzanne," she whispered tearfully.

"Suzanne!" Blade exclaimed, suddenly very concerned.

Turning to him, Molly explained, "Saul told me to come here and ask you to come to the cabin and talk to Suzanne. Neither of us can even get her to respond— she just lies on the bed as though she's in a deep sleep. But we both know she's awake."

"What in the hell are you talking about?" Blade demanded impatiently. "What's happened to her?"

"I'm sorry," Molly murmured. "I should've started

at the beginning. We were visited by Trooper Rowland, who said he was good friends with Trooper Donovan. He started telling us about the Patrick he knew. It seems he often confided in Mr. Rowland about his life at Southmoor." Molly's voice grew tense. "Major Landon, Trooper Donovan told him things he couldn't possibly have known if he were an imposter." A sob caught in her throat, and leaning into Justin's arms, she cried, "Trooper Donovan is Patrick!"

Blade groaned inwardly, his heart aching for Suzanne. Regardless of how she had treated him, he still loved her. He could well imagine the pain she was now feeling. "Why did Saul tell you to come to me?"

"He believes you might be able to help her."

Blade frowned. "Under the circumstances, I'm probably the last person she'd turn to for comfort. Have you and Saul forgotten that I am the man who plans to have her cousin court-martialed?"

"Major Landon," she replied, "I agree with you, and I tried to convince Saul that sending for you could be a grave mistake. But he insists that you come."

When Black Wolf suddenly spoke up, they all turned to look at him. "The Sioux respect the elders in their village, because only with age can a man grow wise." His eyes met Blade's. "Saul is an old man, and a wise one. Go to Little Dove, she needs you."

Blade wasn't sure that Saul was acting wisely in this instance, but it didn't matter. No force on the face of the earth could keep him away from Suzanne in her hour of need. She might turn on him, but nonetheless he'd offer her comfort.

"All right," Blade agreed, "I'll go see her."

"I will walk part way with you," Black Wolf said. He followed Blade across the room and outside.

As they headed toward the cabin, the warrior fell into stride beside his friend. "When I talked to you about loving Little Dove at first sight, why did you let me wound you with words that weren't meant to hurt? Why didn't you tell me that she's your woman?"

"Suzanne isn't my woman," Blade grumbled. "She's free to choose any man she pleases."

"You are in love with her," Black Wolf said firmly. "But your relationship with Little Dove is none of my business, and I'll stay out of it. I only have one more thing to say. It is true that I loved her at first sight, but my love is one of respect and admiration. It was never given a chance to become one of passion." He smiled a little sadly. "Besides, it is best that I never fall in love with a white woman."

"Why do you think that?" Blade asked.

"If I were to marry a white woman, I doubt if she'd want to live with the Sioux. I'm sure she'd be determined that we live in the white man's world."

"Would that be so bad? You certainly wouldn't have any problems adjusting. When you want to, you can act more white than Indian."

Black Wolf chuckled. "My mother taught me well." He paused. "I'll not ask you to be kind to Little Dove, because I already know that you will show her tenderness."

He turned swiftly and moved away. Blade watched him for a moment, then resumed his own strides. The cabin was now in sight, and he could see Saul sitting on the porch steps.

Saul, aware of the major's approach, studied him as he drew closer. He hoped his decision to send for this man wouldn't prove to be a mistake.

Blade came to the porch and looked down at the servant, who hadn't bothered to rise and greet him. Saul's worry was reflected vividly in his eyes as he glanced up to meet Blade's gaze. "She's inside," he mumbled.

Blade felt he should say something to Saul, but he had the feeling that the old man didn't want to talk. Quickly he moved up the steps, across the porch, and into the cabin.

Suzanne was still lying on the bed, curled up on her side. Her back was turned toward Blade, and he couldn't see her face. Carefully he sat down on the edge of the mattress and placed a hand gently on her shoulder. "Suzanne," he whispered.

She flinched beneath his touch. "What are you doing here?" Her voice was unemotional.

"I was hoping you might need me," he said softly.

She buried her face into the pillow, muffling her words, "I don't need anyone."

"Do you think you can hide from life by burying your face in that pillow?" When she didn't respond, he asked, "Where's your spirit, Suzanne?"

"It's dead," she mumbled listlessly.

Studying her, Blade realized if he continued showing her sympathy, her malaise would merely deepen. She needed to release all her bottled-up pain and sorrow. He wasn't looking forward to upsetting her, but he knew that was the best way to help her. "Well," he taunted, "I was certainly wrong about you. I never thought you were a quitter. But then I should have known that your defiance was simply a facade. You're a typical woman—when the going gets rough, you can't take it."

"Go to hell," she muttered, anger seeping into her tone.

Blade grinned. He was getting a reaction. "You don't have to be rude, my defeated little Confederate. After all, I came here to offer you my condolences."

Slowly she rolled on to her back. Blade had expected her eyes to be red and swollen from tears, but they were clear. She hasn't even cried, he thought with concern.

"I don't need your condolences," she said, her adrenalin beginning to flow.

"Of course you do," he argued. "Since you are apparently feeling sorry for yourself, I'm sure you want everyone else to pity you too."

She sat up with a start. "Oh, you unfeeling, heartless, cad! I hate you! Go away and leave me alone!"

"Aha!" he declared. "I thought you said your spirit was dead."

Brushing him aside, she bolted from the bed. She should have known he wouldn't care! He was probably very pleased with himself! Hadn't he always told her that Trooper Donovan was most likely Patrick? Placing her hands on her hips, she said furiously, "I suppose you are thrilled to learn that you were right all along! Well, Major Landon, I concede! The man you want to see executed is my cousin! And when you finally have him standing before a firing squad, I hope to hell you are proud of a job well done!"

Rising quickly, Blade stepped close to her. "I am not in the least thrilled. I was hoping as much as you were that Trooper Donovan was an imposter."

"I don't believe you!" she spat. "If you care, then why are you treating me so coldly?"

"My treatment got you off that bed, didn't it? You are no longer drowning in self-pity. Quite the contrary, you're showing me you still have a hell of a lot of grit."

She raised her chin bravely. "No man can destroy me! Not you or Patrick!"

"Good for you," he encouraged. "But Suzanne, you cannot deny that you love your cousin. He has hurt you worse than you have ever been hurt. Don't you think you should cry and release the pain you're feeling? If you don't find relief, it'll just continue to eat away at you."

She turned away from his gaze, and with her eyes

A <u>FREE</u> ZEBRA
HISTORICAL
ROMANCE
WORTH

$3.95

BUSINESS REPLY MAIL
FIRST CLASS   PERMIT NO. 276   CLIFTON, NJ

POSTAGE WILL BE PAID BY ADDRESSEE

ZEBRA HOME SUBSCRIPTION SERVICE
P.O. Box 5214
120 Brighton Road
Clifton, New Jersey 07015

downcast, she murmured, "I'm afraid to cry."

"Why?" he asked tenderly.

"I'm afraid if I start, I won't be able to stop," she whispered piteously.

Carefully he placed his hand under her chin and tilted her face up to his. "Trust me, Suzanne. Come into my arms and let me hold you." Her vulnerability went straight to Blade's heart. Forgotten was the anger she had provoked in him during their last meeting. Maybe she didn't love him now, but that didn't necessarily mean that she never would.

Suzanne longed desperately to fall into his arms and cry until she had no tears left to shed. But she couldn't trust him; today he'd be here for her, but tomorrow he'd probably return to Almeda Johnson. Abruptly, she whirled about and turned her back to him.

Blade wasn't about to give up. He'd help her in spite of herself. He reached out and grabbed her arm, turning her around and into his arms. He lifted her up, then carried her to the large maple rocking chair, where he sat and cradled her in his lap. "I love you, Suzanne," he whispered, kissing her warm brow.

His tenderness brought on the tears she had kept repressed, and wrapping her arms about his neck, she nestled her head against his shoulder. Blade rocked the chair gently as Suzanne wept brokenly. He held her close, and his own eyes were misty as he rested his cheek against the top of her golden curls.

Suzanne was still cradled in Blade's lap when Molly and Saul entered the cabin. Their eyes sought the major's, their expressions questioning.

He smiled faintly. "She's asleep."

His words arousing her from her restful slumber, Suzanne began to stir. At first her thoughts were muddled, but then, realizing she had fallen asleep in Blade's arms, she felt a little embarrassed. She wondered if he found her behavior childish. Sitting up, she looked into his eyes, but could see only compassion and concern in their depths. Smiling timidly, she left his lap to stand in front of the chair.

"Are you all right, Miz Suzanne?" Saul asked, his tone edged with worry.

Facing him, she answered evenly, "Yes, Saul, I'm just fine."

The servant smiled broadly. He'd been right to send for the major.

Getting to his feet, Blade placed a hand on Suzanne's arm. "Why don't you come with me to my office and have a glass of sherry? The drink will do you good."

"Thank you," she murmured, shyly averting her gaze from his. She was still feeling uneasy about falling asleep in his lap.

Blade smiled understandingly. She was vulnerable in spite of her spirit and defiance. No wonder he loved her so much.

Telling Saul and Molly that she'd see them later, Suzanne allowed the major to escort her outside and to his office. The sentry was still on guard, and as they entered, Blade told him he was dismissed. Locking the door behind them, Blade led her to his liquor cabinet, where he poured her a glass of sherry and a bourbon for himself.

Suzanne thanked him and accepted the proffered drink. She took a generous swallow, finding it soothing.

Raising his glass, Blade encouraged, "Bottoms up!"

Responding, she tilted the glass to her lips and drank it off. In turn, Blade finished off his own drink.

He placed their empty glasses on the cabinet, then, moving smoothly, he drew her into his embrace.

Pressing her tightly against him, he bent his head and his lips descended to hers.

Her arms laced about his neck as she returned his kiss. She needed him with all her heart. Wanting to feel his hardness, she shoved her thighs to his and rubbed against him provocatively.

Responding to her passion, Blade's hands moved to her buttocks so he could press her thighs even closer to his. "Suzanne," he whispered huskily, his lips traveling down to kiss the hollow of her throat.

"Blade," she murmured timorously, "I need you so. Please love me."

"Oh God!" he groaned. "I love you more than life itself."

Taking the initiative, she grasped his hand and led him into the bedroom. She started to take off her gown, but Blade stopped her as he insisted that she allow him to undress her. He removed her clothes slowly, kissing her bare flesh as her beauty was revealed to him. Gently he urged her to the bed, and, as his eyes drank in her loveliness, he hastily shed his uniform.

Now anxious to consummate their love, he laid his muscular frame over her slender one. Wanting him as fervently as he wanted her, Suzanne's arms went about his neck, and her legs parted for his entry.

His mouth came down demandingly on hers as he shoved his manhood deep into her womanly heat. His maleness filling her felt so wonderful that Suzanne gasped as she accepted him, and with her lips still on his, she welcomed his probing tongue. Their kiss was wildly passionate and their thrusting hips moved rapidly.

Suddenly he pulled out, grasped her hips, and turned her on to her stomach.

Suzanne was confused. "Blade, what are you doing?"

"You'll find out, my innocent little Confederate," he

murmured with a tender yet anticipating smile. He encircled her small waist with his strong arm and drew her to her knees. Positioning himself behind her, he guided his erection far into her feminine depths.

"Oh, Blade!" she cried ecstatically, loving the feel of him so deep within her.

He thrust against her time and time again, and matching his sensual rhythm, she equaled his passion. Blade's need to reach complete fulfillment became all-powerful, and he quickly changed their position. Once again he was on top, and as his manhood sought entrance, Suzanne's legs went about his back. Love's ultimate release came to them ardently, causing them to hold desperately to each other as they shuddered with exquisite pleasure.

Blade's lips caressed hers tenderly before he withdrew to lie at her side. She snuggled against him, nestling her head on his shoulder.

Brushing her brow with a light kiss, he whispered, "I could make love to you for an eternity and still want more."

"The feeling is quite mutual," she sighed.

He raised up and looked down into her eyes. "Do you mean that, Suzanne?"

"Yes, I do," she replied.

He was tempted to ask her if she loved him, but his pride kept the question from passing his lips. He didn't want to ask for her love, he wanted her to profess it of her own accord.

Suzanne was longing desperately to tell him she loved him, but she still wasn't sure if she trusted him. Today he had shown her kindness and had been an ardent lover, but tomorrow he might very well spurn her for Almeda's affections.

Silently Blade pleaded with her to make this moment the happiest one in his life and declare her love. But when it became apparent that she had no intention of doing so, he moved to the edge of the bed. How could she give her body to him so completely, yet refuse him her heart?

A bitter frown crossed Blade's face. It's because her heart belongs to her no-good cousin! he thought resentfully. Standing, he reached for his clothes and began to dress.

Watching him, Suzanne was about to ask him not to get dressed, but return to bed and hold her. But suddenly, believing he had only wanted to satisfy his male lust, she bit back her request. When was she going to realize fully that he only loved her in the same way a man loved his mistress? How many times must he callously prove it to her before she'd learn to accept the truth? Why did she continue to let him make a fool of her?

Sitting up, Suzanne left the bed and hastily began to dress.

Blade sat on the edge of the mattress and slipped on his boots. He loved Suzanne, and was determined to hold onto the hope that someday she'd return his affections. He decided to take her to dinner, and during the meal draw her into a serious conversation. Maybe they could rationally discuss her cousin and the part he was playing in their perilous relationship. Having no idea of Suzanne's jealousy toward Almeda Johnson, Blade believed Patrick Donovan was the only obstacle between them.

The moment Suzanne had finished dressing, she said collectedly, "I need to get back to the cabin. I'm sure Saul is still upset, and I'm ashamed to say that I neglected him when we learned about Patrick. I selfishly thought only of myself." Suzanne had spoken the truth, she was feeling guilty and wanted to see Saul, but she wished Blade would accompany her to the cabin and perhaps stay for dinner. She fought back the urge to ask him; he probably already had a dinner date with Miss Johnson.

Well, so much for asking her to have dinner with me at the club, Blade thought impatiently. Slowly he got to his feet, then, placing his hands on her shoulders, he said gently, "If you need me, don't hesitate to send for me."

Feeling as though she had just been dismissed, Suzanne hid her hurt behind a forced, polite smile. "Thank you, Blade, but I'm sure I'll be all right."

She stepped away from him and walked quickly to the doorway. She paused and turned back, and as her eyes met his, she detected a sadness in them that puzzled her. She came very close to rushing heedlessly into his arms and insisting that he tell her why he seemed so unhappy. Could he possibly love her in the same way she loved him? Was she the reason behind his sadness? But afraid of a denial, she looked away from his gaze and left the room. She hastened across the office, unlocked the front door, and stepped quickly outside.

Chapter Twenty

Leaving the cabin, Suzanne sat on the top porch step and tucked her long skirt about her legs. Resting her elbows on her knees, she placed her chin in her hands and stared vacantly. A large part of the fort's courtyard was within sight, but she paid scant attention to the various activities going on within the compound. She had grown accustomed to life on a military post, and had even come to recognize most of the bugle calls. The cavalryman's day was regulated by the fort bugler, who sounded Assembly, Recall, Reveille, Mess, Taps, and other calls. Now, as the bugle sounded loudly over the post, Suzanne knew it was time for the evening meal.

She sighed heavily as she watched the sun begin its descent over the western horizon. For Suzanne the day had been long and depressing. It had only been yesterday that Trooper Rowland had visited her, but it seemed much longer. She was finding it very hard to accept that Patrick was Trooper Donovan, but she could no longer deny that they were the same man. Somehow she had to find the inner strength to face facts, but it was tearing her apart to do so. She loved her cousin and had virtually worshipped him since the day she had first arrived at Southmoor. If only she had

Blade's loving support; perhaps through him she could find the strength she needed.

As her thoughts turned to Blade, Suzanne once again recalled the sadness she had seen in his eyes yesterday when she had left his room. Could she possibly have misjudged him? Did he truly love her? Had she been wrong to believe he was interested in Almeda Johnson?

Suzanne's gaze turned in the direction of Blade's quarters, hoping to catch sight of him heading toward her cabin. She had been expecting all day to receive a visit from him. She knew his job kept him busy, but surely he could've found time to pay her a short call. He knew how troubled she was. Didn't he care about her at all?

Well, she decided firmly, if he won't come to me, then I'll go to him. I think it's time for us to have a serious discussion. I absolutely refuse to share him with Almeda Johnson, and I'm going to insist that he make his choice.

Maybe you've been wrong all along! her better sense intruded. You have no proof that Blade is involved with the colonel's daughter. Just because Captain Newcomb said that Blade is taking the woman to the ball doesn't necessarily make it true. The captain could have been mistaken.

Bolstered by renewed hope, Suzanne bounded from the porch steps and began walking unhesitantly toward Blade's quarters. She would gamble with her pride and tell him how much she loved him. Blade, please, please love me in return! she pleaded silently as she hurried to the man she adored.

Stepping out of the bathtub, Blade walked across his bedroom to his uniform spread out on the bed. He dressed hastily, as he was in a hurry to leave. He was bound and determined to see Suzanne and insist that they have a heart-to-heart talk. He had refrained from visiting her all day, believing she needed time to adjust to the fact that her cousin and Trooper Donovan were the same man.

Blade was fully dressed and had just slipped on his black boots when he heard the door leading into the office swing open. The sentry wasn't on duty, and he wondered who was calling unannounced.

Blade's curiosity was satisfied when Almeda's voice rang out. "Blade, darling?"

Blade grimaced. He could do without a visit from Almeda Johnson!

Her steps were unsteady as she entered the bedroom. Pausing, her eyes roamed brazenly over the major's handsome frame. She licked her lips as though she were actually tasting this superb male specimen standing before her.

Watching her closely, Blade asked, "Have you been drinking?"

"Yes, I have," she answered, her words slurring slightly. "You are driving me to drink, Blade Landon."

He arched an eyebrow.

"Don't give me that innocent look," she scolded affectionately. "You know how I feel about you."

"Almeda . . ." he began.

Interrupting, she remarked provocatively, "After serious deliberation, I came to the conclusion that if you won't seduce me, then I shall seduce you."

Her simply-cut beige frock buttoned in front, and she quickly undid the tiny buttons. Before Blade could stop her, she slipped the garment from her shoulders and let it drop at her feet. Underneath she was naked.

For a moment Blade allowed himself the pleasure of admiring her voluptuous beauty. But although she was the picture of perfection, his passion was not aroused. Glancing away from her, he said impatiently, "Put your dress on."

Neither of them heard the front door open as Suzanne entered Blade's office. Not seeing him at the desk, she headed toward his bedroom, but before reaching it, she detected voices. The door was ajar, and when she caught sight of Almeda standing naked in the middle of the room, Suzanne gasped. She knew she shouldn't remain, but nonetheless she stood riveted to the spot, listening to their conversation.

Approaching Blade, Almeda purred sensually, "Do you like what you see, darling?"

"A man would have to be blind not to enjoy your charms," he answered with a grin, wondering just how far she would go to tempt him.

Smiling invitingly, she reached up and laced her arms about his neck, pressing her bare thighs against him. "Darling, I am on fire for you."

His arms went about her waist, and holding her close, he said thickly, "Are your loins burning?"

"Oh yes," she moaned, feeling victorious. "I am hot, unbelievably hot."

"And I have just the thing to put out your fire," he murmured, shoving her thighs to his.

Suzanne could stand no more, and whirling about, she sped quietly across the office and outside.

"Yes, darling," Almeda was crooning. "Put out my fire."

Moving swiftly, Blade swept her into his arms. She thought he was going to carry her to the bed, but when he headed in the other direction, she glanced into his face with puzzlement.

Taking her to the bathtub, Blade dropped her into it, and as water splashed over the brim and onto the floor, he asked, "Are you quite cool now, Miss Johnson?"

266

She had never been so humiliated. Furious, she cried shrewishly, "You damned cad! I hate you, Blade Landon!"

He went to the dresser and picked up his hat. On his way out the door, he told her, "In a few minutes two troopers will be here to empty the tub, so if I were you, I wouldn't dally."

Blade stopped at the Officers' Club with the intention of having only one drink, but Colonel Johnson had been present and he'd insisted on Blade joining him at his table. By the time Blade could make his excuses, he'd had three glasses of brandy instead of one.

Leaving the club, Blade headed straight for the cabin, and as he drew closer, he was surprised to see Suzanne sitting on the porch steps.

Smiling and doffing his hat, he said politely, "I'd like to talk to you. I'd have been here sooner, but I stopped at the club for a few drinks."

Suzanne glowered. How dare he come here and lie to her! She knew he hadn't been at the club! He'd been in bed with Almeda Johnson!

Puzzled by her angry expression, he asked, "Is something wrong?"

"Of course not!" she denied sharply. She wasn't about to tell him that she knew about his dalliance with Miss Johnson. Why give him the satisfaction of knowing she cared?

Resting his foot on the bottom step, he propped an arm across his bent knee. Eyeing her closely, he said gently, "I know something is bothering you."

"Oh?" She tried to sound insouciant. "Whatever would give you that idea?"

"The daggers I see flashing in your beautiful blue

eyes gives me a pretty good hint that all is not well between us."

"There has never been anything between us, and there never will be!" she seethed.

His patience wearing thin, Blade demanded gruffly, "What in the hell is wrong with you?"

"There's nothing wrong with me that your leaving won't cure!"

"Damn it, Suzanne!" he fumed. Why in the hell was she being so hard to get along with? It must be her cousin! he thought angrily. She's decided to remain loyal to him, which means she's chosen to hate me! "It's Donovan, isn't it?" he muttered testily. "You made your choice between us, and he won!"

Suzanne came very close to telling him that her cousin had nothing to do with this, but then decided it might be best to let Blade believe her present hostility stemmed from her loyalty to Patrick. It was better than letting him know she was jealous of his affair with Almeda. At least this way her pride remained intact!

Her eyes narrowed and she replied angrily, "Major Landon, will you please go away! I have no wish to see you."

Losing his temper, Blade reached out and grabbed her shoulders, jerking her to her feet. "Answer me! Is it Donovan?"

"Yes!" she lied fiercely. "I have no intention of remaining friends with the man who is determined to see him standing before a firing squad!"

"You damned little fool!" Blade growled, his grip on her arms tightening. "Your cousin is a murdering coward, and you don't owe him your loyalty!"

Wresting herself from his firm hold, she retorted, "I certainly don't owe you my loyalty! You two-timing, no-account, despicable Yankee!"

"I'm getting awfully tired of your damned insults!"

he said between gritted teeth.

"If you don't want to hear my opinions of you, then I suggest that you leave!"

"I intend to do just that!" he thundered, turning on his heel to storm away.

"And don't come back!" she yelled furiously.

"You needn't worry, madam, I won't be returning!" Blade promised angrily, heading back toward the compound.

Suzanne didn't watch him leave, but whirled about and went inside. Holding back tears, she hurried past Saul and Molly, who were sitting at the table. Reaching the bed, she fell across it. Then, hardening her heart, she swore to herself that Blade Landon had made a fool of her for the last time. She would never again give him a chance to hurt her. She'd make sure he never got that close!

Expecting Justin's visit, Molly decided to wait outside for him. As she stepped slowly to the front door, she glanced cautiously at Suzanne, who was still lying on the bed. Molly was tempted to ask her friend if something was wrong, but she had a feeling that Suzanne didn't want to talk. Molly wondered if she was still upset over Patrick, or was her present mood connected somehow to Major Landon?

Walking out to the porch, Molly spotted a man approaching. At first she thought it was Justin, but as he came closer, she recognized Captain Newcomb.

Tipping his hat, Gary said pleasantly, "Forgive me for calling unexpectedly, but I was taking a stroll when I decided to stop by and see you for a little while. I hope you don't mind."

Molly certainly didn't object to Gary's visit, but she knew Justin wouldn't be too happy about it. "You called at a bad time," she explained. "I'm expecting Justin."

Casually he remarked, "Well, in that case, I'll keep you company until he arrives."

Knowing the scout's feelings about the captain, she made an attempt to dissuade him. "That won't be necessary."

"Nonsense," he replied. He looked her over closely, finding her very desirable in her printed cotton gown. Her long auburn hair was loose, and the shiny tresses cascaded gracefully over her shoulders and down her back. As his eyes took in every inch of her slender frame, he could feel a hungry longing arousing his manhood. It had been a long time since Almeda had joined him in his bed, and he was desperately craving a woman.

Suddenly catching sight of Justin ambling in their direction, Molly said somewhat apprehensively, "Here comes Justin now."

The scout's expression was far from cordial as he regarded Captain Newcomb. Testily, he muttered, "What are you doing here?"

Gary's smile resembled a sneer. "I was merely keeping Miss O'Ryan company until you arrived."

"Well, as you can see, I arrived, so now you can leave," Justin said ill-temperedly.

Meeting the man's angry gaze, Gary replied smoothly, "How would you like it if I treated you as rudely as you are treating me?"

"How would you like it if I punched in your face?" Justin threatened.

"Justin!" Molly said reproachfully. She moved quickly down the steps and grasped his arm. "I think you owe the captain an apology."

Justin looked at her irritably, "I ain't apologizing."

"Miss O'Ryan, I am not offended," Gary said coolly. "Mr. Smith is entitled to his opinion, for what it's worth."

Before Justin could retaliate, Gary nodded politely to Molly, then walked quickly away.

Frowning impatiently, Molly fussed, "Honestly, Justin, did you have to be so rude?"

"I don't like the weasel, and I don't intend to pretend that I do. And I sure don't like him making a play for you."

"He wasn't trying to . . . to . . ." she stammered. "He simply stopped by to pay his respects."

"Respects, hell!" Justin spat gruffly.

"Justin, your jealousy is unreasonable."

He shrugged. "I can't help it, Molly. That's just the way I am. I don't like another man ogling you."

Giving up, Molly suggested, "Let's take a walk, shall we?"

Agreeing, he slipped her hand in the crook of his arm as he led her in the direction of the post's courtyard. "Molly, I got somethin' to tell you that you probably won't like hearin'."

"What's that?" she asked.

"Black Wolf, the major, and I are gonna be leaving the fort in a few days and we won't be back for three, maybe four months."

Stopping abruptly, Molly stared at him wide-eyed. "Why so long?" she cried, already missing him.

"We're riding into the Black Hills on military business, and we got so many Sioux tribes to locate that there's no way we can get back before early winter."

"Oh, Justin!" she moaned, tears smarting her eyes. "I'm going to miss you terribly."

Her tears touched him deeply, and cupping her face

271

in his hands, he kissed her forehead, her cheeks, and then her lips. "Molly, will you come to my quarters?"

They hadn't made love since that first time, and she wanted him desperately. "But you're staying in the officers' barracks, how can we . . . ?"

"I have my own private entrance. We'll just have to make sure no one sees us when I sneak you in."

"All right," she agreed, willing to take the chance that her reputation could be destroyed if they were spotted.

Holding her hand, he led her to the barracks. Luckily there was nobody around, and slipping her into his private room was easy.

He drew her into his arms, and his demanding kiss quickly aroused their passion. When he released her, she began boldly to undress him.

Her brazen behavior thrilled Justin, and he quickly helped her rid him of his clothes. When he was left standing nude before her, she knelt and took his hard maleness into her mouth. A rapturous moan sounded deep in his throat as he entwined his fingers in her long hair, pressing her closer.

Her mouth and tongue caressed him fully, causing his strong, brawny frame to tremble with uncontrollable desire. Justin's fulfillment soon began to build feverishly, and clutching her shoulders, he drew her upward and into his arms. He kissed her passionately, then with her eager assistance, her clothes were removed and dropped carelessly to the floor.

Justin's room was relatively small, and the furnishings consisted only of the bare necessities. Taking her to the narrow bed, he lifted her onto the soft mattress, then stretched out at her side.

His lips came down on hers with a pressure so aggressive that Molly gasped before moving her hand to the back of his neck, pressing him ever closer. His tongue, entering her mouth, met hers in sensual conflict.

With their mouths still joined, Justin's hand slid down to caress the tight curls between her velvet thighs. Her legs parted, and as his finger probed into her womanly crevice, Molly arched wantonly toward his touch.

"Justin," she pleaded huskily. "Please love me now. I want you so badly."

His large frame once again trembled with need as he mounted, then plunged deeply into her. Locking her ankles about his waist, Molly thrust against him, wanting his full length far inside her.

"I love you, Molly O'Ryan," he murmured.

His confession thrilled Molly, and wrapping her arms about him tightly, she cried happily, "I love you too, Justin!"

"Enough to marry me?" he asked, raising himself up to look down into her passion-flushed face.

"Oh yes," she whispered.

"We'll get married when I come back from the Black Hills."

Her smile was radiant. "Yes! . . . Yes! . . . Now stop talking, and show me how much you love me."

"The pleasure's all mine," he grinned, then encircling her waist with his strong arm, he drew her thighs up closer to his. He pounded into her rapidly, and her passion equal to his, Molly met him thrust for thrust.

Captain Newcomb strolled leisurely past Justin's quarters. He wondered if the scout was at this moment enjoying Miss O'Ryan to the fullest. A smug look crossed his handsome features. Enjoy her while you can, he told Justin silently. Because before you leave for the hills, I intend to tell her all about the woman you murdered, and when she hears about your cold-blooded act, she'll have nothing more to do with you.

Smiling vindictively, Gary headed toward the Officers' Club. He was sure it was only a matter of time before Molly O'Ryan would belong to him.

Chapter Twenty-One

The officials from Washington, D.C., and the two generals had arrived, and thanks to their distinguished presence, the fort was in tiptop condition. All the barracks had been scrubbed until they were spotless, the stables had never been cleaner, and the officers residing at the post had even polished their medals to a glossy shine. The wives and other dependents of these officers wore only their nicest clothes and had their homes cleaned to perfection, just in case they might be visited by one or more of their impressive guests. Everyone was looking forward to the upcoming ball; it would be the highlight of the season.

Suzanne was not in the least impressed by the fort's prominent visitors; as far as she was concerned, they were merely more damned Yankees! She tried to refrain from thinking about the festival ball and envisioning Blade dancing with Almeda Johnson. She hadn't spoken to Blade for days, and had managed to convince herself that she didn't even miss him.

Now, as Suzanne was on her way to the military store to buy a few supplies, she hoped she wouldn't accidently run into Blade. She didn't want to see him! He was a lying rogue, a two-timing scoundrel! Oh, how

275

she wished she could hate him!

As she drew near the store, she saw a man walking toward her. Finding him vaguely familiar, she tried to recall where she had seen him before. He came closer, and she suddenly remembered who he was.

Pausing, he touched the brim of his hat and said, "Ma'am, do you remember me?"

"Yes, I do," she replied. "Your name is Luther and you own a traders' store."

He grinned politely. "I recognized you from that time you came to my store with Major Landon and Justin Smith." He hesitated, then explained, "Ma'am, I came here to see the major, but I've been told that he and all the officers are in conference and can't be disturbed. Well, I ain't got time to linger, so would you mind givin' the major a message for me?"

Suzanne agreed, although with reluctance. She certainly preferred not to seek out Blade, but she couldn't very well refuse the man such a simple request.

"Is Major Landon still searchin' for that deserter?" he asked.

Suddenly very interested, Suzanne answered, "Yes, he is."

"Well, ma'am, a few days ago, this trapper called Indian Joe came to my store. He happened to mention that he camped one night with these two trappers who had another man with them called Donovan. Indian Joe, he knows where these two trappers' cabin is located up in the hills. He told me he had places to go and things to do, but he was plannin' to return to the hills before winter sets in. There's a good chance that he might stop here at the fort before headin' toward the Black Hills. Tell the major to be on the lookout for him. Indian Joe can take him to the cabin where Donovan is holed up. He'll probably have to pay the man to get him to agree, but Indian Joe will do most anything for the right price."

"How will Major Landon know this Indian Joe should he come to the fort?"

"He's easy to identify. He's as big as a bear and has long black hair and a full black beard. He also wears a patch over his left eye. Warn the major that he's a mean one and can't be trusted. He claims his mother was a full-blooded Kiowa, that's why he's called Indian Joe." Once again he tipped his hat. "Well, ma'am, I've got to go. You'll give the major my message, won't you?"

"Yes, of course," she assured him, knowing very well that she wouldn't breathe a word of it to Blade or anyone else.

She watched Luther as he left and walked to his horse. Mounting, he waved to her, then headed for the gates of the fort.

Indian Joe, she thought. I shouldn't have any trouble recognizing him if he comes here. If I offer him money, I wonder if he'll take me to Patrick. Surely he will. Didn't Luther say he'll do anything for the right price?

Suzanne's better judgment told her that taking off to the Black Hills with a stranger could be dangerous, but she chose to ignore her own advice. She would go to Patrick and warn him about Blade. Maybe she could even convince her cousin to return with her to Southmoor. She had been able to find only one logical explanation for Patrick's errant behavior—he had to be emotionally ill. If she could get him to come back home, surely his peaceful surroundings and her love would cure him, and he'd revert back to the Patrick she had always adored.

She knew this plan of hers was very perilous, and that she should try to devise a more sensible one. Well, she wouldn't think about that now. First she'd find Patrick, then worry about the rest.

She refused to let her thoughts linger on Blade. If she

never saw him again, then she didn't care! Besides, he didn't need her; he had Almeda Johnson!

Blade went to the Officers' Club, where he hoped to find Colonel Johnson. The conference had lasted for hours, and he was quite sure the colonel would be relaxing with a drink. Catching sight of him seated at a table with Captain Newcomb, Blade sauntered over to them. The colonel invited him to sit down, and pulling out a chair, he complied.

"Sir," Blade began, "I've decided to leave in the morning. I have already notified Justin and Black Wolf, and they assured me they would be ready."

The colonel was surprised. "But if you leave in the morning, you'll miss the ball. It's tomorrow night."

"Yes, I know," he replied.

"Almeda will be disappointed. I think she was hoping you'd escort her."

"Give her my apologies, will you? But I really think the sooner I begin this mission the better."

The colonel thought for a moment, then agreed. "Very well, you have my permission to leave. I certainly won't order you to attend a ball."

"Thank you, sir," Blade replied.

Gary, listening attentively, realized today would be his last chance to tell Molly about Justin if he wanted her to learn the truth before the scout left. All things considered, he believed it would be to his advantage for her to find out before Justin's departure. His only guarantee that she'd believe him was for her to confront Justin with what he had told her. Knowing the scout, Gary was sure he wouldn't deny what he had done.

Standing, Blade bid the two officers good day, then, anxious to prepare for his journey, he left the club

278

without bothering to have a drink.

After her unexpected meeting with Luther, Suzanne had been so tense that she had returned to the cabin. Having finally calmed herself, she decided to go to the military store and purchase the supplies she had intended to pick up when she'd run across Luther.

To reach the store, she had to pass the Officers' Club, and now, as she was walking briskly past the front door, it suddenly opened and Blade emerged.

Coming face to face with the major brought Suzanne's rapid steps to an abrupt halt.

A cold mask came over Blade's face. His tone heavy with mocking cordiality, he said, "Good afternoon, Miss Donovan."

"Major," she responded coolly, giving him a curt nod. She hoped she appeared more composed than she felt. Her heart was pounding and her knees had grown weak. She wanted to brush past him, but for some strange reason, she couldn't will herself to move.

Blade was unable to tear his gaze from hers, and as he continued to look deep into her beautiful eyes, he felt as though he were losing himself in their azure pools. God, he still loved her! The revelation made him angry, but he was more angry with himself than with Suzanne. He had no patience with this weakness within him where she was concerned. Damn it, he'd get over this defiant little vixen if it was the last thing he ever did in his life!

The silence hovering between them was unnerving to Suzanne, and Blade's piercing gaze was making her feel flushed. In an effort to end the uneasy moment, she stammered, "I . . . I understand you'll be leaving soon and will be gone for three or four months."

"Yes," he replied. "In fact, the others and I are leaving in the morning."

"In the morning!" she exclaimed impulsively. "But

you'll miss the ball!"

"So?" he said uninterested.

Imagining how upset Almeda must be, she smiled a little wickedly. Sounding nonchalant, she murmured, "It's too bad you'll have to miss such a gallant affair."

Fighting an overwhelming urge to take her into his arms and kiss her sultry lips, Blade stepped to one side, nodded brusquely, then mumbled, "Goodbye, madam. I'll see you when I return in a few months."

Without further ado, he turned and stalked away.

Watching his departure, Suzanne had no control over the tears that flowed forth to sting her eyes. She knew she might very well be seeing him for the last time, for if things worked out with Patrick, when Blade returned to the fort she wouldn't be here. I'll always love him! she thought with heartache.

Her vision was blurred, and she wiped the tears from her eyes. As she watched Blade open the door to his office, then step inside and out of sight, she whispered somberly, "Goodbye, Blade."

Dusk was blanketing the fort when Captain Newcomb climbed the short flight of steps leading to the cabin's door. He knocked a couple of times and was pleased when Molly responded.

Holding the door open wide, she said with surprise, "Captain Newcomb, I certainly wasn't expecting a visit from you." She hoped the man didn't plan to stay long, for she knew Justin would be arriving soon.

His smile was engaging. "Miss O'Ryan, may I talk to you privately for a moment?"

"Yes, of course," she answered hesitantly.

The captain moved aside as she walked out to the porch and closed the door behind her. Gazing at him questioningly, she asked, "Why do you wish to talk to me alone?"

Gary had been rehearsing this meeting in his mind all afternoon and knew exactly what he intended to say, and also how he intended to lead up to the shocking conclusion. Forcing emotion into his voice, and feigning a hopeless expression of love, he said ardently, "Molly . . . I'm sorry, I mean Miss O'Ryan, I must tell you what is in my heart. I can no longer keep my true feelings repressed." He reached over and grasped her hands. "I am in love with you."

Molly was totally unprepared for his revelation. She liked the captain and certainly preferred not to hurt him, but in this case she had no other choice. Gently she drew her hands from his. "Captain Newcomb, I am very flattered by your confession, but I am in love with Justin."

He successfully mastered a look of resignation. "Then I have no choice but to bow gracefully out of the picture and concede to the better man." He watched her face very closely as he added carefully, "But I must say, I am surprised that you can love a man like Justin Smith." Raising his eyebrows, he added, "Considering the man's past."

Molly was confused. "What do you mean?"

He gave a casual shrug. "I just didn't think a gentle lady like yourself could love a man who murdered his wife."

"What!" she gasped in disbelief.

He appeared to be surprised. "You mean he hasn't told you?"

"Told me what?" she demanded.

"Justin Smith killed his wife, and afterward he didn't even have the decency to bury her. He set fire to their home and let it burn down over his wife's dead body."

It was a moment before Molly could find her voice. "I . . . I don't believe you!" she choked.

"I'm sorry, Miss O'Ryan, but the story is true. If you don't believe me, ask Justin."

"But why would he do something so horrible?" she cried.

"Well, I heard it from Sergeant Boswell. He isn't at the fort anymore. He retired last year. But the sergeant knew all about Justin and his wife. It seems Justin's wife was a full-blooded Comanche. They had a small homestead in Texas. There was a settlement close by, and Justin had gone there to buy some supplies. When he returned home, his wife told him that she was leaving him for another man. Justin was insanely jealous, and he went into a rage, shot his wife, and then burned down the cabin. Some of the men in the settlement saw the smoke from the fire, and rode out. Justin told them what he had done. Since his wife was an Indian, these men—and a few of them were Texas Rangers—didn't care if he killed his wife. Most of them believed all Indians should be dead."

Molly felt faint, her legs weak. She tottered precariously, and quickly Gary took her into his arms. Needing his support, she leaned against him.

It was at this moment that Justin appeared. The sight of Molly in Gary's embrace sent his jealousy flowing full force. Leaping up the porch steps, Justin grabbed the captain's arm and jerked him around. He had his fist doubled and was about to swing, when Molly shouted frantically, "Justin, no!"

Letting his arm drop back to his side, Justin seethed, "Captain, get away from me before I lose my temper and knock you to hell and back!"

Gary had completed what he had set out to do, and deciding he had handled it very successfully, he was quite pleased with himself as he obliged Justin by leaving.

As Gary was walking proudly away, Justin turned

his wrath on Molly. "I was right about you all along! You don't think I'm good enough for you! Why in the hell would you want to marry a scout when you can be an officer's wife?"

His false accusations angered Molly. "How dare you speak like that to me!"

"It's the truth, isn't it?" he shouted.

"No!" she cried.

"Then why were you in his arms?"

Molly turned away from his furious gaze. Trying to compose herself, she took a couple of deep breaths. Slowly she returned her gaze to his. "Justin, did you murder your wife?"

Her question hit Justin hard, and he staggered backward as though her words had been a forceful blow. He had meant to tell Molly about his wife, but so far he hadn't been able to bring himself to talk about her.

"Well, did you?" she demanded, more harshly than she had intended.

His brow beaded with nervous perspiration, and he wiped his arm across his forehead. He should have known she'd learn about his wife's death. Although it had happened fifteen years ago, it was still a story that people liked to gossip about. He had believed no one on the fort except for Blade knew about it, but apparently he had been wrong. Obviously Captain Newcomb had heard all about it.

Justin's reluctance to answer her sent a cold chill down Molly's spine. Good Lord, the captain was right! Justin had actually killed his wife, otherwise wouldn't he be claiming his innocence?

"My God!" Molly moaned. "You murdered her, didn't you? You went into a jealous rage and killed your wife!"

"You've already got me tried and found guilty,

haven't you?" he sneered.

"Aren't you guilty?" she cried.

"I killed my wife, and then I burned our home with her body inside." A furious glare came to his dark eyes as he yelled angrily, "Is that what you wanted to hear?"

Her hand flying to her mouth to hold back a gasp, Molly said hoarsely, "I never want to see you again!"

"You can rest easy, ma'am, 'cause I won't try to see you. As far as I'm concerned, we're through." He paused, and his eyes stared deeply into hers. "Molly O'Ryan, you think you know me, but you don't."

He took his departure with haste, leaving Molly standing on the porch feeling as though she had just lived some horrible, unbelievable nightmare.

Chapter Twenty-Two

The weather was unseasonably cold for the middle of November, and Suzanne spent most of her time inside the warm cabin, except for her twice daily walks about the fort. Once in the morning and again in the afternoon, she always made it a point to take a stroll about the compound, where she hoped to spot a man who would fit Indian Joe's description. Failing to find him, she'd return to the cabin still determined not to give up her quest. Molly and Saul knew nothing of this, and Suzanne didn't plan to involve them, for she knew they would insist that she not go through with it. They would tell her it was too dangerous and foolhardy, and although she was perfectly aware they would be right, she nonetheless was determined to ask Indian Joe to take her to Patrick. She must find her cousin before Blade did, so she could help him escape! Her conscience nagged at her, telling her Patrick deserved to be court-martialed, but she couldn't be objective where her cousin was concerned; she loved him too much.

During the three months since Blade had been away from the fort, Suzanne had missed him terribly. She tried not to let her thoughts dwell on him, but against her will they continually drifted to the major. If only she could make herself stop loving him! But she realized sadly that he was a part of her heart forever.

Suzanne was not the only one longing for a lost love; Molly was also grieving. She had decided not to confide in Suzanne and Saul about Justin. How could she bring herself to tell them that the man had actually murdered his wife? It was so horrible she couldn't bear even to think about it, let alone discuss it. So she had simply told Saul and Suzanne that things had not worked out between herself and Justin, and they had decided not to see each other anymore. Since Justin's departure, Captain Newcomb had become a frequent visitor to the cabin, and although Molly always welcomed him, the young, dashing captain could not ease the pain in Molly's heart. She still loved the rugged scout in spite of what he had done, but she felt as though she could never marry a man who was capable of cold-blooded murder.

Both Suzanne and Molly pretended all was well with their lives, but their facades didn't fool Saul. He knew they were deeply troubled, and he was quite sure their unhappiness was related to Major Landon and Justin Smith. The old man wished fervently that this trip to Fort Laramie had never been undertaken. It had brought nothing but heartache upon heartache. He hoped with the coming of spring he could somehow convince Suzanne to give up their search for Patrick and return to Southmoor. Saul no longer wished to see his former master; he preferred to remember him as he had been before the war. The servant was emotionally weary and emotionally defeated, and he longed to go home.

*　　　*　　　*

The wind was blowing from the north, and drawing her coat tighter about her, Suzanne shivered as the bitter chill seeped through her wrap. She was standing in the middle of the compound, and this vantage point made it easy for her to study the people moving about in the large courtyard. She had been watching for over thirty minutes, hoping desperately to spot Indian Joe. Finally, deciding it was too cold to remain outdoors, she gave up. Besides, there had been an influenza outbreak at the fort, and she knew standing about in the frigid wind was not a good idea. She certainly didn't want to fall ill.

Suzanne had started toward the cabin when suddenly she noticed a rider entering the fort. He was a huge figure of a man, dressed in buckskin trousers and a fur jacket. His long black hair hung halfway down his back and a full, scraggly beard covered his face. He happened to glance toward Suzanne, and when he did, she gasped sharply. The man was wearing a patch over his left eye!

He was riding a gray stallion and leading a pack mule and an extra horse. He headed for the military store, and Suzanne quickly followed him.

She caught up to him as he was dismounting. He was a threatening presence, and Suzanne asked shakily, "Are you Indian Joe?"

He regarded her suspiciously. "I might be. Why do you want to know?"

"If you are Indian Joe, then I need to talk to you."

"About what?" he asked tersely.

"Before I can explain, I need to know if you are Indian Joe."

He relaxed, and placing an arm across his saddle, he leaned in a leisurely way against his horse. "I'm Indian Joe," he mumbled dryly.

Suzanne's heart raced. "I understand you camped one night with three men, and one of them was called Donovan."

"So?"

"I also understand that you know where these men are staying in the Black Hills."

"You understand a lot of things that ain't none of your business, don't you?" he grumbled.

"But it is my business," she quickly informed him. "Donovan is my cousin, and I have traveled all the way from Natchez to find him."

"What in the hell do you want from me?" He was beginning to sound impatient.

"I want you to take me to him. I'll pay you, of course. I don't have a lot of money, but I can offer what should be a reasonable amount."

"What's reasonable?" he asked.

"Fifty dollars?" she offered, knowing guiltily that it would leave her and the others almost broke.

"Can you be ready to leave at dawn?"

"Yes," she replied unhesitant.

"Let's get one thing straight, madam. I won't be responsible for you. Winter is settin' in, and I can't let no woman slow me down. If you can't keep up, I'll leave you behind."

"All right," she agreed, wishing she was as courageous as she sounded.

"I'll take care of the supplies," he said gruffly. "You just be at the front gates in the morning with your own bedroll and horse."

"I don't have a horse," she told him.

He thought for a moment, then decided, "You can ride my extra horse, but if somethin' should happen to either one of the horses and we're down to one animal, you get left behind."

She nodded her agreement.

"I don't have no extra saddle, so you'll have to give me some money to buy one."

"If you'll go ahead and purchase the saddle, I'll pay you back tomorrow."

"All right, but if you ain't at those gates at dawn, I'll leave without you. Like I done said, you ain't gonna slow me down."

"I'll be there," she promised.

"Make sure you are," he grumbled, then without further words, he left her and entered the store.

Suzanne stood numbly for a moment before willing herself to move. As she walked toward the cabin, her thoughts began to churn turbulently. This quest was indeed a dangerous one, and could very well cost her her life. If she became ill or injured, Indian Joe would callously leave her alone in the wilderness to fend for herself. He'll even leave me if something happens to one of the horses! she thought bitterly. What kind of unfeeling monster is he?

Squaring her shoulders and lifting her chin bravely, she told herself firmly, Well, I'm perfectly healthy, and I'll just have to be extra careful and not suffer a mishap. As her steps took her closer to the cabin, her thoughts added—and pray that nothing happens to either horse!

Suzanne, afraid she'd sleep past dawn, had forced herself to stay awake all night. She slept in the huge bed with Molly, and although she had gone to bed with the pretense of falling asleep, she had not closed her eyes through the long night. An hour before daylight, she slipped quietly from the bed and gathered her belongings, which she had packed soon after talking to Indian Joe. Molly and Saul had been away from the cabin when she'd returned from her meeting with the trapper, and taking advantage of their absence,

289

Suzanne had hastily packed and then hidden the few things she planned to take with her.

Now, quickly putting on her trousers, shirt, and boots, she hoped desperately that Molly wouldn't awaken. Going to where her coat hung beside the front door, she slipped it on. She wished it were a little heavier, but it had been designed for winters in the South, not for the frigid weather in the Black Hills.

Suddenly, realizing she couldn't leave without an explanation, Suzanne stepped furtively to the table and her writing tablet, pen, and inkwell. Hurriedly she jotted a note to Molly and Saul, then, rising, she took the bundle with her belongings and stole undetected from the cabin.

The eastern sky was just beginning to lighten as Suzanne walked swiftly toward the main gates.

The two guards on duty noticed her approach, and wondering why Miss Donovan was up and about so early, they exchanged curious glances.

Suzanne reached the gates at the same moment as Indian Joe. He was riding his gray stallion, and was leading the pack mule as well as the saddled horse for Suzanne.

She started to say good morning, but Indian Joe interrupted shortly, "Tie your bundle on the mule."

Quickly she did as he ordered.

"You owe me ten dollars," he remarked. "The saddle is used, that's why it didn't cost too much. I'll also take the fifty you promised."

Pushing aside her coat, Suzanne reached into the pocket of her trousers and withdrew the money, which she handed to the trapper.

He made a quick count, then shoved the bills into his jacket pocket. "Get on your horse," he said bluntly. "We're already a-wastin' time."

As she was mounting, Indian Joe asked the two

soldiers to open the gates. They did so unquestioningly; the trapper and Miss Donovan were guests at the fort and free to leave whenever they pleased.

Keeping her horse close behind the trapper's, Suzanne rode through the opened gates. She glanced back over her shoulder, her eyes quickly surveying the quiet compound. She had a fleeting impulse to dismount and run back to the safety of the fort, but mustering her courage, she turned her gaze forward. She mustn't allow her resolve to falter. She would travel into the Black Hills and find Patrick!

Molly knocked loudly on the storage room door, which had been converted into a bedroom for Saul. "Saul, wake up!" she called in alarm.

Awaking instantly, the servant slipped quickly into his pants and opened the door. "What's wrong, Miz Molly?"

"This!" she said, handing him Suzanne's note.

He read it hastily. "Good Lord!" he moaned. "I can't believe Miz Suzanne done went and done somethin' so foolish!"

"Neither can I," Molly agreed. "What do you think we should do?"

"I don't know," he said, concerned.

In the note Suzanne had asked them not to let the army know where she had gone. She was afraid Colonel Johnson would order a company of soldiers to pursue them, and then force the trapper to take them to Patrick.

"Do you suppose we should go against Suzanne's wishes and tell Colonel Johnson?" Molly asked.

Saul shook his head. "No, ma'am, I reckon we'd better not. If we do that, Miz Suzanne will never forgive us."

Molly knew he was right. Besides, if they were to notify the army and they captured Patrick, she and Saul would then become indirectly responsible for Patrick's arrest. If it ended in Patrick's execution, how could either of them ever live with what they had done?

Wringing her hands apprehensively, Molly groaned, "Oh, God, I hope nothing happens to Suzanne!"

"So do I," Saul said worriedly.

Indian Joe set an arduous pace, and Suzanne found it terribly difficult to keep up with him without complaining. She now knew that when he had said he intended to waste no time, he had not spoken lightly. He didn't even allow a lunch break, but insisted that they eat cold jerky while still moving onward.

The trapper was a man of few words, and their conversations were short and to the point, which suited Suzanne. She sensed intuitively that Indian Joe was the kind of man she'd just as soon not become too well acquainted with.

By the time dusk began to cloak the vast landscape, Suzanne was feeling extremely fatigued, mostly she supposed from lack of sleep; she hadn't slept a wink the night before. She hoped Indian Joe would decide soon to set up camp, but it was another two hours before the trapper pulled up and told her it was time to stop.

Although Suzanne was anxious to get down from her horse, her weariness caused her to dismount slowly. Feeling flushed, she wiped a hand across her brow and was surprised to feel that she was quite warm. Surely she wasn't running a fever! I'm only tired, she told herself reassuringly. After a good night's sleep, I'll be as good as new.

Feeling Indian Joe's scrutiny, she glanced in his direction. He was watching her closely. Had he noticed her discomfort? Did he think she was ill? Was he considering leaving her behind? Suzanne knew that if he thought she couldn't keep up, he'd have no qualms about deserting her.

Quickly she straightened up and began unsaddling her horse, moving as briskly as she could. As she placed the heavy saddle on the ground, she caste Indian Joe a cursory glance and was relieved to find that he was no longer watching her.

Indian Joe set about starting a fire, and when he had it blazing Suzanne huddled deep into her coat and went to sit beside the flames.

"How far is it to the foot of the Black Hills?" she asked.

"We traveled about fifty miles today, so we got close to fifty more to go."

"How far is it to the cabin where my cousin is staying?"

"After we get into the Hills, we still have about three days' travelin' time before reaching the cabin."

Four days altogether, Suzanne thought. She was sure Indian Joe intended to resume his unrelenting pace and wondered gravely if she'd be able to keep up. I have to keep up, she decided firmly. I have no other choice.

Leaving the fire, Indian Joe went to the pack mule and untied Suzanne's bundle. Returning, he pitched it to her. She had her things wrapped in a blanket, and she unrolled it and removed her belongings, then draped the blanket about her shoulders. The wind was beginning to pick up speed and blew gustily, its cold force penetrating.

Huddled inside her blanket, Suzanne watched silently as the trapper began to cook their supper. He also prepared a pot of coffee, and the aroma from the boiling brew filled the air.

Suzanne was feeling somewhat ill, and wrapping her blanket more closely around her, she lay back on the ground.

She placed her hand on her brow and was concerned to feel that she was still warm. Could she possibly have contracted influenza? The thought sent her heart racing with fear.

"You want some coffee?" Indian Joe asked suddenly, intruding on Suzanne's worried thoughts.

In an effort to cover her weakness, she forced herself to sit up energetically. "Yes," she answered brightly. "I'd love a cup of coffee."

Handing it to her, he looked at her closely. "Are you feelin' all right?"

"I'm just fine," she answered crisply.

He stared at her for a moment as though he weren't convinced, then looking away, he muttered, "Just remember, if you don't keep up, you get left behind."

"Yes, I know," she said somewhat irritably. "You needn't worry, I won't fall behind."

His unexpected grin leered coldly. "I ain't worried. Whether you make it or not don't matter none to me."

She lowered her gaze to her cup and took a drink of the hot brew. In the morning I'll feel much better, she tried to reassure herself. I can't get sick. I just can't!

Chapter Twenty-Three

Gary had been away from the fort on military duty, and Molly hadn't seen him since Suzanne left with Indian Joe. On the third evening following Suzanne's departure the captain returned to Fort Laramie, and immediately after reporting to Colonel Johnson, he paid a visit to Molly.

Upon Gary's arrival, Saul excused himself and went to his bedroom so that Molly could be alone with her caller. Now, sitting at the table with Molly, Gary asked with mild interest, "Where is Miss Donovan?"

Averting her gaze from his, Molly quickly told the story she and Saul had agreed on. "Suzanne left the fort with a trapper. We don't know the man's name or her reason for leaving with him. She went away early in the morning before Saul and I were awake, simply left a note saying she'd explain everything when she returned."

Gary's curiosity was now genuinely aroused. "Good Lord!" he exclaimed, incredulous. "Why do you suppose she did something like that?"

"I don't know," Molly mumbled uneasily. She was uncomfortable with dishonesty.

"Do you think it has anything to do with Trooper Donovan?"

"I don't think so," she replied unhesitantly.

"If there's a chance that she learned Donovan's whereabouts, the colonel should be notified."

"If her departure is connected with Patrick, I'm sure she'd have said so in the note she left for Saul and me."

"But what other reason could she possibly have for taking off with a trapper?"

"Please, Gary, I'd rather not discuss it. I am terribly worried about Suzanne, and talking about her only upsets me more."

"Of course," he said considerately. Leaning back in his chair, Gary looked at her thoughtfully. She was becoming quite a challenge to him. He was used to women going out of their way to vie for his attention and responding ardently when he returned their affection. But Molly seemed totally uninterested in him as a suitor, and perfectly content to keep their relationship merely friendly. He wondered if she was still smitten with Justin Smith. It went beyond his comprehension why she would still long for the scout when he himself had made it apparent that he was romantically interested in her. Initially Gary had set out to court Molly simply because he longed for a wife to share his bed on a permanent basis, but now he had come to realize that he wanted her more than he had ever wanted any woman. Perhaps it was because she was the only woman he had ever truly desired that he couldn't have. He wasn't sure how he had become so enamored with her, but he did know that he must have her. Almeda had resumed her habit of visiting him in the privacy of his quarters, and although she always satisfied him sexually, she hadn't cooled his need for Molly.

Longing to take her in his arms, Gary rose from his chair, took her hands, and urged her to her feet. He embraced her carefully, then bending his head, he pressed his lips to hers.

Accepting his kiss, Molly hoped desperately that he could arouse the passion within her that Justin always had. Her lips parted beneath his, and when he pulled her flush against him, she didn't object. She could feel his male hardness pressed firmly between her thighs, and she waited for the fiery desire, but it failed to ignite. Gently she moved out of his arms. It was no use; she still loved Justin too much to want another man.

Gary, unaware that she had felt no desire while in his embrace, asked pleadingly, "Molly, will you marry me?"

His proposal took her by surprise. "Marry you!" she gasped.

"I love you," he murmured, and for a moment was astonished to realize that he had spoken the truth. For the first time in his life he was actually in love.

She didn't want to hurt him, and replied gently, "I'm not in love with you, Gary. I'm sorry."

His disappointment was sincere. "With a little more time, maybe you can learn to love me."

She smiled tenderly. "Maybe."

"Will you at least think about marrying me before you give me a final answer?"

"Yes, I'll think about it," she murmured. Maybe I should marry Gary, she thought. I'm not in love with him, but where has love ever gotten me? I loved Patrick, and he repaid my love by deserting me. Then I fell even more in love with Justin, only to learn he was not the man I believed him to be. Love! I can do very well without it.

Taking her back into his arms, Gary promised, "I won't pressure you, Molly. But I will be waiting anxiously for your answer."

"Gary," she said collectedly, "there is no reason for you to wait for my answer. I can give it to you tonight.

Yes, I'll marry you."

Elated, he asked, "When?"

"When Suzanne returns," she answered.

Hugging her tightly, he exclaimed, "Molly, you have made me very happy!"

She tried to return his enthusiasm, and she might have succeeded if memories of Justin Smith hadn't suddenly tugged at her heart.

As Suzanne and Indian Joe traveled farther into the Black Hills, the trapper's uncommunicative nature abruptly changed and he became quite talkative about men who had journeyed to the hills looking for gold. It was not easy for Suzanne to listen attentively. She had a natural curiosity about the gold, but she knew now that she had contracted influenza, and her illness made it very difficult for her to concentrate on the information that Indian Joe was giving so freely.

Often Suzanne's attention would fade as she suffered in silence, but nonetheless she was able to grasp most of what the trapper was telling her.

According to Indian Joe, the first prospecting party to venture into the hills consisted of seven men, one of them Ezra Kind. They stayed a year, found gold, and perished. When all had died except for Kind, he had scraped a record on a slab of buff sandstone, which read: "Got all the gold we could carry . . . Our ponies all got by Indians . . . I have lost my gun and nothing to eat . . . Indians hunting me." It was, ironically, the man's epitaph.

Continuing his stories, Indian Joe then claimed that in 1852 a prospecting party of thirty men had gone gold hunting in the hills. Eight men came out and reported gold; the rest were never heard of again.

The trapper continued talking, but Suzanne was no

longer listening. Her illness was making her feel terrible, and she was also extremely tired. The sun had set two hours ago; still Indian Joe had kept pushing onward. Were they never going to stop for the night? Suzanne wondered anxiously. She knew if he didn't soon set up camp, she'd collapse from fever and exhaustion.

As though he had read her thoughts, Indian Joe pulled up and mumbled tonelessly, "Well, I reckon it's time to call it a night."

Reining in her horse, Suzanne sighed gratefully and dismounted. She felt weak, and for a moment, she leaned against her horse. Brushing a hand across her brow, she was alarmed to feel that her fever was raging.

"You look flushed," Indian Joe remarked, ambling toward her. He eyed her closely. "You're sick, aren't ya? You've been sick ever since we left the fort, but so far you've managed to overcome it."

"I'm just feeling a little under the weather," she replied casually. "I'm sure I'll be all right tomorrow."

"I doubt it," he grumbled, taking the bridle reins from her hands. "I'll bed down both horses," he said gruffly.

They were in a wooded area, and Suzanne went slowly over to a large tree, sat, and leaned back against its wide trunk. She knew she should offer to start a campfire, but she could barely stand, let alone handle chores.

The night air was icy cold, and she was chilled to the bone. She wrapped her coat closer about her, but the frigid wind penetrated her wrap. Shivering, she drew up her legs and nestled her head on her knees.

She could hear Indian Joe as he set about making a fire and preparing their evening meal. Suzanne was too sick to eat, and said softly, "Don't cook anything for me. I think I'll just get my bedroll and go to sleep."

The trapper watched her as she rose shakily to her feet and went to the pack mule to get her blanket. When he was at the fort, he'd heard about the influenza outbreak. He was sure his traveling companion had caught the contagious disease, and had no doubt that by tomorrow morning she wouldn't be up to continuing this journey. He shook his head, allowing himself a fleeting moment of compassion. Too bad she had to go and get sick, he mused somberly. But his concern was gone as quickly as it had appeared. Well, I warned her if she couldn't keep up, I'd leave her behind. Mumbling below his breath, he remarked, "So be it."

Sitting about the campfire, the three men drank their coffee. Periodically one of them would make some comment, but mostly they were silent. The travelers were tired and anxious to complete their mission. They had one last stop to make, then Blade and Justin would return to the fort; Black Wolf planned to journey to his father's village.

"We should reach Iron Kettle's encampment about noon tomorrow," Black Wolf remarked.

"The old chief has always tried to avoid war with the soldiers, so we should have no problems getting him to agree to the treaty," Blade replied.

A skeptical and somewhat bitter frown crossed the Sioux warrior's face. "How long do you think the army will abide by this treaty?"

Blade shrugged. "I don't know, but for now, it will mean peace, and that's better than war."

Black Wolf agreed. "We must prolong peace for as long as we can."

"Do you want me to take the first watch?" Justin asked the major.

"All right," Blade answered. He watched his good

friend as he picked up his rifle, then ambled a short way from the fire to take a protective stance close to the camp. Justin had been unusually quiet on their trip into the Black Hills, and Blade wondered if the man's unwonted behavior had anything to do with Molly O'Ryan.

Getting to his feet, Black Wolf said with fatigue, "Well, I guess we'd better get some sleep."

Standing, Blade said, "I think I'll talk to Justin for a few minutes before turning in."

He lit a cheroot before joining the scout. Blade didn't speak immediately, but merely stood beside his friend as he leisurely puffed on his cigar. Then he asked quietly, "What's wrong, Justin?"

"What makes you think anything is wrong?"

"If you don't want to talk about it, then just say so, but don't try to deny that you aren't troubled."

Justin propped his rifle against a tree, and leaning against the trunk, he crossed his arms over his chest. Glancing up at the sky, he remarked, "Looks like it's goin' to snow."

"It'll get here by morning," Blade replied.

The scout pulled up the collar of his fur jacket, then drew his hat down so that it protected his bare ears from the cold air. Finally deciding to respond to Blade's inquiry, he said in a lowered voice, "Somehow Captain Newcomb heard about my wife's death, and he told Molly."

"Surely you told her what really happened," Blade said.

"I guess I should have, but I didn't," Justin muttered flatly.

"Why didn't you?"

"Damn it, Blade, if the woman really loved me, she wouldn't have confronted me in the way she did. She already had me tried and found guilty, so I saw no

301

reason to tell her otherwise."

"Sometimes you can be as stubborn as an ornery mule."

Justin chuckled. "Look who's talkin' about being stubborn." He paused, then continued, "Well, we'll be back at the fort in about a week; maybe then I'll explain to Molly what actually happened with my wife."

Blade dropped his cheroot, and as he pressed it into the ground with the heel of his boot, he said good night to Justin and headed for his bedroll, which was placed close to the fire. He lay down, and drawing up his blanket, he gazed dreamily into the darting flames. As usual, his thoughts wandered to Suzanne. He wondered if she had missed him, for he certainly had missed her. Would she be happy to see him again, or would she greet him with hostility? Considering her obstinate nature, he mused, she'll probably be her usual defiant self. Damn, why must she be so hard to get along with!

Turning to lie on his side, Blade resolutely cleared his thoughts of Suzanne. He needed his sleep, and if he continued to think about her, he'd remain wide awake.

The clouds were heavy in the early morning sky, and the northern wind was blowing briskly. The first winter storm of the season started gently as it released small snowflakes upon the land.

Cuddled inside her bedroll, Suzanne was awakened slowly by tiny drops of snow falling with feather lightness across her fevered cheeks. Drawing the cover up over her face, she shivered as the cold continued to seep through the blanket.

She tried to fall back asleep, but it was no use, she was too chilled, and her body was aching with influenza. Sitting up weakly, she looked toward the spot where she expected to see Indian Joe sleeping.

Finding him gone, she gasped sharply as her eyes quickly scanned her surroundings. The horses were missing too.

Falling back on her bedroll, Suzanne groaned. My God, Indian Joe had carried out his threat and had left her to fend for herself! Tears smarted her eyes, but she bravely fought them back. She couldn't have the luxury of feeling sorry for herself, she must concentrate wholeheartedly on self-preservation. Survival! Dear God, how was she going to survive alone here in the wilderness?

Slowly she sat up once again. Could she find her way back to Fort Laramie? Walking, it would take her several days to reach the post, and considering her condition, she'd do well to walk a mile, let alone over a hundred of them.

Flinging off the blanket, she was about to get to her feet when suddenly she recalled that yesterday Indian Joe had told her there was a Sioux village three miles to the north. Now, thinking back, she remembered that the man had made a point of letting her know that the Indians in this camp were relatively peaceful. When he was telling me about these Indians, he knew he was going to desert me, she thought. He decided to let me know about this village so I would have a place to go.

Three miles to the north, she continued thinking, getting to her feet and gazing in that direction. The snowflakes were now becoming larger, and they brushed against her face. Did she have the strength to walk three miles? If it started snowing heavily, could she possibly trek through the fallen snow and reach this Sioux village?

Well, she told herself, standing here pondering isn't going to get me any answers.

Her mind set, she started packing her meager belongings. She knew she must hurry, but she was so weak that her movements were agonizingly slow.

When at last she had completed the task, she tucked the rolled-up blanket beneath her arm. She headed north, causing the gusty wind to blow directly into her face. Snow was beginning to accumulate, and she hoped her boots would keep her feet dry. Her coat did little to protect her from the frigid elements, and as she forced herself to push onward, she wished she had remembered to bring a hat.

The snow was now falling thickly, making Suzanne's desperate plight even more difficult. Her ears were so cold that they ached. She stopped and unrolled the blanket, and letting her few belongings drop to the ground, she swept the blanket about her, drawing it up to cover her head. She wondered how long she had been walking. It seemed like hours, but she had a feeling it hadn't been nearly that long. She was so exhausted that she had to compel herself to keep putting one foot in front of the other.

The land was eerily quiet, and Suzanne felt as though she were the only living creature in this immense wilderness. The white precipitation clung to the sides of the limestone hills, and to the tops of the pines and spruces that grew abundantly in the area.

Suzanne, walking with her eyes lowered, didn't see the wild animal who was stealthily watching her every move. The beast was in her path, and curious about this figure trespassing on his habitat, he held his ground and didn't run.

The woman was not aware of the mountain lion's presence until suddenly he let loose with a low, vicious snarl.

Her heart jumping with fear, Suzanne looked up and gasped convulsively as she stared at the dangerous creature who was eyeing her hostilely. He was a big lion, weighing close to two hundred pounds. The animal's yellow-brown coat stood out plainly against the snowy background. It had a slender body, and its head and ears were small. The cat's long, thick tail moved back and forth before it bounded forward on its powerful legs.

Suzanne screamed, her piercing cry echoing resoundly. She whirled and began to run, and daring to glance over her shoulder, was petrified to see that the mountain lion was following.

The animal, having an innate caution of man, was merely playing cat and mouse with Suzanne. He wasn't sure if he wanted actually to attack this intruder, but he had no intention of letting her out of his sight.

Panic-stricken, Suzanne was running blindly, and not seeing the protruding tree root, she tripped over it. She took a hard tumble, and the jolt jarred her fever-racked body. She made a wild attempt to get back up, but her wobbly legs refused to support her weight, and she collapsed.

She was trying once again to make it to her feet when all at once, a rifle shot rang out loudly.

Blade and the others had been close by and had heard Suzanne's scream. The moment Blade had spotted the mountain lion, he had drawn his rifle and had sent a shot over the animal's head. He had hoped a warning shot would deter the lion, but if it hadn't, his second shot would have been a fatal one.

Frightened, the animal quickly changed direction and headed lithely for the protection afforded by the dense shrubbery filling the hillside.

Blade rode his horse over to the figure lying on the ground. He dismounted hastily, and kneeling, he asked, "Are you all right?"

Suzanne was lying face down, and he gently turned

her over onto her back. Suzanne was the last person he had expected to see.

"Good God!" he cried.

"Blade," she whispered huskily, tears streaming from her eyes. "Oh God, Blade."

Using what little strength she had left, she lifted herself up and slipped her arms about his neck. He held her close against his chest. He placed his cheek next to hers, but as he did, he realized she was burning with fever. He started to question her, but when he looked down into her face, he saw that she was either asleep or had passed out.

As he was lifting her into his arms, Black Wolf and Justin approached. Recognizing Suzanne, the scout exclaimed, "What in the hell is she doing in these parts?"

"I wish I knew," Blade answered.

"I'd better have a look around," Black Wolf decided. "She might not be alone."

"I'd better go with you," Justin offered. "Blade, can you get her to Iron Kettle's village by yourself?"

"I can make it," he remarked.

Justin took Suzanne from Blade's arms so that he could mount his horse, then when the major was seated, he handed her back up to him.

Justin's brow furrowed with puzzlement. "I wonder why she's here in the Black Hills."

A hard, resentful glare came to Blade's eyes. "I'd be willing to bet it has something to do with her no-good, murdering cousin!"

Chapter Twenty-Four

Suzanne awakened slowly. She realized she was on horseback and was being held gently yet securely by a pair of strong arms. Her eyes fluttered open and she looked up into Blade's face.

He was watching her, and a tender smile tugged at the corners of his mouth, causing his moustache to curl on the ends. "How are you feeling?"

"Terrible," she groaned. "There is an influenza epidemic at the fort, and it seems I was one of the unlucky ones who caught it."

Blade had her wrapped warmly in a blanket, and he carefully peeled part of it away from her face so that he could check her fever. "You're still running a high temperature," he said, worried.

"Where are we going?" she asked.

"To Iron Kettle's village. We'll be there in a few minutes."

Held firmly against his chest, she glanced about quickly. The snow was now less heavy, falling in flurries. "Are we alone?" she asked.

"Black Wolf and Justin were with me when we found you. But they stayed behind to look over the area in case you had anyone with you."

When she didn't respond, he persisted, "Were you by yourself?"

"Since this morning," she murmured, nestling her head against his shoulder. She was sure he'd now start interrogating her. She couldn't tell him about Indian Joe! If she did, he'd probably leave her at the Sioux village, then try to pick up the trapper's trail, and if he caught Indian Joe, he'd make the man take him to Patrick!

"Who were you traveling with until this morning?" Blade demanded. "And why are you in these hills?"

Suzanne knew she couldn't very well skirt the issue; Blade would insist on a direct answer. Deciding there was only one option open to her, she said unyieldingly, "I'm not going to tell you who I was with, or why I'm here, so you may as well stop questioning me."

Blade's anger was quickly aroused, and only Suzanne's illness kept him from losing his temper. "You were looking for Donovan, weren't you?"

"Please don't give me the third degree. You'll merely be wasting your breath. I'm not answering."

Blade scowled. A feeling of resentment welled up within him; he wished she was just half as loyal to him as she was to her unscrupulous cousin.

Iron Kettle's village was located in a glade situated between two towering hills, and as they crested the ridge, Blade pulled up his horse and looked down at the dozens of tepees, which were arranged methodically in a large circle by a river bank. The Sioux dwellings were always set up according to family prestige.

Blade expressed a worried sigh. He wasn't sure if the chief would allow Suzanne to stay in his village. The Indians, with good cause, had a fear of disease. Cholera, smallpox, and syphilis had been brought to their land by the white man and had spread, often wiping out more than half of an Indian village.

Slowly Blade urged his horse forward and down the hillside. He was spotted immediately, and a small group of warriors rode out to greet him.

Lifting her head from Blade's shoulder, Suzanne watched apprehensively as the Indians drew steadily closer. She tensed.

"Don't be afraid," Blade whispered reassuringly.

The riders circled their horses about Blade, and without trying to communicate, they escorted their visitors down the forest-covered hillside and into the village.

The encampment came alive with an excited hubbub as the people emerged from their tepees to stare curiously at the two strangers. Knowing the visitors would be taken to Iron Kettle's lodging, they hurried toward the center of the site.

Suzanne, noticing that many of the people were eyeing them distrustfully, was thankful for Blade's comforting presence. What if she hadn't been found by Blade and had entered this village alone? Would these warriors had offered her an escort, or would they perhaps have run her off—or even worse, have killed her?

The air was redolent with the smell of food cooking, and as the savory aromas assailed Suzanne's nostrils her stomach churned with hunger. Her spirits lifted. Surely hunger was a sign that she was getting better!

They reached the hub of the village and paused in front of a tepee. Its leather flaps swung aside to reveal the old man who stepped outside, followed closely by two young braves. Chief Iron Kettle's eyes met Blade's. Holding up a hand, he said, "How, *kola.*" The greeting was a term of warm good will. The chief had on several occasions met with Blade and had always found the major to be a fair and honorable soldier. "What brings you to my village?" he asked, his English

309

spoken clearly.

"I am here to speak to you about a treaty. Black Wolf and my scout, Justin, are traveling with me. They should be arriving very soon."

Iron Kettle studied the white woman seated in front of the major. "Why do you bring a woman with you?"

"She wasn't with me," Blade explained. "I came across her a short time ago. She's a friend of mine. She was traveling in the hills when she came down with influenza."

The chief looked skeptical. "Why would a woman be alone in this land?"

"She had a traveling companion, but when I found her, she was alone."

"This sickness, it is already in my village, but it does not seem serious. Only one has died. The old woman, Crooked Nose, she went to the spirit world last night. Her tepee is at the edge of my village. You may take the woman there."

"Thank you, Iron Kettle," Blade said, sighing gratefully.

Scanning the people congregating about the area, the chief's gaze fell upon an attractive woman standing in the midst of the crowd. He motioned for her to step forward. "Take Major Landon and the woman to your grandmother's tepee," he told her in their own language.

"Do you want me to take care of the woman?" she asked, also speaking Siouan.

"That is up to you, Prairie Flower," he replied.

Prairie Flower moved to Blade's horse and raised her gaze to Suzanne's. Smiling compassionately, she reached up and laid her hand to Suzanne's forehead. Lapsing into English, she said softly, "The fever, it must be cooled." Turning to Blade, she said, "Follow me, please."

As Blade complied and guided his horse behind the Sioux woman, Chief Iron Kettle watched their departure with reservations. He was wary of whites in his village; too often their presence had brought tragedy to his people. He knew he would not rest easy until these white visitors were gone.

Sitting beside the cooking pit, Blade was watching Prairie Flower tend to Suzanne, when Justin and Black Wolf announced their presence and entered the tepee.

Suzanne was lying on a bed of furs, and glancing toward her, Black Wolf asked Blade, "How is she?"

"Prairie Flower thinks she'll be all right in a couple of days."

Suzanne was awake and she made an attempt to sit up, but was halted by the Indian woman's hands pressing gently against her shoulders.

Black Wolf was carrying the belongings that Suzanne had left behind when she'd decided to use her rolled-up blanket for a wrap. Placing them beside Blade, the Sioux warrior announced, "Little Dove had a companion, but they split up and traveled in different directions." Justin and Black Wolf were experts at reading trail signs, and not even the fallen snow had prevented them from discerning what had taken place.

"Yes, I know she had someone with her," Blade said, "but she refuses to give me his name."

Somewhat perturbed, Suzanne complained, "I wish you two would quit discussing me as though I can't speak for myself."

Black Wolf moved over and knelt beside Prairie Flower. He greeted the woman warmly before turning to Suzanne. "I suppose you had a good reason for wandering around in the Black Hills," he said, grinning wryly.

His smile was so engaging that Suzanne couldn't help responding.

Looking on, Blade fumed inwardly. Why was she always civil to everyone but him?

"Of course I had a good reason," she said. "But I intend to keep the reason to myself."

Justin sat beside Blade and mumbled loud enough for Suzanne to hear, "Trooper Donovan is holed up somewhere in these hills, and it doesn't take too much figurin' to connect him to her reason for bein' here." He glanced at Suzanne and saw that she was looking at him. "Did Molly and Saul know you were taking off?"

"No," she admitted contritely. "I left them a note."

"Good God!" Blade grumbled. "They must be half out of their minds with worry." Speaking to Justin, he said, "In the morning you'd better leave for the fort, so you can let Saul and Miss O'Ryan know that Suzanne is all right. I'll bring her home as soon as she's well enough to travel."

Leaving Suzanne's side, Black Wolf said to Blade and Justin, "I'll go talk to Iron Kettle and see when he wants us to meet with him and the council."

"I'll walk along with you," Justin decided, getting to his feet.

As the men were leaving, Prairie Flower moved to the kettle hanging over the cooking pit and dished out a bowl of broth for Suzanne.

"Would you mind leaving us alone for a few minutes?" Blade asked Prairie Flower, standing and taking the bowl from her hand.

Nodding agreeably, the woman left.

Suzanne sat up, the movement making her dizzy. She watched Blade as he came to her side. Leaning over, he handed her the warm broth before sitting next to her bed of furs.

Hungry, she lifted the round dish to her lips and took

a big drink of the nourishing soup. Blade's scrutiny was intense, and she began to feel uneasy. She wondered if he was about to question her again. Lowering her eyes from his granite-hard gaze, she returned her concentration to the broth and kept her eyes from his until she was finished. Then, placing the empty bowl at her side, she gathered her courage and once again met his unwavering glare. Becoming agitated, she said irritably, "Will you please stop staring at me in such a reproachful manner? You'd think I was a naughty child, and you were trying to figure out the best way to punish me."

"If you weren't sick, I'd blister your bottom," Blade said testily.

"Naturally you would resort to violence," she snapped.

He frowned querulously. "I can't believe you actually pulled such a foolish stunt. Who did you leave the fort with, some trapper who knows where Donovan is staying?"

"I have already told you that I don't intend to answer your questions."

"I want the name of the trapper you left with."

When she didn't reply, he pressed on, "You may as well tell me. I'm sure I'll find out his name when I return to the fort."

"By the time we get to Fort Laramie, winter will be setting in and it'll be too late for you to come back into the hills. So even if you should learn this trapper's name, and maybe even the location of his cabin, there will be nothing you can do about it. But if I give you his name now, I'm afraid you'll try to find him. You'll go farther into the hills and ask every trapper you find if he knows how you can locate this man." Her blue eyes hardened. "I know you, Blade Landon, and you'd not give up until you found this trapper, and then you'd make him take you to Patrick."

Blade could no longer hold his temper in check. "Damn it, Suzanne, sometimes you can make me so mad that I . . ."

"That you what?" she challenged.

Afraid that he would indeed resort to violence, he bounded to his feet. In his anger letting down his guard, he shouted impetuously, "Of all the women I have known, why in the hell did I have to fall in love with a stubborn, defiant Confederate!" Turning abruptly, he stormed out of the tepee.

His declaration left Suzanne perplexed. Love her? Why did he say he loved her? She knew better, for she had witnessed his lustful rendezvous with Almeda Johnson! He probably hopes to weaken my resolve by declaring his love, she decided, believing that will make me given him Indian Joe's name. Well, it won't work! I know him for the sneaky, underhanded Yankee that he is!

While Blade was in a meeting with Iron Kettle and the council, Prairie Flower had Suzanne undress, then covered her with layers of blankets. She gave her patient a bitter concoction to drink, assuring Suzanne that the medicine would bring down her fever.

Suzanne felt warm and cozy beneath her extra covering, and the medicine Prairie Flower had insisted that she drink made her drowsy. Comfortable and relaxed, she soon drifted into sleep.

She had been asleep for hours when suddenly her fever broke. Perspiring heavily, she unconsciously flung off the heavy blankets.

Blade, who was now sitting attentively at her side, watched as she rid herself of her covers. His eyes moved intensely over her sweat-glistened body. Night had

314

descended, but light from the softly glowing lantern filtered across Suzanne's nakedness. Her beauty sent his passion soaring, but controlling his need, he reached toward the pan of water at his side. He took a cloth that was soaking inside it and began wringing it out.

It was a long moment before Suzanne came completely awake. Looking to her side, she saw Blade as he wrung out the cloth. Suddenly becoming aware that she was uncovered, she quickly clutched one of the blankets and draped it over herself.

Placing the wet cloth across her forehead, he said with a smile, "You didn't have to cover yourself for my benefit. I was thoroughly enjoying the view. In my opinion, your body is perfect."

"Really?" she prodded. "I thought you preferred women who are more voluptuous."

"Why would you think that?" he asked.

"Well, Almeda Johnson is quite voluptuous."

"So?" he questioned calmly.

His innocent ploy infuriated her, and grabbing the cloth from her forehead, she flung it at him. "I'm tired of playing your deceitful little games! As far as I'm concerned, you can have Almeda, with my blessings! You two deserve each other!"

His own wrath surfacing, he threw the cloth back into the pan of water. "What makes you think I want Almeda?" he asked irritably.

"Don't you?" she spat.

"Of course not!" he grumbled.

"Oh, you lying cad!" she fumed.

Rising quickly, he said with annoyance, "It's impossible to carry on a civil conversation with you. I'm going to bed."

She watched him as he stepped to a bed of furs that was placed quite close to her own pallet. When he began unbuttoning his shirt, she exclaimed, "What do you think you are doing?"

"I told you, I'm going to bed," he said impatiently.

"You can't sleep in here with me!" she declared.

"The hell I can't!" he replied harshly.

"Why don't you stay with Black Wolf and Justin, wherever they are?"

"Chief Iron Kettle arranged accommodations for them."

"Why didn't he make arrangements for you?"

"He did," Blade answered tersely, now unbuckling his belt. "The chief told me to stay here with you."

"But why?" she gasped.

"He wants his unmarried warriors to believe you are my woman; that way they won't be tempted by your alluring beauty."

When Blade began slipping off his trousers, she turned over quickly, presenting her back to him. "You just be sure you stay over there on your own bed. Don't get any ideas that I might want you to share mine," she muttered tartly.

He chuckled coldly. "I knew you were defiant, stubborn, and sometimes a little daft, but I didn't know you were also hypocritical."

"What do you mean?" she demanded, turning back to face him. He was now stripped down to his long underwear and was in the process of removing the upper half.

"I meant exactly what I said," he replied levelly.

"I'm not daft or hypocritical," she defended herself. "If anyone is daft or a hypocrite, it's you!"

As he pulled down the lower half of his underwear, she promptly closed her eyes. "Have you no modesty?" she fussed, keeping her eyes tightly shut.

"You've seen it all before," he parried.

"That doesn't mean I want to see it again!"

"See exactly what again?" he teased, his grin cocky.

Embarrassed, she stammered, "Are . . . are you under the covers so I can open my eyes?"

"No. I'm not under the covers, but you can still open your eyes. Who knows, you might see something you want."

"Blade Landon, you're insufferable!" she huffed, rolling onto her side. Opening her eyes, she stared at the back of the tepee.

She could hear him moving about and wondered what he was doing, when suddenly the lamp was extinguished. "Good night, my beautiful little Confederate," she heard him murmur.

"Good night," she whispered. "And Blade?"

"Yes?" he responded, crawling into his bed.

"Thank you for saving me from that mountain lion, and for taking care of me."

"I love you, Suzanne, and if you'd give me half a chance, I'd take care of you for the rest of our lives."

Why does he continually lie to me? she wondered wretchedly. I know he doesn't love me; if he did, he wouldn't have been with Almeda!

Blade waited tensely for her answer, but when she didn't offer one, he rolled onto his side and closed his eyes. Hours passed before he fell asleep.

Unknown to Blade, it was also a long time before sleep came to Suzanne.

Chapter Twenty-Five

It was close to noon before Suzanne awoke and looked immediately toward Blade's pallet. Finding him gone gave her a pang of disappointment, and she was perturbed at herself for feeling that way. If only she could stop loving him!

Hearing a movement, she sat up and was surprised to see Prairie Flower dishing up a bowl of stew. She had thought she was alone.

Taking her the food, the Indian woman smiled. "How do you feel?"

Accepting the proffered bowl, Suzanne answered, "I'm feeling much better, thank you."

Sitting, Prairie Flower encouraged her, "Eat, you need nourishment."

Suzanne took a large spoonful of the stew. It tasted delicious. "Prairie Flower, it's very kind of you to take care of me."

"Major Landon told me this morning that your fever broke last night. The sickness has left you, but it will be a couple of days before your full strength returns."

"You speak English very well. Who taught you?"

"My grandmother. This was her tepee. She died a few days ago. She had the same illness as you, but she

318

was an old woman and too weak to recover."

"I'm sorry," Suzanne murmured sincerely.

A look of resignation crossed the woman's face. "Crooked Nose, she was ready to go to the spirit world. She was not happy in this life."

As she continued eating, Suzanne studied Prairie Flower. She was a very pretty woman, her frame slender and graceful. She appeared to be in her early thirties. "Crooked Nose," Suzanne said somewhat distastefully. "Why was she given such an unattractive name?"

"When she was a young woman, she was called Snowbird. I understand that she was very beautiful. She was supposed to marry Iron Kettle. At that time, Iron Kettle's father was still chief. A white man came to the village, and he was very handsome. Snowbird fell in love with him. She had been promised to Iron Kettle, and to jilt the man you are supposed to marry is unforgivable. Snowbird, she ran away with this white man. Her family disowned her, and she brought much shame upon Iron Kettle. Five years later Snowbird returned to her people. She had two sons with her. Her white husband was a cruel man and he had beat her many times. Her nose had been broken. The council decided to let her remain, and her older brother, Tall Elk, took her sons to raise as his own. Snowbird was given the name Crooked Nose, and was told she must live alone in a tepee located at the very edge of the village. Only outcasts are isolated from the heart of the camp. My grandmother's life was spent in repentance. Although her brothers saw to her food, they continued to shun her."

"Is one of her sons your father?"

"Yes, Strong Eagle."

"So she was never forgiven for running away with the white man?"

"No, never."

"How sad," Suzanne murmured.

Taking Suzanne's empty bowl, the woman placed it close to the cooking pit.

"Prairie Flower, where is Major Landon?"

"He is with Black Wolf," she answered.

Suzanne stretched gracefully, saying, "I feel so much better. Do you suppose I could get dressed and go outside for awhile?"

Prairie Flower mulled over the possibility, then answered, "It is considerably warmer today than it was yesterday. Perhaps later, when the sun is at its warmest, I will take you outside."

Suzanne stretched once again. Then, raising her knees, she folded her arms across them. "Prairie Flower, are you married?"

"Yes, I am married to Swift Arrow."

"Do you have any children?"

"I have two fine sons," she answered proudly.

"Someday I hope to be a mother," Suzanne said dreamily.

"Major Landon will make you a good husband."

Frowning, Suzanne asked, "Why do you think I'll marry Major Landon?"

"He told me that you are his woman."

"Hah!" she said peevishly.

Deciding not to pry, Prairie Flower stood and said, "I will return soon. Then you can go outside."

"All right," Suzanne agreed, then added, "Don't stay away too long. I'm anxious to move about. When I'm confined, I get restless."

"I will hurry back," Prairie Flower promised.

True to her word, Prairie Flower returned within the hour. She brought Suzanne one of her Indian dresses, some leggings, and a pair of moccasins. Putting them on, Suzanne was thrilled to find that they fit perfectly. The dress and leggings were made of doeskin that had been worked until it was as smooth as velvet. The outfit was adorned with fringe and colorful beads, and the moccasins were the same soft brown as the clothes. Prairie Flower had also brought a brush, and Suzanne ran it briskly through her long hair. Deciding to let the curly tresses fall loosely, she then wrapped a fur robe about her shoulders and stepped outside with her new friend.

Because the tepee was some distance from the encampment, they had to walk for a few minutes before reaching the other dwellings.

Suzanne's steps were brisk, and the gentle breeze blowing across her face was refreshing. Compared to yesterday, the weather was considerably warmer.

Curiously Suzanne looked about at her surroundings, finding the Indian village interesting. She had never dreamed that someday she'd actually find herself in the middle of a Sioux camp. She noticed women carrying out various chores as children romped and played throughout the site. Continuing to look over the area, her eyes turned toward the communal fire, where she saw several warriors gathered. Giving the men closer scrutiny, she spotted Black Wolf and Blade among them. They were all deep in conversation.

Returning to observing the village, she suddenly became aware of a child standing off by herself. The girl's golden brown hair caught Suzanne's immediate attention. Apparently she wasn't a full-blooded Sioux. Pausing, she touched Prairie Flower's arm, and nodding toward the child, she asked, "Why is she alone? Why isn't she playing with the other children?"

Following Suzanne's gaze, the woman answered, "It is difficult for her to join in with the other children because she does not speak our language. She knows only the white man's tongue. Her name is Kara, and she is Iron Kettle's great-granddaughter. Her mother married a white trapper, and he named the child after his mother. Kara's father wanted the girl to learn only the white man's words."

Thinking of Prairie Flower's grandmother, Suzanne asked, "Did Iron Kettle disown his granddaughter for marrying a white man?"

"No. She was not promised to a Sioux warrior, and her marriage to the trapper brought no shame to her family. I believe Iron Kettle did not truly want her to marry a white man, but he still gave his consent."

Suzanne's eyes had remained on the child. "Where are the little girl's parents?"

"Her mother died a few days ago, and her father brought her here to Iron Kettle. He said he was going away to a distant land and could not take the child with him. Iron Kettle decided Kara should live with her mother's brother and his wife. He has many children, but one more will be no hardship on him. He is a good hunter. Soon she will be given a Sioux name."

"How old is she?" Suzanne inquired, still watching the girl.

"By white man's reckoning, she is four years."

"Four years old," Suzanne repeated introspectively. "I was close to four when I was orphaned." Turning to Prairie Flower, she said, "I want to meet the child."

The Indian woman hesitated. "Kara has been here three days, and so far she has been very quiet. She may not talk to you."

"I think she'll talk to me," Suzanne murmured. "You see, I understand exactly how she's feeling."

Prairie Flower was doubtful; nonetheless, she led Suzanne over to where the child was standing alone, watching the other children at play.

"Kara," the woman began, getting the child's attention. "This is Suzanne, and she wants to meet you."

The girl showed no interest.

Moving slowly, Suzanne stepped closer, then knelt in front of the child. The little girl was quite beautiful, and Suzanne was impressed. She recognized the sadness in Kara's large brown eyes. "May I talk to her alone?" she asked softly.

Prairie Flower gave her permission, then strolled over to pass the time with some of the other Sioux women who were gathered in front of a tepee.

Still kneeling, Suzanne looked deeply into Kara's sad eyes. "Kara is a very pretty name. Can you say Suzanne?"

She shrugged her small shoulders. The child was dressed in Indian garb, and Suzanne noticed that she kept glancing down at her clothes as though she found them strange.

"I'm not used to wearing this type of clothing either," Suzanne remarked.

Kara was surprised that this woman had read her thoughts.

"Didn't your mother wear Indian dresses?"

The girl shook her head.

It then became quite obvious to Suzanne that Kara's father hadn't wanted his wife or daughter to practice their Indian heritage. Strange, she thought, that the man would give Kara to her mother's people. But whatever his reasons, the child was here and apparently felt very alone and out of place.

"When I was close to your age, I lost my parents and was sent to live with my aunt and uncle."

Kara's expression was suddenly one of interest. "Did you live with Indians in a tepee?"

Suzanne repressed a smile. "No, my aunt and uncle

weren't Indians, and I lived in a mansion."

"What's a mansion?"

"A very large house." Rising, Suzanne reached for her hand. "Come, let's take a walk."

Kara fell into stride beside her, and they headed in the direction of the river that flowed close to the Sioux village.

"What's your name again?" the girl asked.

"Suzanne."

She was quiet for a moment. "Did you like livin' with your aunt and uncle?" The child's loneliness was evident.

"No, not really," Suzanne replied gently. "But I had a cousin named Patrick, and he was like an older brother to me. I was happy because I had him."

"I don't have a brother," she mumbled quite seriously.

"But you have cousins," Suzanne pointed out. "Your uncle has a lot of children."

"They don't like me," Kara pouted.

"Why do you think that?"

"They think I'm different."

Reaching the bank of the river, Suzanne noticed the ground was wet from the melting snow, but she found a large patch of grass and spread out her robe. When she and the girl were seated, Suzanne said carefully, "Kara, you are different from your cousins because you have a white father."

All at once tears welled up in the little girl's eyes. "I want my papa to come get me!"

Suzanne had a sense of déjà-vu. Hadn't she once cried those same words to Patrick? She placed an arm tenderly about the child's shoulders, and leaning into her embrace, Kara's tears burst forth.

Suzanne held the girl until her sobs subsided, then she gently led Kara back into conversation.

Responding to the attention the woman was bestowing upon her, Kara was soon chattering freely.

A short time later Blade found them still at the riverbank, deep in conversation. Approaching, he asked, "Is this a private discussion, or can I join in?"

Suzanne watched him as he came closer. He was wearing his buckskins, and the pliable leather clung tightly to his masculine frame. He was such a handsome man; the mere sight of him sent her pulse racing.

"Blade, this is Kara," Suzanne told him.

Finding room on the fur robe, he sat down and joined them. "Yes, I know. Black Wolf introduced us earlier today. But I guess the cat had her tongue, because she wouldn't even say hello."

Blushing, Kara inched closer to Suzanne. The tall man overwhelmed her, but she liked him and thought he had a very nice smile. Watching Blade through half-lowered eyes, she murmured bashfully, "Hello, mister."

He grinned warmly, and in no time at all he had the child completely charmed.

The sun, beginning its descent, shone on the man, woman, and child as they continued to sit beside the bank, enjoying one another's company. None of them was aware of time passing; they were too enthralled with the pleasant afternoon.

When Prairie Flower arrived, saying she had come for Kara, both Suzanne and Blade were surprised to find that it was fairly late.

As the Indian woman reached for Kara's hand, she recoiled and edged her way in between Blade and Suzanne.

"Kara," Prairie Flower said sternly, "it is time for

you to go. Your aunt wants to see you."

"No!" Kara fussed. "I wanna stay with Suzanne and Blade!"

"Can't she stay a little while longer?" Suzanne pleaded.

Prairie Flower shook her head and answered inflexibly, "Sioux children learn to obey." Clutching Kara's hand, the woman pulled the child to her feet and took her away.

Watching them leave, Suzanne said somberly, "Oh, Blade, I can relate so strongly to that child."

"Don't let yourself become too involved with Kara," he advised cautiously. "We'll be leaving in a couple of days, and you'll probably never see her again."

"Yes, I know," she acquiesced. Turning her full attention to Blade, she remarked, "Do you realize we just spent a long time together and didn't even argue?"

He chuckled good-naturedly. "Do you suppose children are a good influence on us?"

"Maybe," she agreed, suddenly feeling a little shy. When Kara had been with them, they had seemed like a family. It had been nice, and she had felt like a wife and mother.

"What are you thinking about?" he asked, wondering where her thoughts were.

Somewhat embarrassed, she answered evasively, "I wasn't thinking about anything important."

Deciding not to pry, he told her, "Tomorrow I'll be gone for the greater part of the day. I'm going hunting with Black Wolf and some of the others."

"Oh?" She smiled pertly. "I didn't know you were a hunter."

He laughed. "That remains to be seen."

"You'll be careful?" she asked, without forethought.

"I didn't know you cared," he replied, his gaze intense.

She rose quickly. "I think I'll go back to the tepee and rest."

Standing, he reached down, picked up her robe, and placed it over her shoulders. She started to walk away, but he gripped her arms. Pressing her back against his chest, he whispered in her ear, "Do you care, Suzanne? For God's sake, tell me the truth!"

Her chin trembled, and tears teased her eyes. "Yes," she sighed, defeated. "I care."

He released her, and she hurriedly moved away. Heading for her lodging, she wondered why she had let down her guard. Was he now gloating? Did it make him feel more like a man to have two women in love with him? Did he plan to make a choice between her and Almeda, or to keep them both dangling?

Meanwhile, Blade had almost gone after her, but caution held him back. She had said that she cared, but what did that prove? Given a choice between her cousin or him, her cousin would win. Knowing that choice was inevitable, Blade saw no reason to pursue her. Her undying loyalty for Donovan had their own love doomed, and a future between them was probably hopeless.

The warriors were still gathered about the communal fire. One of them, a tall, threatening figure, was watching Blade as he remained beside the riverbank. The man's name was Two Moons, and he hated all whites, especially soldiers. He considered Blade the enemy and was angry with Iron Kettle for letting the major and his woman stay at the village. Two Moons had been present when the major had explained the terms of the treaty to the chief and the council. It had infuriated him when Iron Kettle and the others had agreed to this treaty. Two Moons was firmly against peace with the whites; he longed for war!

Now he motioned for his comrades to follow him. He led them a short way from the encampment, then as they circled about him, he announced, "I have made my decision. We will leave Iron Kettle's village and start one of our own."

The others nodded with vigorous approval, their feelings coinciding with his.

"You will be our chief," the youngest one said excitedly.

"When will we move?" another warrior asked eagerly.

"Soon," Two Moons answered. His black eyes shone with a malicious gleam. "When we find a good place to set up our village, we will have a great celebration. We will build our new home where the white soldier's blood will be spilled."

His followers were enthusiastic, but also confused. What white soldier did Two Moons plan to kill?

Seeing their confusion, their leader explained, "Major Landon will be our sacrifice to the spirits."

"How can we capture the major?" The youngest one spoke again. "He has Iron Kettle's protection."

Two Moons frowned distastefully. "Iron Kettle is an old man and a weak one. He no longer speaks the words of a warrior, but those of a woman. Tomorrow, during the hunting, we will find a way to get the major away from Black Wolf and the others. We will hide him in our secret cave, then when we move from this village, we will take him with us. When our new site has been found, the major will die." His hard gaze fell upon two of his men. "Straight Lance, Black Feather, you two will announce that you are not going with us on the short hunt, but have decided to take a long hunting trip. Go to the cave and wait. When we have captured the major, we will bring him to the cave. You two will be his guards. In a few days, when the others and I move from this village, we will bring your families and your possessions with us."

"How do you intend to explain the major's absence to Black Wolf and Iron Kettle?" Straight Lance asked.

The leader smiled coyly. "They will believe that the major had a fatal accident. Do not worry, my friend. I will take care of everything. My plans have been made, now I must set them into motion."

Two Moons glanced over at the quiet village, and catching sight of Blade strolling toward the communal fire, a savage, sardonic expression shadowed his face. Two Moons knew of many different ways to torture a man, and as he envisioned the major suffering these cruelties, he smiled with anticipation.

Chapter Twenty-Six

Night had descended, casting its dark shadows across the quiet Sioux village as Black Wolf and Blade strolled away from the riverbank. They had been discussing a number of things, including tomorrow's hunting trip, and were now heading toward the tepee that Blade shared with Suzanne.

When they reached the wigwam, Black Wolf bade his friend a pleasant good night, then walked swiftly in the direction of his own dwelling.

Pushing aside the leather flaps, Blade ducked his head so that his tall frame could fit through the low opening. He glanced toward Suzanne, who was asleep on her bed of furs. The dimmed lantern shone softly, lighting Blade's way as he stepped soundlessly to Suzanne's side. Love was reflected in his dark eyes as he gazed down at the sleeping woman. He studied her for a long moment, then was about to move away when, suddenly Suzanne began to toss fitfully. He hoped she wasn't suffering a relapse. Kneeling, he gently placed his hand on her forehead, and was relieved to feel that she wasn't running a fever.

Suzanne, remaining restless, clutched her blanket and shoved it downward. She was sleeping nude and her bared breasts were now revealed. Hungrily Blade's searching gaze raked over her tempting flesh. Resisting the urge to bend over and kiss her beautiful bosom, he quickly looked away. Mustering a semblance of composure, he started to wake her from her troubled sleep, but paused when she moaned another man's name.

"Patrick . . . Patrick," Suzanne cried weakly.

Blade's sudden frown was one of exasperation. Damn Donovan! What kind of inexplicable power did he hold over his cousin? Why must she continue to worship him? She knew him for the cold-blooded murderer that he was, yet she still loved him!

Gripping a corner of the blanket, Blade pulled it up over her breasts, then touching her shoulder, he shook her carefully. "Suzanne, wake up," he said gently.

She awoke instantly, her large blue eyes staring into Blade's face with confusion. Then, slowly, her dream came back to her in vivid detail. Sighing heavily, she asked, "Was I talking in my sleep?"

"You called for Donovan," he answered, his tone clipped.

"I was dreaming about Patrick's last day home before he left for the war." Blade was annoyed to see a trace of pain in her eyes. "He didn't want to go into battle and kill anyone."

Making himself comfortable, Blade sat beside her pallet. Taking a cheroot and a match from his shirt pocket, he asked with little interest, "Then why did he join the Confederate Army?"

"He didn't really have a choice. He was young and in good health. If he had refused to fight, people would have branded him a coward. Patrick didn't want to bring down that kind of shame on his father . . . or me."

Blade lit his cigar before declaring bitterly, "Donovan had no qualms about shooting my brother in the back!"

Holding the blanket over her breasts, Suzanne sat up. "Blade," she began intensely, "I think Patrick is emotionally disturbed."

He chuckled dryly. "At last we agree about your cousin! The man is apparently a deranged . . ."

Interjecting, she said strongly, "Don't talk about him as though he's some kind of raving monster!"

"Isn't he?" Blade queried, his expression stony.

"No, he's ill!" she stated firmly.

"Ill?" he snapped. "Like a rabid dog who should be shot!"

"Stop it!" she cried. "Stop talking about him that way! My God, have you no compassion? He's my cousin and I love him!"

Blade was sorry. Why had he hurt her so callously? Was it jealousy that had made him lash out at her? Was he resentful because she didn't love him but could love a no-good murderer like her cousin?

"Forgive me," he murmured. "I shouldn't take out my animosities on you. But surely you can understand why I hate Donovan."

"I do understand," she whispered sadly. "I only wish you'd try to understand why I love him."

Blade took a long drag on his cigar, then expelled the smoke slowly. He drew up his legs and folded his arms across them. Looking into Suzanne's eyes, he said calmly, "Why don't you tell me about the day Patrick left for the war?"

Her face brightened. He was willing to listen, to learn about the Patrick she knew and adored! Smiling faintly, she reached over and placed a hand on his arm. "Thank you, Blade."

He was confused. "Why are you thanking me?"

"For caring enough to listen."

He turned his eyes from hers, and his gaze became fixed on the hot coals embedded in the cooking pit. "Go ahead, Suzanne. Tell me about your cousin, and I'll try to listen with an open mind."

She wrapped the blanket about her more securely, then edging closer to his side, she began telling him about Patrick's last day at Southmoor.

Patrick was supposed to leave within the hour to join his regiment, and Suzanne, anxious to be with her cousin, was searching for him when Lettie informed her that the young master had gone outside.

First Suzanne hurried to the stables, but when she learned that he wasn't there, she suddenly had an idea where she could find him. Quickly she headed for the wooded area behind the house; her destination was the creek, which she and Patrick still referred to as their own special place.

Patrick was standing beside the small stream of water when he became aware of his cousin's approach. Slowly he turned to look at her. At the age of sixteen, Suzanne's beauty was in full bloom. Patrick's gaze trailed over her with appreciation. She was wearing a dress of buff silk. Strips of black lace, ending with large chenille tassels, adorned the flowing skirt. Her hair was arranged in an upswept style, with scarlet and black ribbons looped throughout her golden curls.

As Suzanne came to stand at Patrick's side, her own eyes were filled with admiration. She found her cousin dashing and charming in his lieutenant's uniform. Smiling warmly, she declared, "Patrick, you are the most handsome soldier in the Confederate Army."

He chuckled. "I think you're prejudiced."

"Perhaps," she agreed pertly.

Suddenly the sun, which had been shining brightly,

was eclipsed by an ominous rain cloud. A grayness fell across the landscape, darkening as it cloaked the woods where Suzanne stood with her cousin.

The dismal weather threatening the sky made Suzanne even more aware of her gloomy mood, which she had been trying to conceal from Patrick. She didn't want to send him off to the war remembering her in tears. Her eyes grew misty, and not wanting her cousin to see her sadness, she stepped away from him.

Taking her arm, he deterred her. Her face was lowered and he said gently, "Suzanne, look at me."

Blinking back emerging tears, she gazed up into his brilliant blue eyes.

Suzanne had never been able to hide her feelings from Patrick, and she wasn't surprised that he had read her thoughts. "I appreciate your bravery. But honey, if you want to cry . . ."

"Oh, Patrick!" she cried from the bottom of her heart. "Please, please come back to me! I'm so afraid you'll get hurt or . . . or . . ." She couldn't bring herself actually to speak of his possible death.

"Come here," he coaxed tenderly, holding out his arms.

She went into his embrace, and as he held her close, Suzanne nestled her head against his shoulder.

Patrick's own eyes were tear-moistened as he kept her enclosed within his arms. He knew he would miss Suzanne more than his father or Saul; and even more than Molly. There was no one he loved as much as he loved his young cousin. She had been the light of his life from the first day she had arrived at Southmoor.

Suzanne stepped out of his arms, and wiping at her tears, she said hopefully, "Surely the war will only last a few months, and you'll be back home before we know it."

His smile was wistful. "Honey, this war will probably drag on for years."

"No!" she argued desperately. "It won't take very long for the Confederacy to whip the Union!"

"Suzanne," he began tolerantly, "not only will it take a long time, but when it's all over, the Confederacy will be the loser."

"Patrick!" she gasped. "How can you speak so treacherously?"

Patiently he answered, "The South cannot win this war. When we run out of guns and ammunition, how can we acquire more? We have no factories, only cotton!"

"England," she replied. "They will help us."

"Will they?" he questioned, raising his eyebrows. "I doubt it." He sighed deeply. "Besides, the South deserve to lose this war."

Suzanne was shocked. "I can't believe you said that!"

"This country shouldn't be divided, and every slave should be set free."

"Patrick, if you feel this way, then why are you in the Confederate Army?"

"Just because I don't agree with the South doesn't mean it doesn't have my undying loyalty. I'm not a coward, and I hope I can fight alongside my comrades. Also, I'd rather die than bring shame upon you or father. But this war sickens me."

"What do you mean, you *hope* you can fight alongside your comrades?"

"I've never killed a man, and I don't know if I can bring myself to do so."

"But Patrick, this is war! It's kill or be killed!"

He spoke somberly, "When that time comes, I might choose to be killed."

"Patrick, no!" she exclaimed frantically. "Promise

me you won't let yourself get killed!" When he didn't reply, she grasped his arms and pleaded, "Promise me!"

"I can't make that promise," he sighed.

"Masta Patrick . . . Masta Patrick!" It was Saul calling from close by.

"I'm over here at the creek," Patrick shouted.

Then, before Saul could reach them, he drew Suzanne into his embrace and kissed her cheek. "I love you," he whispered. "Remember me in your prayers."

"I'll pray for you every day and night until you're back home safe and sound."

Coming into view, Saul remarked, "Your papa is waitin' for you, Masta Patrick. It's time to leave."

Thomas planned to ride to Natchez with Patrick, where he was to join his regiment.

Speaking to the servant, Patrick answered, "Thank you, Saul. Tell father I'll be there shortly."

"Yes, suh," he replied, then walked heavily back into the woods. Saul was deeply worried about his young master, and hoped fervently that someday Patrick would return to Southmoor.

Placing his hands on Suzanne's shoulders, Patrick said gently, "I want you to stay here until father and I are gone. I want to remember you here at the creek, in our own special place."

A small smile teased her lips. "I was only six when I decided to call this our own special place."

"I know," he grinned. "You said we would always come here whenever we were worried or needed to think about something. And if we were separated, but needed to feel the other's presence, we could always feel that we are together here in our special place."

Her smile widened. "Patrick, I do believe you can remember everything I've ever told you in vivid detail."

He laughed. "Well, certainly not everything."

Her mood sobering, Suzanne murmured, "I have a feeling I'll be spending a lot of time here at the creek. I'll need to feel your presence every day."

Placing a hand beneath her chin, he tilted her face up to his, then bending his head, he softly kissed her lips. "I must go. Write to me often."

"I will," she promised, sudden tears stinging her eyes. He was leaving, and she might never see him again!

He studied her long and hard as though he were seeing her for the last time, then, without warning, he turned and walked swiftly away.

She almost ran after him, but no, he had wanted to remember her here in their own special place. She mustn't follow him.

Suzanne's whole being weakened, and dropping to a patch of grass, she sat down. Lying back, she rolled to her stomach and cradled her head on her crossed arms. There, alone in the wooded area, the young woman wept heartbreaking tears for the cousin she loved so dearly.

Blade pitched his half-smoked cigar into the cooking pit. He spoke quietly. "I suppose war could take a man like your cousin and turn him into the complete opposite of what he was. Some of this country's most hardened criminals were at one time men of compassion. Who knows what causes a man of peace to become a man of violence?"

Her voice tinged with desperation, Suzanne replied, "I wish I had a shred of hope left that Patrick isn't Trooper Donovan, but I can no longer deny that they are one and the same. Trooper Rowland has visited me several times, and he's told me so many things that he learned from Trooper Donovan. There is no way the man could've known these things unless he's Patrick."

Blade's gaze swept to hers. "I'm sorry, Suzanne, but I hope you realize that your cousin must be brought to justice. He's a murderer and a deserter and deserves to pay for his crimes."

She edged herself away from his side and lay down on her pallet. "I hope you realize that I will never turn my back on him, regardless of what he's done."

He smiled tolerantly. "I am very aware of your loyalty to your cousin, my stubborn little Confederate."

"Well, at least I have loyalty," she said sharply, thinking of his dalliance with Almeda.

He quirked an eyebrow. "Oh? Are you implying that I don't?"

"I won't mince words with you, Major Landon. Instead I'll come right out and tell you exactly what I think."

"Which is?" he probed.

"You're a sneaky, two-timing rogue!" she blurted, tired of parrying with him.

"You have a great knack for calling me names, but you never back up these names with any tangible evidence."

Squinting angrily, she spat, "I know all about your affair with Almeda Johnson!"

"Since you know so much, why don't you tell me about this affair, so I'll know as much as you do?"

Sitting up and holding the blanket over her breasts, she said petulantly, "Don't act so damned innocent! I saw her in your bedroom, and she was naked!"

Recalling the incident to which she was referring, he asked, "Just how much of our encounter did you witness?"

"Enough," she answered. "I came into your office, and when I didn't see you at your desk, I thought you might be in your bedroom. I was heading in that direction when I heard voices, then I noticed that the door was ajar. As I drew closer, I caught sight of Miss Johnson, and she wasn't wearing a stitch of clothing. She told you how hot she was for you, and then you very considerately told her you had just what she needed to put out her fire. Well, I didn't stick around to hear anymore. I rushed out of the office and back to the cabin."

Smiling, he remarked, "So that's why you were so angry when I came to see you. You actually thought I'd been in bed with Almeda."

She found his smile perturbing, and she longed to slap his face. She shouldn't have told him that she knew about his relationship with Almeda. Now he was probably gloating!

"You shouldn't have left my office so quickly, my nosy little Confederate. If you had stayed a little longer, you'd have seen exactly how I put out her fire. I had just taken a bath, and the tub was still in my room. I lifted Almeda into my arms and carried her to the tub and very unceremoniously dropped her into the water. I've always heard that water is the best source for putting out fires."

"You what?" she gasped.

"I dropped her into the tub," he repeated, grinning wryly.

"Blade Landon, don't you dare lie to me!"

"I'm telling the truth," he insisted.

Picturing the scene in her mind, Suzanne giggled. "Oh, I wish I had seen it!"

He told her seriously, "I've never been romantically interested in Almeda. In fact, I try to avoid her whenever possible."

"Then why did you invite her to the ball?"

"I didn't," he answered.

"But Captain Newcomb said that you were escorting her."

"Well, the captain was mistaken. I never had any intention of taking Almeda to the ball. I had planned to ask you, but that was before you decided we were to become bitter enemies."

"Oh, Blade!" she cried, dismayed. "I have been so wrong about you and Miss Johnson!"

"Does this jealousy mean you care a great deal about me?" he asked.

Her eyes met his, and in their depths she could see his need for her. "I love you, Blade," she confessed, her voice trembling.

"God, I've waited so long to hear you say those words," he moaned huskily.

Sweeping her into his arms, he eased her back onto the pallet. As he lay beside her, he pushed aside her blanket, then his searching hand trailed a blazing path across her soft flesh. His lips sought hers, and his kiss was passionate, demanding, and all-consuming.

Returning his ardor, Suzanne's arms went about his neck as she surrendered ecstatically. She loved him, needed him; he was her heart, her very soul!

Anxious to take her completely, Blade rose to his feet and eagerly removed his buckskins. Suzanne's huge eyes were glazed with desire as she watched him shed his clothes. His broad shoulders, massive chest, and long, muscular legs made his manly physique superbly handsome.

"I love you, Suzanne," he whispered, lying beside her and drawing her back into his embrace.

"I love you too," she murmured, pressing her lips to his. She kissed him feverishly, then leaning over him, she urged him to lie on his back. Boldly, she sent fleeting, feather-light kisses over his tight-muscled chest before moving her lips downward, teasing his flat stomach with her mouth and tongue. Blade gasped with pleasure when her head dipped even farther down his body.

Suzanne's exciting and uninhibited ministrations set his passion on fire, and entwining his fingers in her long, curly locks, he moaned thickly, "Sweetheart . . . sweetheart."

Slowly, tantalizingly, her moist lips etched a path upward until they were kissing his mouth with such rapture that Blade rolled her onto her back and shoved his manhood deeply into her warm depths.

Delightfully engulfed in love's passionate union, they met each other's thrusts, giving, taking, and loving all the other had to offer.

Snuggled close to Blade, Suzanne lay with one arm draped across his chest. Basking in the afterglow of their love, they were both physically sated, but their emotions were turbulent. Almeda Johnson was no longer a threat to them, but Patrick's existence still loomed between the couple.

It was Blade who finally spoke what was on their minds. "Suzanne, what are we going to do about your cousin?"

She sighed with exasperation. "Darling, let's just take it one day at a time?"

He frowned impatiently. "But I want to marry you, and we can't build a marriage by living it one day at a time. Marriage is supposed to be for a lifetime."

"Blade," she groaned, upset. "I want to be your wife, but a marriage between us would be so insecure."

"If we truly love each other, we can overcome any obstacles in our path, including Patrick Donovan."

Raising up on one elbow, she gazed tenderly down

into his dark eyes. "We don't have to make any final decisions tonight. Let's give ourselves time to think about it."

"All right," he grumbled. "If you need to think about marrying me, then take all the time you want. But I can tell you right now that I already know where I stand. I love you and I want you to be my wife."

Pleadingly she murmured, "Please don't be angry with me. Try to understand how I feel. The thought of my husband being responsible for Patrick's execution sends cold chills up my spine."

Blade understood, but his discernment brought him no peace of mind. He loved Suzanne and didn't want to lose her, but he knew there was a good chance that he would. For a moment he considered abandoning his search for Donovan, but Major Landon was a man of conviction and he knew the unsavory deserter deserved to be punished. The man had been responsible for too many deaths.

Accepting what he could not change, Blade answered quietly, "All right, Suzanne. We won't discuss marriage until everything with Trooper Donovan has been taken care of."

His acceptance did little to comfort Suzanne. She was helplessly torn between the man she loved and her cousin. There seemed to be no easy solution to her dilemma.

She placed her head on Blade's shoulder and nestled against him. Drawing the blanket over them, he urged gently, "Go to sleep, sweetheart. You need your rest."

"I love you, Blade," she whispered.

His lips brushed across her brow, and his arms held her close. Their love, now so bittersweet, could not ease their troubled hearts.

Chapter Twenty-Seven

The rays from the early morning sun had begun to fall across the landscape. The sky was clear, and the wind was blowing gently from the south. It was going to be a pretty day, pleasantly warm. It seemed as though nature had decided on a reprieve, and the previous cold weather had merely been a warning of what was to come.

The darkness inside the tepee where Blade and Suzanne lay sleeping was slowly consumed by the brightness of dawn. As the sun's brilliant beams drove out the shadows of night, Blade came awake.

The lovely woman snuggled intimately against him caused him to smile contentedly, and turning toward her, he drew her even closer until their bodies were fused, bare flesh touching bare flesh.

Opening her eyes, Suzanne murmured, "Good morning, darling."

Lightly his lips brushed against hers. "What a wonderful way to wake up."

"I agree," she purred, pressing her thighs to his.

"Don't you think we should make a habit of waking up in each other's arms?" he asked, sliding his hand down to cup her buttocks.

343

"It sounds like a good habit to me," she responded. She nibbled playfully at his earlobe.

"If you don't stop, my seductive little Confederate, you will pay the consequences."

"Promise?" she whispered pertly, her hand finding and caressing his rising manhood.

Her touch fueled his passion, and leaning over her, his lips seared hers in a breathtaking kiss.

"Oh, Blade, I want you now," she pleaded wantonly.

"Yes . . . yes," he moaned, as anxious as Suzanne to consummate their union. Whisking away the blanket covering them, he shoved it to the foot of their pallet.

Her legs parted and he moved between them. The feel of him probing against her thrilled her with anticipation.

He entered her slowly, and his intimate invasion was so exciting that Suzanne cried out softly with intense pleasure.

His mouth was again on hers, and she trembled with longing as she returned his kiss with unbridled ecstasy. Blade's thrusts became hard and demanding, and she welcomed his vigorous strokes, her passion equal to his.

Following more rapturous thrusts, she shuddered and called out his name as tingling sensations coursed wildly throughout her body, and achieving his own wondrous release, Blade spilled his seed deep within the woman he loved.

Savoring the moment, he remained inside her as his lips blended with hers in a long, endearing kiss. "I love you," he professed huskily, before withdrawing to lie at her side.

Draping one leg about his, she inched as close to him as possible. "I love you too. So much that I could never find the words to express how deeply I care."

He smiled tenderly, then kissing her brow fleetingly,

he said reluctantly, "I hate to leave such charming company. But," he went on, sitting up, "I have a hunting trip to attend. I'd better get dressed before Black Wolf grows impatient and comes calling."

"Must you leave so early?" she asked, wanting desperately to have him back in her arms.

"I'm afraid so," he replied. He let his gaze sweep over her naked flesh, relishing her womanly curves. As his perusal centered upon the golden V between her ivory thighs, he moaned hoarsely, "I wish I hadn't agreed to accompany Black Wolf and the others. I'd much rather spend the day with you, my passionate little vixen."

She smiled invitingly, and unable to resist the lovely vision before him, he leaned over and placed his lips where his perusal had been centered. Suzanne gasped and arched to his touch.

"You tempting wench," he complained good-naturedly, kissing her softness once again before moving his lips upward to suck gently at her breasts. His need was quickly making itself known, and he had to force himself to turn away from her delightful charms.

Getting to his feet, Blade grumbled, "When I return, we'll take up where we just left off."

"How long will you be gone?" she asked, reaching down and covering herself with the blanket.

"I should be back late this afternoon," he answered, slipping hastily into his buckskins.

"Be careful, darling," she murmured.

He grinned easily. "I'm only going hunting, not into battle. There's no reason for you to be worried about me."

"Yes, I know," she answered, smiling warmly. "But I'm a worrier, Blade Landon, and you may as well get used to it."

"Well, in this case, there's no need for you to worry. I

345

shall return, and when I do, I intend to ravish you completely." With a wink, he added, "You can count on it."

The sun had climbed midway into the sky when the hunting party reached the area where they knew they'd find game. Pulling up their horses, the men decided to split into two groups, with Two Moons and Black Wolf as their leaders.

Two Moons made sure that only his trusted comrades were included in the hunters who were supposed to accompany him. Then, edging his pony alongside Blade's mount, he spoke English as he asked genially, "Major Landon, will you join me on the hunt? This treaty the Bluecoats want the Sioux to consider, there is much that I do not understand. I have many questions to ask. While we wait for game, you can tell me what I do not know."

Blade had no reason to be suspicious of Two Moons. "All right, I'll be glad to answer your questions."

The warrior smiled inwardly. Soon the major would be his captive. "Two Moons is grateful," he replied, his tone laced with friendliness.

The hunters divided into the two parties as planned, and Blade rode his horse beside that of Two Moons as they galloped toward a steep, towering hill.

As they traveled, Two Moons explained their destination. "We will ride to the top of the hill, and from there it will be easy to spot the deer as they venture to the river to drink. We can shoot them from the ridge."

Blade nodded absently. This hunting excursion was not uppermost in his mind. His thoughts were still filled with Suzanne and the love they had shared last night and again this morning.

It took over thirty minutes for the riders to climb the sloping hillside and make their way to the forest-covered summit. Clouds, drifting lightly in the southern wind, billowed peacefully across the azure sky as the sun continued to warm the landscape.

The hunters were now at the very top of the hill, and dismounting, Blade walked carefully to the edge and looked down at the fertile valley below him. The tableau was abundantly supplied with spruces, pines, and firs, and in their midst, a clear, sparkling river meandered through the land.

Studying the countryside below him, Blade found it inexpressibly beautiful. He turned around to relay his thoughts to Two Moons, but the rifle pointed at him caused his words to die on his lips.

Two Moons' hatred for all white soldiers was reflected vividly on his rugged face as he held his weapon on the major.

Blade's holster was strapped about his hips, and Two Moons told him to unbuckle it and drop it gently to the ground. Carefully Blade did as he was told. Then one of the warriors grabbed the holster and flung it over his own horse.

"Why are you doing this?" Blade asked Two Moons.

He answered gruffly, "You will learn why when the time is right." With his rifle, he motioned for Blade to step away from the ridge.

When Blade had complied, Two Moons cautiously inched his way to the very edge of the cliff. With the butt of his rifle he dug at the loose dirt until a good portion of it broke away and tumbled down the side of the hill. Moving to more solid ground, he laughed complacently as he told Blade, "Major, you were very foolish to walk so close to the edge. It is a shame that the dirt floor crumbled beneath you, causing you to fall down the hill and into the river. The last I saw of

347

your body, it was being swept downstream."

"So that's the story you intend to tell Black Wolf and the others?" Blade replied. "Well, it won't work. Black Wolf knows I wouldn't be that careless."

"He will not be able to prove otherwise. So I do not care what Black Wolf thinks! Let the half-breed believe what he wants!"

"I suppose you plan to be the one to push me over the cliff."

Two Moons grinned coldly. "When your death comes, it will not be that fast. You will not die now; you will die later." He beckoned to three of his warriors. "Take him to the cave."

The braves mounted, then motioned for Blade to walk in front of their ponies.

Sitting, Two Moons told the remainder of his men, "We will give them time to reach the cave before finding Black Wolf to let him know that his friend met with a fatal accident."

Sitting beside the riverbank, Suzanne studied the Sioux village, watching with interest as the people carried out their daily activities. Then, as her thoughts turned to Blade, she glanced away from the encampment to gaze vacantly across the rippling water. She was wearing the Indian dress and leggings that Prairie Flower had loaned her, and raising her legs, she crossed her arms over her knees. A becoming blush warmed her cheeks as she mulled over the night before and this morning. Making love with Blade was heavenly! She could make love to him for an eternity and still wish for more.

A wistful smile tugged at the corners of her lips as she recalled that she had once told Blade that if she learned Patrick was Trooper Donovan, she could never love anyone; her heart would be devoid of emotion. How could I have been so wrong? she wondered. I love Blade so much that my heart is overflowing.

Suddenly, hearing someone approaching, she turned, and seeing Kara walking toward her, she smiled happily.

Suzanne was seated on her fur robe, and patting it, she said to the child, "Come sit with me."

Complying eagerly, the child plopped down beside her.

"Good afternoon," Suzanne said warmly. "What have you been doing all day?"

The girl shrugged. "Nothing much."

Noting the sadness in Kara's eyes, Suzanne murmured encouragingly, "Honey, I know you're unhappy now, but in time you'll learn to adjust to your new life. Soon you'll be very happy living with your mother's people."

The child wasn't convinced. She was terribly homesick for her parents and the cozy, rustic cabin that had been their home. Moving to an Indian village had been a drastic change for Kara.

Suzanne's gaze swept to the setting sun. "It's time for Blade and the others to return from their hunting trip."

The words had scarcely passed her lips when they detected the hunters' horses advancing toward the village from the east. Suzanne bounded to her feet, and taking Kara's hand, pulled her to a standing position. Suzanne was anxious to see Blade, and as she gathered up her robe, she decided to wait for him in their tepee.

She was about to tell Kara that she'd see her later when all at once the child's aunt beckoned to her. The child obeyed, but Suzanne noticed that she did so with reluctance. Kara's loneliness touched her deeply, but remembering Blade's warning not to become involved with the child, Suzanne cleared her mind of Kara as she rushed to her tepee to await the man she loved.

Suzanne was sitting on a large buffalo robe, impatiently waiting for Blade's arrival, when Prairie Flower entered the tepee.

Suzanne noticed immediately that the Indian woman looked upset. Getting to her feet, she asked urgently, "Is something wrong?"

Wringing her hands apprehensively, Prairie Flower murmured, "Major Landon had an accident."

Gripped with fear, Suzanne cried, "What kind of accident?"

The woman swallowed deeply. She dreaded telling her friend what had happened to the major. "He fell from a cliff," she groaned.

Perspiration beaded Suzanne's brow and pain shot through her heart. "How badly is he hurt? Where is he? I must go to him!"

She made a frantic move to dash from the tepee and find Blade, but Prairie Flower clutched at her arm. "The major fell into the river and Two Moons said that his body was swept downstream."

"How . . . how far was the drop from the cliff?" Suzanne choked out, paling.

Lowering her gaze from Suzanne's, Prairie Flower whispered somberly, "Two Moons said he does not think there is any way the major could have survived the fall."

"No!" Suzanne cried. "He isn't dead!"

"Black Wolf and my husband, Swift Arrow, are searching for the major. If he lived through the fall and managed to swim to the bank, they will find him."

Suzanne was on the verge of panic. "Blade is all right!" Covering her face with her hands she sobbed convulsively. "Oh God, please let him be alive! I love him so much! Please, please don't take him away!"

Prairie Flower reached toward the young woman to try and console her, but whirling brusquely, Suzanne dropped to the buffalo robe. Turning to lie on her stomach, she began to cry hysterically.

Before Prairie Flower could offer her condolences, she became aware of a disturbance in the encampment. Hoping Black Wolf had found the major alive and had returned with him, she left the tepee.

She ran toward the communal fire where a congested crowd were gathered around Two Moons, who was waving his arms as he talked excitedly. His speech was provoking a stir among his audience. This morning Iron Kettle had come down sick, and Prairie Flower desperately hoped that this unexpected meeting had nothing to do with the old chief. Surely he hadn't taken a turn for the worse! As she drew closer, Two Moons' words became distinguishable.

"Our chief has not grown wise with age, he has grown senile. He thinks like a woman and submits to the white soldiers." Two Moons wouldn't have been spouting off about their chief if the old man weren't ill and delirious with fever. The warrior had an embedded fear of Iron Kettle, but the sickness that the whites called influenza had overcome their chief, and he was now physically unable to stop Two Moons from recruiting more followers. When he left this village to start a village of his own, he hoped to incite more of the people to join in with him. He was glad Swift Arrow had stayed behind with Black Wolf to search for the major; Swift Arrow had a lot of influence with the people and his loyalties lay with Iron Kettle. Two Moons was determined to take full advantage of Swift Arrow's absence. By the time he returned to the village, Two Moons was sure many families would be united with him, and more than willing to leave Iron Kettle

351

and proclaim him as their new chief.

Prairie Flower had never liked Two Moons, and had suspected for a long time that he was planning to leave this village to start one of his own. She didn't mind his leaving, but was afraid he'd tempt too many of Iron Kettle's people to follow him. If they lost a lot of their warriors, their camp would become weak, making them easy prey for any enemy that might decide to strike.

Deciding not to stay and listen to Two Moons' commanding speech, Prairie Flower headed in the direction of Iron Kettle's tepee to check on the chief's condition.

She had only taken a couple of strides when she felt an insistent tug at her arm. Halting, she saw that it was the child Kara who had deterred her.

Two Moons' vehemence had frightened the little girl. "I'm scared!" she cried, trembling.

Prairie Flower had too many pressing things on her mind to take time to try and calm the child. Hastily she assured her, "There's no reason to be scared. Go to your uncle's tepee and stay there."

Without offering further encouragement, the Indian woman resumed her hurried pace to Iron Kettle's dwelling.

Left alone, Kara started to take Prairie Flower's advice, but struck by a sudden idea, she shifted and headed for Suzanne's tepee instead of her uncle's.

Kara was sure that Suzanne wouldn't brush her off, but would give her the comfort she needed. She was so afraid! She didn't like living with her mother's people! She didn't understand them, and warriors like Two Moons frightened her.

Entering Suzanne's lodging, Kara was puzzled to find the woman lying on a robe, crying. Quickly the girl went to her side and knelt down. She laid a hand gently on Suzanne's shoulder.

Aware of someone's touch, Suzanne rolled to her side and sat up. Seeing Kara, she strove to compose herself, but she couldn't stop the flowing tears.

"Don't cry," Kara pleaded, trying very hard to act older than her age.

The child's attempt to comfort her touched Suzanne profoundly. She held out her arms, and Kara went quickly into her embrace. Holding her little friend closely, she murmured tearfully, "Blade had an accident, and I'm so afraid that he may have been hurt very badly."

A vision of the tall, charming man flashed across Kara's mind. "He'll be all right, Suzanne," she said unhesitantly.

Becoming aware that the child was trembling, Suzanne asked pressingly, "Darling, what's wrong?"

"I'm scared!" she sobbed. "I don't like it here and I wanna go home!"

Suzanne wished there was some way she could ease the little girl's unhappiness, but she couldn't find words to comfort Kara any more than she could find words to comfort herself.

Gently she urged the child down onto the robe, and lying at her side, Suzanne drew the small body close to hers. They needed each other, and gaining a certain degree of solace from the other's presence, they clung tightly.

Chapter Twenty-Eight

As she left Iron Kettle's tepee, Prairie Flower was gravely worried over the chief's condition. The man was getting on in years, and she knew that influenza was often fatal to the elderly. Glancing at the communal fire, she saw that Two Moons was still trying to persuade the people to side with him. Her gaze sweeping toward the east, she wished Swift Arrow and Black Wolf would return. Her husband would quickly put a stop to Two Moons' rebellion. Swift Arrow's absence made it easy for Two Moons to incite the people, for there was no one in the village who would openly oppose him.

Iron Kettle had no living sons, and his only surviving grandson, Strong Bull, would not oppose the rebellious warrior. Even though the chief was his grandfather, Strong Bull's beliefs coincided with Two Moons'.

Quickly Prairie Flower passed the communal fire as she headed for Suzanne's tepee, which sat isolated from the camp.

Suzanne was awake and lying on the robe with the sleeping Kara when Prairie Flower entered the dwelling.

Sitting up carefully so she wouldn't disturb Kara, Suzanne asked quietly, "Have Black Wolf and Swift Arrow returned?"

"No, not yet," Prairie Flower sighed. Going to the fire pit, she began to prepare a pot of coffee.

Dusk was blanketing the landscape, and Suzanne rose and lit a lantern. Then, moving to Prairie Flower, she whispered, "If Blade is dead . . ." A sob caught in her throat.

Prairie Flower sat close to the pit and motioned for Suzanne to join her, saying gently, "You must hope for the best."

"Oh, Prairie Flower," Suzanne moaned. "I have been so unfair to Blade. He's always loved me, and I continually rejected his love; hurting him time and time again. He wanted me to marry him, and I couldn't even give him a simple 'yes.' I let family loyalty take priority over our love. A woman should forsake all others for the man she loves!"

"Suzanne," Prairie Flower began softly, "do not torture yourself in this way."

Intensely Suzanne vowed, "If God gives me a second chance with Blade, I swear I'll never again put anyone else before him! And as soon as we return to Fort Laramie, I'll marry him!"

Prairie Flower patted the other woman's hand soothingly. "If the major swam to the bank, Black Wolf and Swift Arrow will find him." She glanced toward the sleeping child. "I suppose I should take Kara back to her uncle's tepee."

"No, please let her stay," Suzanne entreated. "I don't want to be by myself tonight, and Kara's presence comforts me."

"I cannot give her permission to stay, it must come from her uncle and aunt."

"Will you ask them if it's all right?"

Prairie Flower nodded. "They will probably let her stay. Her aunt, Beaded Moccasin, has so many children to tend that she won't mind having one less to take care of. Her uncle, Strong Bull, pays no attention to Kara. He only let her become a member of his family because Iron Kettle ordered it so."

"Why is he indifferent to Kara?"

"Strong Bull harbors much hate for whites, and Kara's father is a white man. If she were a full-blooded Sioux, he would feel differently about her."

Suzanne's tone was tinged with bitterness, "Apparently Kara's aunt and uncle want her about as much as my aunt and uncle wanted me." Her gaze fell upon the child. "I only wish there was something I could do to help her."

"There is nothing you can do. She is Iron Kettle's great-granddaughter, and he has decided that she will be raised as a Sioux."

"What did Iron Kettle say about Blade's accident?"

"He does not know. He is sick with influenza."

Concerned, Suzanne inquired, "Is he seriously ill?"

"Yes," Prairie Flower murmured. Standing, she continued, "I will go talk to Beaded Moccasin and Strong Bull. I think they will let Kara stay the night with you. Before I return, I will check on Iron Kettle's condition."

The coffee was done, and pouring herself a cup, Suzanne replied, "Thank you for helping me, Prairie Flower."

"I will see you later," she answered, slipping quickly from the tepee.

To reach Strong Bull's wigwam, Prairie Flower had to pass by the communal fire, where Two Moons was still talking to the assembled crowd. As the angry warrior's words registered in her mind, the woman

356

halted. Her heart began to pound as she listened closely.

"The white woman has infected our village with her disease, and this sickness is now inside our chief. Soon it will spread and more of our people will succumb. The spirits are angry because Iron Kettle let the sick woman enter our home. We must kill her and appease the spirits."

"No!" Prairie Flower shouted impulsively.

The assemblage turned to stare at the woman who dared to speak up. Two Moons' eyes narrowed resentfully.

Realizing she had thoughtlessly interrupted a speaking warrior, Prairie Flower was shocked by her own boldness. She was suddenly frightened, but nonetheless she stood her ground. "The white woman did not bring this sickness to our village. My grandmother, Crooked Nose, had the same disease, and there are others who have been ill."

"It is not the same sickness!" Two Moons thundered. He didn't believe for one minute that Iron Kettle was ill with any disease other than influenza. He merely wanted the pleasure of killing the white woman and was using the chief's condition as an excuse to justify his means. Continuing, he raged, "The white woman has brought a strange illness to our village, causing the spirits to be angry!"

A large portion of the crowd agreed with Two Moons, but there were others who were undecided.

Prairie Flower, knowing she had already been too outspoken, hastened away from the congregation. She had never been more unnerved and hoped frantically for Black Wolf's and Swift Arrow's return.

* * *

Sitting beside the small campfire with Black Wolf, Swift Arrow remarked, "If Major Landon survived the fall and managed to swim to the bank, or if he died and his body was washed ashore, we would have found him. To continue this search is futile. Tomorrow we may as well return to the village."

Black Wolf's vivid blue eyes turned to his companion. He didn't want to agree with Swift Arrow, but somberly he concurred. His tone was edged with anger. "I do not believe Major Landon fell from the cliff accidentally. I think Two Moons pushed him."

Swift Arrow appeared surprised. Although Black Wolf had been suspicious from the first moment that Two Moons had told him of Blade's plunge into the river, until now he hadn't confided this suspicion to Swift Arrow.

"No," Prairie Flower's husband disagreed. "The major was under Iron Kettle's protection. Two Moons would not defy our chief."

"Swift Arrow," Black Wolf began firmly, "you are judging Two Moons by yourself. You would honor Iron Kettle's word, but you are not Two Moons."

The warrior sighed heavily. He had never especially liked Two Moons, but the man was one of the people, and in Swift Arrow's opinion, all the Sioux must stick together. Their land was being swarmed over by the whites, and if the people became alienated, villages would be too weak in numbers to fight effectively for their homes. "What you say may be true," he admitted quietly. "But if Two Moons killed the major, then he is one less soldier to die later, when the Sioux and the soldiers proclaim a full-fledged war." His black eyes bore into his friend's. "You know as well as I do that war between the Sioux and the Bluecoats cannot be avoided. Someday it will come about."

"That is true. But Major Landon was here as Iron

Kettle's guest. You were the one who invited him on the hunting trip. It was a friendly gesture, and the major accepted your token of friendliness. Now you claim he is one soldier less to kill later. You do not speak honorable words befitting a Sioux warrior. Yesterday you offered the major brotherhood, now tonight you talk as though you are glad he's dead. Swift Arrow, you are letting your resentment for the whites interfere with honor."

"Your words are those of wisdom, my friend. What you say is true. Major Landon is one of the few Bluecoats that I can honestly say I respect, yet I am letting my prejudice rule my judgment. If you want, tomorrow we can keep searching for him."

"One more day," Black Wolf declared. "We'll search through tomorrow, then if we don't find him, we'll return to the village." As his thoughts turned to Suzanne, he added softly, "I will take the white woman back to Fort Laramie."

Black Wolf wondered how Suzanne was holding up. The news about Blade must have been an incredible shock to her. He was glad that she had Prairie Flower to help her; at least she wasn't alone.

Prairie Flower had decided to stay with Suzanne and Kara through the long night. Dawn had just begun to break when Suzanne finally drifted into a restless slumber.

Now, deciding to go to her own tepee and check on her sons, Prairie Flower slipped quietly outside.

Night's chill was still in the air, and shivering, she crossed her arms over her chest and picked up her pace.

The village was still, as people had not yet emerged from their dwellings. In the quiet, Prairie Flower detected the faraway sounds of a horse's hooves.

Peering into the near distance, she was startled to see Two Moons galloping away on his pony. Where would he be going so early? The woman's curiosity was quickly aroused. She didn't trust the mutinous warrior, and wondered if his errant morning ride had anything to do with Major Landon's questionable accident.

Hurrying, Prairie Flower went to her tepee, and moving to her oldest son's pallet, she shook his shoulder.

The boy was sleeping soundly, and it took a moment for him to come completely awake. His eyes opening, he looked at his mother with puzzlement.

"Flying Hawk," she said anxiously, "Two Moons just left the village. I want you to follow him and see where he's going."

The twelve-year-old boy sat up alertly. "I will do as you say, mother."

"You must hurry," she urged. "If Two Moons gets too far ahead, you will lose him."

Flying Hawk bounded lithely to his feet, dressed hastily, then left the tepee to carry out his mother's request.

As Two Moons approached the well-concealed cave, he was totally unaware that he was being followed. Swift Arrow had taught his son well, and Flying Hawk was able to keep his presence undetected.

Reaching his destination, Two Moons dismounted. Shrubbery grew abundantly in front of the cave's narrow opening, and if one didn't know the cave was there, it would not be easy to spot. Straight Lance was standing outside, and as Two Moons stepped away from his horse, he asked, "How is the major?"

"Quiet," the man answered.

Two Moons laughed evilly. "He will not be quiet

360

when we offer him to the spirits. He will beg and scream for mercy."

Unaware that they were being watched, the two men turned and walked into the cave. Squatting behind the lush vegetation that surrounded the region, Flying Hawk continued to look on. He was so close that he had heard the words exchanged between Two Moons and Straight Lance. He had been astounded to learn that these warriors had deliberately disobeyed Iron Kettle. To flout the chief was unthinkable to Flying Hawk.

Slipping soundlessly away from his hiding place, the young Sioux hastened to his pony. He wondered if he should return to the village and tell his mother what he had learned, or if he should try to find his father and Black Wolf. He decided prudently to search for the two warriors.

As Flying Hawk was riding away, Two Moons was taking great pleasure in tormenting his captive.

Blade was sitting in a corner of the murky cave, and the threatening warrior was standing in front of him. Leering wickedly down into the major's unwavering gaze, Two Moons spoke the words that he knew would get a violent reaction from the white man, "Iron Kettle is sick with the illness you call influenza and cannot control the people. I am now their leader, and I have decided that your woman will die when the sun sinks into the heavens."

Blade bolted to his feet. "You have me, so why in the hell do you want to kill her? She's only a woman, she's no threat to the Sioux!"

"As the night emerges, she will die," Two Moons stated, grinning.

The major made a mad lurch for him, but Straight Lance and Black Feather seized him first, pinning him between them.

"Where's Black Wolf?" Blade demanded.

"He and Swift Arrow are searching for your body. Black Wolf will not give up easily. He will search for more than one day. The half-breed will not return in time to try and save your woman."

Blade had never felt so helpless. The thought of Suzanne's possible death weakened his tightly drawn muscles, causing his body to slump.

The two warriors restraining him released their firm hold. Black Feather's rifle was lying within his reach, and picking it up, he held it on the major.

"Tonight I will return," Two Moons said with a complacent smile, "and let you know if your woman died bravely."

His strength renewed, Blade lunged wildly for Two Moons, but reacting alertly, Black Feather struck the butt of his rifle against the major's head. The solid blow knocked Blade off his feet, and he dropped heavily to the cave's dirt floor.

It took Flying Hawk several hours to locate his father and Black Wolf. The two warriors were riding along the river's bank. Black Wolf had Blade's horse and was leading him behind his own pony. Suddenly they became aware of a rider approaching, and glancing over their shoulders, they saw that it was Flying Hawk. Quickly they pulled up and waited.

The boy began talking excitedly before his pony had come to a complete stop. "Father, early this morning Two Moons rode away from the village, and mother told me to follow him. He went to a cave where Straight Lance was waiting. I crept in close and hid myself in the shrubbery. I could hear what they were saying. They have the major inside the cave and are holding him prisoner."

Disgusted with Two Moons, Swift Arrow frowned. "It seems you were right about Two Moons, Black Wolf. He cannot be trusted."

"How far away is this cave?" Black Wolf asked the boy. Learning that Blade was alive had lifted his spirits considerably.

"If we head straight north, we can reach it before the sun sets."

"Good," Black Wolf remarked. He looked at Swift Arrow. "Let's go."

Without further words, the riders turned their horses and began their journey northward.

The radiant sunset was casting its reddish-orange rays across a lurid sky as the three riders advanced upon the cave. The vegetation had Blade's prison almost completely hidden.

Straight Lance and Black Feather were inside. Not expecting discovery, they saw no reason to take turns standing guard.

The riders halted their horses a short way from the cave, then dismounting, they stalked furtively toward the narrow opening. Drawing closer, they could see a soft light glowing from the lantern that Black Feather had lit only moments before.

Swift Arrow was unarmed, not anticipating resistance. As he bent over and entered the damp interior, he said loudly, "Straight Lance, I am coming in."

Blade's two captors had been sitting at their ease, but at the sound of Swift Arrow's voice, they bounded to their feet.

Swift Arrow's dark eyes flitted angrily from one man to the other. He didn't have to voice his disapproval, they both knew exactly what he was thinking. His hard scrutiny made them feel contrite, and they guiltily lowered their gazes from his.

Black Wolf headed toward Blade. At the intrusion of Swift Arrow and the other, he too had stood up abruptly. Shaking his hand, Black Wolf said sincerely, "I am glad to see that you are alive and well."

Smiling widely, Blade answered, "I've never been happier to see you." His face sobering, he continued urgently, "We have to get to the village as fast as possible. Two Moons is planning to kill Suzanne."

He didn't wait for Black Wolf's response, but brushed past him and darted outside.

Swift Arrow and Black Wolf exchanged worried glances, then followed the major. Stepping outside, they almost bumped into Blade, who was standing rigidly staring at the sun sinking farther into the west. Gravely he uttered, "Two Moons said he would kill her when the sun sank into the heavens." A rough groan sounded deep in his throat, and as his gaze shifted to Black Wolf's, he swore, "If he harms her, so help me God, I'll kill him!"

Chapter Twenty-Nine

Suzanne was sitting on the fur robe when Kara approached with a bowl of stew. Offering it to her, the child said worriedly, "You should eat. You haven't eaten all day."

She smiled warmly at the girl, and accepting the bowl, she murmured, "Thank you, Kara. I'm not hungry, but I'll try to eat a little."

Sitting beside her, Kara remarked eagerly, "Suzanne please don't be unhappy. Blade will come back."

The young woman took a small taste of the stew, but although it was quite savory, the food seemed to become stuck in her mouth and swallowing it was difficult. She put down the full bowl. "I'm sorry, Kara, but I can't force myself to eat." Her voice grew intense, "Oh God, please, please let Blade be alive!"

Kara wished there was some way she could help this woman who had been so kind to her. She slipped her small hand in Suzanne's and squeezed gently, her sweet gesture touching Suzanne more than words.

Suddenly Prairie Flower entered the tepee, and they both looked at her questioningly. Her movements hurried, the Indian woman knelt beside them. "Suzanne," she began disquietedly, "the warrior, Two

Moons, plans to kill you!"

Shocked, Suzanne gasped. "B . . . but why?"

Kara's hold on Suzanne's hand tightened. Surely that mean warrior wouldn't kill her friend!

"His reason does not matter. He says he will kill you at dusk. I have a horse hidden a short way from camp. Pack your belongings, then I will take you to this horse. You must find you way back to Fort Laramie."

Everything was happening too quickly for Suzanne, and she was too confused to cooperate.

Taking over, Prairie Flower began packing for her. As she worked, she continued talking. "Two Moons might decide to follow you, but if he does, I think I know of a way to stop him."

Slowly coming to her senses, Suzanne asked, "How do you intend to dissuade him?"

"Do not worry about that." Prairie Flower said no more until she was finished packing. Then she ordered crisply, "It is time for you to leave."

Numbly Suzanne stood. She still hadn't fully grasped the situation. Two Moons wanted to kill her? But why? Why? What had she done to him to make him hate her so?

Insistently Prairie Flower ushered Suzanne outside, and with Kara following, they headed stealthily away from the village.

Prairie Flower had hidden the sorrel mare in a wooded area, tied securely to a tree branch. As the horse came within sight, Suzanne was surprised to see that the animal was saddled. "I didn't know the Sioux used saddles," she remarked.

"Our warriors do not use them," Prairie Flower answered. "But this mare was stolen from a white man, and this saddle was on her when she was taken. Unlike our own ponies, she is used to the whites' way of riding and will not balk at your commands."

Moving to the horse's side, Prairie Flower attached Suzanne's wrapped bundle behind the saddle. Earlier she had slipped one of Swift Arrow's rifles into the scabbard, and gesturing toward it, she asked, "Do you know how to shoot?"

Patrick had taught Suzanne how to handle a rifle, and although she was far from a good shot, she was not entirely unskilled. "Yes, I can use one," she answered.

Urgently the Indian woman pressed, "You must go before Two Moons discovers your absence."

Agreeing, Suzanne stepped to Prairie Flower and hugged her tightly. "Thank you for everything. I'll always be grateful to you." Releasing her, she continued, "I have one last favor to ask. If Blade is alive and returns to the village, please give him a message for me. Tell him I said that I love him and want to marry him as soon as possible."

"I will tell him," Prairie Flower replied.

Suzanne turned to Kara, and kneeling, held out her arms. Hastily the child went into her embrace. "I love you, Kara," Suzanne whispered brokenly.

"Take me with you, Suzanne!" the little girl pleaded.

"Darling, I can't." Her voice cracked. "But God, how I wish I could!"

Touching Suzanne's shoulder, Prairie Flower urged, "You must hurry."

Sadly, Suzanne freed the child and stood upright. She looked beseechingly at Prairie Flower. "Please take care of Kara."

"I will do what I can for the child."

Realizing the woman's ability to care for Kara was limited, Suzanne had no choice but to hope that Beaded Moccasin and Strong Bull would grow to love their niece.

Stepping to the mare, Suzanne slipped her foot into the stirrup. This morning she had changed into her own clothes, and since she was wearing trousers, she mounted with ease.

"When it grows chilly, you'll find your coat wrapped in your bundle," Prairie Flower told her.

Suzanne took one last loving look at Prairie Flower and Kara, then brusquely jerked the reins and began riding away.

The fading sunset was colorful and beautiful to behold, but to Blade it was threatening and ominous. He and the others were still at least two hours away from the village; there was no way they could get there in time to save Suzanne!

The three men and the boy had been pushing their horses to the limit, and the beasts were tiring.

Black Wolf and Blade were riding in the lead, and grabbing the bridle of Blade's horse, Black Wolf pulled up the major's mount as well as his own. Swift Arrow and Flying Hawk drew to a stop behind them.

"Why in the hell did you do that?" Blade bellowed to Black Wolf.

"If we continue this exhausting pace, the horses will drop in their tracks. We must let them slow down to an even canter. We can make better time with the horses galloping than we can on foot."

Blade knew his friend was right, and it would be a mistake to continue pushing the animals. Stiffly he nodded his approval, and as they started forward at an easier pace, Blade groaned deeply. "We aren't going to get there in time to save her!"

Black Wolf wished he could contradict the major's words, but if Two Moons had spoken the truth about killing Suzanne at dusk, then they would indeed be too late. Knowing there was nothing he could say to ease Blade's worry, he remained silent.

Dear God, Blade prayed inwardly, please don't let anything happen to her! His brow broke out in heavy perspiration, and absently he brushed an arm across his forehead. What would he do if he found Suzanne dead? He felt as though he'd lose his mind. God, how could he go on living without her? He didn't want to think about the way in which Two Moons would decide to kill her; it was too horrible to imagine! But aginst his will, the horrid possibilities crossed his mind. Pain gripped his heart like a steel vise, and a cold chill crept up his spine.

Blade had never known such fear; he was on the brink of panic.

Prairie Flower was inside the tepee that had been used by Suzanne when she heard Two Moons and the other warriors approaching. Squaring her shoulders and mentally preparing herself for the upcoming confrontation, she stepped outside.

As she emerged, Two Moons ordered gruffly, "Do not try to save the white woman; my mind is made up! She must die!"

Meeting his steely gaze, Prairie Flower answered evenly, "She isn't here. She has escaped."

Two Moons halted suddenly. He was enraged, and it took all the willpower he could muster not to slap Prairie Flower, then berate her for helping the enemy. But he knew that if he struck Swift Arrow's wife, the people would strongly disapprove, and Swift Arrow would most assuredly seek retaliation.

Turning to his braves, Two Moons declared, "We will pursue her and bring her back here to die!"

Prairie Flower remarked caustically, "Two Moons, you are a very courageous warrior. You are so brave that you will hunt down a helpless woman, and will

369

even take along your men to support you." She laughed. "Oh yes, you are indeed a very fearless fighter."

Anger radiated from his dark eyes. "You are a squaw who does not know her place!"

"And you are a warrior who chases women!" she retorted, undaunted.

The men with Two Moons were quickly losing interest in the white woman. Prairie Flower was right; the chase would be unchallenging and unrewarding. They considered themselves men of valor, and pursuing a woman was not a feat they could later boast about. Some of the men spoke these thoughts aloud.

To save face, Two Moons was forced to agree with them. Besides, he still had Major Landon!

His frigid gaze fell upon Prairie Flower. "The woman can go free."

Inwardly she sighed with relief, but her outward composure remained stoical. She watched Two Moons and the others as they walked swiftly away. When they were a good distance from the tepee, she whirled about and went inside.

Although Prairie Flower was relieved to know that Two Moons wouldn't follow Suzanne, she was still gravely worried about Flying Hawk. Her son should have returned hours ago, and she wondered where he was and if he was well.

Blade kept his horse at an even canter until the Sioux village came within sight, then slapping the reins against the gelding's neck, he broke the animal into a breakneck run.

As the horse thundered through the camp, people moved quickly to get out of the way of the charging beast. Some of them noticed the rider and the way in which his eyes seemed to be glaring madly.

Aware of a disturbance, Two Moons darted out of his tepee. Catching sight of the major racing toward the isolated wigwam, he drew in his breath sharply. How had the man managed to escape? Then, hearing more riders, he turned to look at them. When he saw Swift Arrow, he groaned aloud. He was sure Black Feather and Straight Lance would not be far behind. Swift Arrow guided his pony toward Two Moons' tepee. The warrior braced himself for the lecture he knew he was about to receive.

Pulling up his horse, Blade leaped from the saddle and darted into the dark wigwam. "Suzanne!" he called anxiously. Receiving no answer, he went to the lantern. His hands shook as he lit it.

"Major?" a soft voice sounded from the entrance.

He whirled about. "Prairie Flower!" he said thickly. His voice suddenly weak, he asked, "Is Suzanne alive?"

"Yes," she answered quickly, stepping farther inside.

Blade's relief came to him so effusively that his legs weakened, causing him to stagger. "Thank God!" he moaned.

Hastily Prairie Flower told him how she had helped Suzanne escape.

She had just finished her explanation when Black Wolf and Swift Arrow arrived. As quickly as possible, she then told them exactly what had happened.

Speaking to Blade, Swift Arrow said, "I will have Flying Hawk unsaddle your horse and then saddle you a fresh one. I will also tell him to bring the pack mule that your scout left for your use." His expression stony, he continued in a severe voice, "Do not come back. There is unrest in the village, and you and your woman might not be safe here."

As Swift Arrow was making his departure, Blade asked Prairie Flower, "Do you think Suzanne will stop for the night?"

"I think so," she replied. "By now she knows Two Moons isn't chasing her."

"Then I should be able to catch up to her within a few hours," he remarked. But he was fully aware that Two Moons hadn't been Suzanne's only danger. She was alone in the wilderness, and all kinds of dangers could befall her.

"Blade," Black Wolf began, "tomorrow I'll leave for my father's village. Tell Colonel Johnson that I will come to the fort in early spring."

"All right," Blade nodded. He hoped it wouldn't take too long for Flying Hawk to get him a fresh horse. He was extremely worried about Suzanne and anxious to be on his way.

His belongings were stored in the tepee, and he hastily began to pack. Assisting him, Prairie Flower smiled as she said, "Suzanne left a message for you. She wanted me to tell you that she loves you and wishes to marry you as soon as possible."

Blade grinned expansively. "She wishes to marry me? As soon as possible?"

The woman laughed gaily. "I see her message has made you happy."

"That's putting it mildly, Prairie Flower," he declared.

Clouds had drifted in from the north, blocking what little light afforded by the half moon. Suzanne could barely see where she was going, and afraid the darkness might cause her horse to stumble, she decided to stop for the night. Furthermore, she was sure Two Moons wasn't chasing her, for if he were, he'd have caught up to her by now.

Riding into an area surrounded by trees and

shrubbery, she dismounted. She draped the reins over a limb and tied them securely. Lifting the saddlebags, the canteen, and her wrapped bundle, she stepped a few feet from the mare. She sat and placed the things at her side. Earlier she had looked inside the saddlebags and she knew Prairie Flower had filled them with jerky and pemmican cakes. She was aware that she should eat, for she needed her strength. But she had no appetite, and decided she'd wait till morning.

Remembering her rifle, she moved to the horse and slipped the weapon from the scabbard, then returned to where she had been sitting. Cautiously she placed the gun close to her side.

Her belongings were wrapped in two heavy blankets, and unrolling them, she spread one on the ground and used the other for cover. Lying down, she rolled to her side and drew up her knees. She wanted desperately to fall asleep so the long, scary night would pass.

Nocturnal creatures were making eerie noises in the dark thicket, setting her nerves on edge.

Trying to block the strange sounds from her mind, Suzanne closed her eyes with the intention of willing herself to fall into a deep slumber. She might have succeeded if Blade hadn't painfully entered her thoughts. Oh God, was he dead? Had she lost her love? If she had, how was she to go on without him?

Her grief struck her acutely, and deep, heart-rending sobs tore from her throat. Her cries mingled with the distant sounds of the night prowlers.

Suzanne hadn't been able to will herself to fall asleep, but she was able to cry herself to sleep. Finally, exhausted, she drifted into a deep repose, her cheeks still damp with tears.

Suzanne had been sleeping for a couple of hours when suddenly the mare alertly detected another horse drawing close. She whinnied softly and jerked lightly at her reins.

The mare's warning didn't awaken Suzanne; she continued to sleep soundly.

The advancing horse came into sight, and the man riding him pulled up. Then, dismounting, he stepped lightly to the sleeping woman.

Kneeling, Blade allowed himself the luxury of studying Suzanne at his leisure. God, just the sight of her sent tender, loving emotions whirling through him! He noticed the rifle lying close by. A lot of good that would have done her if she had been approached by a predator, man or beast. A small smile teased his lips. Alone in the wilderness, his defiant little Confederate was indeed very vulnerable.

Gently he placed a hand on her shoulder. "Suzanne," he murmured.

Blinking, she came awake. At first she didn't know what had awakened her, then becoming aware of a hand touching her shoulder, she rolled onto her back. Her large blue eyes were glazed with fright as she stared into Blade's handsome face. For a moment she was too stunned to react.

His grin askew, he said, "I love you, Suzanne Donovan."

"Blade!" she cried softly. Her face now glowing with happiness, she sat up and flung herself into his arms. "Thank God you're alive!"

His strong arms encircling her, he held her as close as possible. He had never imagined he could love a woman as much as he loved Suzanne. God, she was his life, his very reason for living!

His mouth found hers, branding her lips with a fiery kiss that left them both breathless.

Timorously Suzanne moaned, "When I heard you had fallen from a cliff, I was so afraid that you hadn't survived."

374

"I never fell," he answered. "Two Moons took me prisoner."

"What?" she exclaimed.

"Suzanne," he began hastily, "there's an old abandoned cabin a couple of miles from here. I think we should spend the rest of the night there, and on the way I'll explain everything that happened."

Standing, he reached down, took her hand, and drew her to her feet. Once again she went into his comforting embrace. Their bodies flush, they clung together tightly.

Then, with reluctance, Blade released her. "Let's get to that cabin. The last time I saw you I made a promise, and I intend to keep it."

"Promise?" She looked at him quizzically.

"Yes," he replied with a cocky grin. "I promised that when I saw you again, I'd ravish you completely."

She murmured saucily, "In that case, why are we standing here wasting time?"

"My sentiments exactly," he remarked.

Chapter Thirty

Although the abandoned cabin hadn't been lived in for quite some time, it was in relatively good shape. The fireplace and chimney were still serviceable, and Blade soon had a fire blazing. There was no furniture, so Suzanne made them a pallet on the floor, close to the heat from the flames.

Blade had brought in supplies that had been packed on the mule, and as he prepared coffee, Suzanne saw to their meal. There were no lamps, and the only light was afforded by the fire, but it was enough for the small one-room cabin.

Suzanne waited until they had finished eating before asking the question that had been pressing her since she had awakened to find Blade kneeling at her side.

Now, sitting next to him on the pallet, she asked expectantly, "Did Prairie Flower give you my message?"

"Yes, she did," he answered, grinning.

"And?" she prodded.

His smile broadened. "And what?"

She slapped his arm playfully. "Blade, stop teasing!"

Swiftly he drew her close. "Sweetheart, will you marry me when we get back to the fort?"

"Oh, darling, I wish we could marry this very minute!" she cried ecstatically.

"I don't think there are any preachers wandering around in the hills, but there is a chaplain at the fort, and I'll talk to him as soon as we return."

"Where will we live?" she asked.

"Before I left, Captain Donaldson had received a transfer. Chances are good that his house is still available. He had his family with him, and their quarters were quite nice. It has a kitchen, a living room, and two bedrooms." Suddenly a worried frown knitted his brow, and he mumbled a little regretfully, "Compared to the house where you were raised, this home is sorely lacking. There are no mansions on army forts."

"Blade, I could be happy living in a tent if I were sharing it with you!"

He took her hand and pressed it gently. "Suzanne, if you'd rather not endure army life, I can resign my commission."

"No!" she answered immediately. "Blade, you are a soldier, and I know how much the military means to you. And, besides, I'd much rather we shared an adventurous life than a monotonous one."

He studied her appreciatively. "You mean that, don't you?"

"Yes, I most assuredly do," she replied, her tone emphatic.

Struck anew with how deeply he loved her, Blade kissed her ardently. "I love you, Suzanne," he murmured thickly.

She stood without speaking, and her abruptness was puzzling to Blade. Was she having a change of heart? Had her no-good cousin once again interfered with their love?

Suzanne gazed down at him with a dreamy smile as she slowly, seductively began to remove her clothes.

Blade sighed happily; Donovan hadn't come between them. His insecurity dissolving, he became transfixed as he watched the woman he loved disrobe. The flickering light from the fire shimmered on Suzanne's beautiful flesh as she shed her last remaining garment. His feasting eyes devoured her soft, desirable curves before he drew her down to his side.

Their lips blended in a passionate, love-filled kiss. Then, rising, Blade quickly rid himself of his buckskins. Suzanne's gaze fixed on his masculine frame, anticipating the wondrous union they were about to share.

Lying back, she welcomed him with open arms, and placing his tight-muscled body over hers, he entered her deeply, making them one. Their passion and adoration soon consumed them, and together they soared to love's highest plane.

Snuggled closely, the couple stared silently at the darting flames that were crackling in the hearth. They were uncovered and the quivering light fell across their naked bodies.

Blade was reluctant to bring up Trooper Donovan, but he knew Suzanne's cousin was a topic they must discuss before they took their marriage vows. He was determined not to be his wife's second loyalty; he must come first in her life.

"Sweetheart," he began somewhat hesitantly, "we need to talk about your cousin."

He felt her stiffen. "Oh, Blade, what can we possibly say that we haven't already said?"

"Suzanne, I can't marry you if I believe you'll forsake me for Donovan." He sounded a little bitter.

She sat up quickly, and staring into his eyes, she swore fervently, "Darling, I'll never forsake you! I love

378

you, and nothing could ever make me leave you!"

His expression set, he asked intensely, "What if I become responsible for Donovan's execution?"

The warmth from the fire couldn't prevent the chill that ran up her spine. "Blade, I pray that Patrick's execution will never come about. But if it does, and you are somehow involved, it will not make me stop loving you. I intend to spend the rest of my life with you."

Grasping her hand, he urged her to return to his side. Enfolding her in his arms, he hugged her comfortingly. "Maybe I should tell Colonel Johnson that I want to be taken off this assignment. When we are married, he'll understand that I'm too personally involved to remain objective where Donovan is concerned."

"Blade, I would never ask you to give up your pursuit. Patrick killed your brother, and also caused the deaths of many soldiers. I can understand why you feel duty-bound to arrest him and see that he is court-martialed."

"Nonetheless, I'll ask the colonel to find someone else to locate Donovan."

Relief flooded over her, and she felt as though a terrible burden had been lifted from her shoulders. Her voice timorous, she sighed, "Thank you, Blade."

"Honey, I want us to put the past behind us. My brother and your cousin will not interfere with our marriage." Leaning up to look into her eyes, he added tenderly, "Suzanne, you must realize that there is a good chance that Donovan will be caught and brought back to the fort for his trial. If that happens, I'll give you all the support I can."

Sadness shadowed her lovely face, and her sorrow touched Blade. "Patrick is emotionally ill. He must be! There is no other explanation that makes any sense. A man doesn't change the way he did, unless he's unsound."

"Considering what you have told me about your cousin, I'm inclined to agree with you."

"When I recall my last memory of Patrick, then compare that memory to the man he has now become, the difference between the two is a mystery."

"Tell me about the last time you saw him."

"Shortly after he had been wounded, he came home on medical leave. When I heard he was coming home, I was ecstatic. I couldn't wait to see him. I knew I'd have to share Patrick with Uncle Thomas and Molly, but I was sure there would be times when I'd have him all to myself. I made plans for these times when we would be alone, picnics, horseback riding, and . . . and everything I could think of. I imagined us having fun and thoroughly enjoying each other's company. You see, I thought Patrick would be the same as he was before he left for the war. I didn't know his heart would be so troubled that he would find no pleasure in picnics or horseback riding. He had become so withdrawn, and although I tried my best, I couldn't seem to draw him out. He didn't open up to me until his last night home. It was late, and everyone had retired; or at least, so I thought. I was in bed, when I heard a noise downstairs. I knew Patrick had trouble sleeping, and I thought it might be him, so I decided to check."

As Suzanne continued in detail about her last evening with Patrick, Blade listened intently.

The noise she had heard had come from the study, and opening the door, Suzanne peered inside the dimly lit room. Seeing Patrick sitting at Thomas's desk, she went in and closed the door. At her entrance, he looked up to meet her gaze. A bottle of bourbon sat in front of him, and in his hand he held a half-full glass. She noticed that his eyes were bloodshot and glazed from drinking.

Suzanne was then eighteen, and as she hurried gracefully toward Patrick, her clinging nightwear made him acutely aware of her maturity. When she paused beside his chair, he allowed his perusal to linger on the fullness of her breasts and her sensual, curvaceous hips. Then, lifting his gaze to hers, he murmured quietly, "Suzanne, while I've been away, you have bloomed into a full-grown woman. If it weren't for this damned war, you'd probably be getting married." His tone became irascible. "But all the South's eligible bachelors are off getting themselves killed, aren't they?"

She leaned against the desk top, and her eyes pleaded with his. "Patrick, why must you sound so angry?"

"Because I am angry!" he snapped. He helped himself to a generous swallow of bourbon.

"Have I done something to upset you?" she asked pressingly.

Her question took him by surprise. Surely she didn't think she had anything to do with his disposition! Hastily he answered, "Of course you haven't upset me." He reached for her hand and held it tightly. "Honey, you're the only light that is still left in my life. If it weren't for you, I don't think I could continue."

She was confused. "I don't understand. Please tell me what is wrong with you."

"Don't you know?" he queried, his brows raised questioningly.

"The war?" she pondered, her voice almost imperceptible.

He took another large drink of bourbon. "Have you wondered why I'm still a lieutenant? This war has been raging for over two years. Don't you think I should've

381

received a promotion by now?"

"I haven't really thought about it," she replied honestly.

His wound still pained him, and he grimaced as he turned in his chair and stretched out his aching leg. "I haven't made captain because I'm a lousy soldier."

"That isn't true!"

His unexpected laugh was short and bitter, then putting the glass to his lips, he finished off the drink. As he refilled it to the rim, he remarked caustically, "I'm just about as close to being a coward as an officer can become without losing his commission."

Losing patience with him, she said sharply, "Patrick, I never thought I'd live to see the day that you'd be drowning in self-pity! You'd think you were the only man involved in this war who wished he wasn't forced to participate. After two years of fighting, I should think you would have learned to accept what you cannot change!"

"I could never make you understand," he groaned. "You don't know what it's like out there on the battlefield."

"No, I don't, and furthermore, I don't want to know! But I can well imagine what it's like! But Patrick, if you don't learn to come to terms with this war, it will destroy you!"

"It already has," he mumbled.

"No!" she exclaimed. "I refuse to believe that!"

She looked at him closely, and for the first time since he'd come home, she became aware of how haggard he appeared. Placing his glass on the desk, he moved his hands to his lap. Spreading them, he said solemnly, "There's blood on these hands, blood that will never wash off."

Moving swiftly, she knelt in front of him. She slipped her hands gently into his, and a faraway expression came to her face.

"What are you thinking about?" he whispered.

Looking down at their hands, she answered, "I was remembering that time I found the injured bobwhite, and how tenderly you held him. Even then you had a man's strength in your hands, but their gentleness cured a wild bird." Her eyes flew to his as she cried desperately, "Oh, Patrick, there shouldn't be blood on your hands, you should be doing God's work!" All at once irrational anger surfaced, causing her to rage, "Why did God let this happen to you?"

"Don't blame God," he remarked firmly. "Man is born with a will of his own, free to make his own decisions. I chose to appease my father. I wasn't forced to become a planter; I could've carried through with my wish to join the priesthood. Father couldn't have stopped me, and in time, he would have come to accept my vocation."

"Then why didn't you become a priest, Patrick?" she pleaded. "Why did you let Uncle Thomas talk you out of it?"

"Because I'm weak," he murmured. "Some of us are survivors. You are one, but I'm not."

She longed to disagree with him, but she couldn't. Deep in her heart, she knew he spoke the truth.

He went on gravely, "I wanted to help save souls, but instead I'm helping to send many of them, along with my own, straight to hell."

"You won't go to hell," she moaned.

A plaintive smile crossed his face. "Maybe not. God has mercy on the weak."

She studied him through a tearful blur. Was the Patrick she had always known and loved lost to her forever? Even if he lived to see the end of this war, would he ever again be the same?

He stood and drew her into his arms. "Somehow,

before I go back into battle, I must find a way to make peace with God, and with myself."

"You will, Patrick," she cried softly. "I know you will."

By now the fire had burned down to glowing embers, and Blade covered them with a blanket. "Apparently Patrick didn't make peace with God, or with himself," he remarked, but not unkindly.

"Apparently not," she muttered, then signed deeply.

He kissed her brow. "These past few years you have had more than your share of heartache. But from this moment forward, I want you to look to the future, for I aim to do everything within my power to make it a happy one for you." Then, leaning over, his lips sought hers in a long, demanding exchange. Keeping her nestled close to his side, he said soothingly, "I think you should try to get some sleep. We have a long day of traveling facing us, and we'll be leaving at daybreak."

She was feeling drowsy, and cuddling against him, she murmured sleepily, "I love you, Blade."

"I love you too, my beautiful little Confederate," he replied with a warm smile.

They were content, for they believed nothing could ever again jeopardize their love.

Farther up in the Black Hills, a cabin very similar to the one where Blade and Suzanne had found shelter stood in the midst of towering spruces and pines.

As dawn broke over the horizon, the sun's morning rays shone down brilliantly on the lone rider as he pulled up in front of this quiet rustic dwelling.

The man dismounted a little hesitantly, as he was undecided about paying this visit. He shrugged his broad shoulders, and resigning himself to going through with it, he called loudly, "Hello in the cabin!"

The front door edged open and the barrel of a rifle greeted him. "Who's out there?" The inquiring voice was cautious.

"Indian Joe," the man answered.

The gun barrel disappeared, then the door swung open. Showing himself plainly, the man with the rifle extended an invitation, "Come on inside." He lowered the gun, but kept it held loosely at his side.

Casually Indian Joe sauntered to the cabin and entered. Looking about, he saw two other men seated at the table. He nodded cordially to both of them. He was fairly well acquainted with the trappers, but they weren't whom he had come to see. His business was with the one who had opened the door. Turning to this man, he asked, "Have you got a cousin named Suzanne Donovan?"

His listener tensed and his face paled. "Yes, I do. Why do you ask?"

"I was at Fort Laramie a few days ago, and she paid me to bring her to you. Before we left the fort, I told her I wouldn't be responsible for her. Well, I meant what I said, and when she come down sick, I left her about three miles from Iron Kettle's camp. I'm sure she made it there all right. I wasn't goin' to come here and say nothin' to you about it, but for some reason, I couldn't get that little gal out of my mind. So I decided to let you know, in case you might want to go to Iron Kettle's village and get her."

"You left her alone in the wilderness?" the man raged, his blue eyes bulging with anger.

Indian Joe's hand moved to his pistol, his fingers gingerly hovering over the holstered weapon. "I didn't have to come here, and if you lift that rifle, you're gonna wish I hadn't shown up, 'cause I'll blow a hole right through your head. I come here peaceful to offer to take you to this Sioux village to see about your cousin. But if you wanna try and shoot me, then you go right ahead. I know you're a goddamned deserter, and I'd just as soon kill you as look at you."

The taller of the two men at the table suddenly spoke up, "I didn't know you disliked deserters."

Indian Joe cast him a cursory glance. "Ed, there's a lot about me that you don't know. Deserters are cowards, and I ain't never had no use for a man who turns tail and runs."

"What have you got to say about that, Donovan?" Ed asked, grinning largely.

"It seems all men have a certain standard of scruples, even men with reputations like our visitor's." He moved to the corner of the room, limping slightly on his lame leg. Propping the rifle against the wall, he said briskly, "We'll eat breakfast, then head for this Sioux village."

His back was turned, and the others couldn't see his stunned expression. Suzanne here in the hills! Good God, he could hardly believe it!

Chapter Thirty-One

Dusk was casting a gray hue over the fort as Justin rode through the open gates. Guiding his horse to Colonel Johnson's office, he pulled up and dismounted. He was flinging the reins over the hitching rail when the colonel and his daughter stepped outside.

Seeing the scout, Colonel Johnson remarked heartily, "Justin! I'm glad to see you're back." Glancing about, he asked, "Where's Major Landon?"

"He'll be here in a couple of days. He stayed behind at Iron Kettle's village."

The officer was surprised. "Why did he do that?"

"Well, sir, that's why I was comin' here to your office, so I could fill out a report."

The colonel checked his pocket watch. "Well, Justin, it's fairly late." He thought for a moment. "Why don't you come to the house tonight for dinner? Afterward we can come back here to my office and you can make your report."

Justin was hesitant to accept the dinner invitation, and noticing his hesitancy, Almeda spoke up, "Yes, Mr. Smith, please do have dinner with us. We are having other guests, and one more will be so pleasant." She smiled to herself in anticipation. She couldn't wait to see what would happen when Justin came to her house and found that Molly and Gary were the other guests. Would the uncouth scout keep his composure, or would he cause a scene? She could hardly wait to find out.

"I insist that you have dinner with us," the colonel said warmly.

Not giving him a chance to decline, Almeda remarked sweetly, "We'll expect you at eight o'clock." With that, she tucked her hand in the crook of her father's arm and they walked away.

Justin watched their departure with a frown knitting his brow. He wasn't looking forward to the social occasion. He was tired, and would rather have called it an early night and gone to bed. His frown deepened as his thoughts turned to Molly and Saul. He needed to let them know that Suzanne was all right. But he dreaded facing Molly, and decided that a drink or so of whiskey might make the meeting a little more bearable.

His strides long and brisk, he went to the Officers' Club. Going to the bar, he ordered a drink. He was about to down the liquor when someone spoke.

"Hello, Justin." The man had walked up behind him.

Recognizing the voice, the scout grimaced, then, finishing off the shot of whiskey in one gulp, he quickly ordered another.

Moving to stand at Justin's side, Captain Newcomb proceeded in a friendly manner. "When did you get back?"

"A few minutes ago," he mumbled.

"Did everything go all right?"

"Fine," he replied tersely.

"Did the major go to his quarters?"

"He stayed at Iron Kettle's village."

"Oh?" Gary raised his eyebrows. "Why did he remain?"

388

"He wanted to," Justin answered curtly.

Gary found the scout's attitude amusing. Also he was anxious to tell him his news. Smiling tauntingly, he said with pleasure, "By the way, you might be interested to know that Miss O'Ryan and I are engaged."

His words hit Justin hard, but remaining outwardly collected, he muttered, "So?"

"So if you had any intentions of trying to resume your courtship, you might as well forget it. She belongs to me."

Justin's eyes narrowed. "What do you mean, she belongs to you?"

Gary smiled cunningly. "Do I have to draw you a picture?"

Finishing off his drink, Justin slammed the glass down on the bar. "Congratulations, captain," he said, keeping a tight rein on his anger. "You and Miss O'Ryan are two of a kind, and deserve each other."

Justin turned to leave, but was detained by Gary saying, "Justin, for what it's worth, I love her."

Moving with lightning speed, the scout reached out and grabbed the captain by the front of his shirt. Jerking the man forward, Justin leered coldly, "Captain Newcomb, for what it's worth, you're a jackass! And if you're smart, you'll stay the hell away from me!"

Turning him loose, Justin stormed out of the club. As his angry strides took him in the direction of his former cabin, he strove to control his emotions. He didn't know why Molly's engagement had come as such a shock to him. He should've known she'd become involved with the captain. Hell, why shouldn't she? Gary Newcomb was not only young and handsome, but was also an officer. Why should she choose an over-the-hill scout?

Reaching the cabin, Justin walked stiffly to the door

and knocked.

Saul appeared in the doorway. "Mista Smith, suh!" The servant's aged face broke into a big grin. "Come in," he said, moving aside.

Justin removed his wide-brimmed hat and entered. Molly had been sitting at the table, but upon hearing the name of their visitor, she had bounded to her feet.

Now, staring transfixed into Justin's familiar dark eyes, her heart began to thump heavily. At first sight she knew she still loved him, and longed to rush into his arms. Remembering the strength in his brawny arms, and the security and love she had always found in his embrace, she had to fight back tears. Her knees weakening, she dropped back into her chair. She was powerless to draw her gaze away from the rugged scout, and her scrutiny moved intently over his large frame. His buckskins trousers fit tightly against his muscular legs, and his matching long-sleeved shirt was stretched snugly across the wide breadth of his shoulders. His hair and beard had grown longer during the three months since she had last seen him and were in dire need of a good grooming. Wondering affectionately if he realized he resembled a shaggy black bear, a tender smile played across her lips.

Taking note of her grin, Justin looked bemused.

"Your hair and beard need a trim," she explained.

Rubbing a hand over his unkempt hair, he mumbled with a grin, "I reckon I forgot about keepin' it cut."

For a tense moment their gazes locked. It was Justin who managed to look away and regain a casual manner. "I have some good news to tell you both," he announced, glancing at Saul.

"What's that, Mista Smith?" the old man asked.

"Suzanne is with the major."

"What!" Molly gasped, standing.

He explained how they had found Suzanne and had

taken her to Iron Kettle's village. He finished by letting them know that Blade would bring her home as soon as she was well enough to travel.

Saul grinned expansively. "Thank the good Lord that she's all right." Then, as his eyes flitted back and forth from Molly to Justin, he decided to leave them alone. Saul didn't like Captain Newcomb. He couldn't put his finger on a tangible reason why; his dislike for the captain was intuitive. But he did like Justin Smith, and hoped he and Molly would find a way to resolve their differences. "Well," he drawled, trying not to sound too obvious, "I think I'll sit on the porch for awhile." Without further ado, he made his departure with haste.

The moment Saul had closed the door behind him, Justin remarked irritably, "I understand you're engaged to Captain Newcomb."

"H . . . how did you know?" she stammered.

"I saw the captain at the club. When are you gettin' married?"

Her eyes downcast, she murmured, "When Suzanne returns."

"She and the major will be here within a couple of days, so you won't have much longer to wait before tyin' the knot."

Lifting her gaze to his, she began on a pleading note, "Justin, I'm sure you're upset but . . ."

Interrupting, he grumbled, "Molly O'Ryan, you have a bad habit of takin' too much for granted. I told you once before that I ain't jealous of what doesn't belong to me. We had a thing goin' there for awhile, but it didn't work out. You ain't my property, and I don't give a damn who you marry."

A part of Justin knew he most assuredly cared, but he wasn't about to let her see that side of him.

His coldness provoked Molly's anger. For a moment

391

she had hoped that he might still love her. He probably never loved me! she thought heatedly. Hiding her irritation and hurt behind a haughty facade, she said coolly, "You will never change, Justin Smith. You'll always be unnecessarily rude."

"And you'll always be a snobbish southern aristocrat," he retorted, then whirling brusquely, he marched out of the cabin.

Saul, sitting on the porch steps, jumped to his feet as Justin strode outside. "Is somethin' wrong, suh?"

"No, I'm just in a hurry," he answered evasively. "I'm supposed to have dinner with Colonel Johnson and his daughter at eight, and I need to get cleaned up."

"You're havin' dinner at the colonel's?" Saul groaned.

Anxious to be on his way, Justin merely nodded and he walked away.

Slowly Saul sat back down on the steps. He wondered if he should let Miz Molly know that Justin would be at the colonel's tonight. After short deliberation, he decided to keep the information to himself. If he told her, she'd probably refuse to attend, and Saul wanted Molly and Justin to meet each other as often as possible. If they kept seeing each other, surely, eventually, they'd come to realize that they belonged together.

When Molly and Gary arrived at the colonel's house, they were admitted by Almeda, who showed them into the parlor. As she poured a brandy and a glass of sherry for her guests, Molly studied her hostess's apparel with envy.

Almeda was strikingly beautiful in her evening dress. The flowing garment was a heavy white corded silk, trimmed with black lace in a design of dainty leaves.

The gown's décolletage was scandalously low, revealing a shockingly large portion of the woman's ample bosom. Molly was sure the dress was the latest style, and she was a little surprised to learn that gowns were now fashioned to expose so much of a woman's breasts.

As Almeda brought them their drinks, Molly glanced down at her own much-mended and out-of-style gown. Fleetingly she recalled the days before the war and the dozens of stylish dresses that had filled her closets.

At the sound of a few rapid knocks at the front door, Almeda said gaily, "Our other guest has arrived."

"Guest?" Gary asked. "I didn't know you had invited anyone else."

Her eyes gleaming, she replied, "It was one of those last-minute invitations."

Almeda's steps were light as she hurried to greet the caller, and the long folds of her dress billowed gracefully with her lithe movements.

Seated on the plush sofa, Molly and Gary couldn't see the front door and they had no idea who had arrived until Justin's giant frame suddenly appeared in the parlor. Quickly Almeda inched her way around him so that she could see Miss O'Ryan's expression.

Her face turning deathly pale, Molly gasped, "Justin!"

The scout's visage hardened with barely controlled anger. His steely glare went back and forth from Molly to Gary.

Her vision glued to Justin, Molly first became aware that he had trimmed his hair and beard, then her examining eyes took in his attractive appearance. Dressed in fawn-colored trousers and a dark tan shirt, he was handsome indeed.

"Good evening, Justin," Gary uttered with a snicker.

Slipping her arm into Justin's, Almeda remarked, "Father is getting dressed. While we wait for him, may I fix you a drink?"

Removing her hand, he replied gruffly, "Tell the colonel I changed my mind about dinner, and I'll come to his office in the morning."

Repressing her giggles, Almeda watched him stalk to the door, open it, and leave. Then, turning to her other guests, she remarked, "My goodness, the man is certainly ill-mannered. What do you suppose got into him?"

Molly's temper flared. Rising, she snapped, "You know exactly why he left! How dare you invite Justin to your home when you knew I would be here!"

Looking innocent, Almeda replied, "But I didn't extend the invitation, father did."

"But you thoroughly enjoyed it, didn't you?" Molly returned. "I'm leaving!" she said to Gary.

Standing, Gary tried to calm her, "Molly, you're being unreasonable."

He placed a hand on her arm, but flinging it off, she strode across the room and, as Justin had done only moments before, opened the door and left.

Laughing, Almeda moved over to Gary.

"I fail to see any humor in this!" he barked.

Lacing her arms about his neck and pressing her body close to his, she murmured, "Don't be upset, darling."

Her seductive embrace aroused his passion, and lowering his hands to her hips, he drew her against his hardness.

Her gown and petticoats couldn't prevent her from becoming aware of his desire, and she purred provocatively, "The prim Miss O'Ryan is still holding onto her virtue, isn't she?" Almeda hadn't visited Gary's bed since he and Molly had become engaged, and burning for a man, she promised, "I'll come to your quarters tonight."

For a moment, Gary considered going after Molly and smoothing over tonight's incident. But as his manhood grew harder, he decided Molly could wait until tomorrow. Besides, he needed a woman, and so far his fiancée had refused to satisfy his needs, telling him they must wait until their wedding night. Smiling, he recalled the way in which he had implied to Justin that he and Molly were lovers.

Noting his smug grin, Almeda asked, "Where are your thoughts?"

Hearing the colonel leaving his bedroom, Gary broke their embrace. Quickly he whispered, "Come to my quarters at ten o'clock."

Entering the parlor, Colonel Johnson inquired, "Where are Miss O'Ryan and Justin?"

Appearing quite bewildered, Almeda answered, "Mr. Smith said he changed his mind about dinner and would see you in the morning. After he left, Miss O'Ryan became a little ill and went home."

Justin was in his room and had just poured himself a glass of whiskey when a knock sounded at his door. Wondering who could be calling, he stepped to the door and opened it. He was surprised to come face to face with Saul.

"Excuse me, Mista Smith, but can I talk to you for a few minutes?"

"Of course," he answered, showing him into the small bedroom. "I was fixing myself a drink, can I get you one?"

"Thank you, suh," Saul replied.

Justin went to the dresser, where he kept a bottle. Then, gesturing toward the hard-backed chair, he said,

"Sit down, Saul."

Doing as he was requested, the servant moved to the chair. As Justin poured his drink, he remarked, "I kinda figured you would be here instead of at the colonel's."

Handing him a glass of whiskey, Justin asked, "Why did you think that?"

"Well, a short time ago, Miz Molly came home. For some reason that she wouldn't explain, she didn't stay at the colonel's for dinner. It didn't take much figurin' for me to suspect that you left early too."

Justin was amazed to learn that Molly had apparently left shortly after he did.

"I don't know what happened between you and Miz Molly before you left for the hills," Saul continued, "but I sure wish you two would make up. I don't like that Captain Newcomb, and I sure don't want Miz Molly to marry him."

Sitting on the edge of the bed, Justin mumbled, "Saul, if you want to stay and visit for awhile, then you're more than welcome. But there's a stipulation."

"What's that?"

"Leave Molly O'Ryan out of the conversation."

Saul nodded. "All right."

Looking closely at the old man, Justin's expression grew thoughtful.

"Mista Smith, suh, you look like a man who's itchin' to ask somethin' he ain't sure he should ask," Saul said.

"The name's Justin," was the reply, with a smile. "And you don't have to call me sir."

Saul knew it would be impossible for him to address a white man solely by his first name. The words "master" and "sir" had been embedded in him for over seventy years.

"You're right, though," Justin proceeded. "I was thinkin' about questioning you."

"Go right ahead. I won't be offended." Saul took a large drink of whiskey.

"You care a lot about Suzanne and Trooper Donovan, don't you?"

"You know I do."

"How can you love people who once held you in bondage?"

"I didn't belong to Miz Suzanne or Masta Patrick. Masta Thomas owned me."

"But if Patrick had inherited the plantation, then you would've been his property."

"Masta Patrick planned to set me and all the slaves free."

"How do you know?"

"He told me so. He intended to offer wages to everyone who wanted to work for him, and he was gonna give the field hands an acre of land and their own cabin."

"Do you believe he would have done so?"

"Yes, suh," he replied. "Excuse me, I mean Mista Justin."

"You don't need to use the word 'mister' when you talk to me."

"I'm an old man, and it's too late for me to change my ways completely."

Justin nodded understandingly. "Do you still want to find Trooper Donovan?"

"No, I don't. I still love him, regardless of what he's done, but I ain't got no hankerin' to see him. I'm tired, and I'm longin' for home."

"Southmoor?" Justin queried.

"That's my home. Has been for nearly fifty years."

"Donovan's father is still there, isn't he?"

"He's residin' in the overseer's house. A couple of the older slaves stayed on with him, but I don't know if they're still there. I need to get back so I can take care of him."

"I can't understand why you feel obligated to care for your former master."

"Obligation ain't got nothin' to do with it." A sly smile crossed the servant's face.

Comprehending, Justin chuckled.

His grin now sheepish, Saul teased, "This ole nigger is only human, and I'm goin' to enjoy the masta bein' dependent on me for a change."

Studying him with a certain degree of admiration, Justin asked, "Does Suzanne or Patrick know about this resentful streak in you?"

"Masta Patrick, he knows I don't harbor no love for Southerners, but Miz Suzanne, well, that ain't nothin' to discuss with a lady. Besides, I don't dislike all Southerners. Some of 'em are decent folks."

"But you still plan to take care of Thomas?"

"Don't misunderstand my intentions. I'll take good care of Masta Thomas. I got this feelin' that Miz Suzanne will be stayin' here with the major, so Masta Thomas and I ain't gonna have nobody except each other."

"You don't have a family?"

"No, I never had a woman of my own or kids."

"Why not?"

"I was somewhere around twenty years old when I fell in love with a pretty little gal. Her name was Sally. That was before I belonged to the Donovans. I was livin' on the plantation where I was born. Walter Clearfield was my masta. One day he sold Sally to a slave trader. Losing the woman I loved nearly drove me crazy, and I ran away to try and find her. The slave patrollers caught me, and Masta Walter had me whipped." Saul paused to take a drink. When he continued, his tone was edged with unforgotten pain, "Thirty lashes was my punishment. I almost died.

When I was healed, the masta sold me at an auction in New Orleans. That was when I went to Southmoor. I was a young man and I managed to enjoy my share of wenches, but I never let myself care about any of them. I wasn't gonna let my heart be broken again."

"It sounds like you've had one hell of a life," Justin murmured.

Saul stood and placed his empty glass on the dresser. "My life ain't been bad for a slave's. I was luckier than most."

"Do you want another drink?"

"No, thank you. I reckon I'd better get back to the cabin. I don't like Miz Molly bein' there alone at night." He stepped to the door and opened it. "Mista Justin, it's been a pleasure talkin' to you." For a moment he considered bringing up the subject of Molly, then, deciding he shouldn't interfere, he walked out and closed the door.

Chapter Thirty-Two

"Miz Suzanne, I sure hope you don't ever again do somethin' so dangerous. I think I aged ten years while you was away." Saul's chiding was affectionate, but there was truth to his words. He had indeed been gravely worried about his young mistress.

Suzanne had been home for less than an hour. As soon as she and Blade had returned to the fort, he had brought her to the cabin, then left to report to Colonel Johnson.

Hugging Saul briefly, Suzanne replied, "I'm sorry that I worried you." She was anxious to announce her plans to be married, but so far Molly and Saul hadn't given her a chance. They had insisted that she tell them about her journey with Indian Joe and her stay at the Sioux village. Now, as her eyes darted back and forth from Saul to Molly, she exclaimed, "Blade and I are getting married!"

The old servant smiled broadly. "The major is a good man, and he'll do right by you."

Turning to Molly, Suzanne was expecting her friend to be happy for her, and was startled to see a sign of tears in the woman's eyes. "Molly, what's wrong?" she asked urgently.

Composing herself, Molly answered, "For a moment I was so envious of you that I actually felt sorry for myself."

Baiting her, Saul asked cunningly, "Miz Molly, why should you be envious? You got a fiancé, and you two are plannin' to marry real soon."

Smiling happily, Suzanne declared, "You and Justin made up! That's wonderful! Maybe we can make it a double wedding."

"She ain't marryin' Mista Smith," Saul remarked dryly. "She's gettin' married to Captain Newcomb."

Gaping at Molly, Suzanne asked, "Do you love him?"

Flustered, Molly stammered, "Yes . . . yes, of course I do."

Suzanne wasn't convinced. "Molly, you know Blade and Justin don't like Captain Newcomb. Have you stopped to consider that they probably have a valid reason for feeling that way? Maybe you shouldn't rush into marriage with the captain. Give yourself time to get to know him better."

Molly's eyes flared. "I have no idea why the major disapproves of Gary, but Justin's hostility stems from jealousy. I do believe he's jealous of any man who is polished and a gentleman. Justin is rude, uncouth, and totally impossible!" Her expression unyielding, she added, "I do not wish to discuss my fiancé further. It's my life and I will do as I please with it!"

Relenting, Suzanne replied, "All right, Molly." Changing the subject, she asked, "Will you accompany me to the mercantile? Blade and I plan to marry Sunday, and that only gives me three days to sew a wedding dress. Let's go to the store and buy some material."

Molly hesitated, and Suzanne groaned. "How can I be so foolish? We don't have enough money left to

401

spend on material! I gave most of it to the trapper so he'd take me into the hills. Because of me, we're practically destitute. Well, I'll just have to wear one of my old gowns."

Smiling brightly, Molly remarked, "Suzanne Donovan, you're going to be a beautiful bride, and you will wear a gorgeous wedding gown."

Still smiling, she hastened to her cedar chest, which sat at the foot of the bed. She knelt down and flung it open, drawing out her summer dresses and placing them on the floor. Then she carefully brought forth a white gown. Draping the graceful garment over her arms, she went and laid it on the bed.

Going to her side, Suzanne murmured, "Molly, this is your wedding dress. Surely you don't intend for me to wear it."

"Of course I do."

"No," Suzanne protested. "You must wear it when you marry Captain Newcomb."

Molly sighed sadly. "I had servants to help me sew this gown, but I did all the lace by myself. As I took each tiny stitch, I dreamed of Patrick. Even though we hadn't set a wedding date, I nonetheless was anxious to make my gown. I mistakenly believed that if Patrick came home on leave, he'd insist that we marry. Well, as we both know, he did come home, but marriage was the furthest thing from his mind."

Slowly Molly sat down on the edge of the bed and caressing the gown, she continued wistfully, "I'm not sure why I even brought this with me. Maybe in the back of my mind I thought there was a chance that Patrick would still want to marry me. It was a foolish thought, because even if he had wanted to get married, I'm not sure I would've been willing. I stopped loving him before we started on this trip; I just hadn't admitted it to myself." She looked up and met

Suzanne's sympathetic gaze. "I couldn't possibly wear this gown. It holds too many sad memories for me, and a bride should be happy on her wedding day."

"I understand," Suzanne whispered.

Her mood lifting, Molly said cheerfully, "You need to try it on, in case we have to do alterations."

"I'll leave you women alone," Saul said, excusing himself.

After he left, Suzanne hastily slipped off her clothes. With Molly's assistance, she stepped into the formal gown. There was a mirror over the dresser, and anxious to see how she looked, Suzanne hurried over to peer at her reflection.

"Oh, Molly!" she breathed in amazement.

The white satin gown was covered with rows of appliqué lace, and tulle-ruche trim adorned the full skirt. The delicate, lace-bordered bodice barely revealed the fullness of Suzanne's ivory breasts. The short puffed sleeves, gathered with lace, set the garment off perfectly.

While Suzanne had been studying her reflection, Molly had returned to her cedar chest to draw forth another item. Stepping over to her friend, she showed her the final gift.

"The veil!" Suzanne exclaimed. "It's so beautiful!" Yards of white lace had gone into making it.

The unexpected sound of someone knocking on the door, made Suzanne tense. "If that's Blade, don't let him come in. He must not see me in this dress until our wedding!"

Going to the door, Molly assured her, "Don't worry, I won't let him in."

But it wasn't Blade who had called, but three officers' wives, whom Molly had come to know during Suzanne's absence. Cordially she invited them inside.

The sight of Miss Donovan in a wedding gown

struck them with surprise.

Explaining, Molly said, "Miss Donovan and Major Landon are getting married this Sunday."

Then, as Molly began to introduce the visitors, Suzanne nodded politely, but when she heard the third woman's name, she paled and gasped softly. Mrs. Wilkinson. It had been Lieutenant Wilkinson and his men whom Patrick had deserted!

Stepping forward, Shelley Wilkinson said kindly, "Miss Donovan, there are people on this fort who do not hold you responsible for your cousin's actions, and these ladies and I happen to be among them. We would have called months ago if you had given us some indication that we were welcome. We mistakingly got the impression that you preferred not to socialize. Then, while you were away, Molly and I happened to be at the mercantile at the same time, and we began talking to each other." She smiled pleasantly, "To make a long story short, it seems you had the wrong impression of us, and we were mistaken about you. These ladies and I have come here to welcome you to Fort Laramie."

"Thank you," Suzanne murmured. "I appreciate your kindness."

"Now that we have that settled," Shelley declared brightly, "I hope you will invite us to your wedding."

"Of course!" Suzanne cried happily.

"Are you getting married in the chapel?"

"Yes," she replied. Then, glancing down at her gown, she continued, "I was trying on this wedding dress in case it needed altering."

"It's too long," Molly said. "The hem will have to be shortened."

"Miss Donovan," Shelley said, "why don't you step up on a chair, and I'll help Molly pin up the hem?"

"Please call me Suzanne," she told them.

404

They told her that she must use their first names too, then the room became active with everyone bustling about, determined to have the wedding dress altered perfectly before Sunday.

Suzanne had never been happier. Soon she would be Mrs. Blade Landon, and now she had friends with whom she knew she would have much in common. They were all military wives, their husbands' jobs were dangerous ones, and Suzanne realized there would be times when she'd need their support, as they would need hers.

Blade and Suzanne had invited Molly and Gary to join them for dinner at the Officers' Club, and the four of them were seated at their table discussing Sunday's wedding when Justin ambled into the dining room.

The scout's presence caused Molly to tense. She tried to appear undisturbed, but Suzanne noticed her tautness. She still loves Justin, Suzanne thought. So why is she marrying Captain Newcomb?

Justin ordered a brandy, then, glass in hand, he sauntered over to their table. Looking at Blade, he said calmly, "I understand that you wanted to see me. I went to your office, and the sentry told me you were here."

Gesturing to an empty chair, the major replied, "Sit down and join us."

"No, thanks," he said, keeping his eyes on Blade. "Why did you need to see me?"

"As you know, Suzanne and I are getting married Sunday, and I want you as my best man."

He smiled. "I'd be honored, Blade."

With a snicker, Gary remarked to Justin, "Congratulations on becoming the 'best man' for a change."

"Gary!" Molly gasped angrily.

"Captain," Justin began, setting his glass on the

table, "if you want to step outside, I'll show you who's the best man."

Beaming, Gary replied, "Smith, we are in the presence of two ladies. I realize it's difficult for you to act civilized, but in this instance, why don't you try?"

"Stop it!" Molly seethed, glaring at her fiancé. "You are the one who isn't acting civilized!"

"Miss O'Ryan!" Justin sneered. "I don't need you to fight my battles."

Her temper flaring, Molly spat, "Go to the devil, Justin Smith!"

As she suddenly pushed back her chair and rose to her feet, the scout moved to her side. Staring harshly into her angry eyes, he said between gritted teeth, "I'll go to the devil in my own good time, madam! But first I'm leaving this fort permanently! Fort Laramie ain't big enough for you and me both, and that no-good skunk you're gonna marry."

"Great!" she came back. "When are you leaving, so I'll know when to start celebrating?"

"Monday, after the major's wedding."

"I'll be counting the days!"

He turned on his heel to leave, but all at once he whirled back to face her. His expression was threatening, and Molly was suddenly wary. She knew Justin wasn't a man to push too far. Why had she angered him so?

"Miss O'Ryan," he said, his voice level, "just in case I don't get a chance to tell you goodbye before I leave, I'll bid you farewell now."

Justin moved so swiftly that Molly didn't know what had happened until she found herself in his arms with his lips pressed possessively against hers. His kiss was forceful, and he held her so tightly that her frame was molded to his.

For an instant, she fought him, but as his kiss robbed

her of her senses, she leaned into his embrace and surrendered.

Bounding from his chair, Gary rushed to the clinging couple and grabbing Justin's arm, he jerked him around.

Meanwhile, as the patrons in the dining room were looking on with interest, Blade had urged Suzanne to her feet and away from the table.

Gary swung at Justin, but the scout easily ducked the man's wild swing. Then, as the captain was preparing to strike again, Justin's large fist plunged into his victim's face. The solid blow sent Gary careening backward, and losing his balance, he fell across the table, sending dishes and food to the carpeted floor.

Justin turned lithely to Molly, who was wide-eyed and pale. Bowing from the waist, he said smoothly, "Goodbye, ma'am." He gestured toward Gary as he lay sprawled on the table top with blood streaming from his nose. "Your fiancé needs your loving care." With that, the powerful scout whirled about and left the dining room.

Molly and Gary had left the club shortly after the incident with Justin. As they walked up onto the cabin porch, Gary complained bitterly, "If Smith wasn't planning on leaving the fort for good, I'd press charges against him for striking an officer."

"If I remember correctly, you struck first," she declared testily.

"What was I supposed to do? He was practically raping you in the middle of the dining room!"

"You're exaggerating," Molly replied impatiently.

Slowly she moved away from his side, and turning her back, stared thoughtfully into the distance. From the moment that Justin had come back into her life, she

407

had subconsciously known she couldn't bring herself to marry Gary. She had thought she could wed a man she didn't love, but now she had come to realize that it wasn't possible. If she did so, she'd be committing herself to a lifetime of unhappiness. Also, it would be terribly unfair to Gary. He deserved a wife who would truly love him.

"Gary," she said softly, keeping her back turned, "come spring, Saul plans to return to Southmoor, and I've decided to accompany him as far as Natchez. As you know, my parents still live there, and I intend to go home."

Stepping to her, and clutching her arm, he forced her to face him. "It's because of Smith, isn't it? He's the reason you're leaving me!"

"Gary, I don't love you, and a marriage between us would be a mistake."

Sneering angrily, he insisted, "It's because of Smith, isn't it?"

His grip on her arm was painful. Jerking free, she replied sternly, "Let's leave Justin out of this. I've decided not to marry you because I don't love you."

His temper inflamed, he raged loudly, "You teasing little bitch! How dare you lead me on!"

Gary's voice had carried into the cabin, and Saul opened the door and stepped outside.

Hearing Saul, Gary lashed out at him too. "Stay out of this!"

Disregarding him, Saul beckoned to Molly, "Come on inside."

The incident with Justin, together with Molly's rebuke, had the captain so angry that he was beyond rational thought. His true personality flowing forth, he shouted, "I told you to stay out of this, you damned nigger!"

"Captain Newcomb!" Blade's strong, authoritative

voice suddenly bellowed.

The three on the porch hadn't been aware of the major's and Suzanne's approach. Now, whirling about, Gary came to attention. Saluting, he remarked stiffly, "Yes sir!"

Returning his salute, Blade ordered, "Captain, you will apologize to Saul immediately!"

When Gary hesitated, the major threatened, "You will do as I say, or I'll put you on report!"

Turning to Saul and clicking his heels together, Gary said evenly, "I apologize."

Holding Suzanne's arm, Blade led her up to the porch. "Captain, off the record, if you don't leave right now, I'll personally see to it that this time you receive more than a bloody nose."

His eyes bulging with hate, Gary retorted, "Sir, off the record, if it's the last thing I do, someday I'll get even with you and Justin Smith!" Without further words, he hurried down the steps and stalked quickly away.

Suzanne made a move toward Molly to try and comfort her, but the evening had proved to be too much for the young woman, and she fled inside.

Suzanne started to follow her, but Saul said firmly, "Let her be, Miz Suzanne. There ain't nothin' you can say that's gonna help her." An appeasing grin suddenly spread across his face. "But I sure am glad she decided not to marry that Captain Newcomb. Maybe now she and Mista Justin will get back together."

Suzanne sighed with disappointment. "I doubt it. We saw Justin on our way home, and he was leaving the fort. He said he wouldn't be back until Sunday, and then the day after the wedding, he's leaving for good. It doesn't look as though there will be an opportunity for Molly and Justin to reconcile their differences."

"Then it's up to us to make that opportunity for

them," Blade commented.

Saul and Suzanne looked questioningly at him.

"First, if you two will excuse me, I'm going inside the cabin to have a talk with Miss O'Ryan. I'm sure I know where Justin has gone, and after she hears what I have to say, I think she'll insist that I take her to him."

Blade felt uneasy about this talk with Molly. Blade knew that years ago, when Justin had confided in him about his wife's death, he hadn't expected him ever to repeat it. He hoped Justin would understand, and that this night wouldn't somehow end their long friendship.

Gary went directly to Almeda's house, where she showed him into the parlor and fixed him a drink. His hand shook as he accepted the glass of brandy.

"Gary, what in the world is wrong with you? Why are you so upset?"

"Molly broke our engagement," he growled, gulping a large portion of brandy.

"Is that all," she sighed, uninterested.

"I should've known I'd get no sympathy from you, you selfish little cat."

She smiled tauntingly. "You didn't exactly show me any sympathy when Blade announced his marriage to that southern bitch."

He polished off his drink, then went to the liquor cabinet and poured himself another. "I don't know about you, but I intend to get even with both of them."

"Both of them?" she queried, confused.

"Smith and Landon," he grumbled.

"Why are you so angry at Blade and Justin?"

"Never mind," he mumbled evasively, preferring not to recount his losing skirmish with the scout or his reprimand by the major.

But Almeda was not about to be left in the dark.

Going to his side, and grasping his arm, she persisted, "Darling, you know you can tell me anything. Besides, you might need my help getting even with them."

He smiled coldly. Almeda had made a good point. When the time came for his revenge, which he was determined would come about, he might indeed need Almeda's assistance. He decided it would be to his advantage to tell her about the two embarrassing encounters.

Taking her hand, he led her to the sofa and brought her up to date on the night's activities.

Chapter Thirty-Three

When Blade entered the cabin, Molly was sitting on the edge of the bed. Pulling up a hard-backed chair, he drew it close to her and sat down. She looked as though she were about to cry, and he asked gently, "Are you all right?"

"Yes," she whispered. Molly was surprised that the major apparently wanted to talk to her privately. What could they possibly have to discuss?

"I'm sorry about what happened with the captain," he murmured.

"I was aware that you and Justin didn't especially like Gary, and now I understand why."

"Speaking of Justin, he's the reason why I want to talk to you."

She watched him guardedly. "I'd rather not discuss him."

"I insist that you listen to what I have to say," he replied firmly.

Molly sighed. "Major Landon, I have decided to go home in the spring. I do not want Justin Smith in my life, nor do I wish to find Patrick. I hope I never see either one of them again for as long as I live."

He smiled tolerantly. "Well, before you cast Justin

out of your life, I think you should know about his wife's death."

"I already know how she died. Justin murdered her."

"Did he tell you that?"

"When I confronted him with it, he certainly didn't deny that he had killed her."

"Does his lack of denial make him guilty?"

"Exactly what are you trying to say?" Molly asked. She was beginning to feel nonplussed.

"I'm telling you Justin didn't murder his wife." Blade continued forcefully, "Good Lord, he loved her! Furthermore, Justin isn't capable of killing a woman."

"If he was innocent, then why didn't he tell me?" she cried.

"I don't know for sure. Stubbornness, probably."

Thinking back, she replied softly, "And jealousy."

Blade looked at her quizzically.

"The night when I questioned him about his wife, he had found me in Gary's embrace. I'm sure you are aware of Justin's jealousy. He was terribly upset, and I should have known that wasn't the time to bring up his wife's death."

Blade agreed. "It was definitely bad timing. Besides, from what he's told me about that night, you already had him tried and found guilty."

Reluctantly, she admitted, "I might have given him that impression. But you must realize that I was shocked and didn't know how to handle the situation."

"Before I tell you what really happened with Justin's wife, I have a question to ask, and I expect you to answer honestly."

"I will," she replied sincerely.

"Are you in love with Justin?"

"Yes, I love him with all my heart." The look in her eyes confirmed her words.

Blade leaned back in his chair, and stretched out his

long legs. "Justin's wife, North Star, was a full-blooded Comanche. Justin lived with the Comanches for awhile, and that's how he met her. When they married, Comanche-style, he built them a small homestead in Texas. There was a white settlement close by, and although they accepted Justin, they disapproved of his Indian wife. The white settlers harbored a lot of hate for the Comanches. At that time there was violent conflict between the Indians and the whites, and there probably wasn't a family in the settlement who hadn't lost a loved one to the Comanches. Justin and North Star had been living in their home for a couple of months when Justin rode to the settlement to buy supplies. A week before, a young white woman had been raped and killed by a band of marauding Comanche warriors. So needless to say, this had rekindled the hate these white settlers had for the Indians. While Justin was away, four men came to his home. They raped and tortured North Star."

Blade rose from his chair and went to the table. Picking up an ashtray, he returned and lit a cheroot before continuing. "I won't explain the way in which she was tortured. You don't need to hear the graphic details."

"I understand," Molly whispered.

"When Justin returned home, the four men were gone. I can only imagine the pain and horror Justin felt upon finding his wife. She was still alive, and was just able to give him the names of the men who had attacked her. Two of them were Texas Rangers. Before she died, she begged Justin to burn her body so she wouldn't enter the spirit world in the same condition those men had left her in."

Blade paused and took a couple of drags on his cigar. He was finding it difficult to tell this story to a lady. In truth, it was repulsive and horrible beyond words, but

414

for Molly's sake, he must continue.

"After North Star died, Justin set fire to the cabin. The people in the settlement spotted the smoke and a few of the men rode out. Among these riders were the four men who had killed North Star. Justin was beside himself with grief . . . and revenge. He was determined to kill the men who had murdered his wife. He knew the Texas Rangers wouldn't arrest them for they wouldn't care that they had murdered an Indian squaw. If Justin had reported their names, and one or more of them were suddenly killed, Justin would've been the most likely suspect. The whites would have hanged Justin for avenging his wife's death. Most of them believed all Indians should be dead anyway. So when the men rode up to the burning cabin, Justin, on the spur of the moment, told them the first story that came to mind. He said that North Star was leaving him for a Comanche warrior, so he had shot her. Because he didn't want to take the time to bury her, and was leaving Texas, he had simply set fire to their home, with her body inside. Naturally, there were four men among these riders who knew his story wasn't true. But there wasn't much they could do about it, unless they wanted to admit what they had done. They probably believed Justin was willing to let it pass, mistakingly thinking he wouldn't grieve over an Indian squaw any more than he would grieve over his pet hound dog."

Blade put out his cigar, returned the ashtray to the table, then began pacing in front of the bed. "Justin went to the settlement, where he made a point of letting everyone know that he was moving to Wyoming. He rode into the hills and camped for a few days. Then he began his revenge."

"He killed those four men who murdered North Star, didn't he?" Molly interrupted.

"Yes. With the stealth of an Indian he stalked his

415

prey and killed them one by one. He was never a suspect; everyone believed he was in Wyoming. When the last man was dead, he did come to Wyoming, and after a couple of years he hired on as a scout for the army."

"Why hasn't he told the truth about his wife? Why does he continue to allow people to believe that he murdered her?"

"He killed white men to avenge an Indian; there are still people who would want to see him hanged for his actions. Captain Newcomb, for instance."

"He can never claim his innocence?"

"Not where his wife is concerned. There are four dead men whose assailant is unaccounted for. And even after all this time, Justin might be brought to trial for those killings."

"I can't imagine Justin cold-bloodedly murdering four men," she moaned.

"Neither can I. That's why he didn't have to tell me that he gave each man a chance to defend himself. I knew that without being told, because I know Justin Smith."

"If only Justin had told me the truth that night when I confronted him," she murmured regretfully.

"Before we went to Iron Kettle's village he told me he was planning to tell you, but then he came back and found you engaged to Captain Newcomb."

Standing, Molly said, "I'll go to Justin's quarters. I owe him an apology, but he also owes me one for being so hard-headed and stubborn."

Chuckling, Blade replied, "He's definitely hard-headed and stubborn, but you won't find him in his quarters. He left the fort and isn't planning on returning until Sunday morning."

"Oh no!" she cried, disappointed.

"I think I know where he's gone, and if you want, I

can take you to him."

"Where is he?"

"He has a cabin about five miles from here. He calls it his retreat, and he goes there when he wants to be alone."

Anxious to see Justin, Molly asked, "Can you take me there tonight?"

"I'll go to the stable and order a buckboard hitched for us. The terrain we'll travel through is too rough for a buggy." Heading toward the front door, he called over his shoulder, "Bring a coat; it's getting cold outside."

Justin had heard the arriving buckboard and was standing in the cabin's open doorway when Molly and Blade appeared. The night was clear and the moon shone brightly on Justin's two visitors. He studied them suspiciously.

Blade started to climb down so he could assist Molly, but she stopped him by placing a hand on his arm.

"I think you should leave immediately," she began. "If you stay, Justin might insist that you take me back to the fort. If you aren't here, he'll have no choice but to let me remain."

"All right," Blade agreed. He took her hand and squeezed gently. "Good luck."

The night air was chilly, and Molly wrapped her cloak tightly about her as she carefully descended from the wagon. As soon as she was safely away from the buckboard, Blade slapped the reins against the team.

"Come back here!" Justin yelled, but Blade pretended not to hear and kept the wagon moving.

Molly's heart was beating rapidly as she approached the cabin. Was there still a chance that she and Justin might have a future together, or had their misunder-

417

standings put too much distance between them? Could their love close the breach?

Pausing in front of Justin, she lifted her gaze to his. "It's cold out here—do you mind inviting me inside where it's warm?"

He stepped aside, and as she entered the cabin he grumbled, "Why in the hell did you have Blade bring you here? Why aren't you with your fiancé?"

She waited until he had closed the door before answering, "I no longer have a fiancé."

"So you finally wised up and got rid of that no-good son of . . ." He mumbled an apology. "Excuse my language."

Removing her cloak, Molly glanced about the cabin. It had no furniture except for a bed and a table with four chairs. She draped her wrap over one of the chairs, then stepped over to warm her hands at the blazing fireplace.

"Why are you here, Molly?" Justin demanded.

"The major told me the truth about North Star's death," she answered carefully.

"He what?" Justin bellowed.

"He told me the truth," she replied, whirling about to face him. "Which is something you should've told me from the beginning!"

"I know," he admitted. "I had decided to tell you, but when I learned you were engaged to Newcomb, I didn't think you'd be interested." His tone was agitated.

"Then maybe you should stop thinking and start asking!" she retorted.

He waved his arms in despair. "There you go again, acting like a snobbish female!"

"Justin Smith, you're impossible!" she spat.

"So you've told me before!" he muttered angrily.

Silence fell between them, then, composing himself,

Justin asked evenly, "Why did you break up with Newcomb?"

"I don't love him. I knew I didn't love him when I accepted his marriage proposal, but I had convinced myself I could live without that emotion. But now I realize that under no circumstances can I marry a man I don't love."

"If you weren't in love with him, then why did you become his lover?" he asked bitterly.

"I didn't!" she exclaimed. "Whatever gave you that idea?"

"Newcomb," he said gruffly. "The low-down, lyin' weasel!"

"How dare he insinuate that he and I . . ." Her Irish temper flowing hotly, she stamped her foot as her eyes flashed daggers.

"Molly O'Ryan, you got one helluva temper," Justin declared, grinning.

"So do you," she returned.

"I know. No wonder we have so damned much trouble gettin' along with each other."

Her anger now completely forgotten, she asked pertly, "What are we going to do about these tempers of ours?"

"Why don't we get married and merge them into one?" he suggested, his grin broadening.

Molly laughed gaily. "Oh, Justin, what a wonderful suggestion!"

He cocked an eyebrow. "Does that mean you're gonna marry me?"

"Yes, if your suggestion was a proposal."

"It wasn't very romantic, was it?"

"It was the most romantic proposal I've ever received. Do you know why?"

"Why?" he asked.

"Because it came from you, my wonderful Justin Smith!"

In two quick strides he moved over to her and swept her into his embrace. "I love you, Molly," he murmured hoarsely, before pressing his lips to hers.

Lifting her in his arms, he carried her to the bed, where he laid her down with care. Lying beside her, he drew her close, then kissed her once again. Molly's fingers caressed the nape of his neck as she responded ardently to the lips on hers.

"Justin, darling, make love to me," she pleaded throatily, anxious to feel him deep inside her. The three months since they had last been together had seemed an eternity.

Standing, he took her hand and urged her to her feet. He helped her shed her clothes, and when she was beautifully unclad he eased her back onto the bed. Leaning over her, his lips etched a passionate path from her throat, then to her breasts, before moving farther downward.

Writhing with ecstasy, she welcomed his exploration and shuddered when his lips and tongue drove her to a breathtaking climax.

Leaving the bed, Justin disrobed impatiently, now more anxious than ever to enter fully the woman he loved. Molding his body to hers, he sank his hardness deep into her exciting heat. His strong hands, clutching her hips, pulled her thighs up to his, and with each thrust he rekindled Molly's passion until it was revived and equal to his own. She wrapped her legs about him, and together they soared blissfully into their own private paradise.

Molly and Justin didn't return to the fort until late afternoon of the following day. She had thoroughly enjoyed the short journey, as she had ridden in front of Justin on his horse and had felt his strong arms about her for the duration of the trip.

Learning from Saul that Suzanne and Blade were visiting the Wilkinsons, they decided to go to the lieutenant's house. They were eager to let their good friends know that they were planning to get married.

Shelley Wilkinson showed them into her small home and into the parlor. Immediately Molly informed them all of her marvelous news. After Blade and the lieutenant had shaken Justin's hand and the women had hugged Molly, Suzanne inquired, "When do you plan to marry?"

It was Justin who answered, "Well, you and the major are gettin' married Sunday, so we decided to wait until Monday."

"But why wait?" Suzanne exclaimed. "We can make it a double wedding!" She glanced at Blade. "You wouldn't mind, would you, darling?"

"Of course not," he replied. "In fact, I think it's a great idea."

"Oh, I couldn't!" Molly objected. "You two are having a formal wedding. What would I wear?"

"You can borrow my wedding dress," Shelley offered. "We are the same size, and I bet it'll fit you perfectly."

Grinning, Blade looked at Justin. "What about you? Do you have a suit?"

Appearing quite offended, Justin mumbled, "I got a suit. I bought it a couple of years ago. In fact, I bought it 'cause I was goin' to a weddin'."

Blade laughed good-naturedly. "Well, that settles that! A double wedding it will be."

Grasping Molly's arm, Shelley said, "You need to come with me to my bedroom so you can try on the gown."

"That won't be necessary," the lieutenant spoke up. Turning his attention to the other gentlemen, he suggested, "Why don't we go to the club so we'll be out of the ladies' way?"

Justin and Blade gladly agreed, and promising to return soon, they made their departure.

"I'll bring the dress into the parlor," Shelley decided. "There's more room here for you to try it on."

As she was leaving for her bedroom, Suzanne stepped over to the front window and gazed outside. The Wilkinsons' daughter was playing in the front yard with a neighboring child and Suzanne was watching them.

Going to her side, and detecting a note of somberness, Molly inquired, "Suzanne, what's wrong?"

"Nothing," she murmured.

"Are you thinking about Patrick?"

"No," she answered. "Shelley's daughter makes me think of Kara."

"The little girl at the Sioux village," Molly remembered. Suzanne had told her about Kara.

"I hope she's all right, and has learned to adjust to her new life."

"I'm sure she has," Molly said encouragingly.

At that moment Shelley returned with a large box which held her wedding dress. Anxious to see the garment, Suzanne and Molly hurried over to help her remove it from its protective covering.

Chapter Thirty-Four

The double wedding ceremony was held at the huge recreational hall that was used for parties, balls, and other festivities. The fort's military orchestra provided the music that drifted across the large dance floor, which at present was filled with couples waltzing.

As Blade and his bride danced to the music, she gazed lovingly into his eyes and murmured, "Do you realize this is the first time we have danced together?"

"The first maybe," he replied. "But certainly not the last. During the winter months, officers and their families socialize with a whole series of balls."

"Good!" she declared. "I love balls!"

He chuckled. "In that case, Mrs. Landon, you'll thoroughly enjoy this winter."

"Mrs. Landon," she repeated dreamily. "What a wonderful name!"

Meanwhile, as Blade was dancing with his new wife, Almeda and Gary were poised in front of the buffet table. Almeda's eyes were fixed on the newlyweds, her expression malicious. She despised Blade for choosing Suzanne Donovan over herself. Resentfully, she hoped Gary would soon devise a good plan for getting even; when he did, she intended to be a part of his wicked scheme. It would give her great satisfaction to know that she had helped bring revenge upon Blade. She turned to look at Gary, but he wasn't watching Blade and Suzanne; his gaze was glued to Justin and Molly, who were standing off by themselves.

Her gaze meeting his, Almeda pondered, "I wonder why Justin isn't waltzing with his bride?"

Gary snickered. "The clumsy ox probably doesn't know how to dance."

His companion giggled. "Darling, don't you think we should walk over and offer the couple our congratulations?" Her eyes shone mischievously.

"What do you have in mind?" he asked.

"Why do you think I have an ulterior motive?"

"Don't you?"

Smiling vindictively, she answered, "Escort me across the room, and you'll find out what I plan to do." She eyed him challengingly. "You aren't afraid to approach Justin Smith, are you?"

"Of course not," he denied quickly. Taking her arm, he guided her toward the newly married couple.

Conceitedly, Almeda noticed the way in which several men turned to look at her as she moved gracefully across the room. She was exceptionally beautiful; her gown of white crepe was trimmed with violet-colored silk, and the full skirt was gathered with three flounces of black lace.

Close to her husband's side, Molly noticed that Gary and the colonel's daughter were coming in their direction. Placing a hand on Justin's arm, she said apprehensively, "We're about to have company."

"I can hardly wait," he grumbled sarcastically.

"Darling, please try to be civil," she pleaded.

Almeda was all smiles as she arrived and said sweetly, "Mr. and Mrs. Smith, we wanted to offer you our best wishes."

"Yes," Gary added. "We hope you two will be very happy."

"Thank you," Molly replied. She looked at her husband, waiting for him to respond, but he merely glared at the captain and said nothing.

Feigning sincerity, Almeda asked warmly, "My goodness, why aren't you two dancing? The orchestra is playing such a lovely waltz."

"My husband doesn't dance," Molly answered, her tone daring Almeda to come back with a snide remark.

"What a shame!" she declared, her voice heavy with concern. She was completely enjoying the situation, and was pleased to see an embarrassed blush in Molly's cheeks. Serves her right! Almeda thought. She shouldn't have married an uncouth boor! "We have numerous balls during the winter," she rambled on, "and since your husband doesn't dance, you'll have to sit out all the musical numbers."

"Quite the contrary," a deep voice suddenly spoke out.

Spinning about, Almeda saw Lieutenant Wilkinson.

Bowing to Molly, he asked elegantly, "Mrs. Smith, may I have the pleasure of this dance?" He acknowledged Justin. "With your permission, of course."

Receiving permission, the lieutenant then smiled at Almeda. "Miss Johnson, I can assure you that Mrs. Smith will not be sitting out dances. As you already know, there are more men at these dances than women, and a woman as lovely as Molly Smith will be most popular."

With that, he placed Molly's hand in the crook of his arm and whisked her onto the dance floor.

"Miss Johnson," Justin began. As she turned to him, he proceeded in an even tone, "You're a conniving little witch, and I'd appreciate it if you'd stay away from my wife."

425

Aghast, Almeda inhaled sharply. "How dare you speak so insultingly!"

"I was tryin' to be subtle," he returned. "But if you and your conspirator don't get the hell away from me, I'll show you just how insultin' I can be when I set my mind to it."

Taking Almeda's arm, Gary said gallantly, "I should call you out for talking so rudely to Miss Johnson!" Without bothering to back up his threat, he ushered her away.

Watching their hasty departure, Justin chuckled.

Clad in a flowing, sheer negligée, Suzanne left the bedroom and went into the parlor, where she found her husband sitting in an armchair in front of the fireplace.

Aware of her presence, he rose. His dark eyes glazed with desire as his bride moved gracefully to his side. Sweeping her into his embrace, he kissed her passionately.

Suzanne murmured joyously, "Our first night in our new home. Oh, Blade, I'm so happy!"

Stepping back and holding her at arm's length, he asked, "Are you sure you'll be able to cope with army life?" He glanced about the modest parlor. "Military wives don't live in very grand style."

"I have no wish to live elaborately; I only wish to live with you," she assured him, her eyes shining with adoration.

"I love you, Suzanne," he said huskily. Then, drawing her closer, he pressed his lips to hers.

Blade's kiss was fervent, demanding, and Suzanne's arms went about his neck as she returned his passion full force.

He lifted her and cradled her against his strong chest as he carried her to their bedroom. Placing her on her

426

feet, he drew her yielding body flush to his. Entwining her arms about him, her lips sought his with a fierce passion.

Needing her desperately, Blade removed her delicate nightwear, and with loving care, picked her up and laid her upon their bed.

Suzanne's face was alight with anticipation as she watched her husband shed his boots and dress uniform. He was so unbelievably handsome that the sight of him alone could send her pulse racing with wild desire.

She invited him into her arms, and as he entered his wife's embrace, he said thickly, "I love you, Mrs. Landon." Swiftly his lips descended to hers in a deep, love-filled kiss.

His hand traveled agilely over her silken flesh, his touch inciting her passion. Engulfed in the throes of ecstasy, Suzanne responded ardently, returning his fondling as her hand sought and found his male hardness. When she began to caress him, Blade moaned huskily, for her touch was as exciting to him as his was to her.

Unable any longer to resist her charms, he moved over her, and as her legs parted, he entered her deeply. Clinging tightly, Suzanne was swept gloriously away into an exquisite paradise.

The next morning Blade had just finished dressing, and Suzanne, wearing her negligée, was sitting in front of the dresser brushing her hair when they were disturbed by someone knocking insistently at their front door.

A testy frown shadowed Blade's face with annoyance at being interrupted at such an early hour. Leaving the bedroom, he strode quickly to open the door.

"Excuse me, sir," a young trooper said hastily, "but

Colonel Johnson wants to see you at once."

"Very well, soldier," he replied. "Tell the colonel I'll be right there."

Closing the door, Blade returned to the bedroom and said apologetically, "I'm sorry, sweetheart, but Colonel Johnson has sent for me."

Stepping to his side, Suzanne protested, "But darling, you haven't had breakfast yet." She had been looking forward to cooking their first meal in their new home.

"Hopefully, what he has to tell me won't take long, and I'll be back shortly."

"In that case, I'll just tidy up while you're gone, and fix breakfast when you return."

He kissed her long and hard, then with an affectionate wink he turned about and left the room.

Wanting to remain busy until her husband's return, Suzanne made the bed, then slipping out of her negligée, she put on one of her favorite dresses. It was a modestly cut blue frock, but its simplicity emphasized her soft, feminine curves.

Walking into the parlor, she paused to examine the room. It was cozy and comfortable, the furniture in surprisingly good shape. Suzanne thoroughly loved her small home; in her opinion it was the perfect honeymoon cottage. The young woman's happiness was overwhelming, and reveling in her joy, she danced across the floor, her movements as graceful as a swan's. Her bliss was intoxicating, and she laughed gaily.

When Blade suddenly opened the front door, she rushed into her husband's arms and kissed him eagerly. Stepping back, she gazed up into his face. His expression was somber, and she asked with concern, "Is something wrong? Why did Colonel Johnson send for you?"

"Suzanne," he began gently, "I have bad news."

"Bad news?" she repeated, perplexed. She noticed he was carrying an object in his hand, but it was covered with a cloth and she couldn't make it out.

Taking her arm, he led her to the sofa. They sat and he said soberly, "Two of the fort's Kiowa scouts reported in this morning to the colonel. They had been in the hills. A few miles from Iron Kettle's village they came upon a man's dead body. It had been burned beyond recognition. But a few of his possessions were found nearby. Among them were an army issue saddle and blanket, plus his saddlebags."

Suzanne tensed and a foreboding chill coursed throughout her body.

Blade reached into his shirt pocket, and withdrawing a daguerreotype, he continued, "This was found in the saddlebags."

He handed it to her, and her hand shook as she accepted it. She didn't have to look at it to know it was a picture of herself. Nonetheless, she lowered her eyes and looked at her own image. The daguerreotype's corners were frayed, and the picture itself was worn as though it had been handled many times.

Blade removed the cloth covering the hidden object. Numbly, Suzanne saw that it was a Bible.

Placing it on her lap, he said softly, "This was also in the man's saddlebags. I looked inside and read the inscription you wrote to Patrick."

Her voice almost inaudible, Suzanne whispered, "I gave this Bible to Patrick on his twenty-first birthday." Suddenly gasping, she cried, "Oh, Blade, what does all this mean?"

"Sweetheart, you know what it means," he answered urgently. "It's quite apparent that Donovan was traveling alone and for some reason was killed by a band of Sioux. He could very well have been attacked by Two Moons."

"Where is the body?" she asked painfully.

"The scouts buried the man where they found him. Honey, they reported that the body was burned so badly it couldn't possibly be identified."

Tears gushing, she groaned, "Oh no! . . . Patrick!"

Tenderly Blade urged her into his arms. "I'm sorry, Suzanne," he said sympathetically. He held her close as she cried heartbrokenly for her cousin. Blade knew this was not the time to tell her that, callous as it might sound, Patrick's demise was for the best. Later, when she had recovered somewhat, he'd point out to her that her cousin's court-martial had been inevitable, and would have resulted in the death penalty. Now she wouldn't be forced to suffer through his trial and ultimate execution.

Suzanne was silent as she strolled beside her husband. They were on their way to Blade's quarters. Molly and Justin were living in the cabin, and Saul was now staying in the bedroom adjacent to the major's office. Suzanne dreaded telling Saul about Patrick. She knew how deeply the man loved his former master.

Saul had just walked out of the bedroom when Suzanne and Blade entered the office. Smiling broadly, he said, "Good mornin', major, Miz Suzanne." He waited for them to return his greeting, but when they made no attempt to do so, he looked at them closely. Taking note of their somberness, he asked, "What's wrong?"

Stepping away from Blade, Suzanne moved across the floor to Saul's side. Her large eyes were clouded with tears.

"It's Masta Patrick, ain't it?" he guessed. "Somethin's happened to him."

As gently as possible, she told him of the scouts'

430

report and the picture and Bible they had discovered among the dead man's belongings.

A low mournful sob caught in Saul's throat. "Masta Patrick is dead?"

"Yes," she whispered brokenly.

It was a long moment before he managed to compose himself enough to speak evenly. "It's better this way."

Blade was relieved that Saul's feelings coincided with his own. He listened intently for Suzanne's response.

"I agree with you," she murmured sadly. Then she cried piteously, "Oh, Saul, why did Patrick's life have to end this way? Why did he become so evil?"

"Miz Suzanne, we ain't gonna ever learn the answers to those questions. They died with Masta Patrick." He placed his hands on her shoulders. "I don't want you a-grievin' no more for Masta Patrick. Just remember him as he used to be before the war. You got a husband who loves you a powerful lot, and you two shouldn't start your life off with you mournin' for your cousin. The Patrick we knew died years ago. The time has come for you to put the past behind you and live only for the present."

She smiled timorously. "I have already put the past behind me. Blade is now my life and my happiness."

Suzanne's declaration caused her husband to sigh thankfully.

Saul left Suzanne to move over to Blade. "Major, suh, if it's all right with you, come spring I wanna go back to Southmoor."

"Of course," he answered. "I'll make the necessary arrangements."

"Thank you, Mista Blade."

"Saul," Blade began, "I'm sorry everything had to work out the way it did. I know how much you and Suzanne loved Donovan."

"I appreciate your kindness. You're a good man, and

I'm happy that Miz Suzanne found herself a husband like you. When I'm back home, I ain't gonna have to worry about her, 'cause I know you're gonna take good care of her."

"You have my word on it," Blade promised, offering Saul his hand.

In his seventy-odd years of life, Saul had never shaken hands with a white man, and it was with hesitation that he stretched out his hand to take the major's. Their shake was firm and respectful.

"Has Miz Molly been told?"

"No, not yet," Blade answered.

Saul turned and looked at Suzanne. "Do you want me to tell her?"

"Yes, please," she murmured.

Saul left the office so quickly that Suzanne and Blade didn't see the tears that suddenly flooded his eyes. As he headed toward Justin's cabin, with an effort he gained control of his emotions. He would abide by his own advice and not grieve any longer. As he had told Suzanne, the Patrick they had known and loved had ceased to exist a long, long time ago. He would set aside his grief and go home and live out his remaining years at Southmoor. And whenever he thought of Patrick, he'd remember him as the fine, compassionate person that he had once been.

Chapter Thirty-Five

The winter months passed quickly for Suzanne. She thoroughly enjoyed fort life and its numerous social functions. The soldiers seldom left the post, and she and Blade were able to spend a lot of time together. Suzanne utterly adored her husband, and he in turn was totally devoted to his lovely bride.

There were moments when Patrick entered her thoughts and her mood would then become somber, but with the passing of time these moments grew fewer and farther between. Time, the great healer of emotional wounds, worked its magic on Suzanne, and her grief finally dissolved.

With the coming of spring, the parties began to dwindle somewhat as the post became more military minded.

On this particular spring morning, Blade and Justin had gone to Fort Fetterman on business for the colonel. They had been away for several days, and Suzanne desperately missed her husband. It was their first separation since they had married.

Planning to visit Molly, Suzanne left her house and began walking toward the isolated cabin. She was totally unaware of the two trappers who were following her from a distance.

Keeping her in sight, the smaller of the two men asked, "She's the one, ain't she, Ed?"

"As many times as Donovan used to make us look at her picture, I don't see how you can even question if she's his cousin. Damn, I'd know her anywhere." Increasing their pace, he urged, "Come on, Henry, let's catch up."

As they drew closer, Ed called out cordially, "Ma'am, could we talk to you for a moment?"

Suzanne glanced over her shoulder and paused. When they reached her side, Ed asked, "You're Suzanne Donovan, ain't you?"

"Yes, but Donovan is my maiden name. I'm now Mrs. Landon."

"Ma'am, my name is Ed and this here is Henry. We're friends of Patrick Donovan's."

Suzanne stared wide-eyed. "Wh . . . why do you want to talk to me? My cousin is dead."

"No, he ain't dead." It had been Henry who had blurted out this revelation.

She was stunned. "What are you saying?"

Henry continued, "Donovan's alive and wants to see you. He sent us here to get you."

"No!" she retorted. "Patrick was killed. His body was found by two Indian scouts."

"That body they found weren't Donovan's," Ed mumbled.

"Then who was it?"

"Indian Joe, the man who took you into the hills last fall and then left you there," Ed answered.

"I can't believe this!" she cried. Good Lord, could it be true? Was Patrick still alive?

"Mrs. Landon," Henry began, "your cousin will explain everything when he sees you. We come here to get you, and we want you to leave with us in the mornin'."

"I . . . I don't know what to say," she stammered in disbelief.

"Donovan gave us a message to give you," Ed spoke up. "He said to tell you that he's holdin' you to your promise always to be his friend and always to be there for him." He paused, then added movingly, "He needs you, ma'am."

"He needs me?" she repeated vacantly, her mind whirling.

"Ma'am," Henry emphasized, "you can't tell nobody about this. If the army finds out, they'll hunt him down. Can you get away without your husband interferin'?"

"My husband isn't here," she murmured.

"Good!" Henry declared. "Then there ain't no reason why you can't get away. We saw you leave your house, so we know where you live. We'll come by for you tomorrow at dawn."

"Exactly where is Patrick?" she asked.

"He's still up in the hills. It'll take us about three days to reach him. Do you have your own horse?"

"Yes," she replied. Suzanne had kept the sorrel mare given to her by Prairie Flower.

Pressingly Ed reminded her, "Remember, ma'am, you can't tell nobody where you're goin'."

"I understand," she answered weakly. Suzanne was incapable of grasping fully everything they had said. Patrick alive? The burned body had been Indian Joe's? But why had Indian Joe had Patrick's possessions?

"We'll see you in the mornin'," Henry said, then without further discussion, he and his companion strolled away and headed for the enlisted men's bar.

Dazed, Suzanne watched them until they had moved out of sight. Then lethargically she veered from her original course and began walking toward Blade's office, where she was sure she'd find Saul. The servant

435

hadn't yet left for Southmoor, but was planning on leaving early the next month. These trappers had warned her not to tell anyone, but she knew Saul could be trusted. Furthermore, she wasn't about to keep such important news to herself and not share it with Saul.

When she entered Blade's office, she went to the bedroom door and knocked.

"Come in," she heard Saul call.

She went in and saw him sitting in the hard-backed chair beside the opened window. He had been reading, but at Suzanne's entrance he laid the book aside and got to his feet. Her face was noticeably pale, and he inquired hastily, "Miz Suzanne, are you all right?"

Suddenly her knees weakened, and going over to the bed, she sat down on the edge. "Saul," she began, her voice quivering, "Patrick is still alive."

"Wh . . . what?" he cried.

As calmly as possible, she told him about her meeting with Ed and Henry. "They want me to leave with them tomorrow at dawn," she finished.

Moving to the bed on wobbly legs, he sat beside her. "Are you goin'?"

"I have to," she moaned.

"No, Miz Suzanne, you don't have to go if you don't want to."

"I can't turn my back on Patrick," she sobbed.

"How do you suppose Masta Patrick knew you were here?"

"I imagine Indian Joe told him."

"I'm goin' with you," he stated firmly.

Suzanne didn't argue; quite the contrary, she had been hoping he'd offer to accompany her. She didn't care if Ed and Henry approved or not. She was not about to leave the fort alone with two men she didn't know. The last time she had done something so foolish, she had been abandoned in the wilderness and left to

436

fend for herself. Besides, Patrick would be pleased to see Saul.

She placed a hand over his. "I want you to come with me."

Frowning with consternation, Saul asked, "What's the major gonna say about this?"

"I don't know," she sighed, worried. "I'll leave him a note and plead with him to try and understand why I feel that I must go to Patrick. It's not as though I'm choosing him over Blade. After we have visited with Patrick, we'll return to the fort. I love my husband, and I'm not forsaking him."

"I know that, Miz Suzanne, but I ain't sure Mista Blade is gonna see it that way."

She lifted her worried gaze to his. "He'll understand! Surely he will!"

At dawn, Suzanne and Saul left with the two trappers. The servant didn't have a horse and was riding one of the mules they had used to draw their wagon on their journey to Fort Laramie. Except for Molly, they hadn't told anyone about their trip into the Black Hills.

About dusk on the same day of Suzanne's and Saul's departure, Blade and Justin returned from Fort Fetterman. Immediately after making a report to Colonel Johnson, Blade made a beeline for home. He had missed his wife and was anxious to see her.

Swinging open the front door and barging inside, he called loudly, "Suzanne, I'm home!" He was answered by silence.

He wondered if she was visting a friend, and was about to check with his neighbors when he caught sight of an envelope propped on the coffee table. Picking it up, he removed the letter inside. Sitting on the sofa, he began to read:

Dear Blade,
  I've received news that Patrick is alive. Saul and I have gone to see him. Please understand and forgive me for leaving. I love you, and I'll return as soon as possible.

Suzanne

Blade crumpled the letter in his hand and threw it across the room. "Damn Donovan!" he raged. He'd been a fool to think he had his wife's first loyalty. It always had and always would belong to her unsavory cousin!

Blade heard someone entering the house, and glancing up, he saw Justin come into the parlor.

"Molly just told me what happened," the scout said.

"I'm going after her," Blade said tersely.

"I'll go with you."

"Suit yourself."

"Blade," Justin began tentatively, "don't be too hard on Suzanne. After all, Donovan's her kin."

"Oh yeah?" Blade smirked. "Well, Trooper Jones was my kin!"

"Damn it, Blade, you ain't bein' fair!"

Bounding from the sofa, Blade shouted, "I'm sick and tired of fighting Suzanne's love for her cousin! He's always come first in her life!"

"Then why are you goin' after her?"

"So I can pick up her trail, which will lead me to Donovan. Then I intend to arrest him."

"With Suzanne and Saul lookin' on?" Justin asked irritably.

Blade eyed him harshly. "I don't see how it can be otherwise, do you?" When his friend offered no reply, he said briskly, "I want you to tell me everything you

438

learned from Molly. Who in the hell did Suzanne and Saul leave with, or did they take off by themselves?"

Deciding to keep his feelings to himself, Justin proceeded to tell him what he wanted to know.

The hour was fairly late when Gary arrived at the colonel's house and was ushered into the parlor by Almeda. She could sense that the captain was somewhat excited and she asked anxiously, "Is this a social call, or do you have a specific reason for being here?"

"Black Wolf just arrived, and he's at your father's office."

"So?"

"In a few minutes he'll be taking his horse to the stables."

She groaned impatiently. "Honestly, Gary, what point are you trying to make?"

He grinned slyly. "Major Landon and Justin Smith are good friends with Black Wolf. How do you think they'd feel if their Indian comrade was hanged?"

Almeda was at a loss. "They would be devastated, I'm sure," she mumbled, wondering where all this was leading.

"About three hours ago the major and Justin left to ride to the hills. It seems Landon's wife has once again taken off to find her cousin, and they've gone after her."

"I thought Trooper Donovan was murdered."

"Well, apparently he wasn't. But that's beside the point. By the time Landon and Smith return to the fort, their Sioux friend will be dead."

Almeda was enthralled. Black Wolf's death would indeed distress Blade. It would be a good way to get even with him. She cast Gary an inquiring look. "Why is Black Wolf going to be hanged?"

"For attempted rape," he answered.

"Who will he attempt to rape?" she asked, although she had a feeling she already knew.

"Black Wolf will be lynched for trying to force himself on Colonel Johnson's daughter. I want you to go to the stables. At this time of night, there should be no one around. When Black Wolf brings in his horse, tempt him as you know so well how to do. Meanwhile, I'll find a couple of troopers and suggest that they take a stroll with me. Naturally, we'll walk past the stables. When we come near the entrance, I'll find a reason to laugh loudly, which will be your signal to start screaming. The troopers and I will rush inside the stable and save you from the savage's assault. Colonel Johnson will insist on his arrest." Gary chuckled complacently. "In less than twenty-four hours, I will have some of the soldiers so incited that they'll break Black Wolf out of the guardhouse and lynch him before the colonel can stop them. Of course, considering it was his daughter who was almost raped, I'm sure Colonel Johnson will not be too angry."

He waited expectantly for Almeda to agree. Although Gary was relishing getting even with Blade and Justin, he was still more eager to see Black Wolf hanged. He despised all Indians, especially half-breeds who, in Gary's view, thought themselves equal to whites. Black Wolf's intelligence and polished manners infuriated him. He believed all Indians inferior, and half-breeds abominations.

Almeda was finding Gary's plan delightful. That she would be responsible for a man's death made no impact on her whatsoever. Although she had always found Black Wolf savagely handsome, he was, after all, only an Indian, which in her opinion made him less than human. Furthermore, fort life was dull, and she had been longing for excitement. If she agreed to this scheme, it would make her the center of attention. And it would be so thrilling when the soldiers avenged her honor by hanging her assailant!

Smiling wickedly, she answered, "I think your idea is marvelous."

"Good!" Gary declared. Then, taking her off guard, he grasped the bodice of her gown and ripped it all the way to the waist.

Startled, she gasped, "Why did you ruin my dress?"

"I didn't; Black Wolf did," he remarked, grinning shrewdly. "Fetch a shawl and cover the tear. And hurry, because you need to get to the stable and await our unsuspecting rapist."

As Almeda found herself a dark corner inside the stable, she suddenly realized that there was a flaw in Gary's plan. What excuse would she give her father for being in the stables this time of night? After serious consideration, she decided to tell the colonel that she hadn't been able to sleep, and had taken a stroll. She had run across Black Wolf and he had forced her inside the stable by holding a knife to her back.

Detecting someone approaching, Almeda tensed. A horse's soft whinny sounded in the darkness, and as she moved away from the corner, the twilight filtering through the opened door shone upon Black Wolf and his pinto.

He was leading his horse toward an empty stall when Almeda stepped forward and into the light. "Hello, Black Wolf," she murmured, keeping her shawl wrapped tightly about her shoulders.

"Miss Johnson!" he exclaimed. "What are you doing here?"

"I was waiting for you," she replied, smiling invitingly. "I knew when you left Father's office, you'd come here."

Black Wolf was suddenly on his guard. "Why would you wait for me?"

She inched her way closer to the muscular warrior. "Black Wolf, I've always found you very attractive." She pouted prettily. "Don't you feel the same way about me?"

He wasn't about to succumb to her seduction and muttered irritably, "Go home, Miss Johnson. If you're searching for a man to bed, then you're wasting your time with me. For more reasons than one, as far as I'm concerned you're off limits."

Reaching his side, she boldly slid her arms about his neck. Pressing her thighs to his, she murmured daringly, "I want you to make love to me."

Black Wolf was about to disentangle himself from her grip when suddenly a man's boisterous laugh rang out clearly. An instant later, Almeda began screaming at the top of her lungs.

For a moment the warrior was too stunned to react, and Almeda was still in his embrace as the three men rushed inside. Wildly she began to pound her hands against his chest, causing her shawl to fall to the floor. "Let me go! . . . Please let me go!" she cried.

Black Wolf stepped back from her assault, but it was too late; the two troopers with Gary already had their pistols aimed at him.

Stumbling to Gary, Almeda leaned against him and sobbed, "He tried to attack me!"

Glaring at Black Wolf, Gary raged, "You savage son of a bitch!" Then, moving swiftly, he went over to the warrior and doubling his hand into a fist, hit him powerfully across the jaw. To his troopers he said, "I'll take Miss Johnson to her father. You two escort this savage to the guardhouse and lock him up."

Placing an arm about Almeda's shoulders, the captain assisted her from the stables.

"Come on, Indian!" one of the troopers ordered.

The two soldiers Gary had chosen were inexperienced recruits, and no match for the skillful warrior. It took Black Wolf only one sweeping glance to appraise his opponents as insignificant. He stepped forward as though he intended to follow orders. He was now between the two men, and when he made his move, he was so incredibly fast that were taken completely unaware. With his right foot he kicked one soldier in the groin. As he bent over in pain, Black Wolf spun toward the other and sent his fist crashing against the man's face. Dropping his pistol, the soldier fell to the floor. Quickly Black Wolf picked up the gun.

He soon had both men tied up and gagged, then mounting his horse, he rode out of the stable, keeping his pinto at a slow walk until he was safely through the gates. Then, sending his horse into a full run, he quickly left the fort far behind.

Upon hearing the news of Black Wolf's escape, Gary was outraged. He and Almeda had still been in the colonel's office when a soldier had arrived to report what had taken place.

Standing rigidly in front of Colonel Johnson's desk, he said angrily, "Colonel, sir, I request permission to pursue Black Wolf!"

The officer leaned back in his chair and he sighed heavily. Rape was a serious crime, and he knew the Sioux warrior had to be apprehended and brought back for trial. After a moment he turned his gaze to his daughter, who was sitting in the corner crying pathetically. It was hard for the colonel to fathom Black Wolf trying to molest a woman; he had believed

443

an act as degrading as rape to be beneath the Indian's dignity. But obviously he had been mistaken. That Almeda would maliciously lie about something like this never entered the colonel's thoughts.

Returning his attention to Gary, Colonel Johnson complied. "Very well, captain. You have my permission to pursue Black Wolf."

"Thank you, sir!" Gary replied crisply. Then, bestowing Almeda a look of tenderness, he assured her, "I promise you the savage will be brought to justice."

Without further ado, Captain Newcomb turned on his heel and marched out the door. He then set about having the soldiers under his command assembled.

Chapter Thirty-Six

Thanks to the warm, clear weather, Suzanne and the others made exceptionally good time as they journeyed into the Black Hills. It had taken them two days to reach the foot of the hills.

Now, on the second night, Saul and Suzanne were sitting a short distance from the campfire. Ed and Henry had informed them that tomorrow afternoon they'd arrive at the area where Donovan was waiting.

Suzanne, wearing trousers and seated on her bedroll, drew up her knees and folding her arms across them, she said to Saul, "It's so hard to believe that within a few more hours we'll actually be seeing Patrick."

The old man agreed. "I know what you mean, Miz Suzanne. If it was under joyful circumstances, I'd say it was like a miracle."

She sighed unhappily. "If only there were some excuse for Patrick's violent actions. But what can he possibly say to justify what he has done?"

"There ain't nothin' he can say to make matters any better," Saul muttered, his tone edged with disgust.

"Then why are we here?"

"'Cause regardless of what he's done, we still love him." Saul sounded totally defeated.

Suzanne concurred. "Yes, we still love him. But I don't understand why."

"Maybe 'cause we keep thinkin' of him as he was when we knew him, and not as he is now."

She was silent for some time, then said, "I wonder what Patrick's plans are. Do you suppose he still intends to go to San Francisco?"

"I reckon," Saul replied. "He probably plans to ask you to go with him."

"No, I won't go!" she declared hastily. "My place is with my husband. There's no power on earth that could make me leave him."

Saul smiled fondly. "I know that, Miz Suzanne."

"What about you?" she asked. "If Patrick asks you to accompany him to San Francisco, will you agree?"

"No, ma'am," he answered without hesitation. "I'm determined to return to Southmoor."

There was a note of sadness in her voice as she murmured, "We're meeting with Patrick to tell him goodbye, aren't we?"

"Yes, Miz Suzanne. We're gonna bid him goodbye once and for all. Then we ain't gonna let him interfere anymore with our lives. He's done brought us all the pain and heartache he's goin' to bring. We got to cast him out of our minds, and out of our hearts."

Suzanne didn't argue, for she agreed with Saul. "I guess we'd better get some sleep," she said.

Saul stood and said warmly, "Good night, Miz Suzanne. I'll see you in the mornin'."

She watched him as he walked slowly to his own bedroll. She understood why Saul wanted to go back to Southmoor, but she knew she'd miss him terribly.

Lying down, she gazed up at the thousands of stars twinkling in the dark sky. She wondered if Blade had returned to the fort, and if he had, how had he reacted to her note? Was he angry, or did he understand why she was doing this? Oh, Blade, please understand! she pleaded silently. Please!

Suzanne and her party had broken camp and were a good distance away when Blade and Justin came upon the place where she and the others had spent the night.

Remaining mounted, the two men looked over the site. Then, swinging down from his horse, Blade stepped over to the burned-out fire. Kneeling, he sifted the ashes through his fingers and remarked, "They had breakfast about three hours ago."

"We should be catchin' up to them pretty soon," Justin replied.

Blade stood upright. "I don't intend to catch them until they meet with Donovan. That's when we'll make our move."

Justin studied him thoughtfully. The major's cool, stoical manner had him on edge. Beneath Blade's calm composure, Justin knew the man was boiling mad.

All at once, they heard a rider approaching, and reacting defensively, they drew their pistols.

When they spotted Black Wolf they holstered their guns, and as the warrior came closer, Blade asked, "What are you doing here?"

Black Wolf drew up his pinto and dismounted. "I visited the fort and Colonel Johnson told me that you and Justin had left to find Little Dove."

"If you're here to offer your assistance, then it's appreciated, but Justin and I can handle this without help."

"I didn't follow you for that reason," Black Wolf replied.

Becoming aware that his friend seemed somewhat upset, Blade inquired, "Is something wrong?"

The Sioux warrior told Blade and Justin in detail

what had happened between himself and Almeda, then explained how Captain Newcomb had placed him under arrest and the way in which he had escaped.

"Damn Almeda and Newcomb!" Blade snapped angrily.

Getting down from his horse and joining them, Justin asked Black Wolf, "Why in the hell would the captain and Miss Johnson want to frame you?"

"I don't know why," he answered.

"Black Wolf," Blade began firmly, "as soon as I get back to the fort I'll have these charges against you dropped if I have to choke the truth out of Newcomb, and Almeda too."

Black Wolf smiled. "That's the only method of persuasion either of them understand."

"Why don't you come with Justin and me? Then after we catch Donovan, you can come back to the fort with us."

"Are you sure you can force a confession from the captain and Miss Johnson?" Black Wolf asked skeptically. "I don't exactly relish swinging from a rope."

"You can't spend the rest of your days running from the army," Blade remarked. Encouragingly he added, "I know Almeda Johnson, and if I can't convince Newcomb to tell the truth, I can manage to get it from her."

"All right," Black Wolf agreed. "I place my life in your hands, my friend."

Suzanne hadn't been told exactly where they were to meet Patrick, and when they approached a run-down cabin, she recognized it as the same one where she had once stayed with Blade.

Ed and Henry were riding up ahead, and Suzanne

448

was traveling beside Saul. As they approached their destination she began to feel apprehensive. When she saw her cousin, what would she say to him? Considering his past violence, would she find the sight of him repulsive, or would she see him as the Patrick she had virtually worshipped since childhood?

Noting her uneasiness, Saul tried to reassure her, "Everything will be all right, Miz Suzanne."

She forced a smile. She longed to believe him, but she was too distraught.

The four riders arrived and dismounted. Remaining beside her horse, Suzanne watched the front door of the cabin as it slowly began to open. The sun at her back shone on the man stepping outside of the cabin, but its rays were so bright that she couldn't see him clearly as he walked steadily toward her. The sun's brilliance made his blond hair shine like a halo about his head.

Walking with a pronounced limp, the man came closer. Smiling, he said emotionally, "Suzanne, I've dreamed so often of this moment that I can hardly believe it's come true."

He entered the shadowy area where Suzanne was standing. He was now so close that she could almost reach out and touch him. Paling, she looked into his vivid blue eyes, then her legs buckled. He stepped forward and caught her in his arms as she fainted into oblivion.

As Suzanne regained consciousness, her thoughts were muddled, and for a moment she wondered where she was and what had happened. Then, as it all came flooding back, her eyes opened with a start. First, she realized that she was lying on a pallet inside the cabin, and becoming aware of the man sitting at her side, she looked at him.

"Who are you?" she whispered.

"Why, I'm your cousin," he answered, smiling.

"The hell you are!" she spat. She made a move to sit up, but his hands were quickly on her shoulders, pressing her back down on the blanket.

"I love you, Suzanne," he murmured, his voice strangely husky. "I've loved you since the first day you arrived at Southmoor. You remember that day, don't you?"

There was something about him that was terrifying, and Suzanne had never been more frightened. "Where's Saul?" she asked shakily.

"He's outside. I told Ed and Henry to shoot him if he tries to enter this cabin or run away."

Gingerly Suzanne attempted again to sit up, but this time he didn't stop her. "How do you know so much about my cousin?"

"These," he said, reaching to his side and picking up three leather-bound ledgers.

She looked at them questioningly. "What are they?"

"Patrick Donovan's personal journals." Seeing her bewilderment, he asked, "You didn't know he kept his memoirs?"

"No, I didn't," she replied.

"He didn't write a day-to-day account; sometimes weeks would pass before he'd add another entry. He started keeping these the same day you arrived at Southmoor."

"Now I understand why it's been so easy for you to pose as Patrick. You know everything about him that there is to know."

He grinned. "Because I've read his private journals, I probably know him better than you do."

"How did you get his journals? Did you kill him?"

450

He shook his head. "I didn't kill your cousin. I didn't have to; he was already dead."

"How did he die?" she groaned.

"Quite heroically," he answered calmly. "He was in the midst of a battle and was shot while trying to help one of his wounded soldiers reach safety. At the time I wondered why an officer would risk his own life to save a private. All the other Confederates had turned tail and run, but Donovan let the injured soldier slow him down. A helluva lot of good it did him; he not only got himself killed, but the Union troops also killed the injured man he'd been trying to help." The man paused to chuckle coldly. "But after I had read these journals, I understood why your cousin couldn't leave the wounded soldier behind. He was so damned soft-hearted that he wouldn't have left a wounded dog to die, let alone a man."

Patrick's death came as no surprise to Suzanne. From the first moment she had set eyes on this imposter, she had sensed that her cousin was dead. "Who are you? How did you come by Patrick's journals and possessions? Why did you decide to impersonate him?"

"My name is Lyle Watkins. I was deserting the Union Army when I happened to come upon the battle in which your cousin was killed. I was on the run because I had murdered an officer. I hid in the surrounding shrubbery and watched the battle. When it was over and the Union had the Confederates running for their lives, I walked out onto the battleground. There were a lot of dead bodies lying around, but your cousin was the only Confederate officer who had been fatally wounded, and since I had decided to change the color of my uniform, I naturally chose a lieutenant over a private. I stripped Donovan, then put my uniform on him and his on me."

"But why did you want to wear a Confederate uniform?"

"I was being pursued by Union soldiers, and I thought it might be a wise move to change my colors. I didn't have a horse and was about to take off on foot when this saddled gelding comes thundering across the field to Donovan's body. He dipped his head and nudged Donovan with his nose. It didn't take much figuring to realize it was his horse."

"Lightning," she said. "His name was Lightning. He had belonged to Patrick for years."

"I could tell the horse was fairly old, but he looked as if he still had a lot of miles left in him. I swung up onto the saddle and rode away. That night, when I stopped to rest, I noticed a bag attached to the back of the saddle. I was getting ready to examine its contents when suddenly I was charged by a group of Union soldiers. I remounted and tried to make a run for it, but the horse stumbled and threw me. As I was getting to my feet, one of the soldiers giving chase fired his gun and shot me in the leg. When they came up on me, I couldn't tell them who I really was, so I let them think I was a Confederate. I told them I'd gotten separated from my unit. I was damned lucky that these soldiers weren't the ones who had originally been chasing me, because they would've recognized me. These men were a part of the battalion who had been in combat with your cousin and the other Confederates. I was placed under arrest. Your cousin's horse broke his leg when he fell, and one of the soldiers shot him, then gave me the bag."

"Patrick's journals and his other possessions were inside this bag," she finished for him.

"While I was a prisoner of war I had a lot of time on my hands, and I spent it reading these ledgers. Then

452

one day, when I was given the opportunity to take an oath to the Union and head west to join the cavalry, I jumped at the chance. I still had to keep up my new identity, though. I couldn't let anyone at Fort Laramie learn who I really was. That your cousin and I both had blond hair, blue eyes, and a lame leg was ironic, but purely coincidental."

"To protect yourself, you slandered Patrick's name," she said bitterly.

He shrugged. "I had no idea his family had learned his fate until Indian Joe told me you were looking for him."

"Why did you send Ed and Henry for me?"

"Don't you know?" His voice had again taken on a weird, husky tone.

"If I knew, I wouldn't ask!" she snapped.

"I love you," he replied very calmly.

"How can you love me, when you don't even know me?"

"But I do know you," he argued. "I've known you since you were three years old."

"Through Patrick's journals."

"Also your picture, and your letters to him," he added.

"Why was my picture and Patrick's Bible found close to Indian Joe's burned body?"

"I planted them there so the cavalry would think I was the man who was burned."

"Did you kill Indian Joe?"

"Of course," he answered, sounding quite proud of himself.

"Why?" she exclaimed.

"For two reasons. The first of which I have already explained."

"And the second reason?"

A coldness came to his eyes and his lips curled into a

453

vicious sneer. "He left you alone in the wilderness! I killed him because of what he did to you! The fool came to my cabin and told me what he had done. We rode to Iron Kettle's village looking for you, but you had already left. When we were a few miles from the Sioux camp I shot Indian Joe, then tied his body to a stake and burned it. I wanted to make it look as though he were killed by Indians."

"Did you shoot him in the back, the same way you shot Trooper Jones?" she lashed out.

He grinned sardonically. "As a matter of fact, I did shoot him in the back. Indian Joe was the kind of man I preferred not to confront face to face."

"I want to see Saul!" she demanded suddenly.

"You'll see him later," he answered. Reaching over, he took her hand into his. "Suzanne, for years I've dreamed of this moment, but I never imagined it would come true. I have spent endless nights gazing at your picture, envisioning myself making love to you. It was very hard for me to leave your picture behind with Indian Joe's body, but knowing I'd soon have you in the flesh brought me consolation. It was too late in the winter to send for you, and I was miserable all these long, cold nights without even your picture to gaze upon."

She jerked her hand from his, but as she did, he simply moved his hand to her face so he could trace her features with his fingertips. "I have read so much about you that I know you as well as you know yourself."

She pushed him away. "Don't touch me!"

He tensed as though she had suddenly struck him. 'I bet if I was Patrick, you wouldn't object to my touch!" he shouted.

His outrage deepened her fear, but she refused to be intimidated. "But you aren't Patrick! You're an unfeeling, murdering monster!"

He eyed her severely. "I had hoped you'd be a little more friendly. I was planning on taking you with me to San Francisco, but now I see that you won't come willingly. So I have no choice but to leave you behind. It's a shame, for I truly do love you."

"You don't know the meaning of the word!" she retorted.

He lurched toward her, but her reflexes were alert and she eluded him by leaping to her feet.

Rising swiftly, he grabbed her arm. "I didn't want to kill you, Suzanne, but you aren't leaving me any other choice." Roughly he pulled her flush to his body. "But before you die, I'm going to find out if you're as good as I've dreamed."

Fighting helplessly, she cried, "You're insane! . . . You're a raving maniac!"

Suddenly his lips were on hers, kissing her savagely. Using all the strength she could muster, she pushed and fought her way free and began to run for the door. She had taken only a couple of strides before he halted her by clutching a handful of her hair. While trying to force her into his embrace, he pulled her long tresses and jerked her head back so cruelly that she screamed.

Chapter Thirty-Seven

After Lyle had carried Suzanne inside the cabin, Saul found a large pine tree to sit beneath. He wanted to protect his mistress, but Ed and Henry were lounging close by, their pistols strapped to their hips. Saul had overheard their order to shoot him if he approached the cabin or tried to run.

Now he watched cautiously as his guards ambled over to talk to him. It was Henry who spoke, "Why did Mrs. Landon faint when she saw Donovan?"

"That man ain't Patrick Donovan," Saul muttered irritably.

The two trappers' surprise was evident. "What do you mean, he ain't Donovan?" Ed remarked.

"I meant exactly what I said. I don't know who that man is, but he ain't who he's been sayin' he is."

"I wonder why he's been impersonatin' Donovan," Henry pondered. But his curiosity was only mild. In these parts a lot of men pretended to be someone they weren't. If the man wanted to pass himself off as Patrick Donovan, it was all right with Henry.

Ed, whose feelings coincided with Henry's, said with a chuckle, "No wonder he was so anxious for us to fetch the woman." He glanced toward the cabin. "I bet they ain't havin' no family reunion in there, but I reckon Donovan's gettin' to know her real good."

His companion guffawed. "The lucky son of a bitch. Do you suppose he'll let us have a little of her when he's through?"

Their comments sent Saul bounding to his feet, his face enraged.

Ed snickered. "You might as well sit back down, nigger. There ain't nothin' you can do to help your mistress."

At that moment Suzanne's scream sounded from inside the cabin. Love overruled Saul's better judgment, and shoving his way past the two trappers, he ran forward.

Drawing his pistol, Henry aimed the weapon at Saul's back, then pulled the trigger. He hit his mark, and as the bullet penetrated, Saul fell face down onto the ground.

"Dumb-ass nigger," Henry mumbled, holstering his gun.

Blade and the others were approaching the cabin, and hearing the pistol shot, they broke their horses into a full run.

As the riders suddenly emerged from the thicket and into open ground, Henry and Ed reached for their pistols. However, when they saw that the three intruders were armed with rifles, their common sense prevailed, and they moved their hands away from their pistols and into the air.

Meanwhile, inside the cabin, Lyle kept Suzanne in his grasp as he stole a quick look through the window. Peering over his shoulder and spotting Blade, Suzanne screamed her husband's name.

Whirling, Lyle slapped her across the face, his blow

so powerful that she toppled backward.

Quickly the man grabbed his pistol and was about to bargain with the major for Suzanne's life when unexpectedly the front door was thrown open. Lyle fired, but the bullet merely whizzed through thin air before lodging into the cabin wall.

By the time Lyle could see that Blade had dived inside and was on the floor, it was too late for him to fire a second shot. As he was lowering his gun toward his oponent, Blade's pistol went off. Lyle Watkins gasped his last breath, then fell to the floor, dead.

Blade got to his feet, and stepping to the doorway, he yelled to Black Wolf and Justin that he and Suzanne were all right.

Suzanne thought he would take her into his arms, and when he made no move to do so, she looked at him with a puzzled expression.

Moving to Lyle's body, Blade stared coldly down into the man's lifeless face.

Going to her husband's side, Suzanne murmured, "He isn't Patrick. His name was Lyle Watkins, and he was a deserter from the Union Army."

His countenance inscrutable, Blade asked, "Is your cousin dead?"

"Yes, he was killed in battle."

Before she could explain, Blade said brusquely, "Saul's been shot."

"Oh no!" she moaned. Earlier Suzanne had heard a pistol shot, but with all that had happened since then, she had forgotten about it.

"You'd better go see about him," Blade said.

She longed to ask her husband why he was behaving so strangely, but her concern for Saul took priority, and turning away, she hurried through the open doorway.

Black Wolf had placed Saul on a blanket and was

kneeling beside him. When Suzanne reached them, the warrior told her, "He was shot in the back."

Kneeling, Suzanne gazed down at Saul through a teary blur. His eyes fluttered open, and seeing his mistress, he asked weakly, "Are you all right, Miz Suzanne?"

"Yes," she assured him. "Blade, Black Wolf, and Justin have saved us."

Saul smiled faintly, then his eyes closed.

"Is he . . . ?" Suzanne cried.

"No," Black Wolf replied. "He's passed out. We must take him to Iron Kettle's village so the medicine woman can tend to him. I'll make a travois. Since I have to make do with what I can find, it'll be a little crude, but we don't have too far to travel, so it should hold up."

Suzanne remained with Saul as Black Wolf left to carry out his task.

Justin had Ed's and Henry's hands tied, and ordering them to sit down, he told them if they made a move, he'd blow them to hell. Then, keeping a watchful eye on his prisoners, he stepped over to Suzanne.

Looking up at him, she asked, "What's wrong with Blade?"

"He's madder than an old wet hen 'cause you took off to see Donovan."

"The man wasn't Patrick, but an imposter."

"Well, for your sake and Saul's, I'm glad he wasn't Donovan, but that ain't gonna cool Blade's anger. As far as he's concerned, you left him for your cousin."

"But I didn't!" she exclaimed. "I was planning to return to the fort."

"Blade doesn't see it that way. He came home and found his wife gone, and as far as he's concerned, you deserted him. In his opinion, you chose Patrick over him. It's gonna be hard for you to convince him

459

otherwise. When you and Saul rode away from the fort, you believed your cousin to be a murderer. If you look at it from Blade's point of view, it's not too difficult to understand why he's upset."

Suzanne sighed disconsolately. "If Blade had known Patrick, he'd understand why I had to see him one last time."

"But he doesn't know your cousin, and never will."

Before she could respond, Blade walked out of the cabin and joined them. "How's Saul?" he asked.

"I don't know," Suzanne answered. "Black Wolf is making a travois. He thinks we should take Saul to Iron Kettle's village."

Turning to Justin, Blade asked, "Can you manage to take those two men back to the fort? And the body inside the cabin needs to be buried."

"Don't worry," Justin said. "I'll take care of everything."

"Tell Colonel Johnson that Black Wolf and I will return as soon as Saul's able to travel." Then, leaving abruptly, he remarked, "I'll help Black Wolf with the travois."

Suzanne watched him as he strolled away. Would he ever forgive her? If only there was some way she could make him understand! Suddenly, her face alight with hope, she leaped to her feet.

"Justin," she began hastily, "stay with Saul. I need to get something from the cabin."

Suzanne rushed through the open door, and keeping her eyes averted from Lyle's body, she went to where Patrick's journals were placed on the pallet. Quickly she picked up the three ledgers and cradled them against her chest. Then she darted back outside. Although Patrick had been dead for years, Blade would come to know him as well as she herself did.

Surely then he'd understand why she'd had such a compelling need to see her cousin. Somehow she had to convince Blade to read these journals!

Before reaching Iron Kettle's village, Black Wolf let Blade and Suzanne know that the chief's camp was now minus at least half of its previous population. Two Moons had left to start his own village, taking many warriors and their families with him.

Thinking of Kara, Suzanne wanted to know if Strong Bull had joined Two Moons. She was pleased to learn that the warrior hadn't forsaken his grandfather.

When they crested the ridge and looked down upon the scattered tepees, Suzanne was amazed to see how small the village had become. Two Moons' rebellion had been successful, and he had robbed Iron Kettle of more than half of his people.

Months ago, when Suzanne and Blade had approached the Sioux site, several warriors had ridden out to greet them. On this occasion, only four braves arrived to escort them into the village.

Although Iron Kettle welcomed the visitors, he did so with reservations. Whites in his village made him uneasy, but the old chief was a gentle, fair man, and could not turn them away. He ordered Saul taken to the medicine woman's tent, then told Blade that he and his wife could stay in the same tepee where they had stayed before.

As soon as they were settled inside the isolated wigwam, Suzanne gathered the journals, then stepping to Blade's side, she said, "I want you to read these."

"What are they?" he asked, his tone clipped.

"Patrick's memoirs."

He frowned. "I'm not interested."

461

"Blade, the few times you've agreed to hear about Patrick, you tried to listen with an open mind, but I don't think you truly did. You were biased, but I understand why."

"Why do you want me to read about your cousin?" he said gruffly.

"I believe if you read these journals, you'll realize why I was driven to see Patrick one last time. Although I was not choosing him over you, I couldn't completely reject him. Until you came into my life, I loved Patrick more than anyone on the face of this earth. When you read these journals, you'll understand why I loved him so dearly and why I felt I couldn't turn my back on him."

Throwing up his arms with rage, Blade bellowed, "Patrick! . . . Patrick! . . . That's all I've heard since the day I met you! Now I suppose you've convinced yourself that he was a martyr, as well as a saint!"

Her own anger emerging, Suzanne argued, "No, I don't think he was a martyr or a saint! But he was a very compassionate man, and you're wrong to be jealous of his memory! Patrick died years ago, and I'm no longer grieving for him. You're the one who is now keeping him between us; not me!"

She pitched the journals on top of a buffalo rug, then announced sharply, "I'm going to Saul!" As she darted outside, her husband made no attempt to stop her.

Suzanne hadn't walked very far before she spotted Prairie Flower and Kara heading in her direction. Happy to see them, she picked up her pace and met them halfway.

Kara, her face aglow with joy, ran into Suzanne's outstretched arms. Kneeling, she hugged the child eagerly. "Oh, Kara, I'm so happy to see you again!"

Suzanne had to pry the girl's arms from around her

neck so she could stand and greet the Indian woman. "Prairie Flower, I thought we'd never see each other again."

The Sioux woman smiled warmly. "I too believed you would never come back. I welcome you with joy in my heart."

"How are Swift Arrow and your sons?"

"They are fine."

"I was on my way to the medicine woman's tent. Will you please come with me?"

During Suzanne's previous visit, she had spoken to Prairie Flower about Saul. "The wounded man, is he your black servant?"

"Yes, but I don't really think of him as my servant but as my friend."

"Come; we will see the medicine woman."

Holding Kara's hand, Suzanne followed Prairie Flower to the wigwam where Saul had been ensconced. The medicine woman, One-Who-Heals, was stepping outside when they arrived. She couldn't speak English, and interpreting her words, Prairie Flower let Suzanne know that Saul's condition was not too serious, and that the medicine woman believed he would recover.

Suzanne longed to see Saul, and asked permission to enter the tepee. One-Who-Heals agreed, and with Kara and Prairie Flower staying with her, Suzanne entered. Saul was asleep, so they moved quietly to the cooking pit and sat down. A pot of coffee was brewing, and Prairie Flower poured a cup for herself and Suzanne.

One-Who-Heals had not come inside with them, and Suzanne asked, "The medicine woman won't mind us helping ourselves?"

"No, she will not mind," Prairie Flower answered.

The two women began to catch each other up on their lives, with Kara periodically joining in. The child was happy to hear that Suzanne and Blade were now married. She liked the tall, handsome major.

The women were on their second cups of coffee when Kara, growing drowsy, stretched out and placed her head on Suzanne's lap. Within a short time she was sound asleep.

Absently, Suzanne twirled one of the child's braids about her finger. "Prairie Flower, has Kara adjusted to her life?"

"No," she sighed sadly.

"Have Beaded Moccasin and Strong Bull learned to love her?"

"Beaded Moccasin, she is kind to Kara. Strong Bull more or less ignores her. The child is not mistreated. Iron Kettle gives her a lot of attention, but she does not seem to respond."

"Was she given a Sioux name?"

"She is called Morning Star."

"Who named her?"

"Iron Kettle. Before the sun rises, only the morning star can be seen in the heavens. It longs to be separated from the other stars and stands alone in the morning sky. Kara, she is like the morning star and longs to leave the Sioux."

"Iron Kettle gave her a beautiful name, but its meaning is very sad."

"Kara saddens her great-grandfather's heart. It is a shame, for Iron Kettle is a kind man."

Suzanne felt sorry for the chief, but she was more concerned with Kara's feelings. The child's father had taught her to be white, and then with no warning, he had placed her in the midst of a Sioux village. Kara's inability to cope had Suzanne gravely worried.

*　　　*　　　*

Justin had his two prisoners mounted on their horses and was about to start for Fort Laramie when Captain Newcomb and his company of soldiers came upon the area.

Stepping away from his own horse, the scout looked on as the cavalry troop pulled up.

Dismounting along with his corporal, Gary demanded, "Where's Major Landon?"

"What's it to you?" Justin asked disrespectfully.

Pulling rank, the captain commanded, "I order you to answer my question!"

Justin remained calm. "What was the question again?"

"Where is the major?" Gary shouted testily.

"Well," the scout drawled, "I know where he ain't; he ain't here."

"I'm warning you, Smith, your insolence is going to get you in a lot of trouble."

"I don't doubt it," Justin mumbled flatly.

"Who are those men?" Gary asked, gesturing toward Ed and Henry.

Without mentioning Black Wolf's involvement, Justin told Gary what had happened.

Showing no interest, the captain changed the topic. "Have you seen Black Wolf?"

"I wouldn't tell you if I had," Justin remarked.

Ed could overhear their discussion. He wondered if the army would go easy on him if he helped them locate this Indian. Speaking up, he said, "Excuse me, captain."

Turning to him, Gary asked, "What do you want?"

"There was a Sioux buck here. He left with the major, and I heard them say they was goin' to Iron Kettle's village."

Gary's eyes swept back to meet Justin's. "You

465

goddamn Indian-lover!" To his corporal he ordered, "Place this man under arrest." Obeying the officer, the man took Justin's pistol.

"What charges are you usin' for arrestin' me?" Justin asked.

"Insubordination, and aiding and abetting a renegade warrior." Turning to his mounted troopers and speaking to Sergeant Edwards, he issued more orders. "Turn those two trappers loose. They aren't wanted by the army. I want two men guarding Smith." Looking at the corporal, he continued, "We'll ride to Iron Kettle's village and make an example out of the old chief. We'll show these damned Sioux what happens when they harbor one of their own kind from the army."

"What kind of example?" Justin asked hastily.

Smiling, Gary answered, "A few miles back I ran across two of our Kiowa scouts, and they said that Iron Kettle had lost most of his warriors. His village is now weak, and I will take full advantage of it. I intend to wipe him and his people off the face of the earth."

"Good God!" Justin groaned. "You son of a bitch, you can't ride in there and kill at random!"

"Of course I can. Iron Kettle is giving shelter to Black Wolf, and the only way I can guarantee his capture is to take the village by surprise."

"You cold-hearted bastard, there are innocent children in that village!"

Snickering, Gary declared, "Yes, but if we kill them now, then they cannot grow up to kill us, can they?"

"You sorry . . . !" Justin's hands clenched into fists.

"Restrain him!" Gary commanded.

Sergeant Edwards and the corporal quickly responded, and grasping Justin's arms, they led him to his horse. Then the sergeant told two of his men to keep the scout under guard.

For a moment Justin considered reminding Gary

that Blade was at Iron Kettle's village, and that if he attacked, the major might be killed. But he disregarded the idea, for he knew it wouldn't change Gary's plans. He'd merely imply that Major Landon was abetting a criminal and deserved whatever befell him.

Groaning, Justin leaned against his horse. Iron Kettle's village would be slaughtered, and there was nothing he could do to prevent it. He had never felt so helpless.

Chapter Thirty-Eight

The approaching dusk fell grayly over the Indian village as Suzanne walked slowly toward the segregated tepee. She wondered if Blade was still inside. Although she wanted desperately to be with him, she was nonetheless hesitant. Would he treat her with a cold reserve? His stoical aloofness hurt her, yet it also made her angry. Why must he be so stubborn and unyielding? His jealousy toward Patrick was totally uncalled for and unreasonable. If he would agree to read the journals, then surely he'd understand why she had felt such a need to see her cousin. Leaving the fort with Ed and Henry had indeed been dangerous, and she didn't blame Blade for being upset. However, his anger seemed to have nothing to do with her leaving but was fueled by her reason for going.

Reaching the tepee, she took a deep breath and entered. Blade had lit a lantern, and its soft glow fell across the open journal on his lap.

He was sitting on a fur rug, and becoming aware of Suzanne, he glanced up. "How's Saul?"

"He's much better. The medicine woman says he'll recover."

He closed the journal, then motioned for her to join

468

him. "Come here, sweetheart."

Relieved to find that he was no longer angry, she went to him quickly.

"Suzanne," he began, his fingers absently brushing across the leather-bound ledger, "I owe you an apology."

She tried to object, but he held up his hand. "No, don't disagree. I most assuredly have treated you unfairly. I was wrong to be jealous of Patrick Donovan. Not only today, but from the very beginning." He reached for her hand and squeezed it gently. "Lyle Watkins put you through a terrible ordeal, and I didn't even have the common courtesy to ask you if you were all right."

She interrupted. "When I called your name, he slapped me, but other than that, he didn't abuse me; not really."

"Later we'll discuss Lyle Watkins, but now I need to talk to you about your cousin." He lifted the journal and placed it beside the other two. "Did you know Patrick kept these?"

"No," she replied.

"When you have time, you should read them." Blade smiled tenderly. "Your name is mentioned throughout the journals. He loved you."

"Yes, I know, and I loved him," she murmured.

"After reading these books, I can understand why you cared so deeply for him. Also, I now understand why you couldn't forsake him, regardless of what you believed he had done." He sighed heavily. "Patrick Donovan was not only a very compassionate man, but an admirable now. I wished I had known him."

"Blade, he would've liked you," she cried.

He took her into his arms. "Will you forgive me for the way I treated you?"

"Yes, my darling. If you want my forgiveness, then

469

you have it."

"Has Saul regained consciousness?" Blade asked.

"Not yet," she answered. "I stayed with him for hours, hoping he'd wake up. I wanted to tell him about Patrick, and the way he died."

"He was killed in battle?"

"Yes, and he died heroically while trying to save another man's life."

"After awhile we'll go to the medicine woman's tent and see if Saul's awake, then you can talk to him."

Gently he drew her against his chest, and while holding her close, his lips descended to hers. Responding, Suzanne's arms went about his neck and their lips blended in a long, fervent exchange.

He urged her back onto the rug, placing his large frame over hers. Even through their clothes, she could feel his hardness pressed against her.

Taking his time, Blade aroused her slowly, his fondling soothing and gentle. Following several kisses and whispered endearments, their passion began to build toward a crescendo.

Now anxious to make love completely, they helped each other out of their clothes, and then, as bare flesh touched bare flesh, Blade submerged himself deeply within his wife.

Joined together, their bodies thrusting in perfect harmony, Blade and Suzanne were swept away on the ardent waves of passion.

Dawn was just beginning to lighten the horizon when Blade was awakened by Black Wolf calling his name. Suzanne was snuggled against him, and he carefully moved away from her. Slipping into his trousers, he left the tepee.

Black Wolf had his pinto, as well as Blade's saddled

horse. "Will you take a morning ride with me, my friend?" he asked.

Blade grinned, and gesturing toward his own horse, he replied, "Apparently you weren't expecting a refusal."

"We will only be gone a couple of hours. My mother was buried not far from here, and I want to visit her grave. I'd appreciate your company."

"Are we going to sacred burial grounds?"

"No, her grave is located in a peaceful valley where Running Horse had his village when my mother died. My father and I buried her ourselves, and then I read from the white man's Bible. She never fully adopted the ways of the Sioux, and worshipped her own God."

"I'll finish dressing," Blade said, then stepped back inside.

Suzanne was now awake and she asked, "Did I hear you talking to Black Wolf?"

"Yes," he answered.

"Is anything wrong?"

"No, he wants me to take a ride with him. We'll be gone about two hours." As he began to dress, he suggested, "Why don't you get some more sleep?"

"Now that I'm awake, I doubt if I can fall back asleep. I think I'll make some coffee, then go see Saul."

He slipped into his boots, then grabbing his hat, he knelt and gave his wife a lingering kiss. "See you later," he said with a warm smile.

Her heart filled with love, Suzanne watched him as he hurried outside. Flinging off her blanket, she stretched gracefully. She was feeling content and thoroughly happy. Learning the final truth about Patrick had not cast a shadow over her happiness; quite the contrary, she was thankful that he had been innocent of the evil charges against him. Nor had he betrayed the Confederacy. He had always possessed

471

integrity, and now she knew that he had done so even unto death. Her musings turned to last night, when she and Blade had visited Saul. The man had been awake, and he'd listened silently as she told him about Patrick. Then, with a large smile on his face, he had praised, "Thank you, Lord, for lettin' me live to see this day." He had then explained to Suzanne that he had always asked God to let him live to prove Masta Patrick's innocence. Saul, like Suzanne, was not saddened by Patrick's death. The time for mourning had long since passed.

The morning sun had risen and was shining brightly when Captain Newcomb and his men drew up their horses. They had reached the hilltop and had a clear view of the Sioux village that lay within the dale.

Speaking to his corporal, Gary said, "Tell Sergeant Edwards that I want him and ten men to remain here and shoot down the Indians who will try to run. We'll circle around and attack from the east. The ones who attempt an escape will head west, right into the sergeant's path."

"Sir, do you want me to issue orders to kill women and children?"

"All the pestilent savages are to die, regardless of sex or age."

"Yes sir!" the corporal replied, then rode back to relay the captain's order.

Justin had been placed at the rear of the column, and telling his guards that he needed to talk to Captain Newcomb, he urged his horse forward. The two soldiers followed closely behind.

Justin halted his mount beside Gary's. "Captain, I ain't never begged a man in my life, but I'm beggin' you not to go through with this."

"Your sympathy for Indians sickens me," Gary remarked, frowning.

"My God, they're human beings, and you intend to shoot them down like wild animals."

Irritably Gary snapped, "Smith, get the hell away from me!"

Justin's eyes narrowed with rage. "Newcomb, if you butcher this village, so help me God, I'll kill you!"

"Not only are you guilty of insubordination and aiding and abetting a criminal, but also for threatening an officer's life. Smith, if you aren't careful, you're going to find yourself facing a military execution."

"If I don't kill you, Blade will!"

"I don't think so," he answered easily. He leaned toward Justin and spoke so quietly that only the scout heard his words. "The major is down there in Iron Kettle's village, and I intend to see to it personally that he ends up as dead as his Indian friends. His death will not be one of honor, for it will be reported that he fought on the side of the Sioux." Looking at the two guards, he said loudly, "Escort Mr. Smith to the rear of the column and see that he stays there."

Gary watched their departure with a smug smile on his face. After he and his men were finished with Blade and the Indians, he'd conjure up a reason for Justin's demise. He supposed Molly would grieve for a spell, but in time she'd recover. Then, of course, she'd come running to him and beg forgiveness for jilting him. Only when she was thoroughly contrite and submissive would he graciously forgive her.

Suzanne had just stepped out of her tepee when she spotted the company of soldiers advancing. They were arriving from the east, and pausing, she shaded her eyes with her hand as she watched their approach. She wondered why they had their horses at a full gallop. Didn't the officer in charge realize this hurried approach would frighten the Indians?

Suzanne's wigwam was located in the western portion of the village, and because Captain Newcomb and his men were coming from the east, she was quite a distance away from them.

She continued to look on as Iron Kettle's people began to scurry about the village, warriors running for their weapons, and women gathering their children. When the attacking soldiers opened fire, Suzanne became frozen in place. Shocked, she could do nothing but stare incredulously as the mounted troopers charged into the camp, killing indiscriminately.

The sound of Kara screaming her name brought Suzanne out of her trancelike state. Glancing about frantically, she caught sight of the child fleeing from her uncle's tepee and heading wildly toward Suzanne's.

The soldiers were running amuck through the heart of the village where Strong Bull's lodge was located. The invading army was on all sides of Kara as she tried to make her way to Suzanne's tepee.

"Kara!" Suzanne cried. Panic-stricken, she raced toward Kara, praying she'd reach the child in time to keep her from being killed.

Suzanne was wearing her trousers and her long, blond hair was loose, and the soldiers who spotted her running headlong into the village made no attempts to shoot her. They weren't in combat against whites, only Sioux.

It took Suzanne only a couple of minutes to reach Kara, but to the young woman it seemed an eternity. Inexplicably, she felt as though everything was

474

happening in slow motion. As in a dream, her legs seemed to be made of lead, and it was an agonizing effort to keep them moving. The loud, constant gunfire and the frantic screams surrounding her sounded far away. Only the distance between her and Kara existed, and nothing else was real; it was all a hazy, ominous nightmare!

Now only a few feet lay between them, and Suzanne began to believe she'd reach the girl in time. Arms extended, she fell to her knees and waited for Kara to come into her embrace.

Suddenly, a charging horse stirred up loose dirt, sending it flying into Suzanne's face. The grainy particles stung her eyes as she looked up to see a mounted trooper pointing his pistol at Kara. Suzanne's blood-curdling scream emerged simultaneously with the explosive shot that sent the trooper plunging from his horse and face down onto the ground.

Suzanne cried thankfully when she saw that Kara had been saved by Swift Arrow. The warrior, with rifle in hand, lurched for the child, then practically threw her into Suzanne's arms. "Take her, and run from the village!" he yelled.

Kara was clinging to Suzanne with all her might. Lifting the trembling child, Suzanne stood and turned to flee, but Captain Newcomb and his horse thundered across her path. Gary had his pistol drawn, and taking aim, he fired at Swift Arrow. Suzanne gasped convulsively as Prairie Flower's husband dropped to the earth, blood spurting from a fatal head wound.

Gary, showing no interest in Suzanne and Kara, rode on to carry out more merciless killings.

Keeping the child held tightly, Suzanne rushed for the shrubbery that grew thickly over the nearby hillside. Other women and children were also escaping in the same direction, and Suzanne and Kara soon became mingled with them. They and the others had almost reached the foot of the hill when they detected the smell of smoke.

Looking over her shoulder, Suzanne saw that the soldiers were now setting fire to the tepees. Her thoughts on Saul, she resumed her flight into the shrubbery. She knew she had to go back. Saul was too weak to run, and the medicine woman's tepee might be burned with him still inside.

Finding Prairie Flower's youngest son hiding behind a heavy bush, Suzanne placed Kara beside the boy.

"Take care of Kara," she said hastily. "I must go back and help Saul! Where are your mother and Flying Hawk?"

"In village," he answered.

Whirling and heading back, Suzanne wondered if Prairie Flower and Flying Hawk were aware that Swift Arrow had been killed.

On her return, Suzanne had to push her way through the throng of people who were hurrying deliriously for the refuge afforded by the thick shrubbery. The smoke had now become heavier, and peering toward the hub of the village, she was relieved to see that the medicine woman's tent was still unharmed.

Once again the midst of action, Suzanne gave no thought to her own safety; her concern was for Saul. But when she found herself in the middle of the barbarous warfare, her thoughts flew frantically to Blade. Dear God, if only he had been here; surely he could've stopped this bloody massacre!

Within minutes Iron Kettle's peaceful village had become a virtual Armageddon, and the young woman trying desperately to reach her loving servant had little chance of making her way past the raging violence to the medicine woman's tepee. Her path was continuously blocked by charging soldiers, fleeing Indians, or warriors trying vainly to protect their lives and those of their loved ones.

Finally realizing her quest was fruitless, Suzanne dropped to her knees; then, crossing over to borderline delirium, she screamed.

Chapter Thirty-Nine

Justin had ridden at Sergeant Edward's side and was watching the murderous chaos taking place in the valley below. He looked on with surprise when he noticed a large group of Newcomb's men ride away from the village and head for the hillside. He nudged the sergeant, and getting the man's attention, he pointed toward the fleeing soldiers. "What do you make of that?"

"I'd say they have no stomach for this butchering," Edwards answered. "I sure as hell don't blame them."

"If you feel that way, then why ain't you tryin' to stop it?"

"I've got my orders," he replied flatly. "I was told to stay here."

"You were also told to shoot anyone escapin' from the village, but I don't hear you tellin' your men to fire at those women and kids who are runnin' for their lives."

"I refuse to murder women and children," the sergeant declared.

"But there are women and children out there dyin'!" Justin remarked.

"But I'm not the one responsible for their murders."

"If you don't do anything to stop it, then that's the same as condoning it!"

"Damn it, Smith!" Sergeant Edwards yelled. "There's nothing I can do!"

Justin gritted his teeth and held his peace as he watched the mounted troopers climb the hillside. When they reached the top, the soldiers pulled up their horses.

The man in the lead spoke to Sergeant Edwards, "Sarge, I reckon we might be court-martialed, but the others and me we ain't gonna be no part of that massacre. The captain, he's a madman. I done seen him kill two little kids like they was nothin' but animals."

Sergeant Edwards nodded. "I understand. It's too bad your feelings aren't unanimous, then the captain wouldn't have any men joining him in this slaughter."

Suddenly, hearing advancing horses, they looked behind them and saw Blade and Black Wolf arriving.

"Thank God!" Justin moaned. "The major will put a stop to these killin's!"

Reining, Blade comanded, "Sergeant, I want you and all the men here to follow me!"

"Yes, sir!" Edwards replied eagerly, grateful for the major's presence. He outranked the captain, and the sergeant was now free to replace Captain Newcomb's orders by Major Landon's.

Suzanne, fighting her delirium, stood upright and turned her gaze toward the medicine woman's tepee. It still hadn't been set afire, and willing herself to move, she started forward. She had taken only a few strides when she saw Prairie Flower and Flying Hawk assisting Saul from the wigwam. He was between them with his arms draped over their shoulders. Calling out, Suzanne hastened to join them.

Meanwhile, Captain Newcomb had also caught sight of Prairie Flower and her son. Slipping his rifle from its scabbard, he brought his horse to a halt beside Suzanne. Then he carefully centered his aim on Prairie Flower.

Realizing whom Gary intended to shoot, Suzanne made a frantic attempt to jump up and grab the rifle, but she was a fraction too late. The gun discharged, and the fired bullet found its deadly mark. But although Suzanne had been too slow to save Prairie Flower, her sudden grasp of the rifle barrel sent Gary's next shot awry, sparing the life of Flying Hawk. Before the captain could fling off Suzanne's grip, Prairie Flower's son hefted his rifle to his shoulder and fired. Gary fell from his horse, his body landing at Suzanne's feet. She didn't look to see if he was dead, but ran to the others.

Prairie Flower and Saul were both on the ground, and as Suzanne reached them, Saul was managing to sit up. Finding that he was all right, she went to Flying Hawk, who was kneeling beside his mother. She knelt on the other side of the Indian woman's body, and saw immediately that Prairie Flower was dead. Seized with grief, she looked at Flying Hawk. The lad was trying desperately to be brave, but Suzanne detected the beginning of tears in his eyes. She longed to say something to him, but at that moment there seemed to be no appropriate words.

The boy wiped away all sign of tears, then he looked steadily into Suzanne's face. The hate and resentment she saw glaring in the young Sioux's eyes sent a chill down her spine.

"Bluecoats!" he seethed. "I will spend my life avenging my mother! I will not stop killing until all white soldiers are dead!" He bounded to his feet. "Now I must find my father."

"Flying Hawk, your father is dead!" Suzanne cried.

"NO!" he bellowed. He turned and ran away, and Suzanne wondered if he was planning to search for Swift Arrow's body. For a moment she watched his departure, then moving over to Saul, she helped him to his feet.

The change in the atmosphere didn't register at first, and it took a few seconds before Suzanne and Saul became aware that the gunshots had ceased, and only wailing and moaning could be heard throughout the campsite.

Keeping an arm around Saul's waist, Suzanne glanced about the area. In the near distance she saw Blade bringing the soldiers to order.

Suddenly she felt too tired to support Saul's weight, and sighing with relief, she eased him back down onto the ground. Slowly she sat down beside him.

Her emotions numb, she gazed at her surroundings. The massacre was over, but she knew in her mind it would live forever.

"Saul," she whispered. "This all seems like some horrible nightmare!"

He reached for her hand. "Are you gonna be all right, Miz Suzanne?"

Blade was coming toward her, and leaping to her feet, she cried, "Yes, I'll be all right."

She ran to her husband, and as he held out his arms, she flew into his embrace. She placed her head on his broad shoulder, and while clinging to his strength, she wept.

Suzanne and Kara were alone inside the isolated wigwam. The child was sleeping fretfully, and Suzanne was keeping a close watch over her. The young girl had witnessed so much violence that Suzanne was worried that the terrible events might leave a permanent scar.

Hours had passed since Blade had brought his wife and Kara to the tepee. He had told them to stay inside, then before leaving had assured them that he'd return as soon as possible.

Now, hearing a noise, Suzanne glanced up and was relieved to see her husband entering. Slowly he went to her side and sat down. Gazing tenderly at the sleeping child, he asked, "How's Kara?"

"I'm very concerned about her. No child should have to witness what she saw."

"At least she's alive," Blade murmured.

"How many children were killed?"

"Eleven killed and four injured."

"Dear God!" she groaned.

"Twenty warriors perished, three old men and fifteen women."

"Iron Kettle?" she asked.

"He's all right." He paused a moment, then continued, "Strong Bull and Beaded Moccasin are dead."

Suzanne sighed. "Kara is again an orphan. Did her cousins survive?"

"No, they were all killed."

"Oh, Blade!" she cried wretchedly. "What will happen to Iron Kettle's people? His village was almost eradicated!"

"The chief plans to take the survivors to Running Horse's camp. It's located further into the Black Hills and is safe from butchers like Newcomb."

"Does Black Wolf still intend to return to the fort with us?" The night before, Blade had told her about the rape charge against Black Wolf.

"Yes," he replied.

"Do you really believe you can get Almeda to tell the truth?"

"Now that Newcomb is dead, I'm sure it won't be too

hard to persuade her to confess their conspiracy."

"So the captain is dead," she mumbled, feeling no sympathy for the evil man.

Suddenly they heard Black Wolf asking permission to enter the tepee. Blade told him to come in.

The warrior stepped inside, and moving close to the couple, he sat down. Suzanne noticed how haggard he appeared.

"At dawn, we'll leave for the fort," he remarked quietly.

"Black Wolf," Suzanne began, "what will happen to Kara?"

"What do you mean?" He was confused.

"Her aunt and uncle are dead. Who will take care of her?"

"The Sioux take care of their own," he replied. "Another family will adopt her and raise her as their daughter."

Somewhat apprehensive, Suzanne reached for her husband's hand, and as he turned his eyes to hers, he could see her anxiety.

"Sweetheart, what's wrong?" he asked.

"Blade," she cried softly, her tone pleading, "I want Kara to be our daughter."

Her wish caught him off guard, and it took a moment for him to agree. But realizing Iron Kettle might object, he replied, "Her great-grandfather might not let us adopt her."

Suzanne's gaze swept to Black Wolf. "Will you talk to Iron Kettle for us?"

"Yes, I'll talk to him, but Little Dove, don't get your hopes up too high. There's a good chance that he'll be firmly against the adoption. Strong Bull and his family were murdered, and Kara is now the chief's only living relative."

"Honey," Blade said carefully, "Black Wolf is right,

you mustn't let yourself hope too much."

Watching the sleeping child, she answered with a sob, "Darling, I want Kara to be our daughter with all my heart! I love her so much!"

"Yes, I know you do," he whispered. He drew her into his arms.

As Suzanne waited for Black Wolf to return, time passed agonizingly slowly. She tried to abide by her husband's and Black Wolf's advice and guard her emotions, but she found it impossible to do so. She wanted desperately for Kara to be her daughter and prayed to God for Iron Kettle's agreement.

In less than an hour, Black Wolf arrived with the chief. Suzanne hadn't been expecting Iron Kettle, and when he entered the tepee behind Black Wolf, she watched him warily.

The two men sat down on a buffalo rug, placing themselves directly across from Suzanne and Blade. The chief's eyes flitted back and forth from wife to husband.

The old man seemed to be in no hurry to speak, and the silence inside the tepee hovered intensely.

Finally Iron Kettle said, "Major Landon, Black Wolf tells me that you and your wife want to adopt my great-granddaughter."

"Yes, that is right," Blade answered.

"Why?" he asked simply, his gaze on Suzanne.

"Because we love her," she replied.

"I too love her," the chief murmured.

"Iron Kettle," Suzanne began, "Prairie Flower told me that Kara is not happy living with the Sioux."

"In time she will learn to be happy. She is Sioux."

"She is also white," Suzanne argued.

The chief turned his gaze upon the sleeping child. "All my kin are now dead, except for Morning Star.

She is all that is left of my blood."

Suspecting Iron Kettle was about to refuse his permission, Black Wolf decided to intervene. "The spirits, in their wisdom, have made Morning Star's white blood the strongest. She longs to live in the white man's world. Apparently the spirits do not wish it otherwise."

The chief sighed heavily. "I have tried to lead her gently into the ways of the Sioux, but she does not respond. She closes her heart to her mother's people." He looked sadly at Black Wolf. "Perhaps you are right. The spirits do not want Morning Star to be Sioux. Her white blood is too strong."

"Major Landon and his wife will give her a good home and much love."

Iron Kettle spoke to Blade. "I cannot give you my great-granddaughter unless I have your word that you'll send her to me if I should wish to see her."

"You have my word, Iron Kettle," he promised.

The chief nodded solemnly. "Then it is settled. When you leave in the morning, take Morning Star with you."

Suzanne wanted to thank him, but he rose to his feet and left so abruptly that she didn't have a chance to do so.

Smiling at Blade and Suzanne, Black Wolf said, "Congratulations."

"Well, Mrs. Landon," Blade began lightly, "how does it feel to be a mother?"

"Wonderful. How does it feel to be a father?"

"It's a good feeling," he replied.

But their light-hearted mood vanished quickly. The massacre's aftermath was still too fresh to allow any form of happiness to linger.

Kara slept through the afternoon and into the night,

and didn't awaken until dawn. She was disoriented, and for a moment she wondered why she wasn't in her uncle's tepee. Then, as the massacre flashed before her, she sat up with a bolt.

Suzanne and Blade were sitting beside the cooking pit, and noticing that Kara was awake, Suzanne went to the child's side and took her into her arms.

"Don't leave me!" the girl pleaded.

"Honey," she began, "Blade and I are taking you with us. From now on, you're going to be our daughter. Would you like that?"

She hugged Suzanne enthusiastically. "Oh yes!" she cried joyfully. Then, bounding from her bed, she rushed to Blade and threw herself into his embrace.

As he was giving her an affectionate hug, Black Wolf called to them from outside.

Blade quickly ushered his wife and new daughter from the tepee. Black Wolf had his horse, as well as Blade's and Suzanne's. He had also brought Saul's mule and had the travois attached to the animal. "We'll stop by the medicine tent and pick up Saul. Are you ready to leave?"

"As ready as we'll ever be," Blade answered. "Does Iron Kettle wish to see Kara before we go?"

"Here he comes now," Black Wolf remarked, catching sight of the chief and Flying Hawk.

Kara watched her great-grandfather's approach apprehensively. Was he going to tell her that she had to stay with the Sioux? She slipped her hand into Suzanne's and held on tightly.

Suzanne was not worried. She knew the chief would not change his mind, and she gave Iron Kettle only a passing glance. It was Prairie Flower's son who held her attention. The boy's face was so filled with hate that she was shocked.

Iron Kettle went to Kara, holding out his hand.

486

Hesitantly she took her hand from Suzanne's and place it in her great-grandfather's.

"Morning Star, Major Landon and his wife are now your father and mother. Sioux children honor their parents and grow up to make them proud." He knelt, his eyes meeting Kara's. "I hope someday you will learn to accept the Sioux heritage with pride, and I pray the spirits will let me live to see that day. You are of my flesh and blood, and I live within you, as you live within me. I will always be with you, for our hearts beat as one."

Kara was too young to understand fully what her great-grandfather was saying, but the others understood only too well. Suzanne wondered if the day Iron Kettle wished for would ever come to pass. Would someday Kara return to the Sioux and claim her Indian heritage?

Standing, Iron Kettle moved back and stood beside Flying Hawk. Speaking to Blade and Suzanne, he said sincerely, "Go in peace."

Suddenly, with eyes glaring, Flying Hawk turned to Blade. "Major Landon, remember my name, for someday all Bluecoats will speak it with fear. When I reach manhood, I will vow to kill all white soldiers until none of you are left! My mother and father will be avenged!"

He whirled about and stalked away. Iron Kettle offered no apology for the boy's outburst; furthermore, as he turned to leave, Suzanne detected a glimmer of pride in the old chief's eyes.

The soldiers and Justin had camped a distance away, and Sergeant Edwards now rode into the partially burned village and guided his horse over to the major. Pulling up, he said, "Sir, the men are mounted and ready to leave."

Quickly Blade helped Suzanne mount her mare, then

lifted Kara and placed her on the same horse. Settling herself behind, Kara wrapped her arms about the woman's waist.

"Suzanne?" the girl whispered.

"Yes?" she responded.

"Can I call you mama and the major papa?"

Blade, overhearing her question, answered, "Of course you can. You're our daughter now, and as soon as I can manage it, I'll have all the legal papers drawn up."

Kara smiled happily, and recalling her great-grandfather's words, she promised herself that she would make her parents proud that they had chosen her for a daughter.

Chapter Forty

When they entered Fort Laramie, Blade ordered Sergeant Edwards to take Black Wolf to the guardhouse and stay with him, emphasizing that he wasn't to leave the warrior under any circumstances. With Newcomb dead, Blade was fairly sure that Black Wolf was now safe, but he didn't want to take any chances. He then told Suzanne to take Kara home, that he'd join them there as soon as he had reported to the colonel and paid his visit to Almeda.

Blade dreaded telling Colonel Johnson about the massacre. He knew the old man would blame himself because he had been the one to give Gary permission to pursue Black Wolf.

Now, entering the colonel's office, Blade greeted him, then took the chair across from the desk.

Returning to his own chair, Colonel Johnson studied the major's grim expression. When Blade remained silent, he remarked, "Out with it, major. What happened?"

"Well, to start with, I have Black Wolf. Sergeant Edwards took him to the guardhouse. Also, Trooper Donovan wasn't Suzanne's cousin, but an imposter. He's now dead. I shot him myself. It seems he was a deserter from the Union Army and took on Donovan's identity to protect himself." Blade drew a deep breath, then proceeded to tell the colonel the remaining tragic events. He found it extremely difficult to give the officer a vivid account of the massacre. In all his years of military service, he had never witnessed a scene so barbaric.

"My God!" the colonel groaned. It was a moment before he could compose himself enough to continue. "I hope Iron Kettle realizes that Captain Newcomb acted on his own and was not following my orders."

"He knows," Blade replied.

"What does Iron Kettle plan to do now that he's lost most of his people?"

"He intends to move to Running Horse's village."

Remorsefully Colonel Johnson said, "I shouldn't have allowed Newcomb to pursue Black Wolf without sending a superior officer with him. I feel as though this is all my fault."

"Don't blame yourself, colonel. Newcomb was a captain, and he should've been perfectly capable of handling the assignment in the correct military fashion."

"Besides Newcomb, how many of our men were killed or injured?"

"Four dead and three injured. The wounded have been taken to the infirmary. Colonel, you might be interested to know that a large portion of Newcomb's men refused to take part in the massacre."

"I'm glad," he sighed. "My faith in mankind has been restored. I'll personally commend them. I'm proud of those men; damned proud!"

Blade smiled. "So am I, colonel. So am I."

* * *

Almeda was napping on the sofa when she was disturbed by someone knocking loudly on her front door. Annoyed at being awakened, she was cranky as she went to the door. Pleased to find that her visitor was Blade, her sour mood quickly dissipated. "Come in," she said, smiling prettily. Taking his arm, she escorted him into the parlor and asked, "May I fix you a drink?"

"No, thanks," he replied.

She watched him curiously. Why was he paying her a call? Could it be possible that he and his wife were having marital problems? Did he resent it because she had taken off to find her cousin? Was Blade through with Suzanne, and had he come here to pursue her romantically? The possibility thrilled Almeda.

"Newcomb is dead," Blade said dryly.

Shocked, Almeda gasped, "What?"

"You heard me, he's dead."

"B . . . but how?"

"If you want to know how and why he died, then ask your father. I didn't come here to discuss his death."

"Then why are you here?"

"To discuss Black Wolf."

Almeda turned her back. So he hadn't come to pursue her, but to confront her with Black Wolf!

Gripping her shoulders, Blade forced her to face him. "I want you to tell the colonel about the conspiracy you shared with Newcomb. We both know Black Wolf never tried to rape you."

"Are you taking that savage's word over mine?" she asked angrily.

"You're damned right I am!" he retorted.

Involved in their heated discussion, they were not aware of the colonel entering his home. Hearing their bickering, he paused in the foyer and listened.

Blade was saying, "Almeda, you may as well tell the truth; you don't have Newcomb any longer to support you!"

She cast him a smug look. "I intend to bring rape charges against Black Wolf. It will be his word against mine, and the court will believe me." She hesitated, then baited him further. "But strictly between the two of us, you're right, he never attacked me. Gary and I framed him."

"Why?" Blade demanded.

"Out of spite. It was a way to get even with you and Justin Smith." She smiled tauntingly, "But of course, if you should testify to this discussion, I'll firmly deny that it ever took place."

"That won't be necessary!" the colonel spoke up, entering the parlor. "There will be no trial!"

Almeda paled. "Father!"

"At this moment I wish to hell I wasn't your father!" he declared bitterly. "My God, Almeda, how could you have done something so malicious?"

"Honestly, father," she whined, "it wasn't as though Gary and I framed a white man. After all, Black Wolf is only an Indian. His death would've benefited society. All the wild savages should be killed."

Colonel Johnson moved so swiftly that Almeda was taken off guard. His hand shot out and slapped her across the face. "Get out of my sight!" he raged.

Wailing, she ran from the parlor and to her bedroom.

Turning to Blade, the colonel apologized, "I'm sorry about this."

"It's all right," he replied. "I'll go to the guardhouse and obtain Black Wolf's release."

"No," Colonel Johnson remarked. "I'll see to his release, for I owe him an apology."

Blade watched as the man moved heavily over to a

wing chair and slumped into it. He wished there was something he could say to help him, but he knew at this time words would be useless. Excusing himself, Blade left the house and headed for his own home. He was anxious to be with his wife and daughter.

Black Wolf planned to leave the fort, return to Iron Kettle's camp, then escort the chief and his people to Running Horse's village. When he told Blade and Suzanne of his plans, they decided to leave Kara with Molly and ride a short way with him.

Reaching the area beside the Platte River where Black Wolf had once taken Suzanne, the three riders pulled up and dismounted.

They strolled to the riverbank, and Suzanne stood between the two men. Each involved in his own thoughts, they remained silent for a short time as they gazed across the water.

It was Blade who spoke first, "Black Wolf, when will we see you again?"

"I don't know. If the Fort Laramie peace treaty is signed, I suppose I'll see you then."

"Will the attack on Iron Kettle's village be a setback to this treaty?" Suzanne asked.

Black Wolf answered, "It might be."

Suzanne sighed sadly. "I feel so sorry for Iron Kettle. He's such a kind, gentle man. And Prairie Flower was one of the nicest women I have ever met. Her death was so tragic and so unfair." She looked at Black Wolf. "Do you think her son, Flying Hawk, will lose some of his rage?"

"I don't think so," he replied. "He has sworn to avenge his parents, and when he becomes a warrior he will carry out his vow. He is Sioux."

"Which means?" she asked.

"Once a Sioux publicly makes a vow, he does not go back on his word." Turning his attention to Blade, he continued, "Speaking of a man giving his word, you mustn't forget your promise to Iron Kettle. If he should send a message that he wishes to see Kara, you must comply. Regardless of how much time has passed."

"I'll honor the agreement, Black Wolf," Blade assured him.

The warrior smiled. "Well, my friend, it's time for me to leave." He and the major shook hands firmly. Then, gazing down into Suzanne's face, he said softly, "Goodbye, Little Dove."

"Not goodbye, Black Wolf. I'm sure we'll see each other again."

"Let us hope that we are all together again." He smiled at both of them. "Take care of each other."

As they watched the handsome warrior's departure, Blade slipped his arm about his wife's waist.

"I wonder what will happen to him," Suzanne murmured dreamily.

"What do you mean?"

"Will he stay with the Sioux and someday become chief? He's never married; do you suppose he'll ever meet a woman who can win his heart?" She sighed deeply. "He's a wonderful man. The woman he marries will be very fortunate to have him for a husband."

"You sound quite taken with Black Wolf. Should I be jealous?" he asked lightly.

She laughed gaily. "Well, I don't want you to become too sure of yourself. It might be to my advantage to keep you guessing."

"Oh yeah?" he came back. "Well, it might be to my advantage to take you over my knee and give you a sound spanking."

"Blade Landon, you wouldn't dare!" she cried.

"Wouldn't I?" he retorted playfully.

Fleeing from his side, she called over her shoulder, "First, you'll have to catch me!"

Giving chase, his long strides easily caught up to hers, and grasping her arm, he brought her into his arms. His lips descended to hers and their romp was quickly forgotten as they melted into each other's embrace.

His dark eyes filled with adoration, Blade murmured, "Suzanne Landon, my defiant little Confederate, I love you."

Pretending sternness, she replied, "Let's get one thing straight, Major Landon. A Confederate I might be, but I am no longer defiant." Slipping her arms about his neck and pressing close to him, he whispered, "I am compliantly yours, for now and always."

Blade and Justin had invited their wives to dinner at the Officers' Club without telling them that it was an occasion for celebration. Earlier in the day the two men had spoken privately, and then arranged the surprise they intended to spring upon Suzanne and Molly at dinner.

Kara was having her evening meal at the Wilkinsons'. She and Shelley's daughter had become friends at first sight.

After Blade and the others had placed their orders and were relaxing at the table with before-dinner drinks, Justin caught the major's eye.

"Do you reckon we ought to tell them now?" the scout asked, grinning.

"Tell us what?" Molly asked.

Her question wasn't answered; instead Blade said to Justin, "Do you want to tell them, or do you want me to?"

"You talk more than I do, so why don't you tell

them," Justin jested.

"My goodness," Suzanne complained humorously. "You two sound like two little boys sharing a secret."

"Ladies," Blade began, "Saul will not be alone on his journey homeward. We will all be accompanying him. Justin and I are taking you two home for a visit."

"Home!" Molly breathed, gazing happily at her husband. "Oh, it'll be so wonderful to see mother and father!"

Suzanne reached for Blade's hand. "Thank you, darling." Her smile amused, she added, "I only hope Uncle Thomas will treat your cordially; after all, you are a Yankee."

"But Suzanne," Molly began, "when we wrote home about our marriages, and finally received answers, my parents and your uncle didn't sound too bitter about our husbands."

"That's true," she agreed. "I'm probably worrying needlessly."

Speaking to his wife, Blade proceeded, "After we visit with Thomas, we'll travel east."

"To see your mother and stepfather?" Suzanne asked.

"Yes. Sam, mother's husband, is a lawyer and I'll have him draw up adoption papers on Kara. Then she will legally belong to us."

Catching sight of Colonel Johnson approaching their table, Justin remarked, "We're about to have company."

The colonel nodded politely to the ladies, then speaking to Blade, he said, "I have decided to send Almeda to her cousin, who lives in St. Louis. I don't think my daughter belongs on a military fort. Furthermore, I'm sure she'll be happier elsewhere. Life at Fort Laramie is a little dull for her taste."

Blade didn't offer a verbal response, but the

expression in his eyes told the colonel that he understood.

Then, apologizing for intruding, Colonel Johnson bid the diners a good night.

Justin watched the officer as he walked in the direction of the bar. "He's a good man and deserves a daughter better than Almeda."

"We all have our crosses to bear," Molly murmured. "Almeda Johnson is his."

Lying in bed, Justin studied his wife as she stood in front of the bureau, brushing her hair. She was wearing a thin cotton nightgown that seductively shadowed her womanly curves. His eyes raking leisurely over her tempting body soon had him aroused. "Woman, will you quit brushing your hair and come to bed," he grumbled.

"You sound like a grumpy old bear," she replied with a smile.

"I'm not a grumpy old bear; I'm a horny one."

Laughing, Molly placed the brush on the bureau, then whirling around and facing her husband, she exclaimed, "Oh, Justin, my darling, what am I going to do with you?"

Flinging back the covers, he answered, "Crawl in here beside me, and I'll show you what you can do with me."

She held up a hand. "Not so fast, my virile lover. First I have something to tell you."

"Well, you don't have to stand over there to tell me. Come get in bed."

Slowly she crossed the floor, but instead of lying beside him, she sat on the edge of the mattress. "Justin," she began, her eyes shining, "this afternoon I saw the fort doctor. He confirmed my suspicions.

Darling, we're going to have a baby."

Sitting up with a bolt, he stammered, "You're . . . you're pregnant?"

"Yes, I am!" she cried joyously.

He swept her into his brawny arms. "I'm gonna be a papa! Well, I'll be dad-gum!" He moved her gently and looked down into her face. "In your condition, you shouldn't be takin' a long trip. We'll have to cancel our plans."

"Justin, I'm sure the doctor will agree that it's perfectly safe for me to travel."

As he drew her back into his arms, she asked, "Do you want a boy or a girl?"

"It doesn't matter," he answered. "Besides, this won't be our only one. I think we should plan on at least an even dozen."

"I do hope you are jesting," she giggled.

Easing her down on the bed beside him, he asked, "Well, if twelve are too many, how about half a dozen?"

"You're getting closer," she murmured.

"Three and no less," he bargained.

"It's a deal," she agreed.

"So we won't forget how to make babies, don't you reckon we ought to practice?"

"Justin Smith, I reckon you're right."

Lacing her arms about him, she urged his lips down to hers, and soon afterward they were passionately expressing their love for each other.

Epilogue

Thomas Donovan welcomed Suzanne's husband, and within an incredibly short time the two men were on friendly terms, which pleased Suzanne immensely.

Blade, Suzanne, and Saul parted company with the Smiths in Natchez, then traveled nonstop to Southmoor.

Saul had been relieved to find that Thomas Donovan had not been completely deserted by his servants. Lettie and her husband, Joseph, had remained with their former master.

The travelers had arrived at Southmoor early in the evening, and it was late afternoon on the second day of their visit when Blade found Suzanne sitting alone on the front porch. Saul and Joseph had left early in the morning to go into Natchez, and Thomas was in the study with Kara, giving the little girl her first lesson on how to play checkers.

Now, going to Suzanne's side and sitting on the stoop next to her, Blade said with concern, "Honey, you've been very quiet all day. Is something bothering you?"

Her eyes met his tender gaze. "No, not really," she answered, smiling wistfully.

"It's Patrick, isn't it?" he prodded gently. "Coming home has made you think about him."

"Blade Landon, you know me too well," she answered, her smile broadening.

He took her hand and squeezed it lightly. "Why haven't you visited your and Patrick's special place?"

"I can't," she said, sighing.

"Why not?" he asked.

"I'm afraid if I go to the creek in the woods, too many memories will come flooding back to me and I'll start crying." Her hand tightened within his. "Darling, I don't want to cry. I'm happy, truly I am."

"I know you're happy," he replied. "But since you learned what happened to Patrick, you haven't really given in and had a good old-fashioned cry." He raised a brow. "It might make you feel better."

"I feel just fine," she assured him; then, changing the subject, she asked, "Do you know why Saul and Joseph went into Natchez?"

"Thomas mentioned something about sending them for supplies."

Her tone was chipper. "Blade, I'm so pleased that you and Uncle Thomas are getting along so well."

"Thomas Donovan is a survivor, and he has wisely put the war behind him."

The night before, Thomas had informed them that he intended to leave Southmoor. His friend in the North had his own business and had offered Thomas employment. Suzanne's uncle couldn't pay the taxes owed on Southmoor, and until he'd received this offer from his friend, he had been afraid he'd soon find himself homeless. Lettie's and Joseph's plans were to move into Natchez and become domestic servants for Molly's parents.

Thinking of her uncle's decision to leave, Suzanne said with concern, "Blade, I'm worried about Saul. He had planned to stay here at Southmoor."

"Your uncle has offered to take Saul with him."

"Yes, I know," she answered. "But I don't think he'll be happy living in a northern city."

"Saul is also a survivor, and he'll adjust," Blade told her, his mood optimistic.

"As usual, I'm probably worrying needlessly," she replied. For a moment she studied her husband closely. He was dressed in civilian clothing and looked dashingly handsome in his tan shirt and beige trousers. The shirt was partially unbuttoned, revealing some of the dark hair that grew thickly across his muscular chest. Slowly she raised her scrutiny to his face, admiring his deep brown eyes, firm lips, and well-groomed moustache.

"Blade Landon," she murmured, "you are a superb specimen of a man."

He laughed shortly. "Thank you, Mrs. Landon. May I be so bold as to reciprocate and say that you are radiantly beautiful?"

"Yes, you may," she permitted saucily.

Drawing her into his arms, he kissed her soundly. Then, releasing her, he took out his pocket watch and looked at the time. "Sweetheart, it's growing late; don't you think you should go to the creek before it gets dark?"

"I already told you that I don't want to go there," she answered firmly.

"But I insist," he replied. Standing, he grasped her arm and urged her to her feet.

Relenting, she bargained, "All right, I'll go, but only if you come with me."

"You should go alone," he remarked.

She looked perturbed. "If you can refuse, then so can I."

"Suzanne, I've always known you be defiant,

501

stubborn, and unpredictable, but I've never known you to be a coward." He gave her a gentle push forward. "Go to the creek and face your past."

She squared her shoulders and lifted her chin. "Very well, Blade. But surely you must realize how difficult this is for me."

"Suzanne, I read the journals and I know how close you and Patrick were. But honey, trust me. I know what's best for you."

"Maybe you're right," she answered. "Uncle Thomas is moving away, and I'll probably never have reason to return to these grounds. If I want to see our special place, it's now or never."

Blade smiled. "Stay as long as you wish."

She nodded solemnly. "Wait here for me?"

"Of course," he answered.

Blade watched her as she walked away and headed toward the ruined remains of the once-magnificent plantation house. The woods were a couple of yards behind the burned rubble, and he continued to watch until her small form disappeared into the wooded area. Then, detecting an approaching buckboard, he glanced down the narrow dirt road. As the wagon drew closer, Blade smiled expansively.

A gentle southerly breeze was ruffling Suzanne's golden tresses as she stood beside the creek and gazed thoughtfully across the water. A bird chirped musically, causing her to lift her gaze upwards. A noisy bobwhite quail was perched on a tree branch, looking down at her.

Suzanne smiled ruefully. She knew this bobwhite wasn't the one she and Patrick had once saved, but it could very well be a descendant.

She lowered her eyes, for they had begun to fill with

tears. Oh, how desperately she wished Patrick was still alive!

Hearing a fallen twig snap in the woods, she turned around, expecting to see Blade. She was smiling, glad that he had decided to join her.

The smile suddenly froze on her face, and her heart pounded wildly. Her eyes, wide with incredulity, stared at the man who was slowly approaching. He moved carefully, limping slightly on his lame leg. Dressed as a priest, the black cloth made his blond hair seem even lighter than it was.

Suzanne's hand moved to her throat as she watched this man come closer. She was almost choking, her breaths coming in short gasps.

He paused mere inches from her side. "Suzanne," he whispered, his blue eyes misty.

Suzanne's sobs didn't come to her slowly and then build to a crescendo; they broke in a flood. Her tears gushed forth freely, blinding her vision as she flung herself into the man's arms. He embraced her tightly, holding her trembling body close to his.

"Patrick!" she moaned. "Oh God, Patrick!"

Suzanne's knees gave way, and easily her cousin lifted her. Kneeling, he placed her gently on the ground, sat beside her, and drew her against his chest.

Minutes passed before Suzanne's shock began to calm enough for her to regain her senses. She withdrew from his arms, and with tears still streaming down her face, she gazed lovingly into Patrick's watching eyes.

Tenderly he brushed away her tears, then bending close, he placed a kiss against her cheek. "Honey, please don't cry."

She tried to speak, but her voice failed. Taking a deep breath, she made another attempt, this one successful. "Patrick, I thought you were dead."

"Yes, I know," he answered. "When father received

your letter telling him about Lyle Watkins, he brought it to me in Natchez and I read it." He smiled softly. "When I read that you and your husband were coming home, I asked father not to tell you about me. I wanted to be the one to explain everything. This morning he sent Saul and Joseph into town to bring me to Southmoor."

"Saul!" she interrupted, her eyes gleaming. "When did he find out you were alive?"

"Father told him last night; he also told your husband."

"Then Blade knew you were coming home, and that's why he sent me to the creek."

"He thought we should be reunited here in our special place."

She sighed happily. "I think Blade Landon is a romantic."

Patrick chuckled, and glancing at their peaceful surroundings, he said, "This is a perfect place for miracles."

"I do feel as though I'm living a miracle." She grasped his hand. "Oh, Patrick, I have so many questions to ask!"

"I'll try to explain everything, and then when I'm finished, if you still have questions, I'll answer them."

"All right," she agreed.

"First, I need to let you know that my recollections are hazy. I can only remember bits and pieces of my past. And I'm not referring only to my war years, but to my entire life. Slowly, more and more memories are returning, but there are many voids that I cannot fill. Reading your letter about Lyle Watkins explained why I was mistaken for a Union soldier. It's quite understandable why Watkins believed I was dead. I had been shot in the head, and it was weeks before the doctors even knew if I'd live or die. I had been taken to a Union camp hospital, where the surgeon operated and removed the bullet. I remained unconscious, and was finally transferred to a hospital in the North. I was comatose for several weeks, and when at last I regained consciousness I could remember nothing. I had amnesia; I didn't even know my name. My condition was still serious, and I remained a patient for a long time. Although the Union officials tried to learn my identity, they failed to turn up any clues. Since I had no place to go, I was given employment at the hospital as a doctor's aid. I was still working there when the war ended. A couple months later, flashes from my past began to emerge. These fleeting memories soon became more frequent. I was starting to recall my life, but it still took a long time for me to remember finally who I was. I remembered my name, and I also remembered that I had wanted to be a priest. But as hard as I tried, I couldn't remember where I lived, or my family."

Patrick paused, sorting out his thoughts. "I often had visions of a beautiful child with golden curls, and as these visions continued she grew older, until she became a lovely young lady. One day I actually remembered her name was Suzanne."

"By this time did you realize you were a Southerner?"

"No, but I was beginning to suspect that I was. But I had been wearing a blue uniform when I was wounded. I couldn't understand why I would've been fighting for the North if I was from the South. Although I continued to work at the hospital, I often visited with Father O'Brien, who is a priest. I confided in him about my wish to dedicate my life to the Church. With his encouragement and support, I left the hospital and fulfilled my dream. Eventually more and more of my past came back to me until at last I remembered Southmoor and my family. Father O'Brien has a lot of influence with the Church and saw to it that I was transferred to Natchez. First I visited Molly's parents, and they brought me up to date on you and father. They came with me to Southmoor, where my father and I were finally reunited. I love Thomas Donovan with all my heart, but Suzanne, I've never loved anyone as much as I love you. How badly I wanted to see you! Father wrote you a letter, but apparently it never reached Fort Laramie. He was about to write another one when he received your letter, telling him you and your husband were coming home."

"Do you think your full memory will ever be restored?"

"I don't know, but returning home has helped a lot."

Suddenly, her face alight, Suzanne said eagerly, "Patrick, in the letter I wrote to Uncle Thomas, I didn't mention your journals."

"Journals?" he questioned.

"You don't remember keeping your memoirs?"

"No, I don't think so," he replied hesitantly.

"I have these journals with me. After you read them, a lot of these voids will be filled."

His expression grew thoughtful. "Now that you've brought them to mind, I do seem to have a cloudy recollection of them." His eyes lit up. "Yes, I do remember keeping them!"

"Wonderful!" she exclaimed. "Oh, Patrick, with the help of the journals you'll probably begin to recall everything!"

"I certainly hope so," he replied. "These lapses in my past can be a little unnerving."

She regarded him closely. "Do you remember the last time we saw each other? You had come home on leave, and the night before you left to rejoin your regiment, we had a private discussion in the study."

"For some reason, that night is one memory I can

recall vividly."

"The war had you depressed and troubled. You were afraid you'd never find peace within yourself, or with God."

"Suzanne," he said softly, "with God's help, and through prayer, I finally found peace."

Continuing to look at him closely, she said proudly, "I keep calling you Patrick, but you are now Father Donovan."

He smiled. "And you are Mrs. Blade Landon." Taking her hand, he asked, "Did you know that your eyes actually shine when your husband's name is mentioned? You must love him very much."

"Yes, I do," she hastened to reply. "When I first met Blade, I thought him despicable and arrogant. In my opinion, he was a damned Yankee who was bound and determined to capture my cousin and have him court-martialed."

"And you were bound and determined to save me, weren't you?"

She nodded. "The man I believed was you created a lot of tension between Blade and me." She laughed gaily. "Later I must tell you about our stormy relationship."

Suddenly hearing footsteps, they stood and looked behind them. Blade emerged from the thicket and Suzanne raced into his arms.

Hugging him tightly, she cried, "Blade, I'll never understand how you managed to keep this surprise from me all last night and today!"

"It wasn't easy," he told her, smiling.

Stepping out of his embrace, she replied, "But I'm glad you did. Seeing Patrick here, in our special place, was like a beautiful dream come true."

He kissed her lips lightly. "I'm glad to hear that. I was worried that you might be angry with me for keeping such an important secret from you." Placing his arm about her shoulders and leading her back to Patrick, he said, "Your cousin is a very defiant little Confederate, and I'm never sure how she's going to react to certain situations."

Patrick chuckled deeply. "Yes, I can remember even as a child she was usually defiant and unruly."

Suzanne gazed at Patrick with love. It was so wonderful to hear his laughter and see the twinkle that always came to his eyes when he was amused. What a glorious miracle to find him alive! She had thought him dead, buried somewhere in an unknown, shallow grave, his hearty laughter silenced forever.

"Patrick," she began, "have you seen Molly?"

"Yes, I saw her last night, and I also met Justin. She told me she's expecting a child. She seems to be very happy and very much in love with her husband."

"Yes, she is happy." Suddenly Suzanne's expression became one of concern. "But I'm not sure about Saul. I don't think he'll be happy living in the North."

"He isn't leaving with father," Patrick said. "He's going to live in Natchez and work as a handyman for the church; and needless to say, I love that old man and want him with me."

Suzanne was overjoyed, for she knew Saul would be happy with Patrick. Then, struck with an idea, her face took on a special glow as she moved to stand between the two men. Looking at Patrick, she asked, "Do you remember the day when you promised me that if you became a priest, you'd marry me and my fiancé?"

His brow furrowed. "I'm not sure."

"You were in the parlor with Aunt Ellen, and as usual she was complaining about my unladylike conduct. After she left, we sat on the sofa together. You talked about becoming a priest, and I made you promise to perform my marriage ceremony."

"It's somewhat vague, but I think I do have a cloudy memory of that day."

She reached for his hand and grasped it securely. "Patrick, Blade and I were married at the fort by a chaplain. But I'm Catholic, and I long to be married by a priest. Will you marry us?"

He looked surprised. "But honey, if you and Blade were married by a chaplain, then you are legally and spiritually wed."

She placed her hands on her hips and eyed him stubbornly. "Patrick Donovan, you promised me you'd marry me and my fiancé!"

Grinning, he replied, "But Blade isn't your fiancé, he's your husband."

She lifted her chin. "A mere technicality."

Patrick smiled. "If Blade agrees, I'd be happy to marry you two tonight after dinner."

Her gaze turned to Blade, her eyes questioning.

Bowing from the waist, he asked gallantly, "Mrs. Landon, will you please marry me the second time around?"

"Mr. Landon, I'd be honored to marry you the second time around."

His grin cocky, Blade asked, "Does this mean we get a second time around wedding night?"

Blushing profusely, Suzanne exclaimed, "Blade, honestly!"

Patrick and Blade laughed heartily, and losing her embarrassment, Suzanne's laughter was soon mingling with theirs.

Blade carried Suzanne over the threshold and into their bedroom. Placing her on her feet, he took her into his embrace with a deep kiss, which she ardently returned.

"Mrs. Landon," he murmured, "I think marrying a second time calls for an extra passionate wedding night."

"I agree," she purred, pressing her frame seductively against his. Then twirling lithely away, she went to the bedside, and while watching him provocatively, she began to slip out of her clothes. She removed her dress slowly, teasingly; then smiling wickedly, she doffed everything and stood before him completely un-clothed.

Blade's eyes drank in her beauty as she drew back the bed covers and slipped between the sheets.

"Darling, why are you just standing there? If we're going to have an extra passionate wedding night, don't you think we should get started?" She smiled quite innocently.

Blade's clothes were methodically dropped to the floor, the fallen articles etching a path to his wife's bed.

Joining her, he drew her small frame to his side, then leaning over her, his lips branded hers in a fiery kiss.

"I love you, Suzanne Donovan Landon," he said thickly.

"I love you too, Major Blade Landon. With all my heart and soul."

He kissed her again, and their passions emerged fervently as they held tightly to each other. Their bodies blended together, and they became as one.

MORE HISTORICAL ROMANCES
from Zebra Books

PASSION'S FLAME (1716, $3.95)
by Casey Stuart

Kathleen was playing with fire when she infiltrated Union circles to spy for the Confederacy. Then she met handsome Captain Matthew Donovan and had to choose between succumbing to his sensuous magic or using him to avenge the South!

MOONLIGHT ANGEL (1599, $3.75)
by Casey Stuart

When voluptuous Angelique answered the door, Captain Damian Legare was surprised at how the skinny girl he remembered had grown into a passionate woman—one who had worshipped him as a child and would surrender to him as a woman.

WAVES OF PASSION (1322, $3.50)
by Casey Stuart

Falling in love with a pirate was Alaina's last thought after being accused of killing her father. But once Justin caressed her luscious curves, there was no turning back from desire. They were swept into the endless WAVES OF PASSION.

SURRENDER TO ECSTASY (1307, $3.95)
by Rochelle Wayne

A tall, handsome Confederate came into Amelia's unhappy life, stole her heart and would find a way to make her his own. She had no idea that he was her enemy. James Henry longed to reveal his identity. Would the truth destroy their love?

RECKLESS PASSION (1601, $3.75)
by Rochelle Wayne

No one hated Yankees as much as Leanna Weston. But as she met the Major kiss for kiss and touch for touch, Leanna forgot the war that made them enemies and surrendered to breathless RECKLESS PASSION.

Available wherever paperbacks are sold, or order direct from the Publisher. Send cover price plus 50¢ per copy for mailing and handling to Zebra Books, Dept. 1965, 475 Park Avenue South, New York, N.Y. 10016. Residents of New York, New Jersey and Pennsylvania must include sales tax. DO NOT SEND CASH.